FOUR WOMEN

Andy Botterill

APS Books
Yorkshire

Also By Andy Botterill
An Appointment With God
21 Days In Swansea
A Life In A Day
At Heart A Romantic
Miscellaneous Thoughts
Sick Note & Scrapbook
Welcome Lonely Hearts
Years Spinning By Out Of Control
The Wind Changes Direction
The Sands Of Time
Poems Of The Eighties
Rat Trap
Marking The Occasions
Young Punks

APS Books,

The Stables Field Lane, Aberford, West Yorkshire, LS25 3AE

APS Books is a subsidiary of the APS Publications imprint

www.andrewsparke.com

©2025 Andy Botterill

Andy Botterill has asserted his right to be identified as the author of this work in accordance with the Copyright Designs and Patents Act 1988

This is a work of fiction. Any resemblance to actual persons, living or dead, places and events, is entirely coincidental.

First published worldwide by APS Books in 2025

catalogue record for this book is available from the British Library

PART ONE – JUDY

Chapter One

Women were often my downfall. I admit it. I liked women, but all too frequently they were my undoing. I liked how they looked. I liked their clothes. I liked their smell. I liked their company. I liked sex, when I could get it, when it was with someone I knew, liked and felt comfortable with. I wasn't promiscuous. I wasn't good at casual sex. It had to be with someone I loved and cared about. I wasn't a man's man. I didn't like hanging out with groups of males and getting drunk with them. I didn't like being loud, brash or crude. I didn't go to the pub with the lads on Friday and Saturday nights. It wasn't my thing. I preferred to go out on my own. I knew the best clubs to hang out in. I hoped to encounter women I could ask out and date. The trouble was I had a tendency to get too emotionally involved with those I dated. I'd fall for them too deeply. I'd end up getting hurt, if or when it didn't work out. My heart would end up broken in little pieces.

I was twenty-five years old. I was still getting over my ex-fiancée leaving me without warning for a man who'd once been a friend. Now I hated that friend. I wanted to kill him. I was bitter, resentful and full of internal grieving. Outwardly I pretended I was OK. All was fine, I'd tell anyone who asked. Not many did. They mainly stayed away. People generally aren't attracted to those who are full of self-pity, pain and loathing, as I was at that time. I was a failed writer. I was a failed musician. I scratched together a living working part time as a news reporter for a small local newspaper. It wasn't a job I was very good at or very passionate about, but I was just about adequate. I still lived with my parents, something I needed to do something about. I was treading water. I wasn't really going anywhere. I definitely wasn't on any very clear career path. My life wasn't clearly mapped out. If it was, it had somehow departed from the chosen path and was now on something else. I was drifting. I wasn't that bothered. I was still coming to terms with the love of my life leaving me. I drank too much. I wasn't really that concerned what happened to me in truth.

Then I got a lucky break. I began a new if unlikely relationship. I started dating a girl who was just sixteen, nine years younger than I was. It was a big age gap. She was just finishing school. I'd finished university and was now firmly entrenched in the world of work. It should have felt wrong, but somehow it didn't. It felt right. I'd dated other girls, nearer my own age, and it hadn't worked out. Now I was seeing someone who in logic and perhaps by common convention was too young for me. But we couldn't stop ourselves. We wanted to see each other. We wanted to be together. She was called Judy. She lived in the sleepy seaside town where I was worked. She was beautiful, with long, dark brown hair and clear, pale skin. She wore mainly black clothes. She was what was commonly known as a *goth*, a popular alternative youth subculture at that time, or flirted with the look at least. The year was 1990.

I got teased about my new relationship at work. I shouldn't have been, and I paid no attention to it. I realised I was the lucky one. Judy was a creature of rare beauty. I knew she'd only blossom further as she got older. I wasn't a bad looking guy. I was tall, slim and quite fashionable. I knew what clothes looked good on me. I was into music and knowledgeable about it. Some women at least seemed to like me. But I had none of the pure, natural good looks Judy had. She just shone out from the crowd, regardless of her age. She looked far older than she was anyway. She could easily have passed for nineteen or twenty. We didn't look out of place together. We looked like a well-matched couple. Only people who knew Judy's age and the age gap that existed between us thought it was funny we were dating.

'There's been a case of *kidnapping* reported in the town,' one work colleague joked.

The others all laughed. They thought it was hilarious, but the joke was on them. I'd pulled the most beautiful girl in town, sixteen or not. Judy had no trouble getting into pubs or clubs. She never got asked her age. It probably helped she was with someone clearly older, but even so she never once got challenged about how old she was. I didn't give it any thought. We went wherever we wanted. It never even occurred to me we might be refused entry. Surprisingly neither my parents nor Judy's parents outwardly disapproved of our relationship. They seemed OK with it and effectively gave us the green light to keep seeing each other. My parents had disapproved of some of my previous girlfriends in the past. They didn't disapprove of Judy. I think they were deceived by her appearance. I don't think they realised she was as young as she was. I didn't advertise the age gap, though I was truthful if anyone asked. I was just happy to be with someone. I was happy to have found love again. I'd been on my own for nearly a year, wallowing in despair, licking my wounds, waiting to feel like life was worth living once more. Now it was. I'd found something worth living for. She was called Judy. She may have been much younger than me. It didn't matter. We wanted to be together.

Judy was quiet. She didn't say too much. She was modest and reserved. If spoken to she was outwardly polite, but she mainly kept her opinions to herself. Underneath I imagined her to be a more complex and complicated character than she liked to let on. Her alternative fashion sense hinted at that. For some reason she held it in check. In time I was to be proved right. When we first met I liked her quietness. She was sparing with words. She generally held back her thoughts and kept them locked inside. I found myself doing much of the talking. I talked for the both of us. Maybe she was shy. Maybe she was just finding her confidence. I didn't mind. Just her being there was enough. It was enough to make everything feel good. It was enough to make everything feel all right.

Things became easier when Judy left school in the summer of 1990. She came up by train several times every week to see me. Usually she stayed over. She slept in my parents' spare room. I had my own. She normally came up once on a weekday and again at the weekend. Sometimes we stayed in listening to music. Other times we went to pubs in the city centre. We generally chose quiet ones where no one disturbed or bothered us. We largely kept ourselves to ourselves. We were an insular couple. We rarely saw other friends. Judy had one close female friend where she lived. She generally shunned the company of others. I had a few friends, but now I was in a new relationship I wasn't keeping in touch with them so much. I didn't care. I was happy as I was. Occasionally we went clubbing on a Friday or Saturday night. We went to a local alternative club, where everyone wore black. It was the one where we'd met. I was into indie music. Judy was into gothic and rock music. But the music scene was changing. It was becoming more dance orientated. It was being taken over by the *Madchester* movement. Suddenly it was all about raves and ecstasy. Neither of us were into that. We started to lose interest in music.

On Saturdays we went shopping in the city centre, for clothes and records. I couldn't drive, so our options were limited. Sometimes we took a train to Bristol or London just for a change of scenery. Mostly we stayed where we were. We rented old horror movies from video rental shops and watched them at home. They were often flickery and in bad condition from being watched too many times. We watched films like *Dawn of the Dead* and *Day of the Dead*. They reflected our slightly dark

5

outlook on life. My mum made our tea for us. We were lazy. We didn't do too much for ourselves. Life was quite easy. Judy had finished her studies. I only worked part time. On my days off I sat at my typewriter, writing poems and short stories no one was interested in. I was still seeking my big break as an author, one which would never come.

I was inspired by England reaching the 1990 World Cup semi-final. Judy didn't like football. She had no interest in it. Unusually for someone who liked indie and alternative music, I liked sport. I was quite a contradictory person, with sometimes strangely conflicting and unrelated interests. On a sudden impulse I decided to get fit. I cut back my alcohol intake a little and started playing tennis. I even joined a club and started playing some league matches. When the summer season ended I wanted to carry on. I started playing rugby. I played games on some Saturday afternoons, leaving Judy to go shopping or watch television. Sometimes she even came to see me playing. At the time I had long, greasy hair like Bobby Gillespie from indie rock band *Primal Scream*. I looked nothing like the other short-haired, muscular players in my team. I was the oddest, skinniest rugby player they'd ever seen. Luckily I was quick and I used my pace to keep me out of harm's way.

At the end of the summer of 1990 my older sister got married. She was a teacher and much more conventional, sensible and settled than me. She was marrying another teacher. I regarded myself as more of a free spirit. I was a drifter. I didn't want to be too tied down. I was just drifting from one year to another. My life hadn't really taken direction as yet. I had a job, but I was singularly failing to turn it into a career. I didn't really know where I was going or what I was doing with myself. I wanted to be a writer, but it was proving more difficult to break into than I expected. I only knew that I wasn't cut out for conventional work. I didn't want to work as hard as I saw the other members of my family working each and every day of their lives. They were slaves to their jobs. I couldn't follow that pattern. I just didn't have it in me.

'You'll have to get your hair cut for the wedding,' my mum warned me.

I really didn't want to do that. I'd been growing it for some time. I was happy with it as it was.

'You'll need a new suit,' my dad added.

I didn't really want to dress smartly either. I realised I had little choice in the matter. In the end I got my hair trimmed. They took about an inch off the ends. It didn't look too much different. It certainly wasn't the old-fashioned short back and sides my parents would have liked. I had a new suit made to measure, which my dad paid for. It was a dark navy pinstripe. I had it cut skintight and wore it with black Chelsea Boots, in an effort to look like a rock star. Judy wore a fitted navy dress with white polka dots. It was complemented with a white hat and a white flower for the occasion. She wore high heels, which made her seem taller. She was very slim. She looked truly beautiful, quite the belle of the ball. I don't think any of the guests realised she was only sixteen. I happened to see the photos from the wedding again quite recently. She still looks beautiful in them.

The wedding went well. It was followed by a lavish reception at an upmarket hotel. Everything was carefully planned. No expense was spared. Everything was catered for. All was just as it should be. The wedding took place without a hitch, just as my parents hoped it would. By the evening Judy and I had tired a little of the formality. We snuck off into the city centre and went to a club. Nobody missed us. We weren't central to the occasion. We'd enjoyed the day. Now we were ready for a little time alone together. Finally we completed the job of getting properly drunk started at the wedding.

In the autumn of 1990 Judy resumed her studies and started a new course at a nearby sixth form college, in a town a few miles from where she lived. It was more grown up. It wasn't like school. She didn't have to wear a uniform. She no longer looked like a schoolgirl. She now looked like a proper student. I continued to work. Judy didn't have much money, so I had to buy most of her drinks when we went out. Sometimes on my days off I went down to see her. It was fun. I enjoyed the opportunity to go shopping in another town, one I didn't know quite so well. On other days off I continued to write. I started work on a novel, but it wasn't coming together all that cohesively. I kept at it. I was determined to get it finished, even though I realised it was far from a classic.

I sent poems and short stories off to numerous small press magazines in this country and abroad. Quite a few editors accepted the work I sent them. I became quite well known on the underground literary scene, but it meant little or nothing. However many poems and stories I had published, I remained financially no better off, and no one outside this small group of obscure poetry enthusiasts had any idea who I was. I could never quite make the next step. I couldn't make that breakthrough into the literary establishment, however hard I tried. I began to realise, despite my best efforts, this might be as good as it would ever get. I'd never achieve more. I'd never be successful. I'd never make a living as a writer and author.

Over time I started getting poems published in America. They seemed to appreciate my slightly beatnik style of writing more than back home in the UK. I even started getting published in some of the same California based magazines as one of my great literary heroes, the legendary Charles Bukowski. Whilst Bukowski remained an international icon of the written word, I stayed unknown. I didn't always help myself. I could be aloof and standoffish. I didn't play the game very well. I didn't network as I might have. I didn't join poetry groups and societies. I didn't go to live readings. I didn't befriend those I knew locally who were involved in the more established poetry circuits. If anything I shunned them. I didn't really respect what they were doing. I thought what they were writing was rubbish. I only had time for my own writing, and a few other select individuals I published in a small underground poetry magazine of my own. That publication attracted a hardcore of dedicated contributors and readers. They were all writing good stuff, but it was largely vanishing without trace, just as my own poetry was. Only a few similar likeminded individuals were willing to publish such uncommercial and offbeat work back then. I continued to publish my magazine until around the end of 1991, when I lost heart and gave up. It never formally folded. Due to lack of significant interest I just never did another issue.

Instead I focussed on Judy. We were getting on well. We had a more relaxed and easy-going relationship than some I'd experienced in the past. We rarely argued or fell out. It was the polar opposite to my previous relationship with my ex-fiancée, who'd left me for another man now a little over a year earlier. That had been a fraught, complicated and difficult relationship. I didn't feel I could endure another like it. The pain and heartbreak had been too much to bear. I now needed something altogether simpler and gentler. I found it with Judy. We felt content in each other's company. We could quietly cuddle up together and feel happy. Often words weren't necessary. The touch of her soft skin next to mine, her long, cascading hair over me, her thick, pouting lips, were enough. I didn't need more. I didn't think I'd ever get over what had happened to me the previous year. Judy helped me forget. She helped me start a new, better, more positive life. There was little room for anyone else. We had each other. That was all we wanted.

Judy and I didn't rush into a sexual relationship. She'd been just sixteen years old when we'd met. I was twenty-five. I'd now turned twenty-six. She was now seventeen but looked much older. I never pressurised her into sex. I waited until she was ready. One day we were lying on my bed at my parents' house, when things started to happen between us. We were alone. My parents were out. Nothing had been discussed. Nothing had been planned. For once things didn't just stop at kissing. My hands had slipped under her T-shirt. She didn't have a bra on. I accidentally brushed against her naked breasts. She didn't object, so I carried on. Before I knew it we were both pulling each other's jeans down. She touched me intimately for the first time. I touched her back. She let her legs slide apart and I found myself inside her. I was worried I was hurting her.

'Are you OK?' I asked.

She smiled.

'I'm fine. Don't stop,' she said.

It felt amazing. It was a thrill to finally consummate our love after over a year of waiting. Following that we had sex all the time. Judy wasn't quite as shy and retiring as I thought. She was up for trying anything. It made me wonder why we'd waited so long. Perhaps we needn't have, but at least in my own mind I'd done the right thing. I was aware of our age difference. I was anxious she shouldn't feel pressurised to do anything she didn't want to do. In fact I needn't have worried. She herself had grown a little frustrated with waiting. She'd wondered why I hadn't previously made a move on her. She'd wondered if there was something wrong with her. There wasn't. She was just about perfect in every way. I'd simply wished to demonstrate my respect for Judy. Perhaps I'd demonstrated too much respect. It didn't matter now. Our relationship had at last moved to the next stage. It had now developed a sexual aspect to it. It also demonstrated to me that Judy's character had hidden depths of passion I was only just beginning to discover. There was more to her than met the eye. She was the personification of the expression *Still waters run deep*.

I liked to view Judy as my pure English rose, kind-hearted, decent, sweet-natured and innocent, though perhaps not completely innocent anymore. I was an altogether more difficult, challenging and complicated character. Deep down I too was kind-hearted and decent. On a good day I was the perfect gentleman and model citizen. All too often though little or none of that was apparent. I kept my good points well disguised and well hidden. Instead, I could be awkward, tetchy, moody, sullen, rude, profane and childish, or any combination of any of these at any given time. I didn't comply to convention. I didn't care too much what people thought of me. My sense of embarrassment never prevented me behaving badly, if I was in the wrong mood. I struggled to snap out of it, even if I felt sorry afterwards.

I could be aggressive and abusive, if rarely physically violent. I had Obsessive-compulsive disorder and other issues. I could have tantrums like a child. I was often reluctant to tell girlfriends how much I liked them. I didn't always let on how much they meant to me. They often found me intriguing at first. I was different. I wrote poems and recorded music. Eventually the novelty would wear off. I'd become harder work than I was worth. And then they'd leave me, probably not even realising how hurt I was. It had become a pattern. I'd pretend I wasn't bothered. Deep down I was destroyed. I hoped it would never come to that with Judy. Even then I still didn't share my true feelings with her. I held back a little. I still hadn't fully recovered from giving all to my ex-fiancée, only to be brutally dumped for someone else. I remained slightly fearful of a repeat experience.

Chapter Two

In a bid to broaden our horizons I started to learn to drive. I was sick of being stuck in one city and having to rely on public transport if we wanted to go anywhere else. I wasn't quick to learn. I struggled with driving at first, but I stuck at it and continued to take lessons, even during times when I couldn't really be bothered with it. Slowly I learned and got to grips with the art of driving a car. It was harder than I thought. There seemed to be too much to think about at first, but I gradually improved, and by the time I took my driving test I was an adequately competent driver. I passed my driving test first time. I didn't know that I would, though I thought there was a possibility I might. I was still pleased with myself. Judy and my parents were pleased too. It was a small achievement when such things were generally few and far between.

I passed my test in time for us to enjoy the summer of 1991. I still didn't have a car, but my dad was happy to let us borrow his occasionally. For the first time Judy and I were able to get out and about. We were no longer stuck at home or looking round the same tired, over-familiar shopping centre. We could do other things. We could drive to the countryside. We could drive to the beach. We could drive to the moors. We could drive to other towns and villages that we were less well acquainted with. It was fun. We were happy. Life was pretty easy. Neither of us had to do too much or work too hard. Judy was on a course that hardly stretched her. I was only working part time. Both of us lived at home. Our meals were provided for us. Neither of us paid our parents rent. There was an argument they made it too comfortable for us. Judy was only seventeen. I was twenty-six and should have known better. I should have been embarking on a career. I wasn't enthused or bothered by stuff like that. I found it uninspiring and tedious. I was like a little boy who didn't want to grow up. I had no interest in adult things, like getting a good job, buying a house, starting a pension, having a mortgage. I just wanted to write, make music, play sport and get drunk. At times I drove my parents to distraction.

'When are you going to get a proper job?' my mum would occasionally ask with increasing exasperation.

'Soon. I'm looking,' I'd reply.

I wasn't. I had no intention of getting a proper job. I was happy working the part-time hours that I was. My mum and dad had both been devoted to their jobs and worked hard all their lives. My sister and her husband had successfully embarked on careers. I hadn't. They all wondered what was wrong with me. I wondered what was wrong with them. I hated the conversation about what I was or wasn't doing with my life, when it inevitably came up, as it did from time to time. I couldn't really admit the truth, that I didn't really want to work at all. I'd have preferred to be doing absolutely nothing. It was a compromise of sorts that I was even working part time. To me that was a lot. I'd have been even happier just claiming benefits. I had before, and that had been almost more than my parents could bear. They just couldn't understand why I wasn't more like them. They just couldn't understand where my sense of work ethic had gone. I'd never had it in the first place.

On paper my job was a perfectly acceptable one. Working as a newspaper reporter could have been a satisfactory and respectable profession. In my case it wasn't. I was earning peanuts. I was working in sleepy, provincial backwaters. Nothing ever happened in the seaside town where I was based. I was glad it didn't. It suited me just fine that the only news was there was no news. A lot of the reporters spent most of their time in the pubs. They hoped to pick up a sniff of a story, and of course they liked to drink, often too much. I had the occasional daytime drink, but I preferred to save myself for later when I saw Judy. Occasionally there was talk of offering me a promotion at work or making me full time. I always turned it down. Eventually they stopped asking me. They realised they were wasting their time.

Sometimes I did apply for other jobs, just to keep my parents happy. I wasn't really interested in getting any of them. I was just intrigued enough to find out more about them. I applied for all kinds of things, generally the kind of jobs I should have been doing and promotions I should have been seeking. I applied for jobs in radio, television, PR, the media, even film making. Occasionally I even secured interviews for quite prestigious jobs, with production companies and radio and television stations. They were jobs which were much sought after and other young people were falling over themselves to get. I did little in the way of preparation for the interviews. I made little effort to impress when I was at them. I didn't come over as keen or eager. I answered the questions with only minimum enthusiasm. The jobs always seemed like they'd require far too much hard work and would take up far too much of my time for me to be genuinely interested in them. Whilst I was happy occasionally to go to interviews, I didn't really want there to be any serious risk or danger of actually landing one of these jobs. I needn't have worried. I didn't get any of them. I didn't deserve to.

Meanwhile Judy surprised me and got a job. She came to the end of her course and decided that was enough for her. She didn't want to go on and do A-Levels, as originally planned. She had no interest in eventually studying for a degree, as I had. Instead she became a trainee florist. It quite suited her. She worked at the back of a shop putting together floral displays and bouquets. She didn't have to deal with people very much. It also meant for the first time in her life she had money. I no longer had to buy all the drinks when we went out.

'Well done,' I said to her. 'You're now truly grown up.'

Whilst most people socialised at the weekends, we often stayed in and watched television then. Instead we went out on other evenings, when most more conventional people stayed in. Judy sometimes had to work on Saturdays, but that was no bad thing, as it gave her a day off in the week. She generally chose Wednesdays, as I had Wednesdays off too and we could have a day off together. It also meant we could go out on a Tuesday night and have a few drinks, without having to worry about having hangovers the next day. By 1991 the music we liked had started to fall out of fashion. Rave and dance music were beginning to take over the local club nights at weekends. Indie, goth and rock music was being consigned to the less popular weekday nights. That suited us quite well, as a new indie night had begun every Tuesday night at a quayside club in the city centre where we hung out. It was to continue for some years after. It wasn't all that popular, but it attracted a smattering of indie and alternative types, who wore similar style clothes to how Judy and I dressed. We quite liked the music there, and we could be alone together to chat and to cuddle, without anyone bothering us or even talking to us very much. For us it was ideal and a perfect venue.

Judy was quiet and sensible when she was sober. She could hold her drink quite well. But if she had one too many her character transformed completely out of all recognition. She could quickly become out of control. She could turn wild and crazy then, nothing like the girl I knew and loved for the vast majority of the time we spent together as a couple. When she was drunk it was difficult getting her out of the club and home to where my parents lived. She would become loud, unpredictable and highly volatile. It wasn't necessarily a bad thing. It certainly showed there was another side to her than the one I was accustomed to.

13

On many Tuesday nights we wandered drunkenly back through the deserted streets of the city in the small hours. Hardly anyone was about at that time of night. They were all in bed, as they had work to go to the next day. We didn't. We could have a lie-in. It gave us a warm feeling, as if we were somehow better than them. Their rules and values didn't apply to us. We had our own routines, habits and rituals. We mocked people we considered too conventional and normal. We had no desire to be like that. We wanted to be different. We wanted to stand out from the crowd. We didn't care we hardly had any friends. We didn't care we only really had ourselves.

I liked it when Judy was drunk, as it just about guaranteed we'd have sex when we got back. Sometimes I made her a cup of tea first to sober her up. Other times she couldn't wait. Her hands would be all over me and inside my trousers. As my parents slept upstairs we'd make love wildly on their lounge floor for hours. The alcohol would slow our bodies from climaxing and we'd keep going for ages. We were young. In those days we still had the energy. We'd have to keep pretty quiet, so we didn't wake anyone up. Luckily no one ever came down and disturbed us. Perhaps they had half an inkling what we were up to. Eventually, spent and exhausted, we'd go to bed ourselves, with contented, happy smiles on our youthful faces.

As time passed the music we liked became ever less fashionable and the clothes we wore became a bit dated and of another era. I tried to move with the times a little and got my long hair cut shorter. I also updated my wardrobe a bit, to more closely reflect the current trends. I remained alternative. Judy was more resolute. She continued to wear predominantly black. She wasn't in the least influenced by fashion trends and fads. She wore what she wanted regardless of others and their fashion sense.

It became harder to find pubs and clubs to hang out, where we didn't feel out of place. As a result we increasingly started to drink in hotel bars. We found these suited us very well. They were generally quiet and they stayed open late. We could sit in a quiet corner and slowly get drunk, away from other customers and away from other people. We did this a lot. All was fine, unless Judy became too drunk. Then she'd start losing control, and her inhibitions would melt away and fade to nothing. Her wild side would take over. More than once she dragged me into the ladies' toilets for sex. Not that I minded. It was fun. I was just scared of getting caught. Mostly we got away with it, as the hotel bars we chose were so deserted. On one occasion we didn't. An elderly and rather pristine lady realised what we were up to. We locked ourselves in the toilet and hoped she'd go away. She was a determined sort though and didn't disappear as hoped. I wasn't quite sure why it mattered to her. Maybe she was just a custodian of common, public decency. Maybe she just hated the thought we were a young couple having sex and she wasn't. Eventually we had to come out. She chased us out of the toilets and down the hotel corridor towards reception.

'Manager! Manager!' she shouted.

We just giggled and laughed as she continued to pursue us. We went straight past reception and out of the front door into the street. We left it a few weeks before going back to the same hotel. Eventually we did go back. No one seemed to remember us. No one seemed to recall the incident. We were served as usual. We probably did exactly the same thing again, as soon as Judy got drunk. I guess it was exciting. I guess it made us feel daring. We were living for the moment. If you don't do things like that when you're young you probably never will. You may as well take and enjoy the few opportunities you get.

As a goth Halloween was very important to Judy. She spent months planning for the big night. I quite liked it but wasn't that bothered. When I was with Judy I had to be bothered and I had to dress up. Every year we were together our outfits got more striking, elaborate and outlandish. Judy was the queen of Halloween. She always looked magnificent and especially sexy when we went out on All Hallows' Eve. She was tall and skinny and wore clothes well anyway. Her Halloween costumes surpassed anything else she wore the rest of the year. She looked like a cross between the character *Vampira* from Ed Wood's cult B-Movie *Plan Nine from Outer Space*, and Fenella Fielding's *Valeria* from *Carry on Screaming*. Indeed Judy had more than a passing resemblance to Fenella Fielding, when the actress was in her prime. Certainly what Judy wore for Halloween worked for me. On those nights I couldn't keep my hands off her or wait to get her home.

On quiet mornings when I wasn't working I continued to write. Progress on my novel, stories and poems was slow. About that time I put together a new collection of poetry and published a handful of copies of it. It was a long, rambling collection, that had grown out of all proportion. It needed to be edited down, but I no longer had the will, energy or perhaps ability to edit it properly. Amongst the chaff there were some genuine gems, but they were either hidden or needed to be better written. I'd been working on the collection for several years, but every time it neared completion I'd write some more and it kept growing. I no longer knew what to include and what not to include. In the end I included it all. That was a mistake. It was probably the worst collection I ever published. It was called *Welcome Lonely Hearts*. Bits of it were good, but some of it was little better than meaningless typing and me feeling sorry for myself. Some years later I had another look at it. I got rid of all the rubbish and re-wrote and edited the best poems down to two decent slim volumes. Then in 1991 it was little more than an unwieldy pile of random thoughts and lines. My great debut novel was fairing no better. I'd been writing it for several years now, but it showed little promise, form or direction. Disillusioned with writing I turned back to music.

I got the guitar out again and started recording simple, acoustic versions of some of my old indie songs from the eighties. I threw in a few cover versions of bands like *The Doors*, *The Stooges* and *Pink Floyd*. Surprisingly they sounded quite good, and I was even enjoying myself. With the writing hitting a bit of a brick wall it was nice to have a change of direction and do something different. It was a welcome relief. The writing was dragging me down. This was picking me up. Judy accompanied me on tambourine. With no previous musical training she turned out to be a most accomplished tambourine player and percussionist. People without musical knowledge assume the tambourine to be an easy thing to play and not even a real instrument. Anyone who is a musician knows mastering it and keeping in time is anything but easy. It's a rare skill. Judy was a deft tambourine player and accompanied my guitar playing expertly. It was a most unexpected but most welcome surprise she could do it. It was quite thrilling in fact.

As time passed we kept ourselves to ourselves more and more. Then in the middle of 1992 something strange happened. For no real reason other than pure temptation I started an affair. I had no cause to do it. I was happy with Judy. We hadn't argued. We hadn't fallen out. I didn't want to split up with her. I wanted us to stay together. It was just pure lust and nothing more that I strayed. I wasn't intending to. It was just by complete chance that an irresistible opportunity presented itself. It was early summer. On Sunday nights I played badminton, whilst Judy went back home to her mum. One Sunday I went to my club and there was a new player sitting on the wall outside the hall where we played. She was blonde and attractive and had a very nice figure. She was smoking a cigarette, hardly typical of a badminton player. I was immediately attracted to her.

During the course of the evening we played several games together and got talking. Her name was Karen. She was married and some years older than I was, but her marriage had hit the rocks and she'd decided to take up some new interests, including badminton. She was thirty-six years old. I was twenty-seven. Judy was just eighteen, only half the age that Karen was. At the end of the evening Karen said it seemed a shame to go straight home. She casually suggested we go for a drink, so we could carry on chatting. I knew straight away I was in trouble, but I still agreed. Karen changed out of her sports kit and into a pretty dress. She wore alluring high heels and bright, red lipstick to match, as she took me to a quiet country pub. She was just too attractive to refuse and say no to. She had an air of confidence and womanly experience, as she elegantly sipped her white wine and lit another cigarette. The white filter was smeared with the red of her lipstick. I was instantly infatuated. I felt powerless to resist her charms. I felt she was toying with me. I wanted her. I was certain she knew it. She had no doubt toyed with many men's affections before me. I didn't care. I just knew I was longing for her. I knew I wanted to have sex with her.

'You're a very attractive man,' she said, as she stared into my eyes deeply without blinking.

'You're a very attractive woman,' I replied.

She took my hand. We were holding hands and I didn't give Judy a thought. I was too mesmerised by Karen's beauty. I'd forgotten all about Judy for a second. Karen was just so sexy. She was the ultimate femme fatale. She could have told me to do anything and I probably would have done it. I didn't care who was about. I didn't care if we were seen or spotted. I didn't care about Karen's husband, and neither apparently did she. At that moment I didn't really care if Judy found out what I was doing. I was too besotted. I was too caught up with what was happening with Karen. I was just being carried along. I didn't know how to stop. I didn't want to stop. Then our lips touched and we kissed. Outside we sat in Karen's car for what seemed like an age, kissing and letting our hands run over each other. Our breaths were raspy with desire and sexual anticipation. We didn't do anything then. Our passions would have to wait. We decided it was time we both went home.

'Can I see you again?' I asked Karen when we parted.

'Just try stopping me,' Karen replied and smiled.

We agreed to meet for a date in the week. It was easy really, perhaps too easy. Karen lived in a little village on the other side of the city where I lived. Judy lived in a seaside town a dozen or so miles away. Karen's husband rarely went out. No one knew either me or Karen in the rural village pubs where we mostly met up. We had no friends in common. It was highly unlikely the paths of any of the other people in our lives would ever cross. I didn't see Judy every night anyway, so it was relatively simple to find nights to see Karen. It was the perfect arrangement in many ways. I didn't feel guilty, so I didn't act in a guilty way around Judy. I don't think she suspected a thing. Pretty soon Karen joined my tennis club as well as my badminton club, and we sneaked off together every night after we'd played. Pretty soon we started making love in Karen's car. I was having regular sex with an older, sexy, more experienced woman. It was a thrill. It felt great. Karen had lovely breasts and an amazing figure. She was a joy to look at. She was a joy to be with. She was bewitching and a little dangerous. I even liked the way she lit up her cigarette after sex and blew coils of smoke in my face. I felt like I was her sex slave.

Then one day things changed. I met up with Karen and she wasn't quite the same. She seemed a little distant. I asked her what was wrong. She was a little vague in her reply. She said she'd started to worry her husband might find out about our affair. She'd started feeling somewhat guilty about the whole thing. It was making her anxious. I told her not to worry. I told her no one was going to find out about us. We had a nice arrangement. We should carry on as we were. No one would ever discover our secret. I tried to convince her everything was all right. She knew I had a girlfriend, so I was unlikely ever to put any pressure on her, I pointed out. I wasn't asking her to leave her husband or anything like that, and she wasn't asking me to leave Judy. We were fine as we were. Nothing needed to change. Karen was like a drug to me and I couldn't just stop. I needed to keep getting more of her. I wanted our affair to go on forever.

Karen wasn't convinced. She said we should stop seeing each other. I was gutted. I didn't want it to end. I didn't want it to be over. We made love one more time and then things cooled between us. I carried on seeing her at our club sessions, but our affair then stopped, just as suddenly as it had started. It was disappointing, but life carried on. It wasn't long before Karen separated from her husband altogether and moved away. I never saw her again. I just went back to Judy, as if nothing had ever happened. As far as I know Judy never found out or even suspected the truth. I never told her. I just carried on as before. Strangely I didn't regret what I'd done. Maybe it was because I'd got away with it. Maybe it was because life was just too short to have regrets over someone as attractive as Karen. An opportunity had come along, and unusually I'd taken it. But I learnt my lesson. I promised myself I wouldn't let it happen on any future occasion. I was true to my promise. I was never unfaithful to Judy again.

Chapter Three

It wasn't long before I'd forgotten all about Karen. As dramatically as she'd come into my life, so she was gone. As far as I was aware, I'd never given any indication to Judy something was going on and that I was seeing another woman. I'd kept the two aspects of my life completely separate. One was open and respectable, the other a guilty secret. Except strangely I didn't feel guilty. I should have done, but I didn't. It was alarming really. Maybe there was something wrong with me. Maybe I didn't care about Judy as much as I thought I did. I obviously wasn't that concerned about the consequences had she found out, had she discovered my affair. Luckily for me she didn't find out.

I had a pretty, young girlfriend. Why had I even felt the need for someone else? Why had I taken the risk? Judy was like a pure English rose, with long, brown hair, a clear, pale complexion and flawless skin. Karen had been my ultimate fantasy woman. She was blonde and a bit raunchy or at least looked like she had the capacity to be. It had been wrong, but I just couldn't resist. Now she was gone anyway, and I was back being faithful to Judy. She was the only woman in my life. I was the dutiful boyfriend again. I continued as if nothing had happened, as if I'd never been unfaithful in the first place. I barely gave it a thought, despite the fact I would have been terribly hurt if it had been the other way round and Judy had been unfaithful to me. I've had girlfriends be unfaithful in the past, and I knew how utterly devastated I'd been. This time it had been me to stray. I'd been the one to cheat, and I barely felt a thing.

Then something seemingly innocuous happened, that unknown to me at the time was to have a profound impact on my life for many years to come. One Saturday afternoon in the autumn of 1992 Judy came to watch me play in a rugby match for one of the local clubs where I lived. The weather that day had started quite sunny, but it had turned wet by the end of the game. Whilst I was warm running round Judy had got cold watching. She didn't even want to stay in the bar for a drink after. She said she wasn't feeling that great and needed to get home. I was a bit concerned. I checked her temperature when we got back to my parents' house.

'You are a bit hot,' I said.

'I don't feel that good,' she replied.

She went to bed early that night. In the morning she hadn't improved. She hadn't improved the day after, so she stayed off work. When she still didn't get better we decided she should see the doctor. The news wasn't that good, when I rang to find out how she was.

'I've got glandular fever,' she said. 'I'm on antibiotics.'

It hadn't been difficult to diagnose. There was a swelling in the back of her throat the size of a golf ball. I'd never seen anything like it. Luckily, Judy responded well to medication and she started improving quite quickly. Pretty soon she was back to full health, with no lasting ill effects. I wasn't so lucky. I realised I was at risk of catching glandular fever from her, but I'd already kissed her and been exposed to the virus before we'd found out what it was, so I carried on kissing her. There seemed no point stopping, as I reasoned if I was going to get the infection it was probably too late to stop it anyway. It was probably already in my blood. I'd kissed her before we realised she was ill. So I continued kissing her after. It turned out to be a fateful mistake. We never found out how Judy had got glandular fever in the first place. Maybe like me with Karen she too had been kissing someone else.

I didn't fall ill straight away. I was playing so much sport at the time that I was super fit. I was the fittest I'd ever been in my life. It helped to keep the virus at bay and to disguise the symptoms. By the end of the rugby season I started to feel exhausted. I was drained. Training became an effort. I tired easily. I had strange sugar crashes, when I suddenly felt faint. I felt a whole array of symptoms. Strangely none were obviously those of glandular fever. I wasn't struck down in the dramatic way Judy had been. With me the symptoms slowly crept up on me. It actually made it much worse long term, as I didn't stop. I didn't rest. I continued to play tough, competitive sport. I continued to go out. I continued to drink. I complained to both Judy and my parents that I didn't feel very well.

'You look all right to me,' my mum told me.

She didn't really believe in illness. She came from good, old-fashioned, Protestant stock, with the ethic of hard work engrained in her. She believed in just getting on with it, in biting your lip, in suffering in silence, in continuing until you dropped, or got better of your own accord. Unfortunately my symptoms didn't go away. They hung around me naggingly throughout the spring and summer of 1993. I never considered I might have glandular fever. It had been months since Judy had got better. I'd pretty much forgotten she'd been ill at all. I didn't even have the symptoms she had. I had a strange array of odd sensations, including numbness in my hands and mouth. Yet months were passing and they weren't improving. I started to fear there was something really wrong with me. I'd put it off long enough. It was time to see the doctor.

'I think you've probably just got a virus,' my doctor confirmed.

I found they normally said that, when faced with a puzzling list of vague symptoms they couldn't easily explain away. It was partly my own fault. I downplayed to him both how long I'd been ill and how severe the symptoms were. I feared if I told him the truth he might say I was dying. He might discover I had AIDS or cancer or something equally severe. That's what I thought at the time. Even though I wasn't improving I carried on playing sport. I was addicted. I carried on playing, even though there were occasions I felt so faint I thought I might blackout. Of course it made my symptoms worse. I went back to the doctor a second and third time. Still he found nothing. Eventually he gave me a blood test. It also came back clear. I'd been infected with glandular fever so long by this time, it wasn't showing as a new infection. My doctor started to tire of me. He clearly thought I was wasting his time and wanted to be rid of me. He started to suspect my illness was psychological.

'Have you considered counselling?' he suggested.

By this time I was at my wits' end. I knew I was ill, but I didn't know what I was ill with. I knew my own body. I felt ill most of the time, but no one believed there was anything wrong with me. I started to feel depressed. I started to doubt myself. Meanwhile I wasn't getting any better. Judy and my parents were both tiring of my complaining. I think they both started suspecting too that my problems were largely mental. Only I seemed to know there was something physical wrong with me. It was very frustrating. It was dragging me down. It was making me feel lonely and isolated. Faced with no other diagnosis I just had to keep going and battle through it. I carried on doing all the things I always did, despite the fact I didn't feel at all right. I carried on going to work. I carried on going out. I carried on playing sport.

The illness was to have a huge impact on my life for many years to come. I was still suffering ongoing symptoms over twenty years later, although they gradually faded and improved. For the first few years they only worsened. I sought both conventional and alternative remedies and diagnoses, with no success. I genuinely thought I might be slowly dying.

Eventually I changed doctors and had further tests. After some years of worry and mental torture, I gradually started to unravel the truth and get to the bottom of my medical problems. The more detailed tests showed I'd had glandular fever all along. The fact that I hadn't rested and continued to play sport had made it worse. I'd ended up with a kind of permanent post-viral, ME condition, where the symptoms never improved or went away. As time went on it became more obvious it was glandular fever related. I had frequent bouts of tonsillitis and constantly had to gargle aspirin to alleviate the pain and discomfort. When I was having more severe episodes the tiny glands in the roof of my mouth stood up. I could feel them when I ran my tongue over and around them. I felt drained and washed out all the time. It had a bad impact on my mental state. At times I felt life was no longer worth living. It made me realise without health life is nothing. From the spring of 1993 my health failed and was never the same again.

For some years I'd been treading water in journalism. I'd taken postgraduate training to do it, but it was going nowhere. I was in a rut. It hadn't led anywhere. I hadn't moved on. I'd never been promoted. I'd barely had a wage rise in that time. True, I'd hardly made any great effort to advance my career, but by 1993 even I felt it was time for a change. I was ready for something new. I was ready for something different, some kind of improvement in my life. Because of my love of sport I applied to start teacher training in the coming academic year, with the intention of becoming a PE teacher. My illness didn't go away though and so rather put paid to that and my plans to teach. Having fallen ill it was probably fortuitous that in the event I wasn't accepted for the course anyway. I was probably no longer up to the physical demands it would have placed on me. Instead I looked for means of escape. I wanted to get out of myself.

Judy and I no longer went out very often. The club nights where we lived had become boring as far as we were concerned. We didn't like the music. It was too dance orientated. The ecstasy and rave scene had somewhat passed us by. I occasionally went to a rave event, but it did nothing for me. Instead we stayed in a lot and listened to music. We weren't very excited by the latest batch of releases. We ended up listening to a lot of old albums from the seventies; music for parents really, like *Pink Floyd, Jethro Tull* and *Steeleye Span*. Still, it was better than a lot of the new music coming out, much of which was a waste of the vinyl it was pressed on. Or a waste of a CD, if you were into them.

My health had failed anyway, so I stopped watching what I ate and drank so closely. I could no longer stay fit to play sport whatever I did, so there seemed little reason to carry on trying. Being careful and looking after my body had become pointless. It no longer seemed to matter. I might just as well abuse myself, I reasoned. I might just as well drink, smoke, take drugs and have a good time. I wasn't getting any better as it was, so I simply gave up fighting it and started doing whatever I wanted. My parents were in the habit of going abroad to Europe every summer, normally to France and Germany. That year whilst they were away Judy and I took the opportunity to party at home pretty hard. We stayed in almost every night drinking and listening to records. We wandered round the house naked. We felt pretty decadent. We took long baths together, sharing bottles of wine, finishing one after another. One day I brought home a packet of cigarettes. Judy was surprised as I didn't smoke.

'I didn't think you approved of smoking,' she laughed. 'I thought you liked to stay fit for sport.'

'I don't approve,' I replied. 'But I don't really care anymore.'

I lit one for myself and offered the packet to Judy. I was slightly surprised when she took one too. It was actually quite alluring seeing my outwardly sweet, innocent girlfriend smoking. Tasting her smoky breath when we kissed was sexy. It was a turn on. I couldn't wait to get her into bed after and make love to her. The corruption of apparent innocence was always slightly arousing. Though I doubted how innocent Judy really was. She wasn't really innocent in truth. If I thought she was I was probably little more than deluding myself.

A few days later I went one further and brought home some weed. My parents were still away, so it didn't seem to matter. It was unlikely we'd get caught or found out. The smell in my parents' big house would have dissipated by the time they returned, I figured. Judy and I sat upstairs rolling joints together. We were relatively inexperienced, but what we rolled were at least smokable, which was all that mattered. Judy seemed excited by the prospect of smoking weed.

'I can't wait,' she said, as she inhaled long and deeply, before letting the smoke out.

We gently got high together. It was fun. The whole summer and having a bit of time alone, just the two of us, was exhilarating. It made us think it might be nice to live together. The problem was we couldn't really afford it. Neither of us got paid enough. We'd need better jobs.

I'd have to work full time, and I didn't really want to do that. I wasn't helped by the deterioration in my health. Even so I made a mental note to look again at teacher training for the following year. I might get accepted this time. It might also prove to be a stepping stone for Judy and I to forge a proper life and future together.

Even when my parents returned from abroad Judy and I continued our partying when we could. I took Judy with me on a rugby club dinner and dance event, as it meant a weekend away together in an elegant hotel. I wasn't normally into such things. I would normally have been the last person to go. I was one of the least typical rugby players in the history of the game, and I didn't mix all that much with the other players. I just played because I liked playing, nothing to do with the social side. I probably surprised a few people when I said I was going. I did it, as it meant Judy and I could get drunk together and have a lot of sex in a nice hotel room.

We probably surprised a few more people when we agreed to attend a gay charity ball. It was being organised by one of the owners of the florists where Judy worked. It was a lavish event, being held to help raise funds for victims of AIDS and for HIV research. I think he only asked Judy out of politeness. I don't think he expected her to say yes. He was probably surprised when she said she would go. He was probably even more surprised when I said I would go too. Most of the men were going in drag. I was quite open minded, so wasn't too bothered about that. Nowadays such an event would attract an eclectic mix of people. That was less the case then, and when we got there we found we were among just a tiny handful of straight people attending. It didn't matter. We had fun. It was actually held at one of the hotels where Judy and I had previously had sex in the toilets. I don't think we did that night. Judy still managed to shock her boss.

'Are you smoking?' he asked, in a slightly aghast voice. 'I thought you were a nice, sweet girl.'

So had I, until I got to know her well. He had a lot to learn. Despite my ongoing undiagnosed ill health they were good times. We had a laugh, doing things we wouldn't normally do. It helped take my mind off the fact I didn't feel great. It helped me forget I could no longer compete at the same level of sport I had prior to my illness. It helped me focus on other things. It reminded me I really liked Judy. We were well suited. We had fun together. We had almost no one else in our lives, but we didn't seem to need them. Most of the time we were happy just doing our own thing on our own.

As the autumn of 1993 turned to winter I again started thinking long term about leaving my job. As before I applied to do teacher training. This time I applied for a lot more courses, and not just the one or two located near where I lived. I applied to universities and colleges over a much bigger geographical area. It wasn't that I really wanted to be a teacher. I didn't. It was just something I was qualified to do, and it seemed like steady money. The only major downside was that if I ended up studying away, there would be a period of nearly a year when I'd mainly only see Judy at weekends. Still, I believed if our love was truly as strong as I thought it was, we could easily survive that. It might even make us stronger. A change of scenery at weekends could potentially do us some good and give our relationship new impetus.

Judy never said how she felt about the prospect of me going away for an extended period, but she gave little sign it was a problem. She didn't object when I started applying. She appeared to be behind me in my plans. She knew that in part I was doing it to give us a chance of a better future together. I wasn't trying to be selfish. I was doing it for us. I had little doubt that our relationship could survive almost anything thrown at it, including this. I had no doubts we'd be all right. We'd be more than all right. We'd positively blossom, I hoped. Besides, it might not even be a problem. My first choice was to get a place on a course near where I presently lived.

Christmas of 1993 was a good one for Judy and me. We exchanged lavish gifts as always. We went out drinking together. We stayed in drinking. Judy came over and joined us for extravagant festive feasts with my parents. My mum was a good cook and laid on elaborate meals for us all. Apart from my ongoing mystery health problems, which still hadn't cleared up, life was pretty good. I was looking at a change of career. I was reasonably confident about the future. I was in love with Judy. I thought she was in love with me. I just hoped a new year would bring better health. If it did everything else would fall neatly into place, I firmly believed.

Chapter Four

During the early months of 1994 I started getting invited to interviews for teacher training courses to start in the coming autumn. I was particularly pleased and somewhat relieved to secure an interview on the course where I lived. It was not only one of the best, but for me also the most convenient. I prepared well and carefully for the interview, to maximise my chances. I was hopeful of success, but in the event I didn't get a place. I was told I interviewed well, but some of the other candidates were better qualified. It was a setback. It was a disappointment. It meant I'd have to look further afield, if I still wanted to pursue a career in teaching.

Ideally I wanted to teach PE. The problem was there was little in my education, training and employment background to date that qualified me to teach PE, or gave any indication I'd be any good at it if I was accepted on a course. All I had was my knowledge and love of sport. I was adept at playing games, but I had no coaching qualifications as such. I was confident I'd be good at it, but I was expecting course directors and tutors to take something of a leap of faith with me. Why should they do that, when there were better candidates with sports science degrees? I'd studied history. I had a degree in that subject. I could have walked onto almost any course in the country to study to teach history. The thing was I didn't want to do that. I wanted to teach PE.

In the end I had to compromise. It became obvious I'd never get a place on a course teaching PE alone. I'd have to combine it with something else. That would be the best outcome I could possibly hope for. As it turned out I eventually got a place training to teach in primary schools. I'd have to teach a bit of everything, all subjects across the curriculum, but I could at least specialise in PE, history and English. It wasn't quite what I'd wanted, but it was better than nothing. The other thing was the course was in a city seventy miles away. But it was a lively city with a lot going on. I thought Judy and I could have some fun together there. Whilst it was a compromise I for one was determined to make the best of it. When I told Judy she went a little quiet.

'Aren't you pleased?' I asked her.

'Not really,' she replied.

'Why not?' I asked. 'I thought you wanted our relationship to move on to the next level. I thought you wanted us to be able to live together. In a short time this will allow us to do just that. We'll only be apart for less than a year. And we won't really be apart. We'll still see each other all the time.'

'I do want our relationship to move on,' Judy said. 'But I want it to move on round here. I want us to live together now. I don't want to have to wait. I want us to be able to sleep together in the same room, not in separate bedrooms like we do at your parents. I've got fed up with that. We've been together almost four years now. They must know we have sex.'

'I'm sure they do know, but my parents are very old fashioned,' I explained. 'They don't approve of things like that, unless you're married. It's their house, so I guess they make the rules.'

Judy was normally quiet. It was unusual for her to open up with such honesty and say what she really felt; to fully reveal what was really going on in her head and her heart.

'Think about it,' I continued. 'It's only for a year, and then we'll be able to be together and do all that.'

Judy nodded her head but didn't seem totally convinced.

'You'll be able to come up at weekends. We'll be in a bigger city, where we'll be able to go out to better club nights and more big names gigs. It will be fun. We'll enjoy ourselves. When you can't come up I'll come back to see you,' I said.

'Maybe,' Judy said reluctantly. 'I guess it could be all right. I'm just going to be bored and lonely on weekdays, when I don't see you.'

'I'll be lonely when I don't see you too,' I agreed. 'But we'll have the weekends to look forward to.'

Outwardly Judy went along with my plans. She didn't make any more open protestations, but I did sense her growing a little more distant from me. My mum also noticed a change in her.

'Is everything OK between you two?' she asked.

'I think so,' I replied. 'Judy's just found it a little hard adjusting to the idea of me going away.'

'That's fair enough,' my mum said. 'You can't blame her for that.'

'I don't. I've found it hard myself,' I agreed. 'I'd have much preferred to have got on a course round here. But it is what it is. I was lucky to get a place anywhere at all. We just have to make the best of it.'

Then one weekend when Judy came up she dropped a bombshell. It was a Friday night and we'd been out for a drink. I'd felt she wasn't quite her normal relaxed self and had seemed a bit on edge. She didn't want to come back and stay at my parents' house, as she usually did.

'Just drop me at the train station, so I can go home,' she said.

'What do you mean?' I asked. 'I can't do that. You always stay over.'

'I just don't feel like it tonight,' Judy said. 'I need to be by myself. I need some time alone.'

'I don't understand,' I said. 'We've had a nice night. What's the problem?'

'I don't know. I just need to be on my own,' Judy said, half turning away and not really looking at me directly in the eye.

I was shocked. I didn't know what to say. It had come out of nowhere without any warning. I was confused. I was lost for words.

'Look, come back with me tonight and sleep on it at least,' I said at last.

'I don't really want to. I want to go home,' Judy insisted.

'It's late. You can't do that,' I replied.

Eventually I persuaded Judy to stay the night. In the morning her mood had little improved. After breakfast she asked me to drive her to the station. I did what she asked, although I didn't want to. We drove in silence most of the way.

'I just don't understand what the problem is,' I said eventually.

'We need to talk,' Judy said.

'About what?' I asked.

Frankly I was too stunned and too hurt by events as they appeared to be unfolding to want to talk. I didn't really know what was happening. It had come almost totally out of the blue.

'I'm just fed up with this coming up like this every weekend. I need a break from it,' Judy said.

'You've never complained before,' I pointed out. 'We've always had fun together.'

'I'm not having fun now. I just don't think our relationship is going anywhere,' Judy said.

I didn't reply. I was scared what I might say and scared what Judy might say. I was too upset. I was too astonished by Judy's outburst to know how to respond. I thought we were in love. It didn't really sound like the girl I thought I knew and thought I wanted to be with.

'Haven't you got anything to say?' Judy pressed me, when the silence continued.

'Not really,' I replied.

'Don't you want to talk?' Judy asked.

'I can't right now,' I whispered.

'Why not?'

'Because I'm too hurt. I can't believe what you're saying,' I said. 'We can talk about it another time.'

I dropped Judy at the train station as she requested. I didn't say another word. I couldn't think what to say in truth. I was too taken aback. All words seemed worthless and pointless. Instead I just drove back to my parents, to try to make some sense of what had just happened. I sat alone in my bedroom, with just myself and my thoughts. If Judy wanted time apart I'd give her just that, I eventually decided. She'd soon come running back, I thought. She'd be lost and lonely without me. She could have her break, and then soon enough we'd pick up again exactly where we'd left off. By the following weekend she'd be dying to see me. That's what I thought. That's what I convinced myself. So I didn't ring Judy. I waited for her to ring me.

Judy didn't ring me that day, or the following day, or the day after that, or the whole week. I thought she'd ring me to arrange to meet up at the weekend. She didn't. I found myself going out alone on the Saturday night a week since I'd last seen Judy. The next day was Mother's Day. My dad had arranged with Judy to have a bouquet of flowers delivered for my mum. He was now worried they wouldn't come, as we'd fallen out. When they were late arriving the next day he asked me to ring Judy. I didn't really want to, but I felt I had to. Judy answered but was oddly distant.

'My dad is worried about the flowers,' I said.

'They're on their way,' Judy replied.

We then engaged in some small talk.

'When am I going to see you?' I said at last.

'I thought that was it,' Judy replied.

'What, it's over just like that, without even a proper conversation?' I asked, somewhat dumbfounded.

'You didn't want to talk,' Judy said.

'I want to talk now,' I said. 'I need some kind of explanation. You said you wanted a break from coming up, not that it was over for good. Why didn't you tell me the truth?'

'I thought I had,' Judy said, sounding distant and not bothered.

'You can't just break it off like this,' I said. 'Doesn't the fact we've been together for four years mean anything at all? We need to discuss this face to face. You owe me that much at least.'

'I don't owe you anything,' Judy said and hung up the phone.

I tried ringing Judy again at various times during the week. I was in a state. My head was all over the place. I started to feel a little desperate. I really needed to speak to her, to see her, to meet up, to see why she was behaving as she was. I rang at times I was certain she'd be in. She wasn't in. I spoke to her sister, who said she'd pass on a message. I spoke to her mum several times.

'Hasn't she spoken to you? Hasn't she said anything at all?' her mum asked.

'Not really,' I said.

'I'll get her to ring you,' she promised.

I could tell by her tone there was something she wasn't telling me. I'd always got on well with Judy's mum. I could sense that neither she nor Judy's sister were particularly impressed with how Judy was behaving. Something was going on, more than they were saying. Clearly they felt that it was Judy's responsibility to tell me herself. Of course Judy didn't ring me. I had to keep ringing her back, to let her put me out of my misery. Eventually her mum made her speak to me.

'What do you want?' she said. 'You better make this quick.'

She sounded nothing like the person I'd known and been with for four years.

'We need to meet up, to talk this through,' I said.

'I can't, and I don't want to,' Judy replied.

'It's important. I need some answers and I need some closure,' I said.

'I can't meet you,' Judy persisted.

'Why can't you meet me?' I asked.

'I didn't want to get nasty, but it appears I'm going to have to,' Judy stated in a bored, slightly exasperated voice.

She sounded like a stranger, someone twisted, dark and cruel. I didn't really know what she was talking about and where she was going with her train of thought.

'I can't meet you, because I'm seeing someone else,' she said. 'Happy now you know the truth?'

I knew the truth indeed, but I couldn't quite believe it. Of course it all made sense now, why Judy hadn't been in when I'd expected her to be. She'd been staying over with some new man. It had been less than a fortnight, but she was clearly already sleeping with him. It was hard to take in.

'Oh I understand perfectly. It's all falling into place,' I said angrily. 'So how long has this been going on?'

'I've only just met him,' Judy claimed.

It seemed highly improbable.

'Likely story,' I sneered in reply.

'I went out to the pub with my sister the first weekend I didn't see you, and I met him there,' Judy claimed.

'You expect me to believe that?' I laughed.

'You can believe what you like,' Judy replied.

'Whatever, I don't really care anymore,' I said.

Of course, I did care, but it didn't really matter. That was it. She was gone, and there was nothing I could do about it.

'I've still got some of your things. What do you want me to do with them?' I said at last.

'You can throw them away if you like,' Judy answered.

'I'm not doing that,' I said. 'I'll drop them in at your shop.'

'All right, if you must,' Judy said and hung up again.

A couple of days passed before I took her remaining belongings round. When I did I thought about making some great romantic speech to her, proclaiming my everlasting love. In the event I didn't do that. It seemed pointless. I realised it would serve no purpose. She was already gone. She'd moved on. I hadn't even begun to come to terms with the notion of not being with her, and she was already with someone else. She was already having sex with him, whoever he was, wherever and whenever she'd met him. Had she told the truth? It seemed unlikely. If she had, things had moved very swiftly. More likely they'd met a while ago and he was the reason she'd turned cold on me. Whatever the truth there was nothing I could do about it. She'd left me for another man, and I was stuck with it. I had to deal with it, whatever that meant. I thought Judy and I might get married in time. We wouldn't be getting married now. She'd slipped through my grasp. She was gone for good. Suddenly I felt terribly alone. Suddenly the fact she'd left me really hit home hard. When I dropped her things at her work, she grudgingly invited me into the back office, presumably so we could chat in private. I declined. I simply shook my head.

'I thought you wanted to talk?' Judy said.

'It's all right,' I replied.

'You said it was important,' Judy persisted.

'It was, but it's too late now,' I said.

There were loads of things I wanted to say to her about how much she meant to me, but I could tell it would only fall on deaf ears and there was no chance of resurrecting our broken relationship. Instead I left her standing there with her mouth open. Her boss was standing behind her, looking equally bemused. I placed her belongings on the front desk and I just turned on my heels and walked out the door. I didn't look back. I just walked back to my car and drove off. I wanted to talk to her, but the time for conversation had gone. It could achieve nothing now. She'd made her decision. It couldn't be reversed. It couldn't be changed. I couldn't turn back the clock, as if nothing had happened. She'd refused to talk to me on my terms, when I'd wanted her to. I wasn't going to give her the satisfaction and talk to her now on her terms. I dropped her things and that was it. I left and tried to forget all about her. I tried hard to put her out of my head. Of course it wouldn't be quite as easy as that.

Chapter Five

Strangely things weren't that bad at first. Now I didn't have Judy to think about I started going out by myself again much more often. I started to reconnect with friends I'd half forgotten about. Judy hadn't been one to socialise with others. As a result I'd allowed friendships to falter and slip by the wayside. For the last four years it had just been the two of us. My life had pretty much revolved round Judy and hers around mine. There had been little room to let others in. Now I was on my own I had to start reaching out to others again. I had to start doing things I wouldn't otherwise have had need to be doing. In some ways it gave my social life a much needed shot in the arm. I realised Judy and I had become too set in our ways. We'd been taking the easy options. We'd been having too many quiet nights in. We'd become lazy. We'd been taking each other for granted. Maybe she was right. Maybe some of the excitement had gone out of our relationship. We hadn't been sleeping together as much. Perhaps things had gone a little stale. Judy's complaint had been it wasn't moving forward. It wasn't progressing at the pace she needed. There was some truth in her argument. Now I was on my own I could see that myself. Perhaps Judy wasn't alone in growing a little bored. Perhaps I too had become a little bored and needed a change. Maybe I needed something new to reawaken my sense of adventure and excitement in life.

I didn't miss Judy that much at first. It was actually quite refreshing to be single and to be able to go out on Friday and Saturday nights without being beholden to anyone. It felt more like we were just on a break. Perhaps some part of me stubbornly believed she'd still be back, that the split wasn't permanent. I'm not sure what it was. Maybe the reality of the situation just hadn't properly sunk in. On one of the first weekends after Judy and I stopped seeing each other, I went to see some local indie bands I noticed were performing in a function room at the back of a local pub. The live music was being followed by an indie DJ, playing the type of lo-fi, jangly guitar pop I was a fan of. I knew a couple of the guys in the bands, so I thought it might be an entertaining night. I didn't have anywhere else to be. I didn't have anywhere else to go or anyone else to see. So short of other options I thought I might as well check it out.

When I got there I saw a girl I knew sitting at one of the tables. She was drinking and chatting to others, as she listened to the music. She looked like she was having a good time and enjoying herself. Her name was Tracy. I'd fancied her for ages. She was very glamorous and very attractive. She had a distinctive and stylish, sixties influenced look, with high, beehive hair, tight-fitting, stripy top, short skirt and sexy, knee-length, leather boots. She wasn't entirely retro. She'd given her Mod look a slightly modern, indie twist. To me she looked like a goddess. I'd seen a lot of my friends get off with her over the years. I'd always been very jealous, as I'd never been one of them. Maybe tonight would be different. Maybe tonight it would be my turn. As I was on my own, as soon as I saw her I went over to speak to her.

'Hi,' I said, pulling up a chair. 'Do you mind if I join you?'

Tracy smiled. She looked genuinely pleased to see me.

'Of course not,' Tracy replied. 'It's lovely to see you. I haven't seen you out for a long time.'

'I know,' I said. 'I've been seeing a girl, but we're not together anymore.'

'Sorry to hear that,' Tracy said. 'I'm single again myself.'

That news in itself made my ears prick up.

'Must be catching,' I joked.

Tracy laughed. We continued to chat, as one band finished and another started. At one point I got up to get myself and Tracy another drink. She seemed happy. She didn't seem annoyed I was monopolising her company. She continued to chat with the others at the table, as well as talking to me. After a while I got us more drinks. They were slipping down nicely. Then without even looking at me or in my direction at all, Tracy took hold of my hand under the table. She continued to talk to the others, yet at the same time slipped her fingers carefully between mine and didn't let go. My face lit up. I had a beaming smile all across it. It felt amazing holding her hand. Maybe it was fate Judy and I had split up. Maybe it was meant to be, so Judy could find a new man and I could be with Tracy. For a brief second it certainly felt like that. After the music had finished Tracy and I kissed in the street outside the pub. It felt fantastic. For a moment I felt elated.

'I've got to get my taxi in a minute,' Tracy said at last, finally breaking off our embrace.

'When can I see you again?' I asked.

'At the weekend,' Tracy promised.

We made vague arrangements to meet again. As I walked home I felt ecstatic. I thought I was in love. My head was spinning. I couldn't

35

believe it. Judy had left me, but after all this time of longing I was finally with Tracy. Perhaps it was destiny. I soon came back down to reality with a thud. By the following weekend Tracy had cooled on me. I couldn't wait to see her, but she made it clear she wanted to go back to just being friends. It appeared Saturday had been a one off, and there would be no repeat. I felt deflated. I felt like I'd been punched in the stomach.

It was at that point that I realised I truly was alone. It was then for the first time that I fully understood Judy was gone. She'd left me and was never coming back. At first it hadn't felt quite real. It had almost felt like a game. Now it felt all too real. The harsh truth really struck home. I was overwhelmed by a sense of sadness and depression. I felt grey and wretched. I didn't want to get up. I didn't want to go out. I didn't want to do anything. I felt empty inside. A part of me was missing. It was Judy. I missed her now more than I thought I would. I missed her now much more than I realised at first. It wasn't a break. It was permanent. That was it. It was over. I wrote her a final letter, including a poem expressing how much I missed her. She never replied. I tried one last time to ring her. She refused to take my call.

It was a shame. We'd had four good years together, with seldom an argument. It was being soured by a bad and unnecessarily bitter ending. It could have been settled so differently and so much more amicably. Unfortunately Judy handled things very poorly, about as poorly as she possibly could. Of course I hadn't been perfect. I'd had an affair with Karen for a start, but that had been over a long time ago, and Judy had never found out about it. Now it was my turn to feel pain. It was my turn to be hurt. It would have been so much better if Judy had at least met me face to face and spoken to me in person. She'd repeatedly refused. It would have been better if Judy hadn't moved on straight away, if she hadn't already been seeing and sleeping with someone else, someone new, an immediate replacement.

It felt like she was rubbing my face in it. It felt like a kick in the teeth. It felt like she was being as hurtful as she could possibly be. She showed no concerns at all for the harmful and devastating effect that her behaviour would have on me. She could have showed consideration. She didn't show any. She could have met me at least to explain in person. She could have said sorry. She did none of those things. She just became steadily more hostile and more hurtful. Unfortunately things didn't improve. Indeed very quickly they got a whole lot worse altogether.

I could barely face going to work anymore. Everyone there seemed to know my business. It was a small town. People talked. They liked to gossip. My work colleagues seemed to know more about what had happened that I did. It was embarrassing. It was humiliating. I was probably the gossip of the whole town. *Local news reporter has been dumped by young beauty for another man.* I could sense people were talking about it behind my back. No one dared mention it to my face. They didn't need to. There was a kind of hushed silence when I walked into the office. I sensed the chatter before my arrival had been about me. As soon as I was there it suddenly stopped. Worse still I had six more months of this to endure, before I could get away, before I could escape, before I could start again in a new city far away, where no one knew me. The time couldn't go fast enough.

As it was it dragged painfully. Each day felt like weeks. Each week felt like months. It was nothing personal against my work colleagues, but I needed to be somewhere else. I couldn't wait for the six months to pass and my teacher training course to start. I'd outlived my usefulness where I was. Everyone knew I was leaving in the autumn anyway. It was almost pointless my being there anymore. My heart obviously wasn't in it. I was just going through the motions. If I had my time again I wouldn't have stayed. I'd have just left. I'd have done something else for the six months before my course started, something more constructive and rewarding perhaps. But I can't rewrite the past. As it was I stayed. I served out the six months of pain, almost like a prison sentence.

At lunchtimes I took long walks down country lanes leading out of the town, to try and clear my head. I wanted to be alone, to reflect and to come to terms with the hurt of Judy leaving me in the manner in which she had. It didn't get any better. It was made worse by working in the same town, where Judy had got together with her new lover. I worried I might bump into them. All the time I overheard little snippets of information about them, and how rapidly their relationship was progressing. It was hurtful to hear. Things reached a new level altogether, when by chance I bumped into Judy's dad one morning, as I popped out from work to grab some food. I didn't know if he'd even want to speak to me. He did. He was even more anxious to offload than I was, it appeared.

'She's been so stupid,' he said. 'I can't believe what she's done now. I had such high hopes for her. She's thrown away any chance of a future.'

'What do you mean?' I asked, a little bit confused.

I had no idea what he was talking about.

'I had my reservations about you, I must admit,' he continued. 'You seemed like a nice guy, but a bit of a drifter and a dreamer. But at least you looked after her, not like this new fella.'

He seemed genuinely angry and upset. He was finding it hard to hold back his sense of rage and frustration. I wasn't quite sure why. I wasn't sure of the reason for his bitterness. Surely it was just a case that she'd swapped one boyfriend for a new boyfriend. Or maybe there was more to it. Maybe there was something else.

'What's happened?' I asked at last, not 100 per cent sure I actually wanted an answer to my question.

'Well, she's only gone and got herself pregnant,' Judy's dad muttered. 'They're now moving in together of all things.'

There was no sparing of my feelings. It didn't seem to occur to him that it might be very upsetting for me to hear this latest news. We'd only split up two months earlier. There had hardly been any time for her to get pregnant, but apparently she'd managed it. She was barely twenty years old and up the duff. She was moving in with a guy she'd only been with for two months. She hadn't moved in with me after four years. It was a lot to take in. It was difficult to listen to in truth.

'I'm sorry to hear it. I hope she's all right,' I said.

It seemed like the gentlemanly thing to do, to say the appropriate thing to her dad, even though inside I felt totally messed up by what he'd just announced. My thoughts were all over the place in truth.

'I told her she doesn't have to have it. She could get rid of it if she wanted and still have a future. But she's stubborn and won't listen. She's going to have the baby,' her dad said.

I knew if it had been my baby, I'd have wanted her to have it. Of course it wasn't my baby. It was someone else's.

'We had a big row about it and she stormed out,' her dad continued. 'She went round to stay at his place. They're now looking to find a new house together. We're not speaking. I don't know if we'll ever speak again.'

I felt sorry for him. I felt sorry for me. I could hardly believe what I was hearing. But it seemed it was my job to console him. I'm not sure he realised the extent to which my life had been turned upside down, that I'd been planning a future with his daughter that was now in tatters. But I put my feelings to one side. I tried to be the bigger man. I didn't say what I was really feeling.

'I hope it sorts itself out,' I said, before heading back to the office, even more shocked and bewildered than when I'd left.

'Thanks,' he said.

He was clearly as hurt and upset by what had happened as I was. It seemed all our lives had been thrown into turmoil, including Judy's and now every member of her family. In some ways I was relatively unscathed. I was out of it now. She was now lumbered with this guy for the foreseeable future, whether she wanted to be or not. I presumed she wanted to be, however. She hadn't wanted to be with me. When I got home from work I told my parents the news.

'Judy's pregnant,' I said.

'Seriously? She can't be,' my mum said. 'And I always thought she was such a nice girl.'

'Maybe she wasn't such a nice girl after all,' my dad suggested.

'I'm afraid, I don't think she was,' I said.

'Are you sure it's not yours?' my mum asked accusingly.

'It's not mine,' I said.

I was pretty sure it wasn't. We hadn't had sex for a while. I'd have been happier if it had been mine. The next few weeks passed, as if I was in some kind of dream or suspended reality. Nothing seemed quite real. I felt distant and detached from my surroundings. I felt quietly melancholy. I felt lonely and lost. In many ways it was good I was going away. I only had a few more months of this to put up with. To help the time pass I tried to immerse myself in poetry. I reworked some of my best poems I'd written over the last few years and published two small pamphlets of them. The first was titled *Views from an Upstairs Room*. The second I called *Notes from a Broken Home*. They were the best collections I'd produced in a while. I felt depressed but artistically inspired. I wrote lots of poems about my break-up with Judy. I didn't use any of those just yet. I held onto them. It felt too raw and too painful to include them. I'd perhaps use them at some point in the future, when I didn't feel so close to the events that had inspired them.

I finished the novel I'd been working on. It wasn't great, but at least it proved I could write a novel. I could maintain a storyline for the required amount of words. That at least gave me a small grain of comfort. They were hard to find at that particular moment in time in mid 1994. I was twenty-nine years old and was facing the prospect of more or less starting my life again from scratch, on my own. I sent extracts of the novel off to a few prospective publishers and agents. They weren't particularly impressed. There was little interest in what I sent them, so I started working on a new novel. I called it *Beatnik*. It was a largely autobiographical account of launching an underground literary magazine in the 1980s. The subject matter was a little more personal and close to my heart. What I was writing seemed to me at least rather more promising than my somewhat abortive first attempt. I had a little more hope that something positive in the form of publication might come of it. I was trying to be creative, but it wasn't always easy to concentrate. Judy was never far from my thoughts. I felt locked in some kind of dark void from which I couldn't escape. I kept picturing her with her new bloke. I felt like a character from a Jean-Paul Sartre novel, alienated, disillusioned, an outsider, going nowhere.

Worse was to come. We'd only been split up for three or four months when I got more shocking news of Judy. I was at work, when something caught my eye. It was an announcement in the paper. I didn't normally read them, but for some reason I was drawn to this one. My work colleagues tried to stop me from seeing, but it was too late. I'd already seen it. It was a wedding announcement. It carried Judy's name. She'd got married at a small registry office service the previous weekend. It was a congratulations notice from both families. I did a double take. I had to stop and look at it twice. I took a sharp intake of breath. I could barely believe it. Judy was married. As if her falling pregnant wasn't enough. This was truly shocking. I felt like the stuffing had been knocked out of me. I felt like my whole world had well and truly fallen apart. I'd barely started to come to terms with being without Judy. She'd moved on in no uncertain terms. She wasn't only with someone else, she was now pregnant and married.

One of the younger girls at work appeared to take pity on me. She was the same age as Judy. She was called Joanne. They'd been in the same class together at school. They were very different characters from different backgrounds, but Joanne she was good company and not unattractive. She started brushing against me when we were in close proximity at work. She started touching my hand, when there was no real need to. Her body language made it clear she was available, if I was interested. She told me I was welcome to come over to her place at lunchtimes, if I was bored. I didn't take her up on any of her offers. I should have. I regretted it afterwards. It was just too soon for me. I hadn't got over Judy. I also didn't want to date someone else in the same town where Judy lived. I was sure we'd run into each other. With my luck it was bound to happen. It was a shame. Joanne and I could certainly have had some fun, if we had got together.

Instead I resigned myself to being alone. I listened to heartfelt songs of loneliness and longing by soulful American singer-songwriters from the 1960s and 1970s like Tim Hardin and James Taylor. I listened to Carole King, singing her moving melodies of broken love. It seemed to sum up my mood. It was one of loss. I felt like I was recovering from a bereavement. In many ways I was. Then somewhat unexpectedly I started to hang out with an ex-girlfriend of mine called Rachel I'd dated some years earlier, before I'd met Judy. Before I knew it we were dating again, but it didn't feel quite right. I think we both realised we were just friends and would probably never be more than that. Certainly not at that point in time. I wasn't ready. I kidded myself I was, but as soon as I thought about going out with someone different I withdrew into myself. I couldn't commit. My heart was somewhere else.

I spent the last few weeks of the summer back on my own. It was probably for the best. I'd be leaving for pastures new very soon anyway. I'd be starting a new life. I'd be leaving my old one behind. It would be a new beginning. Hopefully the trials and tribulations of the previous few months would be forgotten. Somehow I'd got through them. It hadn't been easy. It had been tough in the extreme. It had been a slow and painful end to over six years working in the same quiet, seaside town. My work colleagues gave me a good send off. It was kind of them. They booked out a room at the back of a local pub for a small leaving function. We had a few drinks and plenty to eat. It was a nice note to part on. They thanked me for my work and told me I'd be missed. I told them I'd miss them too. They hoped I was moving on to better things. Only time would tell, I told them. They realised I needed to get out. I couldn't carry on as I was. I was just glad I had something to go to, something that would take me some distance away. It would be an opportunity to forget all about Judy.

Chapter Six

By the end of September 1994 I was living in a new house in a new city. I rented out the basement of a small, terraced property, with a fellow student. We had one room each, and a shared kitchen and a shared bathroom. It was basic, but it was cheap and functional. After nearly seven years of working I was now a student again. I didn't expect luxury. I didn't need it. It was situated in a quiet, residential street, away from the main road. It was clean, and it was a roof over my head. It was conveniently located, only about a fifteen-minute walk from the campus where I was studying. There were local shops, pubs and cafés nearby, and the city centre wasn't too far away. An elderly lady lived above us, but she largely kept herself to herself, just as I kept myself to myself. I played my music quietly. I rarely strummed my guitar. I didn't want to draw undue attention to what I did and when I came and went. I didn't want to be an annoyance to anyone else, and I didn't want them to be an annoyance to me.

In some ways I was quite happy to have moved as a single man. I wasn't tied down to anyone. I didn't have anyone waiting for me back at home. I was free. For the first time in some years I could do whatever I wanted when I wanted. I could go out anytime I liked. I could date anyone I met who seemed interested. I could explore new possibilities at last. Naturally I missed Judy. I still felt a huge hole in my life that hadn't been filled. But it was a real chance to forget and move on. I was determined to try and do that. The fact that I'd moved helped a little bit. I was now living somewhere that had few connections to Judy. I'd left behind all the places, memories and faces I associated with her. It was an opportunity to start again. In some ways I was quite excited. I knew that the women outnumbered the men on my course by about four to one. They'd be falling over themselves to compete for the available males, I naively thought. I'd be fighting them off. In all probability I could have my pick of the single girls. Surely there would be someone there for me. Given the odds there was bound to be. Of course it didn't quite work out like that. I couldn't have been more misguided and more wrong. Things weren't quite as I'd hoped and expected to find them.

As is often the case when splitting up with a long-term partner, there is an inclination to go for a new and more extreme look. That was my first mistake. I wanted to make a bold statement. I wanted to update my wardrobe, revamp my appearance and freshen up my image. I realised that in a relaxed and comfortable relationship with Judy, I'd allowed myself to become a little too safe and middle of the road. I was much taken with *Primal Scream*'s latest album *Give Out But Don't Give Up* at that time, which had been released in the March of that year. I started dyeing my hair darker brown and letting it grow longer, to look more like singer Bobby Gillespie. I started wearing similar clothes to the styles he favoured. Whilst the look might have been a hit in an alternative or indie nightclub, it was unlikely to score many points with a class of young, female trainee teachers. It didn't.

Then I made my second mistake. I was like a child in a sweetshop. I was faced with too much choice. I made my intentions far too obvious. I was too keen. I didn't play it coolly and cleverly, as I normally did. I played it very badly. Young women aren't stupid. I put them off. They could sense I was a little desperate. Every new girl I met I saw as a potential girlfriend. They could see right through me, and each one ran a mile. I was stupid. If I'd been more aloof, more mysterious, as I normally was, I might have stood a chance. Here, faced with what seemed like an abundance of riches of the opposite sex, I couldn't make progress or headway with a single one. Maybe I'd been out of the dating game too long. I'd always done quite well with women in the past. Maybe I'd lost my looks. Maybe I was getting too old. I was after all a little older than the rest of the students on my course. Here, in a situation where I was surrounded by young women and thought I couldn't fail, I failed hopelessly. Still, I learnt my lesson. I vowed I'd never show my desperation again. I'd never chase women. I'd let them come to me another time.

Whilst I didn't help myself, and I went about finding a new girlfriend in entirely the wrong way, it wasn't entirely my fault I didn't meet with more success. For a start most of the attractive girls on my course were already taken. They were in long-term relationships. They weren't looking for anyone else. Others just wanted to concentrate on their studies. They didn't want the distraction of a relationship, whilst trying to pass what was a very intense course. Some just weren't into men. I was soon to learn it was a somewhat strongly feminist college that I was attending, and for quite a number of them men just wasn't their thing. Fair enough. It meant my odds of finding someone weren't quite as high as I'd hoped. No one else was into the kind of indie and alternative music and fashion that I was. They largely had quite conventional tastes.

Whilst everyone was pleasant enough to my face, I was a bit of an outsider and an odd one out. I was a square peg in a round hole.

For me part of the appeal of being a student again was to be able to go out and socialise once more. I wanted to party, get drunk and have some fun. It seemed I was somewhat alone in this. Whilst fellow students were happy enough to go out on a Saturday night, the majority had come to study. Their priority was to complete the course and get a job teaching. They weren't like me. I would have been happy going out drinking most nights. Very quickly it became apparent that wasn't going to happen. Or if it did I'd be largely drinking alone. I socialised with the other students as much as I could. If there was a party or a gathering in a café or pub I went. There were a few single girls I liked. The problem was none of them seemed to like me back. And for me the amount of socialising and going out just wasn't enough.

I quickly established a routine. The college course was hard work, relentless and exhausting. We had a full timetable of classes to attend on a myriad of different subjects. There was more studying and preparation to be done every evening. I generally didn't finish working until around half past nine each night. Afterwards I'd drink beer in my room. Occasionally I went for a walk outside in the dark, nighttime air. Sometimes I'd stop at a pub and have a drink by myself. I'd meet up with fellow students, if they happened to be going out. Mostly they went to bed early, as we had classes again first thing the next day. That wasn't sufficient for me. It wasn't what I'd come for. I needed more. I found the course quite boring. It wasn't as much fun as I'd hoped. I wasn't sure I was cut out to be a teacher.

I scoured local listings and what's on magazines for interesting things to do. I looked for indie and alternative music nights I could go to. I found one or two, but it was only limited pleasure going on my own. I went to see arthouse movies when they were on. I always went by myself. I never went with anyone else. I was still feeling the effects of glandular fever quite badly, though I was still yet to be officially diagnosed. Even so I looked to play some sport to relieve my slight sense of boredom and loneliness. I joined the college badminton club. I joined a local rugby club and played a few games on Saturday afternoons. Mostly when I wasn't working, I sat in my room by myself listening to music and drinking. I liked the city I was living in. I could see it was full of possibility for socialising and entertainment. I just needed someone to socialise with. It was a shame Judy hadn't come with me. But she hadn't. She'd made her choice. I didn't much like the course I was on, but I liked where I lived. I tried to make the best of it. I hoped in time I might meet someone, someone into the same things, who I could share my new life with.

After I'd been away for about eight weeks, I was sent on my first school-based teaching practice. It was deemed I was now sufficiently experienced to be let loose in a classroom, to teach real kids on my own. I was sent to a struggling inner-city school, where the children were largely from poor and disadvantaged backgrounds. I had an unsympathetic and mostly disinterested class teacher as my mentor. She gave me little guidance in how or what I should be teaching. She mainly left me to my own devices and to get on with it by myself. I got the firm impression she was happy just to be shot of the pupils in her class for the few weeks I was there. It was a nice break for her. It wasn't for me. I found it a depressing and disheartening experience.

The children had no interest in what I was trying to teach them. It wasn't surprising. Many were from the homes of single or unemployed parents, in some cases drug addicts and even prostitutes. They hadn't been given the greatest start in life. I tried to enthuse them. I tried to give some of the most disadvantaged words of encouragement, but it was difficult. Whilst I felt sorry for them, my enthusiasm for the course and teaching in general quickly dissipated. I carried on, but my heart wasn't really in it. I started to have severe doubts if I'd done the right thing in taking a place on a teacher training course in the first place. I realised I'd probably made a big mistake. Though I hadn't made a mistake leaving my job. I'd been right in doing that. I couldn't have carried on as I was. I'd needed to escape all memories, connections and associations with Judy and the town where she lived. I just doubted I'd chosen the best profession for me personally to replace it with. I should probably have done something else. I just had no idea what I should have chosen or looked at instead. Teaching had been a compromise. It was beginning to feel more like it with every week that passed.

At the end of my first teaching practice, a report was completed on how I'd performed. It was disappointing and nowhere near as good as it should have been. In fact it was so far below the level I should have been achieving, that I was called in to discuss it with one of the tutors at a special meeting. There was a general feeling I'd tried too hard to be a friend of the children and not a teacher to them. There was some truth in that. I'd felt sorry for them. Part of me wanted to fix them. Of course it wasn't as easy as that. A lot of them couldn't be fixed. There was an acceptance too that it wasn't entirely my fault. I hadn't received the support I should have. The teacher I'd been left with had been entirely unhelpful and uncooperative. She hadn't even been cooperative with the college in returning her report or answering the questions on it. Even college staff had found her offhand and generally evasive. In the end I faced no further action. It was just hoped I'd perform better at my next placement. I'd actually worked quite hard. It just wasn't really my thing. I didn't really know what I was doing there.

I was faring little better in my college-based work. Despite my best efforts nothing I did quite seemed to hit the right note or the right mark. Privately I was told the heavily outnumbered male students had a history of struggling in this particular college and on this particular course. I was just another example in a long and well documented line of them. I was a case in point. I was academically more than sufficiently qualified to do well, but I wasn't doing well. I was failing. I didn't quite fit in with the somewhat feminist ethos that was being promoted on the site or the overly politically correct doctrine we were being fed. Frankly I thought a lot of it was bullshit, though I kept quiet. Maybe my facial expressions or general demeanour somehow betrayed what I felt underneath. Whatever the reasons, as my first term started to draw to its conclusion, it was clear I could and should have been doing an awful lot better than I was.

I looked for avenues of activity to take my mind off my college woes. Increasingly I went for late night walks by myself. I liked to feel the cold, evening air on my hands and face, as I strolled at a leisurely, relaxed pace, lost in my own thoughts. I liked to see the city at night; the illumination of streetlights; speeding cars and taxis taking people to all kinds of different places, venues and destinations; laughing faces in pub windows; the reflection of moonlight on water; the constant high energy, metropolitan hustle and bustle contrasting with the relative silence of parks and open spaces. There was much urban variety to investigate, depending on where I was and where I walked to.

I kept in touch with as many of my fellow students outside of college hours as I could, some of whom I genuinely liked, even if we weren't entirely alike as people or in our interests. I continued to go out with them at least once most weeks. A few were genuinely good company, but they still didn't go out enough for me. I'd given up trying to land any as a girlfriend. It was quite apparent there was no one there for me.

I wasn't their type. I was surrounded by young women, but none had any interest in me at all as a potential boyfriend. I'd now accepted that and moved on from my initial disappointment. As a result I started to branch out more and more. I moved further away from the narrow confines of the college and the people there. I increasingly started to explore the city by myself. I started going out alone more often. I'd done it to some extent from day one. Now it was all the time. It was better than staying in. I didn't care if I didn't have anyone else to go with. I'd go anyway. That was how I viewed things. I wouldn't be held back. I wouldn't be stopped because of a shortage of drinking buddies.

An old university friend lived quite nearby. Before starting the course we'd discussed meeting up once I'd moved. It never happened. He was always too busy. Someone else from my hometown was also there in the same city. I thought I might spend time with her. She was too busy with her boyfriend. It was fair enough. I was left to fend for myself. I'd now found two arts centres, where I could watch the latest arthouse movies. Conveniently both had enticing and appealing bars. They were cool places to hang out. I spent many pleasant evenings in one or other of them. On other nights I hit the clubs. I'd now found three that played alternative music, although I normally went to a pub first. There was one city centre pub in particular, where the local indie and gothic types seemed to gather. It was always very busy. I liked the music and atmosphere there. There were many interesting and attractive alternative girls to look at too. It was a just shame I was too shy to speak to any of them. It didn't matter. I was happy just finding a place to be on a Friday or Saturday night. It was better than being alone in my room by myself.

Afterwards I often went to a club which was located on a boat moored to the harbourside nearby. It was strangely disorientating, because once inside it there was nothing at all to suggest it wasn't on dry land. It was an interesting concept and venue, which I liked a lot and I went there quite regularly. There were other venues I liked too, perhaps as much or even more. On occasion I went to a small live music venue I'd found located in the partially derelict, former industrial quarter of the city near the railway station. Here I saw old punk bands like *999* and the *UK Subs* that I'd loved growing up as a teenager.

My favourite club, however, wasn't an alternative club at all. It was a mainly dance-orientated venue, but once a week hosted an old school, punk music night, where they played records by the likes of *Stiff Little*

Fingers, *The Ruts*, *The Stranglers* and *The Buzzcocks*, in many cases songs I hadn't heard in years. It was never busy or popular on the nights I went, but I absolutely loved it. Very quickly I became a regular there. I eagerly looked forward to the night. I couldn't wait for it. It helped me get through my somewhat depressing week. I started to go so often, some of the regulars there even started to recognise me and speak to me. On one occasion an attractive, blonde girl spoke to me. She was a little older than me and looked like she'd been a punk when she was younger, as I had myself. She was sitting with a couple of friends and smoking a cigarette when she spoke.

'I saw you here last week, and the week before,' she said. 'Why are you always by yourself?'

'I like the music, but I've got no one else to go with,' I confessed.

'What do you do?' she continued.

'I'm training to be a teacher,' I replied.

'I thought it might be something like that. You look the well-educated sort,' she observed.

'I don't know about that,' I laughed. 'I'm barely passing the course. I've been a bit of a failure so far.'

'Too much going out,' she suggested.

'Probably,' I agreed

I saw her a couple of times afterwards. We spoke again. She was friendly and pretty. I was just worried she was a little too mature, experienced and world weary for me. Judy had been a lot younger than I was. Now I was chatting to an older woman, more like Karen, whom I'd had an affair with. I probably should have asked her out. If nothing else, she would have been someone nice to go to the pubs and alternative nights with. For some reason I didn't. Something stopped me. Maybe I was waiting for something more. Maybe I was waiting until I was certain. I wasn't quite sure. I regretted it a little after. To date she was the only woman who'd shown even the slightest interest in me since I'd moved away. Yet I hadn't acted on it. I'd found her attractive, but I hadn't taken it any further. Maybe I wasn't as over Judy as I thought.

When I wasn't clubbing or watching films I browsed the city's vintage clothes shops and record stores. I was always on the look out for something striking to wear, and interesting music to listen to. It helped to take my mind off the fact the course wasn't going quite as I hoped. I think mentally I was increasingly distancing myself from it. It was almost as if I inhabited two totally separate and independent lives in the same place. On the one hand I had a life on a teacher training course that I more or less loathed. At the same time I was discovering a new and exciting life in a city I liked, that had no bearing or relevance to my daily struggles in my college work. It was an odd position to find myself in. I couldn't quite make sense of it or where I was going. I hoped in time things would become clearer, and I'd realise what needed to be done, to renew my feelings of self-belief and purpose. I needed to find a concerted direction to move forwards in. I hadn't found it yet.

I should have been concentrating on my studies. I was after all a failing student. I should have been focussing all my energies on the course, to get back up to speed. I'd fallen behind. Despite my best efforts, some of my assignments needed re-doing. They would have to be edited, improved and submitted again. I needed to work harder. I needed to devote even more hours to my teacher training. True to form of course I did the opposite. If anything I put in less time. Rather than working harder to catch up, I continued writing my new novel *Beatnik* I'd started before moving away. It was slowly coming together and taking shape. It was broadly the factually accurate account of running an underground poetry magazine, which I'd edited with a friend and fellow poet some years earlier. It concerned the adventures we'd had and the ups and downs that followed.

The magazine had been quite successful in its own way but had eventually ceased publication after my co-editor suffered a tragic accident. He was left confined to a wheelchair and was sadly to die from his injuries some years later. The novel was in part a eulogy to my lost friend. It wasn't a commercial work. I never tried to be commercial or popular in my writing. I believed in following my instinct. I was dedicated to writing what I wanted to write, whatever the consequences, or indeed lack of them. I expressed the thoughts that came into my head, whether or not they were the ones I thought people wanted to read or hear. Largely they weren't. I hoped in time I would find a natural audience. Sadly for the most part I didn't. That didn't put me off. It didn't deter me. I had my own quest. I had my own path to follow, which I did more or less regardless.

Things didn't improve greatly for me in my second term of teacher training. They continued much in the same vein. Whilst I struggled to reach the required standard in the work, I wasn't quite hopeless enough to be thrown off the course. My failing health didn't help. I was still experiencing a myriad of varied and unexplained symptoms, that seemingly could be neither diagnosed nor treated. Throughout that winter I suffered from a hacking and persistent cough, which refused to go away. It was now 1995. I hadn't been well for nearly two years, since the days when I'd been with Judy. It did occur to me I might be dying. The intensity of the course wasn't conducive to getting better. I had to be up early in the morning to go to teaching placements, and often worked late into the evening both on my college work and novel. When I had time off I gave myself little rest. I still hadn't found a girlfriend. In fact I'd given up on that. I knew I wouldn't find one where I was. I started to wonder if I'd ever date anyone again. I longed for the Easter break, when I'd have a chance to recuperate and recharge my batteries. When it finally came it led to my life taking an unexpected turn.

PART TWO - ROXANNE

Chapter Seven

It made a pleasant change to spend a few weeks back with my parents. It was nice to be in a warm house and to have a warm bed to sleep in. My living arrangements away at college were pretty basic. Now I had room and space again, and someone to cook for me. I couldn't complain. The two terms that I'd completed had been hard work and hadn't gone as I'd anticipated. I now had some time off, when I could rest and enjoy myself. Of course I still had college work to complete. I had to prepare for my final term's teaching placement, but that could wait. I wanted to relax and have a bit of fun first, at least for the early part of my holiday. I'd worry about lesson preparation nearer the time I had to go back. Until then I wanted to forget all about it. I wanted to put it out of my head completely for a bit. I didn't like teaching anyway. For a while I didn't want to give it a moment's thought. It had taken up enough of my time of late. Instead I wanted to do something else. I wanted to let my hair down. I wanted to go out drinking and socialising, and perhaps even meet women. There had been none where I'd been living. Perhaps it was an opportunity to start again.

Every Thursday at my favourite alternative club they held a retro sixties music night, where they played old Motown dance numbers, bits of Northern Soul, easy listening and even kitsch theme tunes from cult television series and the movies. It was an offbeat, eclectic and slightly eccentric mix of music, but I liked it. It was popular with the local indie kids and the art college students. On the first Thursday after I arrived home I decided to go along. There was a bar downstairs, and upstairs there was a dancefloor. It was the same place I'd met Judy some five years earlier, but that had been on a very different sort of night. This particular evening it was quite quiet in the bar, so after buying a drink I went straight upstairs, just as I had done when I'd met Judy for the first time. Now I was out on my own again. I'd dressed for the occasion in my best paisley shirt. Perhaps I was hoping to meet someone. Perhaps I was hoping to impress somebody new.

When I went in my eyes were immediately drawn to a girl standing near the dancefloor. She wasn't a regular, but she stood out from everyone else. She had an air of dignified confidence about her. She had blonde hair and was wearing a long, fitted, navy blue dress and high heels. She could have been attending a ball, not a midweek night in a cheap, rundown club. She was more striking and more stylish than anyone else there, many of whom were dressed down in scruffy jeans and trainers. She didn't look overdressed. She just looked cool and glamorous. I felt instantly drawn to her. My eyes barely wavered from her. She took my breath away with her chic beauty. Of course I didn't go up and talk to her. I didn't go over and introduce myself, as I might have done. It wasn't my style. I'd learnt my lesson with my abject failure with the girls on my course.

Then I got a lucky break. She was joined by an old friend of mine called Matt, who I'd once played music with. I got the impression they knew each but weren't a couple. I thought if I went over and talked to Matt, a chance might present itself to talk to the fascinating girl by his side. So I strolled over at a leisurely pace and exchanged pleasantries with Matt. I pointedly didn't speak to the girl. I hoped she might just be intrigued enough to make the first move and speak to me. I was right. My plan worked. She leant over and said hello. I said hello back. She told me her name – Roxanne. I told her mine.

'Are you a regular?' she asked.

'When I'm home,' I replied. 'I'm away quite a lot at the moment, studying to be a teacher.'

'That sounds interesting,' Roxanne said, her attention momentarily captured.

'Not really,' I laughed. 'It's not as interesting as it sounds. I don't really enjoy it to be honest.'

'That's a shame,' she said.

She looked genuinely sorry for me.

'What do you do?' I asked.

'I did my art degree here. I've just come back, as I couldn't get a job in my hometown,' she explained. 'I've just started a short business training course, which will hopefully lead to a job.'

'Jobs are overrated if you ask me,' I said.

'I know, but I need the money,' she said.

'How long have you been back?' I asked.

'Only a couple of weeks. I don't know anyone else here except Matt. Everyone I knew has moved away,' she said.

'I don't know many people here now either,' I said. 'But if I hear of anything exciting going on I'll certainly tell you.'

'That would be great. I have no idea where to go these days,' Roxanne said. 'I feel a bit overdressed for this place. I wasn't quite sure what to expect.'

'You're not overdressed. Everyone else is underdressed,' I said. 'You look fabulous.'

'Thanks,' she said, looking happy to be complimented. 'You look pretty good yourself.'

Once we started talking we didn't stop. It was almost as if we were the only ones there. We only had eyes for each other. I felt slightly sorry for Matt. He may have been interested in her too, but he didn't get a look in. I felt a bit bad for taking over, but it was as if Roxanne and I were meant to be together. At the end of the evening, when it was time to go I offered to walk her home. We walked slowly, as we were still finding things to talk about. I'd only just met her, but I immediately felt relaxed and comfortable in her company. I'd been away for two terms on a teacher training course surrounded by young women, but I hadn't met anyone like this. She was different. She stood out from the crowd. I definitely liked her, and I got the feeling she liked me back.

When we reached her house I asked if I could have her phone number, so we could arrange to meet up again very soon. She seemed happy to give it, and I gave her my number in return. I didn't wait long to ring her. I got the firm impression we were both equally interested in each other. There seemed no point and no reason to play games. She was just as relaxed and talkative on the phone. We had no difficulty in maintaining a conversation. She asked me if I'd like to come over for lunch one day in the week and she'd cook for me. We arranged a convenient day and time. It was to be our first proper date.

I was a little nervous when I went round. I'd only met her once, and in a club at that. I took a bottle of wine to share to ease any nerves. I needn't have worried. We carried on exactly where we'd left off. The food was good and the time with her passed pleasantly. It was blissful and exactly as I'd hoped. When we finished eating I didn't want our date to be over so soon, so I asked if she wanted to go for a drive somewhere. She happily agreed. I briefly popped home to pick up my dad's car and came back as speedily as I could to collect Roxanne. She didn't know the wider area that well, so I took her to the some of the local sights and landmarks she hadn't visited when she'd been at college in the city. I took her a little further afield than she was previously familiar with, into the countryside and to the sea, and to some of the quieter, more scenic places she didn't know. The afternoon went quickly. We had a lovely time together. When we got back, I could sense neither of us was ready for our date to end just yet. So I asked her if she wanted to go for a drink that night. Again she happily agreed. I returned my dad's car to him, tidied myself up a bit, and went back to collect her for our night out.

After our first date Roxanne and I didn't really look back. We quickly became inseparable. My parents weren't best pleased, only because of the timing of my starting a new relationship. They wanted me to be concentrating fully on preparing for my impending final term of teacher training, which both they and I knew would be nothing but hard, unrelenting slog. Roxanne was bound to be a distraction. I was spending all my time with her, but she was a distraction I welcomed even if they didn't. By our second or third date Roxanne and I were kissing. A day or two after I was staying over and we were sleeping together. It felt very natural in bed with her. We were very compatible. We were spending every moment together we could. It was an unseasonably warm Easter that year. It was lovely lazing in bed naked with her. I couldn't get enough of being with her. The only downside was that my break went too quickly. Before we knew it the weeks off had passed and it was time for me to go back to college. We both felt devastated. Already we couldn't bear to be apart at all. We wouldn't be for very long. Roxanne arranged to come up and see me the very first weekend after I'd gone back to resume my studies.

My final term was all school based. Yet again I was sent to another deprived, inner-city location, which was certain to be challenging at the very least. It was all I expected it would be – hard work, arduous, relentless and a largely depressing experience. It was simply something to get through and not to be savoured or enjoyed in any way. It was a ten-week ordeal to be survived; nothing else and nothing more. Only the prospect of seeing Roxanne again got me through the first week. Everything else in my life at that time was just hard, solid graft.

It wasn't doing my health any good. I was suffering. My undiagnosed symptoms of general malaise only worsened. I was under intense pressure. I wasn't getting enough rest. I was working with children and exposed to their germs and infections, which only made me worse. I was getting ill all the time. I was lonely without Roxanne. I was now almost completely cut off from everyone else on my course. We all were. We were all at different schools, engrossed in our final teaching placements. We hardly saw each other. I was just happy Roxanne was coming up to look after me. I couldn't wait to see her. I couldn't wait to pick her up from the train station and take her to where I lived.

Roxanne was only meant to stay for the weekend. In the event she stayed longer than that. She didn't want to go back, so she stayed for a few extra days. She even tidied my room for me when I was out teaching and cooked for me when I got back. It was lovely having her about. It lifted my mood. Finally after more than a year I forgot all about Judy. She no longer meant anything to me. She'd treated me badly, and I had someone else now, someone I felt I was falling in love with. In many ways our meeting had turned my world upside down. At the back of my mind, I'd been thinking of getting a job where I was studying when my course ended. Now I knew I'd be heading straight back to Roxanne and would be looking to get a job wherever she was. All my plans had suddenly changed overnight. Roxanne was now at the very heart of all of them. I didn't mind. To me love was everything. It meant more than anything else. Being with the person I loved was suddenly my number one consideration. Nothing else really mattered. Nothing else was important.

It was bad timing of course. I couldn't have met her at a more inconvenient time in truth. My course, which had been intense from start to finish, was drawing to its even more intense conclusion. It now required my full focus. I'd struggled almost from day one, but I was aware if I gave the final ten weeks my full concentration I could still pull it off and achieve an unlikely pass. It all hung in the balance. With the correct degree of effort and application failure could be avoided. It was by no means a certainty. I knew there were several pieces of work I still needed to re-submit, but I was confident I'd now brought them up to the required standard. I just had to get through my final teaching practice. The problem was I now had a distraction. After a year of being on my own I had a girlfriend. And with the pressure I was under on all fronts, my health was suffering and worsening daily. It didn't matter. If I could only get the final term out of the way, I could then get back to Roxanne and be with her permanently.

One of the best things of having her around was that I now had someone I could share all of my city discoveries with. Slowly I introduced Roxanne to the interesting pubs, cafés, clubs and urban sights and sounds I'd uncovered over the previous ten months, but to date had only visited on my own. I'd been longing to have someone to share my world with, and now I did. I took her to cinemas, arts centres, galleries and theatres, to restaurants and bars, to exciting shops selling fabulous vintage clothes, to second-hand record shops and locations of cultural interest. I was sorry when she had to leave. She'd stayed longer than she should have, but eventually even she realised she had to go back.

I immediately missed her, but I realised I needed to knuckle down to my work. I did my best to do that, but it was hard to concentrate. I couldn't wait until I could see Roxanne again. It wasn't long. I went home the very first weekend after that I could. We spent several more lovely days together. We went back to the club where we'd met. We spent a magical afternoon at a small petting zoo, set in the middle of a picturesque, fishing village. The weather was fine and we made the most of it. We maximised the short amount of time we had together, before all too soon I had to head back, just as she had several weeks earlier. We carried on like this for the rest of the month and eventually made it through to half-term. I had a week off. I was delighted. My first thought of course was to head straight home to see Roxanne.

When I got home my body went into meltdown. I'd been running on empty for longer than I cared to remember. I hadn't been well for over two years. I'd tried to fight it. I'd tried to battle on. I'd tried to pretend that I was all right, when I wasn't. I tried to kid myself there was nothing wrong. It could no longer be denied. I'd pushed myself as hard as I could. I'd reached my physical limit. My body was no longer willing to go on. It simply stopped. It ground to a halt. I went home to see Roxanne, but almost immediately I found myself confined to the couch, unable to move. I sensed this was it. I had a feeling straight away I wouldn't be going back after half-term to finish my course. I could feel it was more than just a passing blip. I wouldn't be well in a week, a fortnight, even a month. I'd been in denial too long. My parents couldn't quite believe it. They thought I'd just snap out of it. I'd wake up the next day and would be well again and be off to resume my course. I didn't share their confidence. I didn't improve. In fact I worsened daily.

I made several more fruitless trips to my doctor. Again I got nowhere. The best they could do was to recommend counselling. They were convinced it was a mental problem, perhaps a nervous condition, anxiety or depression. I was certain they were wrong. Being ignored and dismissed only served to increase my sense of frustration. I felt angry and let down. I wanted to lash out at them. I was sure there was nothing wrong with my mental state. I had a physical illness. No one else, apart from Roxanne, seemed to believe me.

On Roxanne's recommendation I changed doctor. I'd gone as far as I could with the one I had. They hadn't achieved anything. They'd failed me completely. Roxanne knew a good doctor, who'd helped her when she was a student. I immediately found the new doctor more sympathetic and more willing to listen to the myriad of strange and unexplained symptoms I presented her with. Meanwhile the weeks were passing. Half-term had finished. I hadn't returned to complete my teaching practice. I'd had to contact the school and the college to explain my absence. Fairly soon it became apparent my illness wouldn't be a passing one. I wouldn't be returning anytime soon. I was barely able to leave the house.

My social life with Roxanne quickly ground to a halt. She'd only just met me. She could have used my illness as an excuse to end the relationship. It would have been fair enough. It wasn't exactly what she'd signed up for. She chose not to do that. Instead she cared for me as best she could at my parents' house. They didn't know how to react to seeing their son in such miserable plight. They found it hard to deal with. They stayed in denial, as I had been. They kept telling themselves I'd be better soon. The problem was they didn't know how long I'd really been ill. I'd only ever told them half-truths about how I was feeling. I'd never told them how ill I really was and how long I'd been ill for.

I underwent all kinds of medical tests. My new doctor was willing to believe there was a physical cause and it wasn't all in my head. She agreed I was very run down. She soon discovered I had a number of infections, for which she prescribed antibiotics. I had tonsillitis and a urinary tract infection. It still didn't explain why I was in as bad shape as I was, and why with rest I continued to fail to significantly improve. The results of the blood tests were inconclusive. There was no great indication of anything serious. It remained a mystery. Occasionally I showed a small improvement for a day or two, only to wake up worse than ever. The weeks passed. I began to feel depressed. I felt sorry for Roxanne. She was young. She was just twenty-three. I'd just reached and passed my thirtieth birthday. I hadn't been well enough to celebrate it.

Roxanne deserved a social life. She wasn't getting much of one. Most of the time she just stayed in and watched television or listened to music with me. That was about all I was up to doing. I didn't feel well enough to do much else. When I had the energy I did a bit of writing or played my guitar or did some reading. I tried to do things to take my mind off feeling ill, but it was hard. It was on my mind all the time. It was hard to take my mind off the symptoms I was experiencing. I obsessed over them. They became all consuming. I kept thinking I might be dying. I thought I probably was, but I didn't die. I carried on. I just didn't get any better. I imagined I might have all kinds of weird and wonderful diseases. My parents had to take medical dictionaries away from me. I imagined I had every illness they described. Finding a diagnosis became an obsession, because I wasn't getting any better. I tried to distract myself further by watching sport on television, but it only added to my sense of frustration that I wasn't well enough to play myself.

Roxanne was just about the only thing that kept me going. Without her life wouldn't have been worth living. Without good health life was nothing. I was coming to realise that. I felt like I had flu all the time, flu which never went away. My head was permanently fuzzy and foggy. I didn't feel like I was in my own body. I was having out of body experiences. Yet at the same time I felt trapped in a body that was behaving badly. I wished I could climb out of mine and into someone else's. Without Roxanne I'm not sure I could have carried on.

Thoughts of suicide seriously crossed my mind. I just couldn't get better. And no one knew what was wrong with me. Only the pain that it would have caused Roxanne and my parents prevented me from possibly killing myself. I was desperate. My quality of life was meaningless. At one point I didn't leave the house at all for a whole month. My course was now a distant memory. I'd put in so much effort for nothing. Even if I ever got better I'd have to repeat my final term at the very least. I couldn't face it. I realised it was a lost cause. The very thought of it reduced me to blind panic. My nerves were out of control. I felt so weak and ill I was having regular, severe panic attacks.

On one of my slightly better days my parents drove me up to my student house to pick up my stuff. I hadn't been there for weeks. Sadly my elderly landlady had passed away since I'd last been there. She'd died suddenly and unexpectedly from a stroke. But everything else was just as I'd left it. It was a strange feeling being back and collecting my things. It was like an admission of failure. Almost everything had gone against me since moving there. I should have jacked in the course months before, I realised. Teaching just wasn't for me. It wasn't my thing. Everything that had happened on the course had been telling me that.

I'd refused to accept it. I'd refused to give in. It was down to my stubborn nature. I found it hard to accept defeat. I'd pushed myself too hard. I'd pushed myself to breaking point and beyond to complete the course. But I'd fallen at the last. My body had broken down. It couldn't go on.

I popped into the college too, to pick up some of my work. My fellow students were just passing out, having completed the course. No one spoke to me. No one acknowledged me. No one ever got in touch afterwards to see how I was or what had happened to me. I felt quite let down. I felt quite hurt. No one cared. No one was bothered. It was over. It was finished. I knew then I wouldn't be going back. My parents hoped I would, but I knew it was never going to happen. Instead I headed back to Roxanne, to an uncertain future and to battle my illness together.

Chapter Eight

My parents remained convinced that a little more rest was all I needed, to get better and to get back on my feet. They believed once the pressure of the course was removed, I'd quickly improve and before long I'd be right as rain again. They found it hard to take my illness seriously. They found it hard to believe there was anything physically wrong with me. They remained in denial, as I had been when I'd first started getting ill. They pointedly didn't tell friends and relatives that I'd given up my course because I was unwell. They were too embarrassed. They suspected the source of my problems was mental. They thought I was having some kind of breakdown, and that physically I was actually fit. My old doctor had thought the same. They were guided by him. My new doctor wasn't so certain. I remained adamant the source of my problem was physical not mental. I wasn't losing my mind, as some thought I was. Though at times it felt like it.

Roxanne was great. She did everything she could. She was very supportive. She did everything in her power to try to help get me better. She tried her best to nurse me back to good health. She researched possible causes of my malaise. No illness or disease was too far-fetched to be considered. I appreciated her efforts. She really was the only thing keeping me going, but nothing seemed to work or assist me in improving. It was the summer of 1995. My parents had been planning to go abroad. They had to abandon their plans. I wasn't well enough to be left. I needed constant looking after. The weeks and months continued to pass. My abortive attempt to train as a teacher soon became no more than a vanishing recollection. Memories of the course started fading into the past and into the distance. I no longer even thought about going back to finish what I'd started. It wasn't even a consideration. The only thing I thought about was getting better. I thought about that, and about Roxanne. I didn't think about much else.

I became a virtual recluse. I stayed in almost all the time. I hardly ever went out. When I did it was probably just for another trip to see the doctor. I didn't socialise at all. Old friends wondered what had happened to me. They wondered why they didn't see me anymore. I didn't really want to speak to them. I preferred to keep myself to myself. I didn't really like having to explain what was wrong. It was embarrassing. I could tell them I was ill, but I couldn't even tell them what was wrong with me and what I was ill with. My condition remained unexplained and undiagnosed. I was depressed. I was desperate. I could see no future in my life. I was thirty years old and it felt like it was over. I still wasn't getting any better. I'd almost given up hope of ever improving.

With Roxanne's help I tried all kinds of potential cures, treatments, remedies and therapies to get well again. I was willing to try anything. I explored hosts of natural and herbal supplements from the health food shops, mainly to boost my immune system. It seemed almost every week I was afflicted with some new infection. I took a concoction of drugs, both herbal and pharmaceutical, to try to rid myself of them. It wasn't really working. Nothing was. Eventually, against my better judgement I consented to counselling. I even attended hypnotherapy and anxiety management classes. It helped me understand some of the feelings I was experiencing, but they were just a by-product of the fact I felt unwell. They weren't the cause. I remained convinced a physical illness lay at the root of my woes and predicament. Only Roxanne seemed to believe me, and even she'd started having her doubts.

They were desperate, lonely and thoroughly miserable times. I spent every day at home. It was a struggle to get out of bed in the morning. I felt absolutely wretched and could never get moving. When I had the energy I did a bit of work on the novel I was writing or worked on some poems. On other occasions I got out my guitar and started composing some new songs. I drew inspiration from the *Britpop* movement, which was just taking off. I tried to write tunes in the same style and vogue. I never worked very long. I tired quickly. I found it hard to get interested in what I was doing. My awareness of being ill was overwhelming. I couldn't get it out of my mind. I couldn't concentrate on anything else.

My mum cooked me lunch, but I found it hard to eat. My appetite was always subdued. In the afternoons I just read or dozed or watched films. Roxanne lent me videos of dozens of classic, old movies. I enjoyed watching them. They did cheer me up a bit. I then waited for her to come over. That was the best part of the day. Her business course was drawing to a close. She only had a couple more weeks to complete. She'd shortly be looking for a job. In the meantime, as soon as she finished every day she came round to see me. I wasn't well enough to go out. We just stayed in watching television or listening to music. My dad normally dropped her back at her bedsit at the end of the night. My parents didn't like her staying over. They were old fashioned like that. It wasn't helping our sex life. Neither of course was my illness.

I struggled to sleep at night. I often lay in bed for hours in a pool of sweat, unable to switch my brain off and relax. My mind would be full of torturous thoughts. I wished I knew what was wrong with me. I wished I could start feeling better. My imagination would run riot and out of control. My head would spin with notions and speculations of all the exotic diseases I thought I might have. I was convinced I was dying. This was it, I thought. Sometimes I hoped I wouldn't wake up. I thought it might be easier if I simply died in my sleep. But I always did wake up. I woke up to another torturous day, just as the last, and the one before that, and the one after, and the one after that, et cetera, et cetera, it seemed, going on forever. When ill in the past I'd been accustomed to getting better after a few days or at worst a couple of weeks. This was entirely different. It was beyond anything I'd previously experienced. I no longer expected to feel better the next day. I knew I wouldn't. I knew there wasn't the slightest chance of it. I'd just be faced with more of the same; of lingering, debilitating, depressing sickness.

As the weeks continued to pass and I still failed to show any signs of improvement, my new doctor decided it was time to undertake further tests. This time I was subjected to more detailed and comprehensive blood and urine tests than I had been before. It was at this point that a breakthrough of sorts was finally made. I finally started to get some answers to what had afflicted me for almost two and a half years. When the blood results came back, it was finally confirmed that I'd had glandular fever all along. I'd contracted it from Judy when she'd had it, when we'd been dating each other several years earlier. I just hadn't known it, so I'd struggled on going to work and playing sport, despite feeling pretty wretched, when I should have been resting. The blood tests also revealed something more. The hacking cough I'd had during the previous winter, when I'd continued to struggle into schools to teach, had actually been pneumonia. If that wasn't enough, the urine tests showed the result of all these assaults on my body was that my kidneys weren't now working as efficiently as they should be. Furthermore, as the glandular fever hadn't been treated I'd been left with some kind of post-viral *ME* condition, which was never likely to go away.

It was a lot to take in. At least I now had some kind of explanation as to why I'd felt as I had done; why a once fit and healthy young man had been so completely struck down. I also felt vindicated. I'd proved there was something physically wrong with me. It wasn't just in my head. I also felt very, very angry. I felt let down by my previous doctor, who'd sent me away and dismissed me as either a hypochondriac or a mental health patient. I felt I might not be in the predicament I was, if I'd had a correct diagnosis in the first place. I felt lots of things, including a small sense of relief. At least I now knew what I was dealing with. It only helped so much. I still didn't get better.

I documented some of my experiences in a collection of poetry I suitably titled *Sick Note*. It mainly contained a mixture of poems written about being ill and about Judy leaving me, although there were some other things too. It felt therapeutic to get my feelings out. With her permission I put a picture of Roxanne on the cover. It felt a bit like the end of one thing and the beginning of another. I still felt ill. I still felt depressed. I even tried antidepressants for a short period, but I decided they weren't for me, so I stopped taking them. It was the late summer, early autumn of 1995. With Roxanne's help I was ready to move forward with my life. I was ill, but I decided to make the most of what I had. I'd start again, within the limitations and confinements that my illness placed on me. It was hard, but I'd try to be positive. I had to embrace the lot I'd been given and get what pleasures and satisfaction out of life that I could.

The first step on the road to recovery was acceptance. I was forced to accept my health was no longer what it had been, and it was highly unlikely I would ever return to the full fitness I'd taken for granted prior to my illness. It was a painful admission to make for someone who had been a healthy, virile sportsman, bursting with energy, as I was at twenty-seven. At thirty I was no longer like that. I was more like an old man. In all probability my health was permanently damaged, I realised. It would never be again as I'd known it for the first half of my life and as I'd so casually taken for granted. I now had barely twenty per cent of the physical capacity I'd enjoyed before. That was the reality I faced and was stuck with. It was hugely frustrating. It was deeply depressing for someone who just wanted to get out and play sport again. It wasn't going to happen. I just wasn't up to it.

I dreamt of returning. I prayed for a speedy return to rugby, tennis and badminton. My dreams and hopes were constantly dashed. I wasn't suddenly going to be well and outside playing in the fresh air. Even though I now had a better idea of the cause of my affliction, there was still no magic wand to be waved to make me better. I had to understand and acknowledge that fact. It hurt me to do so, but until I did no significant improvement could be made. Without a degree of acceptance of the position I found myself in, progress would be minimal, even non-existent.

As well as acceptance I had to learn there would be no gain without pain. I was constantly forced to push myself through the pain barrier and not give into it. I had to ignore the physical feelings and discomforts I was experiencing. I had to divorce myself from them and carry on regardless. It was the only way to improve at all. I had to push myself harder than I wanted. I had to keep battling and keep fighting. I gradually went for longer walks to improve my fitness. I wandered to the city centre shops, even when I didn't want to. I had to resist my instincts to turn and run home as soon as I began to feel unwell. I had to subdue my sense of panic, when I was overcome by feelings of peculiarity. I had to ride them out. I had to maintain my regime of going out on bad days as well as good ones. I had to stick to it, even though I continued to be dogged by minor infections. I got new colds, bugs and viruses all the time. My immune system had taken a battering and couldn't fight them off. Rarely a week passed when I didn't feel my temperature rising, to announce the onset of some new sickness.

Despite this I grew physically and mentally a little stronger over time. It was mainly due to my change in attitude. Very slowly I became better able to cope with the feelings of illness I was experiencing. To some small extent I learnt to manage my symptoms and not be controlled by them. I tried to push them to the back of my mind, so they were no longer all consuming. I learnt to carry on doing things despite being unwell, when previously I might have taken straight to my sickbed. I refused to be ruled by ill health. I tried to fight back. I no longer wished to be defined by physical feelings I couldn't control. I realised that whilst my illness might have been out of my hands, how I dealt with it and how I reacted to it wasn't. That part I had some degree of control over. It required huge mental effort for me to keep fighting back, but I did just that. I used all the will and determination I could muster to stick with it.

Sometimes I felt weak and wanted to give in. Sometimes I felt I was about to succumb again. Roxanne tried to keep me strong. She encouraged me to keep at it and keep going. She bought me self-help guides and books on self-healing. I read them with interest, keen to learn and to act on them. I would never have believed I would have needed to read such material. At that point in time I very much did. It was vital. It was an essential part of my therapy and treatment. My mental state was as fragile as my physical one. It was a side effect of physical sickness you don't always hear about. I remained perilously close to a total mental breakdown through all those months of gradual rehabilitation. Somehow I just about retained my sanity. It wasn't a smooth path to recovery. My improvement wasn't a steady one. I had ups and downs. I had constant setbacks. I slowly became more active, however, and left the house more often. A return to work or finishing my course remained out of reach and out of the question. Before I could consider any of that, I needed to wrestle my life back at least to some extent from the months of illness that had enveloped me.

As time passed Roxanne and I gradually started going out together occasionally again. For a long time we'd only gone out when my mum or dad had taken us. I hadn't been well enough to drive. Now we occasionally took the car out on our own. I felt just about confident enough to do it, if we weren't going very far. It was part of the slow process of building my confidence back up. On other occasions we'd go for a quiet drink in a pub. It wasn't that I really felt well enough to do it. I just wanted to prove that I could. As more weeks passed I eventually returned to gentle exercise. Again I didn't feel well enough to do it, but I forced myself. I'd take a rugby ball or football to the local playing fields during the daytime whilst others were at work and do some modest ball routines. It hurt and I felt weak and I often felt wretched afterwards, but I stuck at it. Once I started exercising again, I kept it up and went out several times every week throughout that autumn and winter.

Meanwhile Roxanne had finished her course and got a job. She was working for an exclusive women's fashion shop in the local High Street. It wasn't quite what she wanted, but it was a start and there was potential for improvement. It was a classy establishment and a nice environment to work in. She seemed quite at home when I visited her there. I was pleased for her. She also moved into a new shared house in line with her sudden, relative affluence. An improved income meant she could now afford somewhere slightly nicer to live. Ironically she chose to move into the same house, where an ex-girlfriend and ex-fiancée had both lived almost a decade earlier. For me it was a slightly strange feeling going back there. There was no denying, however, that it was a nicer location and a nicer house than she'd had, so it made good sense to move.

After a couple of weeks in her new job, Roxanne wasn't sure she liked it quite as much as she hoped she would. It wasn't turning out to be everything she expected. She was bored a lot of the time, as when there were no customers there wasn't much to do. It was repetitive and lacked variety, she found. She still resolved to stay though, to see if things improved or until a better opportunity came along. We both agreed that was the best plan. The downside of her working was I didn't see her quite as much as I would have liked or as I had done. We remained close. We spent as much time together as we could manage. I was so grateful for everything she'd done for me. I felt very much in love with her. I believed she loved me back. As a result we quickly took the next step in our blossoming relationship.

'You've been so kind. You're someone I could imagine being married to,' I blurted out, when we were alone one night.

'I could imagine being married to you too,' Roxanne replied.

'Does that mean you want to get married?' I tentatively enquired.

'You'd have to ask,' Roxanne said.

'Well, would you like to marry me?' I asked.

'Yes,' Roxanne replied, giving me a huge kiss.

Before I knew it we were engaged. Within days, using some money I'd saved and some more I borrowed from my dad, I'd even bought Roxanne an engagement ring. There was no going back. I'd been engaged once before, a decade earlier. This felt different. I had a feeling we'd see it through this time and get to the altar together. I had no idea how I was going to support her. I still wasn't well. I didn't have a job. I still hadn't recovered enough to work. Despite that my need for money forced me to go to the local unemployment benefits office and sign on. I didn't mention my illness. I reasoned it would take a while for them to find me work or for me to find a job myself. I hoped in the meantime my health might further improve. I did consider applying for sickness benefit, but that in itself would have only led to more questions and medical investigations I didn't want to be subjected to.

Instead I decided just to take my chances and trusted that I would remain unemployed for the relative foreseeable future. I was fairly certain that whatever followed, no job would be immediately forthcoming. Luckily that proved to be the case, and I now had a small source of income once again, which I hadn't had for months. Despite my ongoing problems, things were looking up a little. Progress was slow, but it was apparent and evident. Bit by bit, piece by piece I was getting my life back. I was moving forwards. There were small causes for hope and optimism. Things were falling back into place. My life would never be the same. It would never be what it had been, but at least it was moving in the right direction once again.

As time passed I slowly returned to doing more things that I'd once done without even having to think about them. My life regained a degree of normality. I kept up my light training, however poorly I felt. I was no longer willing to give into my feelings of sickness. I wasn't well enough for competitive sport, but I did what gentle exercise I could manage. I did at least some exercise every week that passed. When she wasn't working or going home to see her parents, Roxanne and I got in the habit of taking the car out on Saturday afternoons for little trips to nearby picturesque towns and villages. It was a habit I was to continue for years and a sign I was steadily becoming more family orientated. Saturday afternoons were no longer about shopping or playing sport. Without being fully aware of the change it slowly became family time I would guard over jealousy. Roxanne and I gradually went out more often in the evenings too. We'd go for quiet drinks together or occasionally to see a film. Now and again we even went to gigs or out clubbing. I didn't always feel well, but somehow with Roxanne's help I managed to do it.

My sickness continued to afflict me badly for over twenty years. It was generally worse in the morning, when I'd just got up, and in the early evening, when I was starting to get tired. It was particularly bad throughout my thirties. It improved a little in my forties. It improved a little more in my fifties, when it became more of a hindrance and irritation than a constant affliction. In all that time it never totally left me. It was always around me to some degree. Mainly I just learnt to live with it. I learnt to carry on regardless. By the time it improved a little more noticeably in my fifties, sadly I was afflicted by other illnesses. For so many years it just became my normal state. I could no longer even recall what it felt like to be 100 per cent well. I no longer expected it even. I knew it would never happen. When it was at its worst it would really get me down and I'd be sad and depressed. I realised then I would never feel truly well again. What health I had was as good as it would ever get for me. At other times I felt a little more optimistic and believed there was a chance I might improve.

There were periods when the symptoms eased at least a little bit. I'd start to think I was actually getting better. Then they'd come back and be with me worse than ever for months, even years, on end. It was normally a virus that triggered the return. During the periods of remission I eventually attempted to play competitive sport again. It took five long years of recovery to get back to league tennis and badminton. The problem was I'd play a couple of games, only to be taken ill again. I could never rely on my health. I could never tell when it was going to fail next. It made it hard to commit to anything. That was one of the most frustrating parts and almost worse than not doing anything at all. I'd commit to playing a game, only to be too ill on the day and be forced to cancel. I was never well enough to play serious football or rugby again. For years I dreamt of making a return to the rugby field, but my dreams were always dashed and I was never well enough. Eventually I became too old. Even then I still dreamt of a return. Amazingly I managed it once. I was just a month short of my forty-ninth birthday, far too old to be playing full contact rugby, when I played a whole game for my old team against another local club side. I didn't do it again. I realised at that age I was risking serious injury. At least I managed it once and didn't disgrace myself in a 5-10 defeat.

Twenty years earlier, back in 1995, I had no idea what the future might bring. I was still hoping to resume a much more active football and rugby career at some point. It just wasn't to be. My extreme post-viral sickness caused by glandular fever continued to afflict me badly. It would be boring, tedious and pointless to continue to mention it at every point, but it hung over every act and every event I describe for the rest of this book like a dark cloud. I was never free of it and it tarnished and affected everything I did. It affected my confidence and personality. It made me less outgoing. It made me less sociable. It restricted what I attempted. Afterwards I kept things basic and simple and within the narrow confinements with which I felt reasonably comfortable. It made me less ambitious and less spontaneous. It made me fearful of travelling and going abroad. It prevented me from taking opportunities I might otherwise have grabbed. It made me scared to move away or apply for more demanding jobs. I no longer felt I was up to them. It ruined my chances of being successful or achieving very much at all. I was no longer the energetic, carefree person I'd been when I was dating Judy. I was someone else, someone I didn't really recognise.

I rarely discussed my illness, except with Roxanne. Other people, even my parents, didn't really understand, and it was hard to explain. They couldn't grasp the fact that I had something that was both difficult to define or treat and that didn't go away. It was particularly hard for old friends to comprehend, who only knew me as someone fit and healthy who played lots of sport. It became boring trying to explain to be honest. As a result I withdrew from some friendships and kept myself to myself. To new people I met I barely mentioned it. If pushed I'd mutter something about glandular fever. I preferred not to discuss it at all. I hoped by doing that it might just disappear. Of course it didn't. It stayed with me, like an unwanted guest. However hard I tried, it simply refused ever totally to vanish from my life and leave me in the peace and better health I craved so much.

Chapter Nine

I started applying for more jobs. Not because I really wanted one, but because I felt I should be doing something. I still wasn't well enough to work, but it was a condition of receiving unemployment benefits. So I looked for jobs I didn't want and applied for them anyway. I even had the occasional interview, which I attended in a half-hearted way. I didn't mention my health problems. I didn't really feel I needed to. With several million unemployed desperate to work, I reasoned it was unlikely anyone would give a job to someone who wasn't that bothered. Luckily I wasn't offered a single thing. Occasionally I attended an interview for a job I was slightly more interested in. I didn't get any of them either. I wasn't offered anything at all.

Roxanne and I continued living our sheltered life. We had each other, but not much else. We barely saw another person beyond ourselves and our immediate family. It was restricted and limited, but it was enough for the moment. We liked to go out in the car on Saturday or Sunday afternoons when we could. We browsed the craft centres and galleries of small country towns and villages. We occasionally visited *National Trust* estates, with their quaint tearooms and gift shops. It was safe, comfortable and faintly reassuring. We both had our health issues. I was recovering from complications induced by glandular fever. Roxanne was plagued by chronic asthma and stomach problems. In our own ways we were both as nervous as kittens. We sometimes ate out in quiet, scenic cafés and restaurants. Circumstances had forced us into an almost middle-aged lifestyle, more suited to our parents than a couple the age we were.

In the evenings we tried to stay in touch with our youthful sides to some small extent. We both enjoyed dressing up for a night out. It was almost as important and as enjoyable to us as actually going out. We both liked to look chic and stylish. *Britpop* was all the rage and the clothes associated with the guitar-driven music suited both my and Roxanne's fashion sensibilities. I liked wearing classic *Fred Perry* T-shirts, tight jeans and Chelsea Boots. Roxanne enjoyed wearing her fitted, sixties dresses. We were a glamorous looking couple. Roxanne's high heels made her appear taller than she was. When we went out we almost looked like models. Together we could turn heads. It belied our almost total lack of confidence inside. Inside we were nervous wrecks, but we wore our clothes well and enjoyed being seen out. As time passed we began going out clubbing quite regularly on Saturday nights. We didn't dance or drink much. Neither of us were up to it, but we liked being spotted and being part of the crowd. Afterwards I'd get the pleasure of taking Roxanne back to her bedsit and slowly undressing her. Despite our issues we'd enjoy gentle sex long into the night.

We also started going to more gigs and saw many of the *Britpop* bands popular at the time, like *The Bluetones, Lush, Gene, Space, Sleeper, These Animal Men, Elastica* and a host of others. It was always fun and entertaining. Roxanne and I were one of those mysterious couples that would always be there, but no none knew who we were. We didn't mix or talk to anyone else. We just kept ourselves to ourselves. But we were happy that way. It suited us. We only needed each other. We didn't need other people in our life. We were aware that others on the scene knew us by sight. For us that knowledge was enough. We didn't feel the urge to socialise or be sociable. We didn't feel the need to make ourselves known beyond that. It wasn't part of our plan. We only had eyes for each other. It was reminiscent of when I'd first dated Judy, except for the time being Judy and my other ex-girlfriends were all forgotten. It was almost like I'd never been with them. I only had feelings for Roxanne.

Christmas came and Roxanne got a new job. The high end, ladies' fashion shop hadn't worked out quite as she hoped. She found it dull and unrewarding. To my surprise she went to work for the Benefits Agency instead. I didn't feel it was quite the right move for her, but it was more money and she was keen to give it a try. Despite my reservations I had no intention of standing in her way. It was regular nine to five, weekday hours, which would leave her evenings and weekends free for us and our plans. Though she still regularly went home to see her parents every few weeks when she could manage it. On those occasions I had a weekend to myself and would go home and see my parents. Most nights I spent with Roxanne.

Just as she had done previously, now she had a new job Roxanne decided to move again. She had a better income, so she could afford somewhere slightly nicer to live. She finally moved into her own flat, where she didn't have to share a kitchen or bathroom or shower, or anything like that. It was only small, but it was entirely self-contained, where we could be alone together. It was also the last flat Roxanne would rent on her own. By the time she moved again we'd begin living together full time. As it was I increasingly stayed the night with her, until it reached the point that I was staying with her far more often that I stayed with my parents. They didn't seem to mind. They were old fashioned, but they appeared to accept it. They could see it was a serious relationship that in all likelihood would end in marriage. As I was staying with Roxanne so much, I even started giving her small amounts of cash to help out a little with the rent. It wasn't much, but it was what I could afford.

Roxanne returned to her parents for Christmas. She'd always spent it with them and wasn't ready yet to spend it anywhere else. Even so she rang me all the time she was away. She missed me a lot, she said. I missed her too. My parents always made a big thing of Christmas, and that particular year was no exception. Even so I couldn't wait for it to be over and to get Roxanne back. When she returned we went out on New Year's Eve to celebrate. I was happy to be seeing the back of 1995. In many ways it had been a terrible year, the worst year of my life. Meeting Roxanne had been the only good thing to happen in a sorry twelve months. She'd helped get me through it. Without her I dreaded to think how bad it would have been, and what would have happened to me. It didn't bear thinking about. As 1995 ended and 1996 began I turned and kissed Roxanne on the lips.

'Let's make this a better year, our year,' I said, and she nodded.

I was determined it would be a better year. It couldn't be any worse. It was a chance to start again and put some of the pains and troubles of the previous twelve months behind us. I wanted to forget all about so much that had happened. I wanted to concentrate on the future instead. I wanted to forge a better one. I wanted to be in control of my life again and not be ruled by illness. I didn't want to be at the mercy of the whims of my failing body. I wanted to be able to enjoy myself with this terrific girl I'd met. I wanted us to find happiness. I wanted us to have the life we deserved. I just hoped the new year would be able to give us that. It was a lot to ask and expect, but there was no harm hoping. I wanted to be positive. I'd spent too much time being ruled by negative thoughts. 1996 would be different, I told myself. I told Roxanne too. For the first time in a while I felt a small grain of optimism. I trusted that optimism would prove well founded.

During the early months of 1996 I gradually got a little stronger and slowly a little of my confidence returned. I maintained my strict regime of exercise, which I completed whatever the weather and however I was feeling. Only on days I felt truly awful did I allow myself to miss it. I continued to have regular setbacks, but my efforts did produce gradual dividends. I was slowly able to get out more and do more normal things. I wasn't controlled by illness, quite as I had been the previous year. I started applying for more jobs. I started getting a few more interviews too. I even reached the point I was willing to give a part-time job a go, if I could get one. That had been pretty much unthinkable since I'd given up my teacher training course. I now felt almost ready, or as ready as I was likely to get. Naturally I didn't apply for anything full time, stressful or pressurised. I wouldn't cope with that. I realised I'd have to ease my way back, working a couple of days a week at most. I knew anything more than that and I'd end up having to give up again. I'd be back where I started before I knew it. I didn't want that to happen. I wanted to maintain my sense of steady progress.

As luck would have it, as winter slowly faded and spring began to arrive, bringing with it an improvement in the weather, I saw an advert for part-time, temporary work at our local arts centre. I was genuinely excited. It was just the kind of place where if I'd had a completely free choice I would have chosen to get a job. I instantly applied. Of course I'd be starting at the bottom of the ladder. I'd been a journalist. I'd been a trainee teacher. Now at the age of thirty I'd be starting again in something rather more humble. I didn't really care. I liked the venue. I liked to go there as a visitor, to see films, gigs and to the café bar. I imagined I'd also like working there. The pay wasn't great, but it was a start. I'd also find myself beneath people who were younger and less well qualified than myself, but again that couldn't be helped. Beggars couldn't be choosers. It would be a start. It might lead to better things. I could see myself in a career in arts administration. This could potentially be a way in. The work was pretty simple and basic – answering the telephone, selling tickets on the box office, dealing with general enquiries from members of the public. But I didn't mind that. In fact I thought it could potentially suit me quite well. That was if I got the job. Only time would tell. I kept my fingers crossed.

I was pleased to be called to an interview. It was probably the first job interview I'd attended in years where I actually wanted the job. Both before and since my teacher training debacle, I'd attended job interviews in a very half-hearted way for jobs I had little interest in getting. And unsurprisingly I hadn't got any of them. This was different. I was actually going for an interview for a job I wanted. I prepared carefully. I dressed tidily. I wanted to create a good impression. I hoped I wouldn't be scuppered by nerves or ill health. It was a concern to me whether I'd even be well enough to attend. I was fortunate. On the day of the interview I felt reasonably OK, at least for me. It wasn't one of my worst days, and that was the main thing. I felt I performed quite well at the interview. I gave it my very best shot. I endeavoured to come across as keen and enthusiastic, a rarity in itself. I believed I achieved that. I was lucky in one sense. I wasn't asked too many awkward questions about why I'd abandoned my teacher training course. I didn't feel the need to mention it myself, or my health issues. I simply said I'd worked as a newspaper reporter but was seeking a change of direction. They seemed to accept my explanation. They seemed reasonably impressed by my level of eagerness to work there. At the end of the interview I thanked them and said I looked forward to hearing from them.

I didn't have to wait long. A letter arrived in the post only a day or two later. I was one of several candidates being offered a job. I was very pleased. The only downside was that it was only being offered on a temporary basis, but there was a small possibility it might get extended. Roxanne and my parents were quick to congratulate me. My mum was particularly relieved I'd be back in work, even if it was only part time and temporary. I hadn't done anything for nearly a year. Now at last she could talk about me to relatives and neighbours in some kind of positive way again. She wouldn't feel embarrassed when people asked after me. She came from good Protestant stock, with a strong work ethic, who had a knuckle down and get on with it attitude in the face of adversity or bad fortune. They didn't believe in ill health. They believed in stoically maintaining a stiff upper lip whatever the circumstances. Her father had struggled on with heart problems to an early grave. That was what was expected. My mum could never accept I'd been ill. In her head I was too young for any of that. It was just too hard for her to believe any different. She couldn't even bear to talk about it. At least now I was making a return to work of sorts. That gave her a small degree of comfort.

I liked working at the arts centre. I immediately felt at home there. I took to it straight away, and I seemed to fit in. I liked the atmosphere and the people were all right. The work wasn't too demanding, but neither was it boring. Of course it wasn't perfect, but it suited me as well as I could have expected. After just a few days I was confident I'd mastered the basic demands of the job, and it felt like I'd been there longer than I had been. It wasn't as strange going back to work as it might have been either. Indeed I only wished I'd thought of a career in arts administration before. It was probably the kind of work I should have been doing for the past decade since leaving university. It suited my temperament much better than either journalism or teaching had.

There were some downsides. The hours were erratic. I never knew in advance which days I'd be working. It was never the same from one week to the next. It made it harder to make plans with Roxanne. One week I'd be working quite a lot of hours, the next week only a few. The rota only came out just before the week started. I never knew until then when I'd be working or how much I'd be working. Inevitably there were also days when my health wasn't good and I'd struggle just to get through a shift. If it was quiet and I was on my own, which I often was if I was working an evening, I'd ring Roxanne and tell her I was really struggling. Somehow I always made it through to the end of the day and made it home to her, even when I doubted I would myself.

Often it wasn't easy. At times it required every ounce of effort in my body. I refused to give in. I stuck at it. I put on a brave face. I never admitted to any of my colleagues I had health issues. I preferred they didn't know. They didn't need to. But overall I was happy. I liked working there. I was thankful and glad I'd got the job. I enjoyed the benefits of the café bar. Staff got a reduction on food and drink. If I was working a day shift I availed myself of this and had my lunch there. The portions were large and generous. The food was tasty. For the first time in several years I found myself putting on weight. That in itself was a sign I was slowly getting better.

I worked at the arts centre right through the spring and summer of 1996, and as I turned thirty-one years of age. I was pleased to see the back of being thirty. It hadn't been a very happy time. Now at last things were looking up a little. Roxanne still had itchy feet and moved flats yet again. We finally got a place together of our own, although we shared it with a work friend of hers. She had the spare room. It didn't matter. We barely saw her. Now I was working again I could pay a little more towards rent and I could afford to live with Roxanne. At last I felt I was growing up. I was escaping my parents' clutches, though I still stayed with them from time to time when Roxanne went home to see her mum and dad.

Throughout the time I'd been with Judy my parents' house had been just too comfortable to leave. In retrospect that had been a mistake.

Now at last and rather belatedly I was making my first real steps towards achieving true independence and making a family life of my own. After leaving home this time I'd never live with my parents again. It had been a long time coming. No doubt for them too it was more than high time. I'd been slow leaving the nest. Though only ill health had driven me back there in the first place. Now at last I was truly independent and was living with Roxanne. We could start making very real plans to get married.

Roxanne threw herself into organising the wedding with the same flurry of energy she did everything. We started looking at dates and venues, potential guest lists, transport, rings, accommodation and options for reception food and drink. It wasn't long before we had much of it organised. We weren't spending too much. With contributions from her parents and mine, and a little bit of money I'd saved up when I was ill and couldn't leave the house, we could just about afford a pleasant but modest do in the setting of a nice country house, with a barn dance afterwards. Whilst Roxanne got most of it booked straight away, as her energy faltered I looked after some of the finer details over the months that followed. We set a date. We'd be married in September the year after. We started telling some of our closest friends and relatives to keep the day free. It was something for both of us really to look forward to. It would be the start of a new adult life. I finally felt truly grown up.

Life continued to improve. During the summer of 1996 I finally re-joined a local tennis club. I wasn't really well enough to play, but I was determined to make the effort and give it a go. I went back to the first club I'd ever played at, which was small and friendly and of a fairly low standard. That suited me perfectly, as it was just another stage on my gradual road to recovery. I wasn't ready to play seriously again. I just went along one or two nights a week and played a couple of sets. It was about the most I could manage really. I didn't even care if I won or lost. In the past I'd always been very competitive. I hated losing. I'd always given each game I played every ounce of energy I had, as if my life had depended on it. Sport had involved total commitment, to the point of losing my temper, getting aggressive, being sullen afterwards, even feeling something bordering on hatred for my opponent or opponents. Now I no longer cared. It was irrelevant. Just being out there on court was all that mattered. That was an achievement in itself. I no longer played competitively. I barely followed the score of the games. Hitting the ball was the important thing and became a form of therapy. I didn't always feel well when I played, but the longer I could stay out there was another small step on the path to getting better.

Other players seemed impressed by my calmer demeanour. They probably wondered just what had happened to the angry young man they'd known before. He'd gone. He'd disappeared for good. I explained I'd been unwell and was slowly trying to get back to full health. I didn't give all the details of my illness and my months off doing nothing. I didn't really like talking about it, if I could possibly avoid it. The irony was I now came across as a more mature, rounded individual. It wasn't really the case. It was just illness had given me a new perspective on life. My view of what was relevant and what was irrelevant had altered. The physical playing of a game for a period of time during an evening was my sole focus, not the individual points, the totting up of games, the final score, who won and who lost. I didn't care. I went home happy if I'd managed to play for an hour. I was thrilled if I played for even longer. If I didn't feel unwell afterwards that was an added bonus. In some strange way illness had made me a better, slightly more considerate person. I'd just been a highly competitive brat when I'd played before.

At the end of the summer, when the tennis season finished, I realised I needed to find something else I could play in the same low-key, non-strenuous manner. I still wasn't well enough for football or rugby, so I went back to badminton. It fulfilled the same role and purpose as tennis had. It allowed me to continue to play something during the autumn months, when it was too cold and dark to play outdoors. It meant I could continue to get some physical exercise, without feeling completely exhausted and wretched afterwards. It was also beneficial for my mental health and wellbeing. I realised some people hated sport. I on the other hand felt depressed when I wasn't actively involved in playing sport. It was almost slightly at odds with the person inside me who liked loud indie rock music, clubs and drinking. But that's how I was. I was a mass of contrasts, contradictions and conflicting interests that didn't quite fit together.

As the summer ended, so too did my contract at the arts centre. I'd been desperate to be kept on. One or two colleagues on temporary contracts were being retained. Most weren't. I'd really put myself out and given the job my total dedication and enthusiasm in the hope of being one of them, but it wasn't to be. I just missed out. It wasn't entirely bad news. The job had at least given me an opportunity to start working again, when at one time that had looked like it might never happen. It had also given me a chance to get valuable experience in an area I was actually interested in. Previously I'd worked for years in jobs I'd loathed. I'd finally found something I actually enjoyed doing. That was a major change and improvement in itself. As it happened, I discovered that even if I'd been retained at the arts centre it would only have been for a short period. Towards the end of my time there it was announced the centre would shortly close for an extended period for an extensive refurbishment. Only a small handful of staff were being kept on during the closure. Most faced redundancy.

As fate would have it, just as my time at the arts centre drew to a close, I saw an advert in the local paper to work at a new arthouse cinema that was due to open shortly in the local area. I liked alternative cinema. The fact that the city where I lived was getting its own independent cinema was exciting news enough. The fact I might get to work there made it even more exciting. I'd sometimes had fantasies of opening a small, independent cinema myself. The city would certainly have benefited from one. Of course it had been nothing more than a pipedream on my part. I had no finances to invest in such an enterprise. I had no backing. But as chance would have it, it was now actually happening. And with my recent experience at the arts centre, where they also showed independent and alternative films, I did at least have a chance of getting a job at the new, purpose-built venue that was rapidly nearing completion.

I applied for the job immediately. To my pleasant surprise I was invited for interview straight away. I was interviewed by a confident young man, younger than me, who'd been put in charge of the project. He was smartly dressed and clearly upwardly mobile, eager rapidly to advance his career. He was the polar opposite of how I'd been at his age. He was self-assured, even a little arrogant, but at the same time he was chatty and had a friendly and easy-going manner about him. I felt I could work with him. He didn't ask me all that much. He said I had the job and could start straight away. I could even help get the building finished and ready. Furthermore, I could do pretty much as many or as few hours as I wanted. With my health issues that suited me ideally. It sounded like a highly worthwhile project. I was delighted to be involved. I couldn't wait to get started.

'Well done. That's great news,' Roxanne said, when I arrived home to tell her I'd got the job.

'I think this might actually work out rather well,' I replied.

I felt good. I finally had a job I really wanted for once, doing something I was genuinely interested in. At last my luck was changing.

Chapter Ten

I enjoyed helping get the cinema ready to open to the general public. It was rewarding seeing it all come together, as the day of its official opening drew ever nearer. When I started my new job, parts of the structure still resembled a building site. As the days passed work progressed quickly. Before long it was mainly just the finishing touches that were needed. I ran errands and helped with the general cleaning, tidying and preparing. It wasn't work that taxed the brain, but it was fun. I liked most of the people I worked with. One of the project managers, however, was a thoroughly objectionable individual. He was a brusque, gruff, rough and ready Antipodean, who didn't have a polite word to say about anyone. I couldn't stand the man, so mainly stayed out of his way. He was possibly the rudest man I'd ever met. The only saving grace was that as soon as the project was finished and the cinema was open he was off to work on another one. It was a good thing. If he'd been there all the time I would probably have quit. Luckily I soon found out I only had to put up with the bore for a couple of weeks. That was more than enough. In the meantime avoidance and biting my lip in his presence remained my main strategies to get through my time with him. He was loud, lewd, sexist and crude. I wasn't alone in forming a negative opinion of him. Almost everyone there was just counting the days off until he was gone.

When the cinema was finally finished it looked amazing. It truly was an impressive addition to the city's cultural facilities. It had two luxury screens, complete with the latest in comfort seating, and an equally lavish, purpose-built bar with stunning views. It was just what the city needed. I was confident it would be a success. I was certain the city's more artistically minded residents would take it to their hearts and flock there in large numbers. I knew I'd be a regular visitor myself, if I wasn't already working there. It had the smell of newness and of quality upholstery and carpets. It hadn't been done on the cheap. Award-winning architects had been employed to draw up the plans for the building. They'd now realised the dreams of the owners and turned it into reality. The frontage was mainly glass. It was very open plan. But in 1996 it looked elegant and modern.

On the day of the official opening there was still much to get ready and clean. I was worried we wouldn't manage it all, but somehow we got it done just in time. We had a briefing with all the other new staff.

Some like me had been working there for a few weeks. Others were only just starting, now the cinema was ready to open. They had employed a good team. There was a great sense of camaraderie and excitement among all of us. We genuinely believed we were part of something important that was happening. The city was gaining something new, dynamic and significant. We felt like the chosen few to be working there. Most of us were in our twenties and thirties. Quite a few were students. There were one or two who were older, from different backgrounds and life experiences. But we felt bonded and bound together, with a united sense of purpose.

The official opening was a grand affair. Local dignitaries and celebrities were invited. Some executives from the national film industry even travelled for the occasion. An elaborate spread of food and drink was provided for them. Speeches and words of welcome were made formally to declare the cinema open, followed by a special screening of one of the latest high quality film releases. There was a wonderful atmosphere that evening, both among staff and guests. The vibe was good. Everyone was happy. Everyone was pleased to see the cinema open. We all went away with contented smiles on our faces. The event had run smoothly. It was a job done well. It was one of the only jobs I ever had where I actually looked forward to coming back the next day, to see the cinema open its doors to the general public for the first time.

I'd enjoyed working at the arts centre. If anything I enjoyed the cinema even more. Of course I had my bad days, when I didn't feel well, but I always got through them. The general feel-good air that surrounded the cinema continued for some months. Just about all the staff seemed thrilled to be working there. The customers who came in were equally delighted to be able to take advantage of the new facility. Many joined as members. News of the cinema's opening travelled far and wide and quickly spread round the county. Many came from miles away to sample the new cinematic experience and enjoy a drink in the bar before or afterwards. Some came just to drink in the bar. For a while it became a trendy place to hang out. On days I didn't work I almost felt I was missing out on something that might be happening in the cinema. Of course that feeling wore off in time, but not for a while.

On my days off I often went in to watch films free of charge. It was a staff perk. I watched as many as I could. Sometimes in the evenings Roxanne came to a film with me. We usually made a night of it and visited the bar both before and after the film. At the end of most of my

83

shifts I stopped for a quick beer and chatted to the bar staff before heading back. It was a very sociable job. Sometimes it didn't feel like a job at all. I felt relaxed and at home there. On weekends Roxanne went to see her parents, if I wasn't working I'd go in and watch the films. I spent many Saturday nights there on my own, viewing the latest releases and having a drink afterwards. Roxanne was a little possessive. It was one of the few slight flaws of her character. We all have some. She didn't like me going to a pub or club without her. She thought I might chat to other women. She didn't mind me going to the cinema. So that's what I did whenever she was away.

They were good times. Plans were progressing fast for our wedding the following year. The job was going well. I was just a general front of house assistant at first. It wasn't long before I was given more responsibility. Only a month or two had passed when I was promoted to the role of Box Office Manager and given a set of keys to the building. Shortly after that I was made a Duty Manager and had responsibility for cashing up and locking up the cinema at the end of some shifts. I also had responsibility for distributing the cinema's printed programmes. Every six weeks or so I spent a couple of days taking them round the nearby towns and villages in my car, dropping them off at related businesses and other venues, where passers-by could pick them up. I quite enjoyed getting out and about. I felt like an ambassador for the new cinema. I wasn't the General Manager, but many saw me as the public face of the business. I was very pleased to be working there. It had all worked out rather well, just as I'd hoped it would. The cinema's opening couldn't have come at a better time for me. It felt like fate had done me a favour for once. I was happily working somewhere that hadn't even existed a few months before.

At the cinema I generally worked either afternoons or evenings, and quite often both. I normally had mornings off, when I had the flat to myself. Once or twice a week I went out to do a little light training, as I continued my recuperation from illness. On other mornings I sat at my desk writing, sometimes in silence, sometimes listening to music. Writing a few more pages each week I eventually finished the second novel I'd been working on. I'd titled it *Beatnik*, as I thought of myself as something of an underground poet and beatnik. As well as being an autobiographical account of running an underground poetry magazine, as I had done with a fellow poet and friend in the years immediately after leaving university, it was also something of a criticism of the 1980s and its ideologies. I was a particular vehement critic of the Margaret Thatcher years of greed and monetary aspiration, and that provided the background which the novel was set against.

As previously alluded to the novel didn't have a happy ending. Unfortunately most of mine didn't. It finished, as so much of my writing tended to, with my girlfriend of the time leaving me. Even more tragically it finished with my magazine co-editor attempting suicide. Worse perhaps than dying, he ended up paralysed from the neck downwards and confined to a wheelchair for the rest of his life. This was perhaps not the subject matter for the most uplifting novel of all time. Yet much of what we'd published in our magazine had been full of parody, dark humour and satire. We'd had much fun and hilarity writing it together. It was perhaps at odds with the tragic way things had ended. I'd even continued to publish the magazine by myself for some years afterwards, as a tribute to my friend. Eventually I ran out of steam with it and it simply stopped, without ever officially ceasing publication. My finished novel was a fairly accurate and faithful account of that period of my life, but it failed truly to convey the amusement that had also accompanied compiling the magazine. To that extent it was another failure. I still sent sample chapters off to potential publishers and agents. One or two showed some initial interest, but as with my first novel ultimately it was passed on by all of them and I received no offers of publication.

I wasn't downcast for long. In a sudden burst of energy and frenetic typing I quickly launched into writing a third novel. I'd recently seen Danny Boyle's film adaptation of the Irvine Welsh novel *Trainspotting*. It had struck a chord with me. It was original, entertaining, uncompromising, funny, fast paced and poignant. I didn't want to write about drugs, but I could write about young people who were into music, going out and having a good time. Taking a little inspiration from *Trainspotting*, and a little from Roddy Doyle's *The Commitments*, which I was familiar with through Alan Parker's big screen version, I started working furiously on my new project. I called the novel *Ravers*. It was more light-hearted and less autobiographical than *Beatnik* had been, and it was more fun to write. Unlike much of my writing it wasn't really autobiographical at all. It was just about a group of young misfits who liked what most young people like – music, getting drunk and having sex. It was about pubbing and clubbing. It was about avoiding getting a job. It was about enjoying being unemployed. It was about putting a band together, just for something to do.

For once the main character wasn't me, though perhaps a version of me in a parallel universe. I too had enjoyed extended periods on the dole, when I didn't really want to work. Like the lead character, I too loved classic punk rock bands like *The Clash*, *The Ruts*, *The Buzzcocks* and *The Stranglers* and wanted to emulate them. The novel drew on some of my experiences playing in bands as a teenager, hoping without success to secure a record deal. There the similarities ended. Most of my early bands hadn't even got as far as doing gigs. They'd split up long before that became reality. Perhaps writing *Ravers* I was writing what might have been.

Either way work progressed really quickly on it. Within a month or two I'd written a hundred or so pages. I'd never written so much so quickly. I felt quite inspired. I was sure this was the novel with which I'd finally find success. This was the novel that would land me a contract with a major publisher. I was as certain as could be. I had total faith. It was strange. I never really doubted myself. Through all my ups and downs, and through all the setbacks I'd had, my belief remained undiminished. As quickly as one novel was rejected I moved on with another one. It was remarkable that I carried on believing really, but carry on I did. I had unshakeable confidence I would eventually be discovered. I believed I would eventually be noticed, and I'd be transported from the life I lived into one of glitz and glamour, of book launches, award ceremonies and parties. I never once doubted it. And when it happened I could laugh at those who'd doubted me, and the girls who'd ditched me on the way. That's what I thought. Except of course it didn't happen. I remained in the more humble reality in which I was living.

When I wasn't working on the new novel I started putting together a new poetry collection, tentatively titled *Scrapbook*. Hopefully it was a little more optimistic than my previous effort, *Sick Note*, had been, when I'd been caught in the depths of severe illness. Hopefully it reflected the fact my life was now on a slow upward path of sorts, as my gradual progress towards recovery continued. Another indication I was slowly improving was my sudden decision to sign up to a couple of casting agencies, specialising in film and television extra work. I'd always been interested in film and even owned a cine camera as a young man, when I'd considered myself something of an amateur filmmaker. Now inspired by the films we were showing at the cinema, I decided it was time to take my hobby further. I even got a few professional photographs of myself taken to improve my chances of getting work. To my surprise it wasn't long before I got a little extra and bit part work, mainly on television dramas and foreign language films, where they took advantage of the ample local scenery to provide settings and backdrops. This was despite the fact I had no acting experience whatsoever. But it provided a bit of extra cash and was a boost to my confidence.

As 1996 rolled into 1997 Roxanne and I moved again. I'd started to lose count of the number of places she'd rented in the small time I'd known her. This was at least the fifth different location, but it had become necessary to move yet again. Roxanne's work colleague we'd shared with since moving in together had started to resent our presence. She clearly disliked our closeness. Perhaps it just emphasised to her that was she was single and on her own. Perhaps she'd hoped to spend more time with Roxanne herself. We were so inseparable that was virtually impossible. Whatever it was, the relationship between us and our housemate had deteriorated to the point that we barely talked and mostly just stayed out of each other's way.

Roxanne realised before me it was time to go. It made sense. We decided to get a new place, where we'd hopefully be living when we got married. This time we rented out the whole floor of an old Victorian house, which we had entirely to ourselves. For once we really didn't have to worry about anyone else. The quietness was serene. I even had a little study at the back where I could write. In the daytimes before I went to work the silence was simply marvellous. We could finally relax. It really was just the two of us. At last we could complete the final preparations for our wedding, which was edging closer and closer. It was now just a few months away, and it was time for the invitations to be sent out. It really was happening. I was thirty-two years old, and I was going to be married. There was no backing out now.

We'd chosen an old, historic mansion as the venue for our wedding. It was situated on a family estate about fifteen miles from where we lived. It was quaint, rustic and hidden away. The house itself wasn't normally open to the general public. The estate grounds were open for walks and had a few native animals scattered here and there to look at. In our experience it was rarely busy. That suited us ideally. The estate was a little overgrown and in need of some minor care and attention, but for us that was just part of its charm and appeal. It wasn't to everyone's taste, but we found it peaceful and relaxing. It had been the location for one of our early dates and so made perfect sense for us to get married there. For some reason it wasn't especially well known locally. Whilst available for wedding hire it wasn't a hugely popular venue, as few seemed aware of its existence. For us that made it even more perfect. It was also relatively inexpensive, compared to most of the other more favoured, local wedding venues. All in all it was a natural choice. It just felt right. We had no hesitation at all in choosing it for our special occasion.

A few months before the big day we visited the venue to discuss the finer details of the wedding ceremony itself, and the food and drink choices for the reception afterwards. Roxanne's parents came with us, as they were paying for the venue hire and reception. I was paying for wedding cars, photographer and rings, from a little money I'd saved up. My parents were paying for the flowers, drink and for our honeymoon afterwards. We weren't having a huge wedding, but we were still inviting eighty guests to the main ceremony and reception. A further forty guests were coming to an additional party in the evening.

Roxanne was a committed atheist and didn't want any religious content included in the ceremony. It was another reason we'd deliberately chosen a civil wedding venue as opposed to a church setting. There would be no hymns or religious readings at our wedding. Instead my dad and Roxanne's chief bridesmaid agreed to recite some carefully chosen poems and poignant texts on love, marriage and commitment to mark the occasion. Atmospheric background music was being provided by an accomplished harp player. Roxanne was being transported to the venue in a classic, vintage car. The same car was transporting us to a quiet, village manor house afterwards for our official wedding night. Our evening do was going to be an old-fashioned barn dance. We hoped everyone would get up and join in. Nothing was over formal. We hoped it would be a relaxed occasion. We wanted everyone to have fun.

It took Roxanne and I several nights to write and send all the invitations out. We wanted to give everyone plenty of notice, as a number were travelling from distance. I was aware quite a few of my relatives had never even met Roxanne. The wedding day itself would be the first time they'd meet her. I still wanted them there. I wanted them to celebrate our big day with us. I even invited some of my old university friends I hadn't seen for a few years. I thought it would be a nice opportunity to see them again. I only had a small family, so on my side choosing the guests was relatively straightforward. Roxanne had a far larger family, with many more aunts, uncles and cousins, so for her it was a rather more complicated task. With a larger family also came more black sheep. There were a few relatives she wasn't desperate to invite, but for one reason or other she felt obliged to.

Weddings can make or break friendships. Those you can't invite, as there is simply no more room, never forgive you. Some guests are put out as you don't have room to accommodate all their children too. The bride and groom often struggle to forgive those who don't put themselves out to be there. Of the university friends I invited, they all originally agreed, only to drop out one by one. One said they were still coming, simply not turn up on the day itself. You don't forget. Two of my oldest friends from school, including one of my official ushers, only put in brief appearances and left early. You don't forget easily. Conversely you remember the ones who clearly had a good time, who joined in, who had fun, who were the lives and soul of the party, who stayed until the end. You remember and are thankful to them. Yes, weddings are strange things.

The 1990s was a period of transformation. In May 1997 there was a sea change in British politics. Tony Blair and New Labour were swept to power on a tidal wave of popular enthusiasm and optimism. They secured a landslide victory in that month's General Election. The country had tired of eighteen years of Conservative government, firstly with belligerent Prime Minister Margaret Thatcher and more recently with the rather grey and dour John Major. Young and old alike were ready for an alternative and something different. New Labour seemed to provide it. Somehow a youthful Tony Blair managed to attract support from all quarters. Rather cleverly he was able to align himself with the popular music and fashion cultures of the day. Somehow they became entwined with politics in a way they hadn't been before. It was a return to the *Swinging Sixties*. London was cool again, once more the cultural capital of Europe. Phrases like *Cool Britannia* were coined. It was hip and trendy to be British. The Union Jack flag suddenly became iconic. It was OK to be nationalistic, to celebrate British culture, as it was a new, more inclusive form of nationalism. This was a groundbreaking movement that welcomed Brits from ethnic minorities and our European cousins too.

When Roxanne and I looked at potential honeymoon destinations it made perfect sense to choose London, the European capital of the moment, the epicentre and heartbeat of everything that was modern and happening in music and fashion. Roxanne and I were both keen on clothes and music. Where better for us to go than London? It also made good practical sense. I hated flying. Roxanne disliked boats and water. Going to London on the train we didn't have to negotiate either. There were many very much cheaper places to go, but in a funny way it suited us. We booked an expensive, central London hotel for our first night. Then to save money we booked a more modest hotel a little further out for the rest of our week's stay. We couldn't wait to go. We were really looking forward to it.

The wave of optimism and general sense of goodwill and happiness that was sweeping the country didn't extend to the weather. The summer of 1997 was an unusually wet one. We started to worry our big day would be a washout. In the event we were lucky. There were only about two dry weeks the whole of the summer, one of which coincided with the week of our wedding and honeymoon. There were other obstacles for us to overcome, however. As September came and with it an Indian Summer the country plunged into national mourning. The feelings of joy and optimism had been short lived. Princess Diana suddenly died in a car crash in Paris. Her death and funeral coincided with our wedding. There were calls in the national media for those with weddings planned to cancel them as a mark of respect. Ours had been booked and paid for. There was no way we were doing that. We had to get on with our own lives. We had to carry on regardless. We weren't Royalists. I was no admirer of the Royal Family. I had no wish for Diana to be dead, but her life and death had no bearing on my life and our happiness. We both agreed there would be no mention of Princess Diana at our wedding. We had other things on our mind. We remained pretty much oblivious to it and events going on in the rest of the country, as we continued to prepare for our special occasion.

Even the day before something suddenly went wrong, something I was most fearful of. After a number of years fighting illness my biggest fear was my health would fail me on the day, that I wouldn't be well enough to go through with the ceremony. The day before, as we had a wedding rehearsal at the venue, I was struck down by a high temperature. I think the stress of the build-up, the enormity of the impending event, had got to me and I'd become sick. I went home and went to bed early. I was genuinely concerned I wouldn't be well enough for the wedding and we'd have to cancel, with guests already setting out and on their way. My health was so fragile it didn't take much to set it back. When I woke up the next day I was only a little better. But I was determined to go through with my wedding anyway, and I was determined to enjoy it.

Chapter Eleven

Despite my worries my wedding to Roxanne went just about as perfectly as it could have done. Even though predictably I didn't feel very well on the big day, everything went smoothly and according to plan. My adrenalin and my excitement got me through it. To ensure we didn't see each other before the ceremony Roxanne got ready at our flat, whilst I stayed at my parents' house. In the morning I went out for a little walk by myself, to collect my thoughts and clear my head. Quietly I contemplated the enormity of what lay ahead and what I was about to enter into. I had no regrets and no last-minute second thoughts or doubts. I was happy with my choice. I was content Roxanne was the right person for me. I was confident we were doing the right thing.

Despite the summer being largely a washout I woke up to glorious sunshine. It was a beautifully warm, early September Saturday, when I went out to breathe in the fresh air. No one could have asked for a better day for their wedding. It was balmy and sunny, but not so hot as to be uncomfortable. It was ideal weather for a wedding. Although I didn't feel right my high temperature had receded a little. It was much closer to normal. I took some aspirin to try and ensure it didn't begin rising again. Any thoughts of cancelling had now been forgotten. I was totally focussed. I was ready to get married. I was going through with it. I hoped Roxanne felt the same.

I got ready slowly. I ate a light lunch in the late morning, so I didn't feel hungry before the main reception meal. It was just enough to fill me up, but not enough to make me feel over full or sick before the big event. As I got ready I ran through my speech once more. It was relatively short and to the point. I was no public speaker. My dad was that. He enjoyed it. I didn't. Yet I hoped my speech would hit the right note, thank all the right people that needed to be thanked, and contain at least a little humour. I'd spent several months working on it and was just about happy with the wording. I wasn't looking forward to delivering it. I knew I'd need a few drinks beforehand, to give me the confidence to get up and address the waiting audience.

I wore a new, navy blue, pinstripe suit and waistcoat. I had a new shirt and tie. I had new socks and shoes, only the best, which my mum had helped me to buy. I had a silk handkerchief in my top pocket. I had a white flower in my pinhole. My hair was cut short. It was shorter and neater than I normally had it. I looked smart. I looked the part.

Being tall I wore my suit well. I occasionally wore a suit jacket. I occasionally wore suit trousers. I rarely wore both together. It was unusual for my parents to see me so dressed up. For once I think they were proud of their only son.

'Are we ready to do this?' my dad asked, when we'd all finished getting ready and checking ourselves in the mirror.

'I think so,' I replied.

'Have you got the rings?' my dad continued.

'I have,' I replied.

'Then let's go,' he said. 'And let it be a wonderful day.'

'Good luck,' my mum added, giving me a kiss on the forehead, as we left the house together.

We'd booked a taxi to take us to the venue. We were meeting my ushers and best man there. We arrived early. Everything was ready. The room where Roxanne and I were to get married was laid out perfectly. The flowers looked lovely. An adjacent room was exquisitely prepared for our guests to eat. The historic ancestral home looked amazing. It was a wonderful setting. Every small detail had been carefully attended to. It almost brought a tear to my eye, taking it all in, as we waited outside in the garden for our guests to arrive.

Slowly cars and taxis started to pull up. Well-dressed guests got out and began to make their way to the house. It was time to go inside. I gave the wedding rings to my best man. He was an old friend called Richard I knew from my bachelor days. He performed his duties well, but strangely we saw little of him after the wedding. He got married himself several years later, and didn't even invite us, which was something of a surprise. But negative thoughts of future events as they'd unfold were far from my mind at that moment. My parents and I made our way to the front. The ushers stood at the back and started to direct guests to their seats. It began to fill up. The time of the ceremony drew near. There was still no sign of Roxanne. The room was full. I began to get worried. My nerves started to get the better of me. Perhaps she'd changed her mind. Perhaps she wasn't coming. Perhaps it was all off. I turned to my mum to share my concerns.

'Don't be so silly. Of course she's coming,' my mum reassured me.

'Why isn't she here then? It's time,' I pointed out.

'It's fashionable for the bride to be a little late,' my mum explained.

She'd never been that keen on Roxanne in truth. My mum tolerated her rather than really liked her. But she didn't want to see her only son left standing alone at the altar now. She tried to assure me everything would be all right. Time just seemed to be going so slowly. I kept looking at my watch. Another minute, then another minute passed. I was standing in a room full of people waiting to see me get married. But there was no bride. There was no Roxanne. Where was she? Then I saw the vintage car transporting her pull up in the grounds outside. I saw the driver open her door. I saw her get out in her white dress. I saw her dad. I saw her chief bridesmaid. Even then they seemed to take an eternity to come up. She explained afterwards that they'd had to stop to take photographs. It only heightened my sense of panic.

'Why is she taking so long?' I asked my mum again. 'Why hasn't she come up? She must have had second thoughts. She must have changed her mind.'

I even started to get my mum worried there might be some truth in my fears. There was frantic activity outside. I could see Roxanne's bridesmaids rushing about. Were they trying to talk her into going through with it? They weren't. I was mistaken. There was no problem. I needn't have worried. There were no foundations to my concerns. They were just getting themselves sorted. Roxanne seemed to take what seemed like an age, but eventually she was ready. The music changed. The room hushed. Roxanne's dad emerged to walk Roxanne down the aisle, followed by her troupe of bridesmaids. Eventually she reached me.

'I thought you weren't coming,' I said, as I took her hand in mine.

'I wouldn't leave you on your own,' Roxanne replied.

She wore a fitted, white wedding dress of an almost sixties' style. It suited her to a tee. Her blonde hair had been carefully coiffured by a stylist that morning. Her make-up was flawless; her red lipstick perfectly applied on her lips that I wanted to kiss. She looked magnificent.

'I'm very glad you're here. I'm nervous,' I said.

'I'm nervous too,' Roxanne replied.

'We'll be nervous together then,' I said.

I don't remember the wedding ceremony very well, though much of it was captured on video camera. Thinking of it later it all seemed slightly unreal and a bit of a blur. I don't recall the exact words we'd practised and which we said to each other in front of our gathered audience of family and friends. But we dutifully followed the prompts of the official registrar and recited aloud our wedding vows one after the other and exchanged rings. At different points in the ceremony there were readings by my dad and Roxanne's chief bridesmaid, as well as passages of atmospheric music played on the harp, creating the right tone for the occasion. I do remember the registrar saying *You may now kiss the bride!* when it was all over. There was a loud cheer from those gathered. That was the cue for us to relax. Beaming smiles started to spread across our faces. We were now legally married. There really was no going back.

The rest of the day was pretty fabulous. It was relaxed and good natured, as the drink flowed and everyone enjoyed themselves. Immediately after the ceremony there were canapes and sparkling wine outside on the lawn in the sunshine. Then the guests were called in for the main reception. I sat with my parents, best man and Roxanne. We enjoyed a full formal meal of starter, main course, dessert and coffee. I drank copious amounts of wine as we ate. I wanted to be relaxed before delivering my speech, the bit of the day I was most nervous about. I kept looking across at Roxanne. She looked beautiful in her wedding dress. I could hardly believe we were married, but we were.

I was happy. I was pleased with myself. She was a good catch. I'd done well for myself. It had been a difficult few years, with Judy suddenly leaving me and marrying someone else. I'd been plagued by ill health. My attempts to become a teacher had failed. Yet since then I'd found a different job, perhaps one I was better suited to, and now I was married myself. Something good had happened, in front of all my family and friends. Things were working out at last. The day was pretty much perfect. The sky outside was blue. We were bathed in glorious sunshine. It shone in through the open windows. It felt like it was shining on me and Roxanne at that moment in time. We felt blessed. We couldn't have been happier.

Roxanne's dad delivered his thoughtful and carefully prepared speech. He had some kind words to say about me, probably more than I deserved. Then it was my turn. I kept it fairly short and sweet as I'd planned. With the help of the wine I'd consumed I actually felt more relaxed speaking to the assembled audience than I'd expected. When I watched the video recording back, in the quiet privacy of our home at some later date I seemed quite confident, far more confident than I actually was or had anticipated being. I was perhaps just caught up in the magic of the occasion and simply enjoying it. Perhaps I was relishing being the centre of attention. It doesn't happen very often. Perhaps I was subconsciously making the most of the moment. It would be a while before it would happen again. I even forgot how poorly I'd felt only the day before, when I'd had genuine fears the wedding might have to be cancelled. All that was now a distant memory. Everything was going just as we'd hoped it would. My speech was well received. There were laughs and cheers in all the right places. That was all I could expect and ask for. I was happy when I could sit back down and leave the rest to my best man. I took another large sip of wine. As I did so Roxanne gave me a kiss. I hoped I'd said some suitably lovely things about her.

'Thanks,' she whispered.

After the reception there was a small gap in proceedings, when guests could relax and look around the house and grounds. I got myself a beer and took the opportunity to mingle properly with our guests, with Roxanne by my side. We could now chat to them as legally wed man and wife. As afternoon ran into evening the wedding relocated to an outside courtyard taproom and function room, where our evening reception got into full swing. More friends and work colleagues joined us there. Some of our guests were quite drunk by this stage. An old school friend, a college friend of Roxanne's, and one of my dad's former work associates, all stood out as having taken full advantage of the wide selection of drink on offer. By then they were noticeably tipsy. It didn't matter. They were enjoying themselves. That was what they were there for. There was a good atmosphere. There were no underlying tones of bad feeling or ill temper. We wanted people to be tipsy. We wanted them to have fun.

Having a barn dance in the evening turned out to be an inspired choice. It was much better than having some mediocre, middle of the road disco. It meant everyone could join in. Everyone was a beginner. Everyone was the same. It didn't matter who was a good dancer and who wasn't. Everyone was on a level and equal plain. The caller explained the basic dance moves and then the Celtic folk band behind him struck up the music. Everyone started to dance. Roxanne and I joined in. My mum joined in too. Roxanne's dad got energetically and enthusiastically involved. It was thirsty work. I quickly needed more beer. It was hilarious watching people go round the wrong way, bump into each other, and sometimes even fall over. They quickly got up to carry on. It reminded me of the country dance festivals I'd attended whilst at primary school. The worse people danced the funnier it was.

Midway through the evening the band took a break, and more food and drink was brought out. Surprisingly I found I had room to eat again.

There was plenty to go round, and it gave our evening guests an opportunity to eat too. Then the band began their second set. Some of our more elderly relatives started to leave. They were worn out by the busy day and retired to their hotels and guest houses. A little after eleven the music stopped. The evening started to wind down, as slowly more people began to leave. The bar was still open, and I carried on drinking, as did the hardcore of our friends and relatives. Around midnight our chauffeur-driven, vintage car arrived to take us to the destination for our wedding night. It was funny driving off from our own wedding, with our guests waving goodbye to us, as they slowly vanished into the distance. The thing I remember most is my dad chuckling to himself. He'd had a good day. His only son's wedding day had been a success.

We arrived safely at the impressive, old manor house that was our sleeping place for the night. Our luggage was already waiting for us, as we checked in. It was the small hours when we finally made our way up to our bedroom. Our wedding night wasn't quite what it would have been in generations earlier. We already lived together. We had no bedroom secrets from each other. We were hardly virgins. Even so we took advantage of our spacious and luxurious four-poster bed and made love to each other for the first night as man and wife, as was the custom for newlyweds. I'd have been disappointed if we hadn't. I'd have been disappointed if we'd let the moment pass. We didn't. We explored each other's bodies lovingly, as was expected, and it did feel a little different having sex as a married couple that it had done before.

In the morning I drew back the curtains and sunlight flooded into our room. It was another beautiful day of glorious blue sky and sunshine. The weather was being kind to us. Clearly someone up there approved of our marriage. We looked out onto undulating farmland. I could hear a cockerel somewhere in the distance heralding the start of a new day. The adrenalin of the day before was still flowing through our veins. We could still feel the sense of excitement it had generated. There were beaming smiles of relaxation and happiness on our faces. We got dressed at a leisurely pace and went down to breakfast. When we'd eaten and were ready, we called a taxi to take us and our luggage to the train station. There we got a train to take us to London Paddington to begin our honeymoon.

For the first time we travelled as man and wife. There was no doubt it felt different. We were now legally married. We were officially Mr and Mrs. When we boarded the train and showed our tickets to the conductor, Roxanne even referred to me as her husband for the first time. It was funny to hear, but I didn't mind. That was what I was. I was her husband. She was my wife. We were now bonded closer than ever. Now we were married we should do nothing to spoil it, I thought to myself. We should never have a cross word. We should never argue again. Not that we argued all that much as it was. But all couples have disagreements sometimes. Now we were married I was determined not to. I was determined there would be arguments on our honeymoon. Even if I was tempted or felt irritable I'd just bite my tongue, I decided. And if we ever did go through rough times, if ever things did get strained between us in the future, we should just sit down and watch our wedding video again together. We should remind ourselves what we went through on our special day and the vows we'd made to each other. Hopefully that would always be enough to bring us back together. We would instantly remember how much we were in love.

When we arrived in London we got another taxi to take us to our hotel. We weren't short of money. My parents had ensured that. We could afford to relax and enjoy ourselves without worrying too much about our cash situation or the cost. London was expensive, but it didn't matter. We were there to have fun. Whilst some were still mourning the recent death of Princess Diana, London was still very much swinging. It was the London of *The Spice Girls* and *Blur*, and the Union Jack flag was very prominent in the fashion, advertising and visual images on display around the city. The film *Austin Powers*, which tapped into that sense of nationalism and nostalgia, was playing in all the movie houses. Posters for it adorned the walls of all the tube stations. People were proud to be British. For once it was something to shout about, not to be ashamed of. London was the cultural capital of Europe, if not the world. And we were part of it, at least for a brief moment in time.

That evening we enjoyed a lavish meal in our hotel restaurant. The food was elegant and delicate in its preparation and presentation. We were waited on by staff in neatly pressed uniforms, who attended to our every need, bringing wine and beer to our table. We were referred to as *Sir* and *Madam*. We were made to feel quite special. For the short time we were there we did feel a bit unique. For the first time in our lives we felt truly grown up. I was thirty-two. Roxanne was twenty-five. We were married. We really were adults, or felt like we were.

On the first full day we were in London we went shopping. We were anxious to spend some of the money we'd brought with us. It was burning a hole in our pockets already. We browsed the shops of Oxford Street and Carnaby Street and bought clothes to wear on nights out when we were back home. We both enjoyed dressing up to go out. We liked to look good in the latest indie fashions. We were pleased with our purchases. We hoped to impress the clubbers at our regular haunts on our return. We had lunch at the *World Food Café* in Covent Garden. Roxanne was an ardent vegetarian and was slowly turning me into one. I had a coconut and sweet potato curry. It was nice. Roxanne had a copy of the café's cookbook and promised to make me something from it when we got back. I looked forward to that with eager anticipation. This week, however, there would be no cooking. We would be eating out every lunchtime and every evening.

Our itinerary was very full. Roxanne and I had organised a very busy programme of events and activities for our stay. There was little opportunity for downtime, as we went from one tourist destination and location to another. We did so much I can no longer recall everything we crammed in, or the exact order we did them in. Suffice to say we kept ourselves very active and engaged throughout the week. Towards the end of our first day, having wandered the streets of Regent Street, Piccadilly, Soho, Shaftesbury Avenue, Charing Cross Road and Trafalgar Square until we were exhausted, we returned to our hotel. There we collected our luggage, to transfer it to a cheaper hotel for the rest of the honeymoon. It made sense, as it gave us more spending money to enjoy. The first hotel was luxurious, but we'd had two nights of luxury now. We didn't really need any more. Clean and functional was enough for us moving forwards, so we could spend our money on other things for the remainder of our time in London.

On our second day we visited Kensington Market, and the Natural History Museum and the Science Museum in South Kensington. In the evening we saw the musical *Oliver!* at the famous London Palladium. I wasn't a huge fan of musicals, but I liked that particular one. I'd always been an admirer of the film version with Oliver Reed, so I was more than happy to see it performed live on stage. I knew all the Lionel Bart songs from the film at least hum to, so I was able to follow the performance easily and enjoy it. I'd never read the Charles Dickens novel. I still haven't. I'd never been a Dickens enthusiast in truth, as my dad was, and even watching the musical didn't encourage me to want to become one. Still it was a fun evening. It was a pleasurable experience to go a grand, old London theatre with Roxanne.

On our third day we went to Madame Tussaud's Waxworks and The Planetarium in Marleybone. I particularly enjoyed The Planetarium, as I had an interest in cosmology and the stars. That night we had our first minor disagreement, despite both of us vowing we'd have no arguments on honeymoon. I wanted to go to Wembley to see England play a World Cup qualifying match. The game wasn't full and we could have got cheap tickets. Roxanne didn't want to go. She wanted to go to Rock Circus instead, which was a pop and rock version of Madame Tussauds, with waxwork figures of some of the most iconic stars from the history of popular music. The highlight was a performance by life-size models of *The Beatles*. It was good, but we were both a bit too tired to enjoy it fully. By the end of the day we both got a bit tetchy with one another, as tiredness started to take over. We'd done too much in too short a space of time. It was good to get back to the hotel and get some much-needed sleep. We were both ready for it. We needed to recharge our batteries.

On our fourth day we decided to go outside the boundary of London and we took a train down to Brighton, where we enjoyed browsing the cafés, record shops and clothes shops. It was my first visit to the legendary town and I found it quite fascinating. I'd always loved the Mod-influenced film *Quadrophenia*, and Roxanne and I had fun spotting the locations and sites used in the film. They were so well known they weren't too hard to find. Wearing slightly Mod influenced fashions ourselves we felt a little like the film's stars Phil Daniels and Leslie Ash, as we wandered the Brighton streets. We didn't look so unlike them either. My hair was short, dark and neatly cut, rather like a Mod. I wore a pale blue Fred Perry T-shirt under my jacket. Roxanne was a platinum blonde and wore a fitted sixties dress and suede coat. She could easily have passed for a Mod herself. It probably looked like we were paying homage to the Mods, who'd regularly visited the town and battled with the Rockers of the day some thirty or more years earlier. We weren't. We were indie kids really, but we didn't look too out of place. Cultures and fashions had become very merged by the nineties.

On our penultimate day we browsed the numerous clothes stalls of Camden Lock, before going on to London Zoo in Regents Park. The zoo seemed to go on forever. Until we got there I didn't even realise it had two parts, one either side of the main road. I was particularly impressed by the huge variety of small mammals they had on display, many I hadn't seen or even heard of before. I loved small mammals -

rodents, mustelids, civets, genets etc. Whilst I had mixed feelings about animals being kept in zoos, it was a thrill to see them in the flesh. I had a keen love of wildlife and nature. London Zoo was better than I expected. For me it was one of the highlights of our week away.

We had a leisurely final evening and day together. We'd done a lot. We'd spent a lot. Now we just wanted quietly to enjoy each other's company before heading back. The honeymoon had gone so quickly. Our weekend away had been packed with so many exciting things to look back on and savour. The weather had been perfect. All had gone pretty much to plan. We'd never forget it. It would be engrained in our memories forever. Now it was over. Now we were heading home, to begin our married life proper. We were both happy. We were both looking forward to it.

Chapter Twelve

The first couple of years of our marriage were definitely the best. They're the ones I look back on with most affection and the fondest memories. It was a good time. Things generally went pretty well for us. We were at our happiest. Roxanne and I both quickly settled into our new life of domestic contentment and wedded bliss. The transition from being engaged to being married was smooth. We both took it comfortably in our stride. It seemed easy and natural to adjust to for us. There were no issues or adjustment problems that couples can have. We were both confident we'd done the right thing in getting married. We were both content with the choice we'd made.

We returned from honeymoon to the flat we'd recently taken on, and things seemed idealistic and how married life was intended to be. We did our best to turn our surroundings into a home. We wanted it to be a comfortable, cosy and pleasurable space to live in. We bought a large, new sofa, new bed and new furniture. Roxanne used her passion for art to add the finishing touches. I left her to it. That was her department. I let her decorate exactly as she wanted, with little comment or input on my part.

To make it even more homely we decided to get some pets. We bought two pedigree guinea pigs named Molly and Florence. I loved them and let them run unchecked around the flat. Roxanne wasn't quite as keen as I was and largely left looking after them to me. Still they fitted in with the sense of cosiness and homeliness we were trying to create. We figured they would also be nice for a child, if we ever had a family, which we both knew we certainly wanted to have one day. We didn't have long to wait. Just a couple of months into our marriage Roxanne dropped an unexpected bombshell, and everything changed.

'I'm pregnant,' she announced.

'Surely not?' I said.

I knew she was late for her period, but I imagined it was just a false alarm. There had been one or two before, and I just assumed this was another one. I never thought for a moment she was actually pregnant. The home pregnancy test kit she'd bought begged to differ, however. It suggested she was very much pregnant. Roxanne hastily arranged an appointment with her doctor, who duly confirmed the pregnancy. I was shocked, but also rather delighted. I'd always wanted to be a dad, and although this was somewhat sooner than we'd planned we'd just have to make the best of it. We had intended to enjoy a year or two of just being married before starting a family, but it seemed those plans had now altered irrevocably. Neither of us was too concerned or upset. I was really thrilled, and Roxanne seemed OK with it too, if a little concerned about the nine months of actual pregnancy that had to be negotiated first.

'It will all be fine,' I tried to reassure her.

'Let's hope so,' Roxanne replied, a little nervously

To our surprise when Roxanne went for scans and due dates were discussed, it seemed the baby had almost certainly been conceived on honeymoon, or very soon after. What were the odds of that? How terribly quaint and old fashioned, we both agreed. It was a strange quirk of fate, but it had happened. Roxanne and I had been having sex for a number of years, with no serious thoughts of her getting pregnant, but it appeared that in the week of our actual wedding and honeymoon she had conceived. The baby hadn't been planned, but we were both very happy to be having it. It did change our outlook a little. Very quickly we had to start making serious plans to become parents. It was barely seven months away, and the days and weeks were flying by. We waited until the doctor had checked everything was in order and as it should be, before telling friends and family our good news. They were as delighted and excited as we were.

Whilst we were both thrilled Roxanne was expecting, we soon both discovered there was a downside to Roxanne being pregnant. Roxanne suffered morning sickness almost straight away. She went from being a young, healthy newlywed, to being sickly and ill most of the time. We'd always enjoyed our leisure time together. We'd tried to make the most of it. It was one of the things that bonded us to each other. Almost overnight that completely vanished. All too often when we had time off Roxanne was simply too ill to do anything. She was getting her own back on me, I teased her. It was just like the days and months after we'd first met, when I'd dropped out of my teacher training course and been too ill to do anything. It was exactly the same again now, but in reverse. Roxanne was still well enough to go for little day trips out in the car from time to time, but doing anything in the evening simply became out of the question. Roxanne wasn't allowed to drink anyway, because she was pregnant. But all that was irrelevant. She simply wasn't well enough.

I tried to be supportive, just as she'd been when I'd been at my worst, but it was hard. At the blink of an eye our social life ended. I loved going out pubbing and clubbing with Roxanne, and showing off the latest clothes we'd bought. I'd hoped we'd be able to carry on for a couple more years yet, but overnight it ended. Roxanne simply wasn't up to it. In theory I could have gone out by myself, but firstly Roxanne wouldn't have liked that, and secondly my place was at home, looking after her. Roxanne didn't have many faults, but she was a little possessive, as I was myself. We were both inclined to get jealous. If Roxanne couldn't go out, there was no way she was going to let me go out and enjoy myself without her. It was out of the question. I didn't mind. We were having a baby. That was the priority. I knew I should be at home, making sure she was as healthy and comfortable as she could be. All the same it wasn't always easy.

When Saturday night came round and Roxanne took herself off to bed early, I found myself sitting on the sofa watching *Match of the Day* on my own. It was difficult then. I still got the urge to go out and drink. I missed it. It had been cut off so suddenly and without warning I felt a little lost, like an addict whose supply had abruptly ended. I was being denied my drug of choice. I had no option but to rein my impulses in. I had to fight them. At first it was hell. I told myself it would all be worth it though, and it was. In the end I got used to staying in, but Saturday nights were never quite the same again.

Even after we were married, every third weekend or so Roxanne continued to go home to see her parents and spend Saturday and Sunday with them. It was normally when I was working at the cinema anyway. Sometimes she got the bus or train. On other occasions her dad came to collect her in the car, before dropping her back on Sunday evening. Although it meant I spent the weekend alone, I didn't mind too much. At least Roxanne could relax and get some much-needed rest at her parents' house, and be pampered and looked after as she deserved and craved.

Meanwhile I generally did a long shift on the Friday and Sunday and then had the Saturday to myself, if Roxanne had gone away. On some Saturday afternoons I went to watch a local rugby or football match. On other occasions I just went for a walk or a potter by myself in the car. On Saturday night, if I was on my own, I went to see a film at the cinema where I worked. I went regardless of what was on. Whatever it was it was better than staying in alone. As a staff member I didn't have to pay.

I could see as many films as I liked for free, as long as they weren't full. And they seldom were.

Sometimes it would have been nice to meet up with friends, to go to the pub or even a club, but I never did. I knew it would upset Roxanne. She was pregnant. She was carrying my child. I was a father-to-be. I didn't want to do anything to anger or worry her. I didn't want to do anything that might disrupt the pregnancy. Staying in was a small sacrifice, but it was one I was willing to make. It was a minor price to pay for having a happy family life, a contented wife, and a baby on the way. Roxanne was concerned about the impending birth. I still wasn't in perfect health. But we stayed close. Our relationship remained good. We were upbeat and positive. On the weekends Roxanne didn't see her parents, we enjoyed cosy, little trips out together, as much as our respective physical limitations would allow. Home life was comfortable and pleasant. We had much to be grateful for,

As we entered 1998, personally and professionally my life began to come together probably better than at any point to date. There had been many ups and downs before, as many backward steps as forward ones. Moments of promise hadn't developed or lived up to expectation. Promising openings had closed no sooner than they'd opened. I'd done well enough academically, but in the world of work I'd never lived up to my academic potential. That was partly my own fault. I'd always struggled to truly dedicate myself to any job. As a writer I'd got a lot published, and at an early age. It had given me hope. It had made me believe I might be successful and I might be able to make a career at it. But one false dawn had followed another. Nothing had ever come of any of it. It hadn't kickstarted a career. Now in 1998 things quite suddenly started coming together a little more.

Professionally things were going quite well. My cinema work had raised my profile on the local arts management scene. In my small and limited field I'd become quite well known, so much so that I was approached by programmers at the local BBC Radio Station to make guest appearances on their arts-based radio programmes. They wanted me to talk about cinema, music, theatre and literature. They were all fascinating subjects to me, so I was only too happy to oblige. I'd always been attracted to broadcasting, so I jumped at the chance. I didn't tell them, but in fact it was fulfilling a secret ambition of mine. For years I'd had more than a passing interest in working in radio, so privately I was delighted to be asked. I was both flattered and pleased to be given the opportunity. I suspected one or two of my work colleagues were jealous that I'd been approached and not them. It wasn't my fault I'd been asked and they hadn't. It was no reason to decline the invitation and I was determined to make the most of it.

Although I was a little nervous going live on air I found I enjoyed the experience. I'd been a regular presenter on my university radio station many years earlier, and it stood me in good stead for the new venture. The local BBC presenters considered me something of a natural. They kept asking me back and inviting me to appear on other shows. Pretty soon as well as being a guest on the arts programmes I found myself regularly reviewing the morning papers. I was discussing all kinds of topics, way beyond the realms of what I'd first envisaged. It helped being a trained journalist. I knew all too well what I legally could and couldn't say. The BBC found they could trust me. I was articulate and informative. I prepared carefully and returned to the station frequently. My voice was often to be heard on the local airwaves at that time. Frankly, after a lot of setbacks it was a helpful boost to both my ego and confidence. Occasionally people even stopped me in the street to tell me they'd heard me. It was nice to hear. For the first time in a few years it gave me something to feel good about myself. My parents were also pleased. For once they didn't have to feel embarrassed about their only son. They could ask friends and relatives if they'd heard me on the radio. It was something for them gently to boast about.

My volume of film and television extra work was also increasing, much to my delight, and about that time I was approached by the editors of the *Poetry Now* series of poetry anthologies, to contribute to a special, new book they were compiling. I'd been a regular contributor to their books in the past, but only contributing one poem for each anthology among dozens of other poems, to the point each individual poem became lost and none stood out. Although it was nice to be included and to see them stocked in the established bookshops like *Waterstones*, nothing ever came of it. This was different, however. The proposal was to launch a series of books showcasing the work of just four or five promising, new poets in each, with each individual poet contributing around twenty of their best poems per book. This seemed a much more promising and worthwhile project to get involved with. I was very happy to be asked.

The series was being called *Spotlight Poets*, and immediately I went to work carefully selecting some of my best poems for inclusion, together with a photograph that portrayed me in a flattering light. The finished collection was called *With Grace and Harmony*. It was well compiled and presented. It was published to high standards. I felt honoured to be included. I was given a number of promotional copies to circulate among friends and family. I was happy to distribute them. It made me feel like a genuine published poet, at least more than I had in my stuttering literary career to date.

Meanwhile Roxanne was getting bigger. There was no doubting she was pregnant now. It was plain to see. I wanted a boy. Roxanne wanted a girl. We couldn't both be pleased. The latest scans revealed in all probability we were having a girl. Roxanne was thrilled. I was pleased too in fact. I didn't really mind. I just wanted a healthy baby. We started discussing baby names. Nothing to do with the book I'd just been in, but Grace was one we both agreed we liked. The pregnancy was gathering pace. We started accumulating baby clothes and toys, including many that were gifts from friends and family. We started making plans to acquire all the things a baby needs. Even though we didn't have much money, somehow we got just about everything we required.

As spring turned to summer and the clocks went forward I started playing tennis again. I didn't agree to playing any competitive matches. On the one hand it was doubtful if I was well enough. On the other hand I was the one who'd be taking Roxanne to hospital, when she went into labour. Until then I couldn't agree to anything that I might be called away from at the drop of the hat. I had to be alert. I had to remain on call at all times. Work of course were notified. They were aware I could be called away at any moment with no notice. I also had to make arrangements for paternity leave, which would begin as soon as the baby arrived.

In the weeks leading up to the birth Roxanne and I attended regular antenatal classes. We prepared as best we could. As the day drew nearer our expectations rose. We anticipated Roxanne going into labour any second. For some reason we thought she'd be early. She wasn't. In the event she was late and passed her due date. We had to go in for check-ups. The doctors became a little concerned, after several more weeks passed and still nothing. There were signs the baby was getting distressed. There was nothing else for it. Roxanne would have to be induced.

We were given a date the following week for Roxanne to go into hospital to give birth. It was a Thursday. We had to take her overnight bags with us, as she was expected to stay in hospital for several days afterwards. We were called in first thing in the morning and drugs were administered to Roxanne to induce the labour process. Roxanne's waters broke, so we knew things were underway. We'd be coming out with a baby. We had no idea how long it would take. Things progressed slowly. We remained calm. We were given a room to ourselves to wait in, where we chatted and read to help the time pass. Although things were happening the serious stage of labour still hadn't fully started.

Morning turned to afternoon and turned to evening. The contractions were now getting faster. The discomfort for Roxanne was increasing. She decided at the last minute to have an epidural to ease the pain. We'd now been transferred to a labour ward in the maternity unit. Doctors and nurses fussed around Roxanne, as I hovered in the background. As Roxanne was asthmatic they had to keep a special eye on her, to ensure her breathing remained steady and there wasn't undue stress on her heart. As Roxanne was told to push I could sense the worried look in her eyes. She wasn't enjoying the experience. I held her hand when I could. It seemed to be taking an age. There was still only minimal sign of the baby. I guessed there was still some time to go before delivery. Roxanne was suffering. I felt for her, but there was little I could do apart from offer words of encouragement.

Early evening turned to late evening, and still no baby. We'd been in the hospital for around fifteen hours. I could now see the head, but the numbing impact of the epidural was making it difficult for Roxanne to push it out. Gradually inch by inch the baby was emerging. Roxanne was struggling, but there was no going back. The end was in sight. I implored her to hang in there. It wouldn't be much longer, I promised her. Eventually in the early hours of the Friday morning our healthy baby daughter, Grace, was born. She was pulled out like a rabbit from a hat, warmed under a heater, wrapped in a blanket and handed to me to look after. I couldn't quite believe or comprehend it. At last I was a dad. Her baby blue eyes were staring up at me. She had a confused expression on her face.

Meanwhile, there was a problem. During the final delivery Roxanne had suffered a tear. She was bleeding quite heavily. There was a pool of blood on the sterilised, vinyl, tile flooring under the bed where she lay. The medical staff worked feverishly to stem the flow. The doctors stitched furiously. As a precaution they gave her blood to compensate for the blood that she'd lost during the birth. Roxanne looked pale and worried. She felt feint, she said. I think we both did. I wasn't prepared for this added drama, but I tried to reassure Roxanne all would be well. After working on her for a while, the doctors and nurses were satisfied they'd stabilised Roxanne's condition. She was now able to hold the baby herself. After all she'd been through she appeared hesitant and somewhat reluctant at first. She seemed awkward and uncertain, as if her motherly instincts were yet to kick in. Again I encouraged her. I wanted to see mother and baby together, and eventually she took Grace in her arms. After a while more had passed and they were out of any danger, Roxanne and Grace were transferred from the delivery room to the maternity ward, where they could rest and sleep. I was allowed to stay a little while longer whilst they settled, before being told it was time for me to leave.

I got home to our flat at around 4am in the morning. It was strange being there alone without them, but fathers weren't allowed to stay over. I felt tired, almost like I'd given birth myself. It had been some ordeal, even to me. I wasn't great with blood. It had been hard to watch at times. I'd just been the witness, the almost helpless onlooker, offering vocal support and encouragement as best I could. Roxanne had done all the difficult work. Now it was over. It was time to go to bed and sleep myself. It wasn't easy. The adrenalin was still pumping. It was tricky to switch off. I got into bed and tried to sleep as best I could. I was just dozing off when the phone rang. I glanced at my watch. It was 6am. I picked up the phone. It was Roxanne.

'Can you come back? I hate it here on my own,' she said. 'I need you with me. I can't bear it by myself.'

'Will they let me come straight back?' I enquired, feeling a bit dazed and not yet fully awake.

'I've asked them. They say it's all right,' Roxanne assured me.

'OK, I'll come immediately,' I said, and jumped out of bed.

Suddenly a wave of nausea engulfed me. I ran to the toilet. I thought I was going to be sick. It occurred to me that I might have picked up a hospital bug. I think in fact the events of the previous day had just been too much for me, and now I was suffering an adverse reaction. I couldn't let Roxanne down. I had to go back to the hospital, however ill I felt. I didn't know what to do. There was nothing else for it. It was still early, but I rang my mum. I'd already given my parents news of the baby's arrival in a brief phone call in the small hours. I now explained the situation and how ill I felt and asked if my mum could accompany me back to the hospital. She came straight away.

As dawn gave way to the bright sunshine of a new summer's day, my mum and I sat with Roxanne and Grace by her bed in the maternity ward. Roxanne was feeling a little more comfortable and settled now. I was learning to change Grace's nappies. They were filled with a black, glutinous substance that resembled tar. Apparently that was normal during the first hours after birth. We prepared for a day ahead of visitors - my dad, my sister and her family, Roxanne's parents and sister, and various friends and other relatives. They'd be coming in one after another, with cards, flowers and gifts. Roxanne found it all a little daunting and overwhelming. She longed to get home.

Roxanne didn't like it in the hospital. Very quickly she talked of coming out. She said she was considering discharging herself that day and taking Grace back to the flat. My mum implored her to stay in for a couple of nights at least, so she could get some rest and sleep and where the nurses were on hand to help. Roxanne wouldn't be put off. She felt the nurses weren't being that helpful anyway. They hadn't even called her for meals, she said. She kept on repeating that she wanted to go home. The doctor looking after Roxanne examined her and Grace again. He seemed reasonably happy. All appeared well, and as we lived only minutes away from the hospital he reluctantly agreed that Roxanne could leave if she really wanted to. If there were any problems we could come straight back, we were told. So slightly contrary to plans, as the day ended we packed up our belongings and took Grace back to our flat. We laid her down in her travelling cot on the floor in the middle of our front room. Grace started to cry.

'What do we do now?' I asked.

'I have no idea,' Roxanne replied.

Chapter Thirteen

During the first few weeks there were a lot of adjustments to make. Whilst having Grace was a joy there was no denying it was tough. Grace was a good baby, but of course she didn't settle down into any kind of established sleep pattern straight away. As with all things it took time. At first she struggled to sleep and woke frequently at night, crying for milk. As Roxanne had chosen not to breast feed, we took turns feeding Grace formula baby milk in a bottle through the small hours. Night after night I found myself awake at one, two, three in the morning, pressing a bottle to Grace's lips as she drank, barely able to keep my eyes open. A couple of hours later it would be Roxanne's turn. We were both exhausted. Roxanne was still recovering from the trauma of giving birth. I was tired too, having been up night after night with the same demanding routine.

During the early days of my paternity leave I found myself regularly having to take trips to the shops, for more nappies, bottles, more formula milk, more baby suits, more toys, and food for me and Roxanne to eat. The list was endless. There was always something we needed. I tried not to leave Roxanne too long. At first she was worried looking after the baby on her own. It was definitely a two-person job most of the time. In the afternoons I'd take Grace out in her pram, if the weather was fine. I'd walk the quiet, residential streets near where we lived, and through the tree-lined paths of the local park. The movement of the pram normally sent Grace to sleep. It would also allow Roxanne to get an hour or two of rest at home, before the trials of the evening began. Grace rarely settled at bedtime. As a result I often let Roxanne go to bed, whilst I stayed up late with Grace on my lap. To help time pass I'd watch re-runs and recordings of the football World Cup taking place in France, through to the small hours. Eventually Grace would finally nod off to sleep and I could get some sleep myself. A couple of hours later it would be Roxanne's turn to get up, before mine again before dawn.

Of course we had regular visitors to fit in; more friends and relatives bringing gifts and keen to meet the new baby. Naturally they only meant well, and we tried to be good and appreciative hosts. It wasn't always easy, however, when we felt and looked exhausted, and our flat smelled of changed nappies. When there was one visitor after another and all we wanted to do was sleep, it was hard being sociable. I'm sure it's the same for all new parents. We were novices. There was much to learn.

Winding the baby was an important one, to avoid her immediately throwing her milk up down your back the moment she'd finished drinking it. We soon learned not to be too precious. Our clothes became covered with little marks and stains, where Grace had brought her milk back up. After a while we ceased to notice or care. It was hard to keep on top of our washing. There were things to wash and clean all the time, and bottles and soothers to sterilise. Grace quickly became attached to her dummy. She loved it. It helped to calm her much of the time. We were always having to buy new ones, as she dropped them from her pram, or they simply disappeared, probably behind the back of a sofa or similar place. I in turn became an expert at nappy changing.

Even when I returned to work our routine didn't change too much. I often found myself getting in late at night, to take over from Roxanne and look after Grace until she finally settled. I rarely got to bed before two in the morning and would be up again about seven. Then I'd help out with Grace again for a few hours, before starting another long shift at work. I did get some time off. Occasionally Roxanne would take Grace out for a walk or take her into town in her pram. Once in a while I'd arrange a game of tennis or badminton with a work colleague. It was a nice way to relax and get a break from looking after the baby. When Grace did fall asleep I'd retreat to my study and try and keep up with my writing. I'd snatch any moments I could. It was the only way to keep it ticking over. If I hadn't done that I wouldn't have got any done at all.

We'd earmarked a space for Grace's cot, but more often than not we brought it in with us. When she wouldn't settle we brought her into our bed. If she wouldn't settle in my lap it was often the only way to get her to sleep. Pretty soon we realised that we'd outgrown our flat. It had been quite nice for the two of us, but now with a baby and all her things it simply wasn't big enough. We were also aware other people lived in the building on other floors. Grace could be keeping them awake with her crying. We needed somewhere bigger, we decided. We had jobs. We were both working, although Roxanne was presently on maternity leave. We were just about in a position to get a modest mortgage on a house. I still had some savings put back for a small deposit. It was time to buy our own place.

Things became more pressing when our landlords suddenly gave us notice. They needed the flat back, as they wanted to move back in again after a period of working and living away. With a new baby it was rather a worrying situation to find ourselves in. It meant finding a house to buy was suddenly a major priority. We weren't desperate. We always had the emergency backup of living with my parents for a short period, if we had to, but it wasn't a contingency plan I was desperate to have to put into operation. It had taken me years to finally move out. I didn't want to move straight back in with them. As a result we began looking for a home to buy in earnest.

We went to see a mortgage adviser and found out what kind of mortgage we might get based on our combined incomes. We also found out about the different kinds of mortgages that were available. It was all new to me. Unlike for other members of my family buying a house had never previously been that important to me. Now with the responsibility of a child to look after it suddenly was important. We scoured the local papers and property pages, looking for potential homes to view based on price, location and convenience. We arranged a number of viewings as soon as we could. It at least gave us some idea what kind of properties were on the market, and what we might expect to get for our money. Some properties we ruled out straight away. Others had potential and were maybes. Most of them had something we didn't like about them.

Eventually we found a terraced property not that far from where we presently lived. It wasn't perfect, but it was certainly adequate. It had been carefully looked after. The rooms were reasonably spacious and it had been well maintained. It was near to a major, local bus route, ideal for Roxanne, as she didn't drive. It was also well located for me to get to work. There was a large park behind, where we could take Grace to play. It was certainly the best we'd seen. After just a brief conversation and with time pressing we put an offer in on it. To our surprise the offer was accepted. We were delighted. We were moving. We were going to own our own house. We got reports and surveys done. We arranged the mortgage. Everything seemed to be progressing well. The only snag was the middle-aged owner seemed in no particular hurry to move out.

The weeks began to pass. They turned into months. It became apparent they never were going to move in any circumstances. They were planning to stay put exactly where they were. Quite why they'd put their house on the market in the first place was a total mystery. It was senseless. As time was running out on the flat where we lived, we reluctantly had to abandon our plans to buy that particular property.

In desperation we started to look elsewhere. We were lucky. We found another similar house not that far away. We put in an offer on that. After some negotiation it too was accepted. We started to go through the same process with the new property as we had before. Having had our fingers burned we proceeded with an increased degree of caution second time around. Our doubts proved well founded. This time the owners came back and said they'd now had a better offer and were going with that instead. We'd been gazumped! We couldn't believe it. It seemed we weren't lucky after all. We had no idea how complicated and hard this house buying lark was. We had to start looking again, all the time whilst we were caring for a young baby.

Then we did get a lucky break. The couple who'd gazumped us had been turned down for their mortgage. The seller came back apologetically and said the house was ours if we still wanted it. They promised not to mess us around again. We readily accepted. Surveys showed there was some damp that needed attention before we could move in. Otherwise the building was structurally sound. We agreed everything we had to, and arrangements for the damp proofing work to be done were made. Contracts were exchanged. Funds were transferred, and finally we were given the keys to our new house. We'd spent several weeks packing up the possessions of our flat into boxes. We were ready to go. Now, with the help of Roxanne's dad we were set to move in. We didn't hire a removal firm. We didn't have that many possessions. We were reasonably confident we could do it all ourselves. It was one way of saving some much-needed money. What with the wedding, a new baby, and now buying a house, we didn't have too much left.

On a pleasantly mild Saturday morning in the autumn of 1998 we moved into our new home. Roxanne's dad had borrowed a van from work, to transport the few larger items of furniture we had, and I had my car, which we crammed full of our smaller possessions. I knew it would take multiple trips back and forth to get it all moved, but I was confident with a bit of effort, commitment, sweat and hard work, I could get it done in a day. As Roxanne's dad and I concentrated on moving all our belongings, Roxanne and her mother looked after Grace and worked on getting the flat we were leaving clean and spotless. We knew if it wasn't left in a reasonable state there was a possibility our deposit, or at least some part of it, wouldn't be returned to us. Hard up as we were that wasn't a risk we wished to take or a prospect we were anxious to face. We needed every penny we could muster, to spend on getting our new home decorated and up to scratch.

Roxanne's dad was now in his sixties and close to retirement. I'd had health issues and was still some distance from full fitness. Negotiating the narrow doorways, restricted hallways and small and awkward spaces, that was necessary to move everything we had to, wasn't easy. It was sweaty and exhausting. Having worked late at the cinema the previous night, I found myself quickly tiring and getting a little fed up with all the lifting and carrying. Pretty soon my arms, then my legs and back and pretty much everything else, started to ache. But I stuck at it and bit by bit we got it done. By the end of the morning our larger items had been packed into the van and moved. By the middle of the afternoon, after numerous car trips, all the smaller things had been transferred. The old flat was now clean and empty, ready for the owners to move back in. It had served us well. It was time to say goodbye to it.

We looked around one last time, to see we had everything and were leaving it in a reasonable state. Then we shut the front door and posted the keys through the letter box. I felt a tinge of sadness. We'd been happy there. It was the home we'd brought Grace back to. It would always remain the first house she'd lived in. I'd always enjoyed the peace and quiet of my little study in the back room, where I'd worked on my poetry and fiction. Now we were leaving. We were leaving some small part of us behind too. But hopefully at the same time we were moving onto bigger and better things. We had a new house, one we actually legally owned.

It was exciting setting foot in our new home for the first time. I was thirty-three years old. Roxanne was twenty-six. Neither of us had ever been homeowners before. It was a new experience for us both. The house was modest – a front room, a dining room and a kitchen downstairs; two bedrooms and a bathroom upstairs; a small yard at the back. But it suited our needs. It was a start. It was ours. That was all that mattered. We got all our suitcases, bags, boxes and other containers, all full of our assorted possessions, into the house and collapsed exhausted. It was over. It was done. I let out a small sigh of relief. A contented smile started to spread across my face. It was then that things took an unexpected turn for the worse, and a sour note entered the proceedings.

'You're not leaving them there like that, are you?' Roxanne's mother suddenly and abruptly snapped.

'I thought I might,' I replied, barely able to find any energy even to look up at her.

'Oh no you're not. You're unpacking everything and putting it all away right now,' she demanded.

It was an odd thing to say, particularly for an overweight, middle-aged woman, who'd spent most of the morning sat in a chair, keeping an eye on Grace, as the three of us had worked tirelessly around her. I liked Roxanne's dad. He was a decent, honourable and courteous man. I was less enamoured with her mother, whom I tolerated rather than liked. She hadn't worked since she was nineteen years old, and it showed. She'd had the luxury of being able to live her life in the relative comfort of being a suburban housewife, who only had limited domestic demands and expectations placed on her. Cleaning a room, from top to bottom as she called it, was the highlight of her week. She wasn't a particularly keen cook. She did little in the way of gardening or other domestic chores. Most of the time she was happy to sit at home knitting and watching television. She believed those fortunate people who went to work did so for the enjoyment of it, not because they had to and because they had to earn a living and had bills to pay. She'd lived a very sheltered existence, one somewhat divorced from the realities of what most people had to face and deal with on a daily basis in their normal, everyday lives. But from the comfort of her chair she still felt more than able to bark out her orders to others. I was now finding this out to my cost. I was now seeing her in a rather new light.

'No, I'm pooped. I'm done. I'm not doing another thing,' I said. 'Thank you for your help. It's been great, but we've done enough. We can unpack everything tomorrow.'

'You'll unpack it now, or you'll leave this house,' Roxanne's mother announced.

I could hardly believe my own ears. Was she actually ordering me out of my own house, the one we'd just bought with a deposit I'd saved up? I believed she really was. What a cheek! What a nerve! I thought. I was incredulous. It was the most arrogant and impertinent remark I'd ever heard in my life, both before or since. I simply couldn't comprehend it.

'This is my house. I'm not going anywhere,' I said. 'It was bought with my money. If anyone should leave, you should!'

She clearly wasn't in the mood to listen.

'Right, out! Off you go. Get out!' Roxanne's mother shouted.

I looked at Roxanne and Roxanne's dad for support, but I could see I wasn't going to get any. They just looked away. I didn't want to see the situation deteriorate or escalate any further, so I thought I'd just go out for some fresh air. The atmosphere was already bad enough. You could cut it with a knife. I didn't want to make things any worse than they were. There was nothing else for it. I got up and left.

'Well, I'm off to see my parents, while you calm down,' I said, as I walked out the door.

I half expected Roxanne to come running after me. She didn't. She let me leave. She let me get in the car and drive off. It was all very odd and awkward. I'd actually been kicked out of my own home on the day we'd moved in by my overbearing mother-in-law. It really was hard to take in. It was hard to believe it had actually happened. The cheek of the woman was beyond all comprehension. It had certainly taken the shine off buying the new house. It had very much taken the pleasure away from moving in. Afterwards owning the new house was never quite the same. Something had been lost. In some ways I felt her actions had cursed it. I felt she'd cursed us.

When I arrived at my parents and explained what had happened, they were equally aghast. My dad was straight on the phone. He was an articulate, intelligent and well-respected man. When he spoke people listened. Though now retired he still had a voice of authority from many years' experience at the highest levels of his profession. He wasn't pleased. He was horrified. He said what had happened was totally inexcusable, and that there were no circumstances where it was acceptable that I be banished from my own home. He made it clear in no uncertain terms I would be returning immediately, and that I should be given full and complete access to my own property, where Roxanne's mother was the guest not I. They couldn't really disagree. I said I was only going back if my parents came with me. They got their coats and followed me in the car. I no longer felt outnumbered, as I nervously returned to where I'd so recently been ejected.

When we arrived at the house we were welcomed back in, but an air of tension persisted. My parents stayed for a while, both to have a look around and until things appeared to have calmed down a little. They liked what they saw of our new home. They didn't like what had happened, but for the health of our marriage and in the interests of Grace it was best for all concerned that a line be drawn beneath it immediately. Everyone needed to move on as quickly as possible and forget what had occurred as soon as they could. Even so I never quite forgave Roxanne's mother for what she'd done, and ruining the enjoyment of moving into our new home. My relationship with her never fully recovered. An unspoken dislike simmered underneath. Even my relationship with Roxanne was strained for a few days. Nothing was said, but I could tell things weren't quite right. I was angry she hadn't supported me. I was annoyed she hadn't stood up to her mother. I was disappointed she'd let her kick me out of my own house. Maybe Roxanne was upset we'd had the argument in the first place. It had come out of nowhere. It had been a shock. I'd been totally unprepared for it. It had left me quite stunned.

Ironically Roxanne's mother still got her own way. She didn't leave until everything was unpacked. She sat and watched over us until we'd done the lot. She didn't help of course, but she made sure we did it all. It was getting late by the time we finished, after 9pm. We still hadn't eaten. I popped to a nearby Chinese takeaway to pick up some food before it closed. We sat around in the front room afterwards, replenishing our energies with some much-needed nourishment. Superficially relationships had been restored and things had returned to normality. Polite conversation returned. It was almost as if nothing had happened. But something had happened, and underneath it wasn't quite the same. For me at least such things weren't quite so easily forgotten. I couldn't totally forget or forgive. I didn't. I retained a small grudge and sense of resentment against Roxanne's mother for her bizarre outburst for as long as I knew her.

Chapter Fourteen

As Roxanne was an art graduate I let her decide the colour scheme for our new home. I had no input. I gave her complete free rein to do whatever she wanted. My mum told me I was silly. She said I should have some say. I wasn't bothered. I did have some ideas of my own over how the house should look, but I let Roxanne decide instead. I didn't really mind what she did. If she was happy I was happy. I also let her make all the decisions regarding any new decorations and furnishings. Her style wasn't my style. It was lighter and more feminine. That was fine by me. I would have turned our house into more of a sixties' style pad. In my hands it would have been a homage to everything that had been iconic and cool in popular culture since the second world war. I'd have adorned the house with bold images from classic film, fashion, design and music. I'd have loved it, but it wouldn't have been to everyone's taste.

Roxanne had other ideas. We went with them. She liked silk, softness, swirling patterns, pastel colours, sea blues and greens, and nautical finishings. I had no problem with that. It mattered much more to her that the house looked as she wanted than it mattered to me. Since graduating she'd kept up her skills in needlepoint, but had put her other artistic interests on the backburner. This was a project to reignite her passion and enthusiasm. It was something she could really get her teeth into, and she did exactly that. I did make one mistake, however. Whilst I knew Roxanne was passionate about design, I soon found out she was less keen on the actual painting and hard work that had to go into bringing her visual ideas to fruition. She just wanted it to be done. She didn't want to put the time and effort into actually ensuring it was done properly. It was a pity.

Both myself and my mum, who was a keen amateur painter and decorator herself, were willing and ready to help. We put ourselves at Roxanne's full disposal in every spare moment we had. My dad also helped, by keeping half an eye on Grace and ensuring she didn't get too distressed, whilst the rest of us worked on decorating the house. As my mum and I carefully concentrated on a room each, following Roxanne's designated colour scheme, Roxanne raced ahead. She just wanted it finished, but she wasn't prepared to give the dedicated attention to detail needed to make it look as it should have looked.

Watching her paint was almost like seeing someone throwing paint at the walls rather than painting them. There were drips and missed bits everywhere. Roxanne wasn't concerned. She rampaged on regardless, jumping from room to room, barely spending an hour in each before declaring it done. My mum and I both looked at each other with eyebrows slightly raised. We couldn't stop her. Roxanne was someone on a mission. She carried on oblivious to our concerns. Whether it was matt or gloss it made no difference. It was applied in the same casual, slapdash way. By the end of one afternoon Roxanne declared the painting and decorating finished. She had as much paint on herself and on the floors as she had on the walls. It was a good job we hadn't had the new carpets fitted yet. They would have been ruined.

'It looks awful,' my mum whispered to me, when she was out of Roxanne's earshot. 'I've never seen painting like it.'

'I know,' I said. 'But don't worry, I'll sort it out.'

'How can you?' my mum asked. 'It's been done so quickly and so badly. I don't see how it can be rescued. It needs to be re-done. You may as well just start again and paint over it all.'

'I'll go back over the worst bits and tidy it up as best I can,' I promised. 'It will be fine. It will look all right in the end.'

My mum remained unconvinced.

'I don't see how,' she said.

'Roxanne's happy with it, so I can live with it,' I said, though I wasn't sure I could.

I liked things done neatly and precisely, if I was going to do it. Otherwise there was no point. This was anything but neat and precise. Some of it looked like it had been done by a child. Perhaps Grace had picked up a brush and helped. It was carelessly painted in the extreme. But it was our home. It was a place to live in for Roxanne, Grace and myself. I'd just have to learn to get used to it, though when I looked at the particularly badly painted bits I found that a difficult prospect to digest, I must admit.

In the event I spent weeks and months going over the painting, neatening it up and trying to make it look a little better. I persevered long after Roxanne had downed brushes, and indeed after she'd finished maternity leave and gone back to work. I carried on in odd moments. My mum continued to come over too when she could and do bits and pieces of neatening work here and there, to gradually make it look nicer.

Between us, over an extended period of time we pretty much repainted and touched up everything until it looked all right.

Roxanne was happy in that she could consider it her work. My mum and I were much happier in that it now looked almost acceptable. I no longer found myself drawn to spills, drips and white spaces, that had been missed, out of the corner of my eye every time I looked up at the walls and ceilings. I only finally gave up, when having spent weeks touching up the blue in our front room, Roxanne decided to paint it yellow instead. That was it for me. I'd had enough. I couldn't be bothered to go through the whole process again. The yellow would have to stay as Roxanne painted it, with little bits of blue showing through here and there, where, she'd failed to cover it fully. I thought if I carried on she'd only paint it again, so I left it as it was. It would have to do. I didn't like painting and decorating anyway. I'd seen it as my domestic duty and I'd done my best, but now I'd had my fill of it. It was time to turn my attention back to other things, including my writing endeavours, which I'd been neglecting of late.

When Roxanne returned to work I had to re-arrange my working hours a little to ensure Grace's childcare was fully covered. There were certain daytime shifts I could no longer do, but I had to do a disproportionate number of evenings and weekends to compensate. In general I looked after Grace every morning, as well as Wednesday and Friday afternoons. Most days when Roxanne got home and took over, I had to head straight off to work and stay late. Grace was a good baby, but still woke up at night of course. I was always tired. I never got enough sleep. It was always an effort to open my eyes in the morning, when Roxanne went to work. Often she just put Grace into bed beside me, until I'd fully woken. I'd then get up and get Grace her breakfast. Through a combination of help from my parents, Roxanne's parents and Roxanne's aunt and uncle on her dad's side, all assisting where they could, we managed just about to cover the afternoons when I had to work.

Things weren't too bad. I still managed to play a little tennis or badminton every Wednesday night, and even played the odd game in the mornings before work, when I took Grace with me. Most weekends I tried to grab a few minutes to go over to the nearby park, where I did a little light training by myself, working on my football and rugby skills. It was important to me, after all my health struggles, to stay as fit as I possibly could. I feared if I stopped making the effort my body would seize up and I'd go back to the bad old days of being little better than housebound. I feared that more than anything.

I took Grace out in her pram most days; into town, to the shops, to play areas or just for a walk. Sometimes I took her out in the car. Sometimes we visited my parents and had lunch with them. There were always some moments during the day when Grace slept. I made the most of those times. Whereas other new parents would have used the time to catch up on their rest themselves, I used the time to keep up with my writing. I worked at it any odd moment I had. I still harboured ambitions of becoming an established writer. I still dreamt of being a successful novelist. Whilst I enjoyed being at the cinema my first choice remained making a career out of the written word. I continued to be quite widely published, but I still wasn't making money out of it in any meaningful way. It was frustrating, but still I persisted. I refused to be downcast or dejected. I believed in myself. I believed it was just a matter of time and I'd get some lucky break. Suddenly opportunities would open up for me. I was convinced of that. Eventually I'd get a chance to make something of myself, and I'd have to be ready and able to take it.

Making the most of the little time I had I eventually finished writing and editing the latest novel I'd been working on called *Ravers*. I'd deliberately made it a little more commercial and accessible than some of my previous efforts, in the hope that it might attract genuine interest from prospective publishers and agents. I hoped to some extent it caught the mood of the moment. Novels about music and young people were quite fashionable. The subject matter was moderately in vogue, more so than some of the previous novels I'd written. Perhaps this was the novel that would finally get accepted? Perhaps this was the novel that would finally make my name in the world of books and publishing? This was the one that would get me well known?

As I started to prepare sample chapters to send off I was already getting ahead of myself. I should have learnt from past failures. These things were never as easy as I expected them to be. It seemed a straightforward thing to get a novel published. You wrote something reasonably good. You sent it off. It got accepted and then published. Of course in reality it was nothing like as simple as that. Most publishers wouldn't even consider manuscripts from unknown writers, unless they came recommended from an agent. Most agents' books were full and they weren't taking on new writers to represent at present. It was a kind of *Catch 22* situation. You needed to be very good or very fortunate or probably both to get anywhere at all. Failing that you needed to know someone in the trade; perhaps a family member to give you a leg up and to help you get your lucky break. I had no one to help me. I didn't know a soul in the trade. I was never that lucky. And I probably wasn't that good anyway.

Even so I still sent sample chapters of my new novel off with a sense of confidence, moderate hope and optimism. This was the one. I was certain of it. The novel was easy to read. It was entertaining. It wasn't too long. It wasn't too short. It was quite well written. Of course no sooner had I started sending it off than the inevitable rejection letters immediately followed. Most said they hadn't even read it. They simply weren't considering new proposals at present. It was a little soul destroying. How could I tell if it was any good or not if they wouldn't even read it? I got no useful feedback at all. How could I get a foot in the door if I couldn't find any publisher or agent taking on new writers?

Still I persisted. I pushed Grace to the post office in her pram several times a week, where I dropped off a bag full of manuscripts. It was an expensive business sending them off, particularly as it was generating no interest. Eventually I received a couple of replies from literary agents, which were a bit more encouraging. Several actually said they liked it. One from Edinburgh confirmed my belief it was *an entertaining read*. Even so it proved difficult to place. The agent in question retired before he had any luck finding a publisher for it. Typical of my luck! It wasn't for want of his or my efforts in trying though. I did my best. I gave it everything I could. I carried on sending it off for years and got nowhere. Eventually I had to move onto other projects and accept *Ravers* would never find a proper publisher.

During the afternoons when Grace went for her nap I started feverishly working on another novel. It was about a failed writer and his relationship problems. Where did I get that idea? It had the working title *Writer's Block*. I set it in Paris, a city I'd visited and knew in some detail. It made a change from setting it in good, old England and the places I knew so well. I felt my writing needed a change of scenery. A change could be as good as a rest perhaps. It might give my prose fresh impetus, I thought. As ever I started writing with the same false confidence I always had, and with all the hope I'd felt for the last novel and the one before that. My optimism would of course be as misplaced as it previously had been. *Writer's Block* would eventually end up on the scrapheap too, together with all my other projects.

I also started work on a new collection of poetry. I decided to compile an anthology of all my best published poems to date. I'd put them together in one slim volume. I started reading through all my old poems to make a suitable selection. I picked out a number I was pleased with and then gradually whittled it down to the required amount I needed. Using my connections with the *Poetry Now* publishers I managed to arrange for a small, limited edition print run to be published. I called the collection *Moments and Observations*. It was actually stocked by several reputable book outlets and it was reviewed in a number of poetry magazines. The reviews weren't very good. They complained it was too narcissistic and the poems were too similar. They had a point. On reflection many of my best poems stood out in their own right, but when they were put together the feeling of similarity was amplified. I was happy with the collection at first, but after the reviews came out I realised it was another failure.

Meanwhile away from literature our home life had settled down. A lot had happened over the last couple of years. We'd got engaged. We'd got married. We'd had a baby. We'd bought a house together. We needed a period of calm and reflection, to take it all in and come to terms with everything we'd done. We'd achieved a lot. Much had taken place in a short space of time. We needed to take stock and recharge our batteries. I felt this quite strongly. I think Roxanne did too. Our world had been turned upside down. A lot had changed, in a good way. We needed to adjust, to make sense of it, to accept how far our lives had moved on, and that they'd never be quite the same again.

'I think we need a period of stability before we do anything else,' I said to Roxanne.

She seemed in agreement. It made sense. We'd now established new patterns and new routines, to take account of Grace. We still needed to get used to them. Whereas once we used to get dressed up to go out on Saturday nights, now we got dressed up to go out on Saturday daytimes. It was a kind of compromise. It was hard to get babysitters for evening events, so instead we did what we could with the time together we did have, and we tried to make the most of it. In the months and early years after Grace was born, most Saturday mornings we put on our best clothes and went into town as a family. Smartly dressed as we were I think we were making some kind of subliminal statement, though I'm not quite sure what that statement was. We generally went to our favourite French restaurant, where both Roxanne and I normally had a baguette and fries. Afterwards we'd go off for a drive in the car, to a seaside town, country village or somewhere scenic. By early evening we'd be home and getting Grace ready for bed, just as our other friends who didn't have children were getting ready to go out.

Very occasionally my parents would babysit so we could go out too. We didn't like to ask them too much, as they were already babysitting several afternoons in the week when I was at work. That was far more important. Our social life was very much secondary. We were anxious not to trespass on their goodwill too much. Even so three or four times a year we did go out. These occasions became big events for us. We'd let as many people know in advance as possible, so we could catch up with them in a social setting. We didn't see people very often. It was nice on the odd occasion that we did. It was also nice to revisit our old haunts; the pubs and clubs we'd lovingly frequented before we were married.

Most of my friends and work colleagues at the cinema were single. They could go out whenever they wanted. By contrast Roxanne increasingly started to befriend other married couples at her work. As a result we occasionally started having dinner parties in each other's houses, or occasionally going out for meals with these other couples, where we could take Grace with us. There were two couples in particular we started spending a lot of time with. It seemed quite an adult thing to do. It was a new experience for me and I think for Roxanne as well. I'd grown up going to pubs, going to gigs, and going clubbing. Now we were hosting dinner parties. It was a new life altogether. It was very different to the one we were used to. I didn't mind it. It was actually all right in many respects. We settled into it quite easily and quite comfortably in fact.

By the beginning of the summer of 1999 Roxanne had been back at work for six months. I'd adjusted to my new role as a father, and indeed because of working shifts I spent more time looking after Grace during her waking hours than Roxanne did. During the weekdays I was Grace's principal carer. Grace was developing fast. She was nearly a year old. She was starting to eat more solid food. She was beginning to crawl. She was making noises like words. She was sleeping better. She was calmer. She cried less. She woke less at night. It hadn't been an easy year, although special in its own way, but it was getting better. Our efforts were slowly being rewarded. Our baby was becoming a child, with a distinct character, with hair and with striking pale eyes.

There had been times when she'd cried incessantly, when I was on my own with her and I had no idea what to do. I didn't have a clue how to calm her or stop her. In desperation I'd even called my mum over once or twice to help. After the first year all that improved. It happened less and less often. Things became easier, so much so that in the summer of 1999 I finally returned to playing competitive tennis after a break of five years. I'd remained a member of a club during that period, but because of persistent health issues and work and family commitments I hadn't played any local league tennis. At last I felt just about well enough. I also felt Grace was now old enough and calm enough to be left alone with Roxanne whilst I played. Generally Grace was in bed and asleep, so it was no great inconvenience to Roxanne. So that season I finally became a regular competitive tennis player again.

In the summer of 1999 we went on holiday as a family to North Somerset with Roxanne's parents. I imagined it was a sign of things to come. The disagreement we'd had when we'd first moved into our new home had at least been superficially forgotten. We hired a holiday cottage in a little village near the coastal town of Watchet, in an area I wasn't that familiar with, which we could use as a base to make day trips from. I couldn't complain. Roxanne's parents were paying for the accommodation. Besides it was nice just to get away. Apart from our honeymoon it had been years since I'd enjoyed much in the way of holidays. I had to go back to my childhood years, when I used to go abroad with my parents, to recall any meaningful breaks of that kind. Apart from the honeymoon I'd had no holidays for over a decade. Now I was starting to have them again. From our base we visited the nearby picturesque locations of Dunster, Minehead, Lynton and Lynmouth, Exmoor, Glastonbury and Wells, and many more. It was fun. It was nice to get away as a family. When we got back I imagined years like this one stretched out ahead, of blissful, happy marriage. Unfortunately things don't always work out quite as you expect and hope. And in this case they didn't.

Chapter Fifteen

As the year 2000, the Millennium as it was referred to, drew relentlessly nearer, for many it did so with a mixture of excitement and trepidation. It had been talked about and discussed for what seemed like an age. Now at last it was here. Some made extravagant plans that had been hatching in their heads for years. They wished to celebrate the Millennium in Paris, in Tokyo, in Las Vegas, in Australia, New Zealand, Africa, Asia, South America, on top of a mountain, in a jungle, on a desert island, in Antarctica. You name it; someone planned to go there. Others threw lavish parties, as if this was it. The end of the world was coming. Some predicted meltdown and chaos. The so-called *Millennium Bug* was meant to stop all computers from working and cause systems, networks and institutions to grind to a standstill. In the event none of these fears materialised. It was a new year pretty much like other new years. And afterwards when people woke up the world hadn't changed. It carried on pretty much as before.

Whilst many had exotic and grandiose celebrations planned we had altogether more humble plans for New Year's Eve 1999. For a start we had no chance of getting a babysitter. If we could have got one we probably couldn't have afforded to pay them. They were charging triple or quadruple rates for such services, just as taxis for the evening were doing. Not that we would have left Grace with someone we didn't know anyway. We only left her with trusted members of the family. If we had made it out, pubs and clubs were demanding ridiculous, inflated entry fees. It just wasn't worth it. In the event we enjoyed a pleasant but low-key family dinner party at my sister's. She was kind enough to invite us over to see in the new year at her house, with her, her husband and two young daughters. My parents were also invited, and with myself, Roxanne and Grace, it made nine of us in all.

It was an evening of convivial conversation, fine, home-cooked cuisine and good wine. It also proved to be the last time I ate meat. I'd already decided some months earlier I was giving up meat for the Millennium and I stuck with that decision. Like a condemned man I enjoyed one more meal of cooked animal flesh, and then no more. Roxanne and Grace were already vegetarian. Now at last I was joining them. I was becoming a vegetarian too. I realised I simply liked animals too much to carry on eating them. I'd already given up red meat some years before. I only ate poultry and fish as it was, so it wasn't that difficult giving up the rest. Afterwards I never really missed it.

My sister served goose for the occasion. It was something of an extravagance, but also fitting to mark the start of a new century. None of us were very likely to see in another. I was used to eating duck, but had rarely if ever eaten goose before. It was very like duck, I found. I enjoyed it. I made the most of it and savoured my last meal as a carnivore. I knew from the following morning, having made up my mind to give up meat, I wouldn't return to it and would in future remain strictly vegetarian. And indeed I've remained so ever since, even as I write all these years later. I'm proud to be vegetarian and not a meat eater.

Once the bunting, banners, flags and fairy lights had come down things returned to normal pretty swiftly. As the year 2000 got into full swing we carried on in our new, family routine, looking after a baby who was fast becoming a walking, talking toddler. After so much change in such a short time we continued our period of consolidation. I think in some ways I found life easier than Roxanne. I looked after Grace in the mornings and some afternoons, before going to work. Roxanne had her in the evenings, when I was at the cinema. I think Roxanne struggled on her own when I wasn't there. She sometimes felt lonely. She bemoaned the fact that I had to work nights. She suggested it might be better if I got a day job with normal hours. I said it wasn't as easy as that. It wasn't really practical. If I worked days, who would look after Grace? I asked. Neither of us were in particularly well-paid jobs. We could never have afforded the childcare costs if we worked the same hours. Even so she continued to raise the matter from time to time. Besides, I liked working at the cinema. It was true to say I'd pretty much hated every other job I'd had before. I wasn't that eager to revert back to an office type job.

On a couple of occasions Grace was taken poorly, and I had to come rushing home from work to take her to the local hospital's accident and emergency department. She had croup more than once and struggled to breathe. It was horrible hearing her wheezing, and for us her parents it was very alarming. It wasn't until she received strong medication to relax her windpipe that she could inhale more air in, and we could begin to calm down. Another time she had a severe stomach infection and had to be treated for dehydration. It was always worrying. I hated it when Grace was ill. Roxanne was ill too sometimes. She was prone to

128

asthma attacks, sometimes requiring hospital treatment herself. She was plagued by digestion issues. Far too late and after far too many years of suffering she was diagnosed with celiac disease.

Despite these issues there was joy being a parent. I found that to be the case at least. I seemed to adjust to our new life and cope better than Roxanne in some ways. Playing a bit of tennis or badminton proved a handy distraction for me and helped to keep my body and mind healthy. Roxanne's downtime involved more solitary occupations, like reading and doing her needlework hobbies. Whilst outwardly she was happy, perhaps she needed more active forms of distraction herself that would get her out of the house more often. The problem was she wasn't really interested in the kind of sporting leisure activities I enjoyed. It was hard finding comparable things that interested her and that she could do with her asthma. In retrospect both of us should have tried harder, to find interests that could have broken up her day more. I was slow to realise she needed them. I should have realised, as I needed them myself. Roxanne didn't speak up. She suffered in silence. She kept her thoughts to herself. She probably needed more friends to do things with, but she wasn't that sociable. She was a little reticent and withdrawn, unless she knew people well.

I had my writing, which I continued to work on during Grace's nap times. Fairly regularly Grace would fall asleep for relatively long periods during the mornings and afternoons, which allowed me to get quite a lot done. Sometime during the course of 2000 I finished work on my novel *Writer's Block*. As with previous efforts I send it off diligently to would-be agents and publishers. It garnered little interest. Undeterred I ploughed straight on with another novel. I was absolutely convinced one day I would write something good, something which would get published and achieve recognition. I was naïve in the extreme. My next novel had the working title *Daydreamers*. It was about exactly that. It told the parallel stories of two daydreamers, one male, one female, who lived in the same town, but didn't know each other. They were very different and lived very different lives. The young man was a nerdy office worker. The girl was a young, unmarried mum. They weren't really suited to each other. The question was would they get to meet anyway? And if they did finally meet, how would they get on?

I had different versions in my head, of them finally meeting and liking each other, or alternatively hating each other, or indeed having no feeling for each other one way or another. In another version the twist was after all the suspense and big build up, they don't actually get to meet. In a cruel turn of fate at the end, I would create a scenario where they just missed each other by a fraction of a second or a minute. As I started writing I wasn't even sure which ending I'd use. But as with all my novels I began writing it with a surge of enthusiasm and optimism. Perhaps this would be the one?

I also put together a new poetry collection, including all the poems I'd written for magazines and anthologies since my last one. It was titled *Water Under the Bridge*. I felt it was a nice piece of work, but I knew it wouldn't bring me any new readers. It would only appeal to those few people and literary editors who'd enjoyed my work before. There would be no new ones won over. It didn't matter. I wrote out of a feeling of compulsion. I had no choice in the matter. I felt there was something I had to get out. I didn't really care if no one read it. I had to write anyway. I wasn't happy unless I was writing. I was dead inside.

At the end of the summer of that year we again went on holiday with Roxanne's parents. This time they rented a holiday cottage in Beaminster in Dorset. From there we enjoyed trips to Bridport and West Bay, Dorchester, Weymouth, Shaftesbury and Salisbury. We visited some of the landmarks and locations made famous in the novels of Thomas Hardy. Grace was now older and more grown up and could enjoy it more. Again it was nice to get away, but I felt the relationship between Roxanne and myself wasn't quite the same as it had been the year before. Something was missing. We weren't quite as close. We'd drifted apart. It was a little more tense and strained. I was right. My intuition was correct. When a family holiday was booked again the following year in 2001 they left me at home. They went without me. Of course there was nothing in the year 2000 to give me any idea of what was to come. I had no clue what was to unfold and happen between us, and leave our marriage perilously close to collapse. I just had a vague sense things weren't quite as they had been.

Perhaps we'd spent too long consolidating. Perhaps we'd allowed things to stagnate. Perhaps they'd grown stale. Perhaps the magic spark that had brought us together and kept us as a couple through the ups and down of the previous five years had started to flicker and fade. Perhaps it needed to be reignited. Perhaps neither of us were quite capable of that. We were tired. We both worked long hours. We had a young daughter to look after. Things weren't always easy.

Perhaps superficially everything had appeared to be all right. Perhaps deep down it wasn't. It was hard to put my finger on quite what the problem was. It just felt different. Something had changed. I think I was happier than Roxanne was. Perhaps I'd underestimated the negative impact the irregular hours of my job had on her. I had to do them to help support our family, to keep food on the table and a roof over our heads. Perhaps I'd closed my eyes to how lonely Roxanne felt in the evenings when I was at work. It was easier just to ignore it than recognise she felt alone, sad and hurt. I couldn't understand why she'd feel like that. She should be happy, I thought. She had a husband, a child and a house to be content with. Perhaps that wasn't enough. I was confused. Why wasn't it? I wondered. It was for me.

Summer and autumn passed and winter arrived. Our hectic working lives continued with little let up. Roxanne prepared for Christmas with her usual energy and gusto. Heaps of presents were bought for Grace, far more than we could reasonably afford or even store in the limited space we had. Still, we wanted her third Christmas to be a memorable one. It was important for Roxanne too that Christmas was a big success. I was slow to recognise how much emphasis she was placing on it this particular year, as if her entire state of happiness was intrinsically tied up with how Christmas went. Roxanne organised a host of events both with friends and family to ensure it went as she hoped. Indeed she organised far more than she had for the Millennium, which others had made a big deal of celebrating. A year later it was Roxanne's turn. She had various things lined up for us, apart from the obvious, including a night out on the town, a family meal at an expensive restaurant, and a dinner party at our house with another similarly aged couple with a young family.

Unfortunately disaster struck. Just before Christmas I was struck down by a flu bug. It wasn't just a cold or sniffle. It was one of those nasty viruses that does the rounds every few years. I felt absolutely terrible. I carried on struggling to work for a few days, but it was proving impossible. I felt hot, sweaty, weak, unsteady on my feet and like I might pass out. I couldn't even walk to the corner shop to buy food. I didn't feel strong enough. I didn't want to eat anyway. I felt too sick. Each day I went in I had no idea how I got to the end of my shift. I felt like I was undergoing an out-of-body experience. I was there, but I wasn't there. It was like I was hallucinating. After my health issues of recent years I'd learnt to soldier on through almost anything, to push physical symptoms out of my mind, but on this occasion I couldn't keep doing so. I had to succumb to the inevitable. Reluctantly I was forced to take time off. I hoped to be better for my staff Christmas party. I wasn't. It took place without me. The night out Roxanne had planned with friends was still a few days away. I hoped to be better for that. Roxanne was convinced I would be.

'You'll be fine,' she assured me. 'You don't want to miss two nights out. Besides I've put a lot of time and effort into organising this. You can't cancel at the last moment.'

I didn't want to cancel. Roxanne was right. But I had no choice. I simply wasn't well enough. On the night I even thought about trying to get ready, but I realised it was pointless. I was still running a high temperature. With the best will in the world there was no way I was making it out.

'You go without me,' I told Roxanne. 'I simply can't manage it. But you have a nice time anyway.'

Roxanne was gutted. We always went as a couple. It wasn't the same if I wasn't going. I got through Christmas Day a few days later, but that was about it. When Roxanne's parents arrived at our house to take us for the family meal Roxanne had arranged I had to go back to bed. I'd even tried to get ready. I just wasn't up to it. I had to let them go without me. The only blessing was that Grace hadn't caught whatever I had. That was a small relief. I hoped to god she wouldn't get it. It could be serious for a small child, I realised. I tried to avoid going near her whilst I was still ill. I don't think Roxanne understood how poorly I felt. I got little sympathy. I think she thought I was exaggerating and putting it on to some extent. She was angry I'd not only missed the night out, but I'd also missed the meal with her parents. There was no way I'd have missed any of it if I felt all right. Unfortunately I didn't.

'You can't cancel the dinner party. You really can't do that,' Roxanne threatened.

I wanted to cancel, but I couldn't. Two of our closest friends, another couple with young children, were coming to the house for new year. I'd just have to grin and bear it. I'd just have to grit my teeth and somehow get through it. They were a nice couple. I liked them, but to me the evening was purgatory. Every second seemed like a minute. Every minute seemed like an hour. Every hour seemed like ten. I pretended to be happy and to be enjoying myself. I pretended to be having a nice time. Inside I felt like I was dying. I felt awful. I just couldn't wait for them to leave and for the evening to be over. I spent a lot of time in the kitchen, doing the washing up, just to help the time pass and to disguise how wretched I was feeling. Eventually, not a moment too soon, they had to head home.

'Thank god for that,' I announced. 'That really was one of the worst evenings of my life.'

Roxanne didn't even reply. She just gave me a hateful look and stomped out of the room and off to bed. After that, as we entered the new year, I finally began to feel a little better. I'd been ill at least a month, since the beginning of December. Unfortunately the same couldn't be said of Roxanne. She plunged into a great and terrible depression. She was signed off work as clinically depressed. I tried to snap her out of it. She refused or perhaps couldn't snap out of it. She just stared vacantly and blankly at the walls and ceiling. She became almost incapable of looking after Grace. I had to do almost everything for our daughter. It was as if a light had gone out in Roxanne. She was just a shell. The person I'd known was missing.

'I know you placed a great deal of emphasis on Christmas, but these things happen. It can't be helped,' I told her. 'I'm better now. We can organise other social events if you want.'

I tried everything to get through to her, to wake her up from her strange, vegetative slumber. She was unresponsive. She wasn't listening. I took her and Grace out for drives in the car. I took her to some of her favourite places. Perhaps too late I became the model husband. I was determined to fix whatever was broken. It appeared it wasn't as easy as that. It wasn't so simple to fix things like depression. I couldn't get through to Roxanne at all. It was as if she was in the room but was absent at the same time. Even the medication wasn't really working.

What was odder, when Roxanne did finally start to get better she re-emerged almost as a different person. I didn't really recognise her. She was cold and distant, not at all like she'd been in the past. She seemed intent on reinventing herself, with a new hair colour, new look and new clothes. She got her nose pierced and talked about getting a tattoo. It wasn't really like her at all. She started to listen to completely different music; new raucous bands like *Sum 41* and *Linkin Park*, not the gentle indie music of the ilk of *Pulp* that she'd liked before. It was strange and hard to make sense of how much she'd changed. I tried my best to ignore it, to pretend she was the same and everything was OK, but it wasn't. It wasn't OK. She was different. We were no longer close. She no longer really felt like my wife.

I hoped she'd eventually just wake up. She'd somehow return to how she'd been before. Unfortunately she didn't. Instead things got steadily worse, despite my very best efforts to get things back on track. I was failing. I was fighting a losing battle. The girl I'd known and married was slipping away. She was drifting further from me. I was getting worried now. There was clearly no easy fix. This was a problem that was here to stay. It wasn't going to vanish in a hurry, as I'd first anticipated. It seemed that as a family we were stuck with it. Depression had muscled into our home and lives. It wasn't about to disappear any time soon.

Chapter Sixteen

Things took a further turn for the worse when Roxanne bought herself a new computer. For a start we couldn't afford it. We simply didn't have the cash. Despite my concerns and reservations she just put it on a credit card. One day we'd have to pay that money back, I pointed out. Then Roxanne became hooked on the internet, which in those days was still in its relative infancy. People were only just starting to get online. There was no social media and other temptations we're now so accustomed to. It was just getting started as a platform for people to interact with each other. Roxanne was one of the first, at least in the circles I moved in, to get into it in a big way. There were no cheap *Broadband* deals back then. Roxanne started to rack up hefty bills on our telephone line, not even realising she was doing so. That was soon the least of my concerns. Very quickly she became addicted to these newly burgeoning chatrooms, where she could chat live with other lost souls, who had nothing better to do with their time. She started to shut herself away in her room, away from Grace and me, and chat for hours on end without us. It started to become a worry. She was secretive about who she was chatting with. She was distant and evasive when asked about it. Soon she spent longer and longer online. It seemed to me it was becoming a dangerous obsession. From the outside it seemed very unhealthy. It didn't seem to be helping to cure her depression. It seemed to be giving her a platform to revel in it.

As the weeks passed Roxanne spent more and more time conversing in these online chatrooms. It became her main interest. In the past she'd always gone to bed early, often before I came home from work. Now when I came home she was still on the computer, feverishly typing away. Despite the fact she had to be up first thing she would refuse to go to bed. She stayed up later and later into the small hours, still chatting long after I'd gone to bed myself. Sometimes I'd wake up at three or four in the morning to find she still hadn't come to bed, even though she had to be awake again in just a few hours. It couldn't be doing her health any good, I thought. Yet, she still refused to stop. When confronted about her addiction she became feral, like an addict questioned about their favourite drug of choice.

'It's none of your business. Go away!' she shouted, her face distorting in anger and hatred.

'It is my business. I'm your husband. You're the mother of my daughter,' I replied.

It was no use. Things didn't improve. The depression was merely masked by medication. I could tell by looking at Roxanne's eyes it was present in her as powerfully as ever. She looked drugged. She looked like she was in another world, her own little world we no longer had access to. Even when she seemed superficially all right I could tell she wasn't. She'd changed. She was no longer the same person. The chatrooms and the furtive, secretive way that she was engaging with them proved a source of growing tension and friction between us. I wanted to know who she was talking to, and what she was talking about. She refused to divulge. Occasionally she mentioned names of people, as if they were best friends of long standing, when in fact they were people she'd just chatted to online. She'd never met them in person. More worryingly she started talking about meeting up with them. I was so concerned that I rang Roxanne's mother, to express my concern about Roxanne's growing addiction. Foolishly I thought she might be able to help. It was a mistake. Of course it backfired. Roxanne's mother was no help at all. She simply rang Roxanne to say I'd been telling tales on her. I was at my wits' end. Roxanne was livid.

'How dare you ring my mother. Just stay out of my life!' she screamed.

I started to do that. I turned a blind eye to it. I buried my head in the sand. I pretended it wasn't happening. I thought about the good things in our life, like Grace. I tried to concentrate on them. I couldn't even admit to myself how perilous the state of our marriage was, let alone confess to my parents, friends or work colleagues. Although I started to give little hints to my parents that things weren't entirely rosy. Outside of the house I mostly stayed protective of Roxanne. I stood up for her. I didn't admit there was anything wrong. Of course our sex life was suffering. We had been very close. Now we hardly ever went near each other. She just turned me away. I stopped trying. I didn't need the rejection. I felt bad enough as it was.

Roxanne began considering leaving her job. She scoured the job vacancy pages in the local paper every time they came out. She could never find anything to suit her. She pressed me to get a new job. I was resistant. I liked my job. I didn't want to leave it and get one I hated, only to find Roxanne and I didn't stay together anyway. I was desperate to hold onto the few things in my life that were a constant. In a turbulent marriage the familiarity of the cinema and things like playing tennis and writing remained a much-needed comfort, compared to what I was going through at home.

If the chatrooms weren't bad enough there were other unpleasant surprises to come. Roxanne stopped wearing her wedding ring, even though I still wore mine. She started giving off the vibe she was single, whether it was a deliberate plan or merely accidental. Several times when my mum brought Grace home after babysitting her for the day, she was surprised to see Roxanne being dropped off by male work colleagues in their cars. My mum thought it was odd for a married woman, but she didn't say anything. What was even odder, on other occasions I came home from work late only to find Roxanne entertaining men with candlelit meals in our dining room. It was very peculiar. I just tried to shut it out and pretend it wasn't happening. Roxanne's behaviour was becoming so erratic and unpredictable I almost ceased caring. She could do what she wanted, I told myself, and I would too. Several times, as she entertained, I just sat down in our lounge and put the television on until they left.

'Who the hell was that?' I asked afterwards.

'They're just friends from work,' she replied.

Whatever they were it wasn't right and I didn't like it. Maybe Roxanne just liked the attention. Maybe she had no plans to actually act on it. Even so I could see these various men getting their hopes up. They clearly considered Roxanne to be unattached and fair game. It certainly wasn't what I expected and wanted out of married life. I was starting to get seriously disillusioned. Yet I carried on trying to make things work, for Grace's sake as much as anything. I told myself Roxanne was sick. She wasn't herself. She didn't know what she was doing. Unfortunately things didn't improve. Roxanne announced she was taking a holiday, by herself. She'd booked time off work and was going away. She refused to say where she was going or who with. She said something vague about going with an old university friend, but it was hard to tell if she was telling the truth. She provided no further details and refused to do so. Perhaps she was meeting up with someone she'd met online? I never found out. To this day I have no idea where she went and what she did. I was stuck at home with Grace.

We'd talked about going away as a family at the end of the summer, as we always did. It had even been arranged and I'd taken time off work to go. When the holiday came round Roxanne announced I wasn't going. She was still going with her parents of course, but she was taking Grace on her own without me. I was being left behind. It was just about the final straw for me. Instead of going on holiday I spent the week going out and getting pissed with a work colleague called Paul I'd grown close to. He was a relaxed, easy-going fellow. He was laid back and good natured. He was single and he was up for partying. He introduced me to a host of new people he liked to go clubbing with. He was also into music, so when Roxanne was away we got the guitars out and started jamming songs together. Roxanne had always mocked my musical efforts. It was nice to be doing it again after a lengthy break. It was also a useful distraction to take my mind off things. Roxanne had always been funny about me going out without her. Now I was going out with Paul all the time. We went to see bands and to indie club nights. As Roxanne had now gone on holiday without me twice I vowed I'd never stay in for her sake again. I'd go out whenever I wanted. I'd do exactly as I liked. It was a change of outlook for me and one for the better. To some extent it put my marriage woes out of my mind. I started to forget all about them and enjoy myself.

After Roxanne and Grace had gone on holiday without me, I could no longer pretend to my parents that everything in the garden was rosy. There were major problems between us, I admitted. Roxanne's depression had got no better, and I had no idea if we were going to stay together. My dad's seventieth birthday dinner followed soon afterwards. Roxanne had even got us to change the date to suit her, only to refuse to go on the night. She was too embarrassed. When my parents drove round to pick us up she hid in the back room of the house. She didn't want to see them or speak to them, or them to see her. My parents still sent us a wedding anniversary card, to celebrate our fourth wedding anniversary. It was hardly a celebration. Roxanne's parents didn't send us a card. Neither did Roxanne give me a card, though I gave one to her. In my eyes we were still married. Nothing had been said to change that. We still lived together. Despite all that had happened we had made no plans to separate. Yet just as Roxanne was doing I too was increasingly living the single life. I went out with Paul and his friends more and more often. I reconnected with some of my old acquaintances, whom I'd enjoyed the company of before I'd got married. I no longer saw our marriage as untouchable and above question.

Then Roxanne dropped another bombshell. She said she was leaving her job to embark on a teacher training course. She'd made little mention of this, but had been making plans behind my back. Initially she'd planned to enrol on a course where we lived, but she hadn't got a place. She had got a place at a college near where her parents lived, however, some fifty odd miles away. Initially she planned to commute. As time passed she talked about taking Grace with her and spending the weekdays staying at her parents. They'd only see me at weekends. On five days out of seven I'd be on own, living in our newly bought house alone. It was a lot to take in. I was far from happy, but raising objections was futile and pointless. It was a fait accompli. It was happening. I was stuck with it, whether I liked it or not. They were going to another town. I was staying. It was hard to see how our marriage could survive it.

Roxanne had a leaving do with work colleagues to say goodbye. I was present, but she completely ignored me. She acted like she was single and not married at all. I just left her to it. I couldn't be bothered. She was annoying me now. I just went off with my own friends and tried to forget all about her. She'd upset me enough. It was getting to the point where I wasn't prepared to be upset anymore. I'd had enough pain. I'd done enough suffering. I'd shed enough tears. I went home without her. I just left her there to do whatever she wanted to do. To my surprise I no longer cared. I no longer really felt married. I'd tried my best, but my best simply hadn't been good enough. I was a failure. Where marriage was concerned we both were.

When Roxanne left to start her course Grace was just three years old. Luckily she wasn't really old enough to be aware of what was happening. I was grateful for that small mercy. She stayed with her grandparents some weekends anyway. She'd just be staying with them more often. She still had a home with me. She still had a bedroom, with her books, toys and clothes, lovingly decorated to suit and engage the tastes and interests of a child. It would just be much more seldom that she was there to make use of it. She still had a bed. Only most nights it would lie empty. Most evenings when I got home from work there would be no one there. The house which we had bought so relatively recently would be dormant and quiet. I'd be alone with my thoughts. I'd have time to wonder what I'd done wrong to deserve such an outcome. I'd got married in good faith. We'd had a child together. Now for all intents and purposes I was on my own.

For Roxanne's part she seemed excited at the prospect of starting a new life. The thought of going back to college and being a student again seemed to thrill her. She no longer wore her wedding ring, even though I did. It was clear to me she planned to make the most of being in a new environment. At the end of the first week of her course Roxanne didn't bring Grace back to see me for the weekend as promised. She suggested instead that I drive down on the Saturday and see them then. I wasn't even invited to stay the night afterwards. After taking them out I was left to drive the fifty odd miles back in the twilight of the early evening to our empty house.

A pattern soon emerged. The same thing happened the following weekend. As things panned out Roxanne and Grace only came home to me once or twice in the whole of the first term. It was far from satisfactory. I became totally disillusioned with this sorry imitation of a loving family life. As a result I went out more and more by myself. As soon as I got home after seeing them I'd hit the town. I no longer gave any consideration to what Roxanne thought. I imagined she was doing the same with fellow students from her course, as her parents were left to babysit. I went out with Paul, together with another work colleague called Sandy. Sandy lived with a gentle, kind-hearted girl called Joan, but the freshness and excitement had gone out of their relationship. He suffered from commitment issues and subconsciously was ready to move onto something else. He was loud, jolly and always the life and soul of the party. He was only too happy to come out drinking with us. We were often joined by Paul's friend, an alcoholic, former Goth called Steve; an unassuming indie musician called Cliff, who Paul and I had both known for years; and a pair of attractive girls called Cally and Mattie. We were quite the party gang, and all of us had a leaning to the alternative side of the fashion and lifestyle spectrum. As I spent more time with them I started having fun. I started to forget my problems at home.

Most Friday and Saturday nights we went to our local indie club, where they played music by bands like *The Strokes*, *The White Stripes*, *The Hives* and other similar rocky acts. It was energetic and lively. For the first time in an age I danced. I was going out so much it was inevitable I started feeling single again myself. Roxanne and Grace were fifty miles away. Roxanne certainly wasn't thinking much about me, though I imagined Grace missed her daddy. My attention started to be drawn to a tall, slim girl I guessed to be in her mid twenties we started to see out most Friday nights. She had slightly wild hair and was always with two female friends. All three were attractive to my eye, though I hadn't talked to another girl in that way for seven or eight years. I wasn't about to start now, but there was no denying I'd noticed the tallest one in particular. She had long, dark hair, and had a slightly strange, demonic look about her. She wasn't a Goth, but at the same time she could have been into the occult or white witchcraft. There was something exciting yet also dangerous about her. She had the kind of face you could just as easily be attracted to or repulsed by. I later found out it was a mixture of her mother's beauty and her father's ugliness. I personally found the combination alluring. I was beguiled by her. I had a strange feeling she'd also noticed me too.

I still wasn't ready to act on such thoughts. Far from it. I was still married to Roxanne. She was my wife. We had Grace. I had to remain faithful. I had to do the decent thing by my daughter, however far my marriage had fallen apart. One night when I finished work slightly early I took the opportunity to watch the evening screening of the latest film version of the classic *Moulin Rouge*, which we happened to be showing. I was much moved by it. It seemed to sum up my position perfectly. I was being destroyed by the futility of love. Inspired by what I'd seen I went straight home and wrote Roxanne a letter. I told her I still loved her. I told her we should try and make things work between us. I reminded her how close we'd once been. I said we should start again. Touched by the sentiments of the film I hoped my letter shared some of those same sentiments of true love. I certainly did my best to ensure that it did. The letter was truly heartfelt and was an honest expression of what I felt.

Roxanne never replied to my letter. Indeed she never even mentioned she'd ever received it, although I knew she had. For me her failure to reply or acknowledge what I'd written was the final nail in the coffin of our dying marriage. It was my last shot, my final effort to repair the damage and put things right. I'd given it everything I had over the best part of a year. It wasn't enough. I had nothing left to give. It was clear to me, despite my best efforts, our marriage was dead. It couldn't be revived. New life couldn't be breathed into it. Roxanne had given up. She'd given up many months ago in truth. It was time I accepted that fact. It was time I did the same. It was time to move on.

The next time I went out on a Friday night, when the tall, demonic girl with flowing, almost black hair looked in my direction I didn't look away. I returned her gaze. We stared at each other. I felt something pass between us. I was sure I hadn't imagined it. There was a definite spark. There was something there. I felt quite excited by it. I hadn't felt like this since first setting eyes on Roxanne nearly seven years earlier. Since then I hadn't so much as looked at another woman. Now here I was doing just that, for what seemed like the first time in as long as I could remember. Later that evening one of the companions of my mystery girl wandered casually over to speak to me.

'I want to introduce you to a friend,' she said. 'She wants to meet you.'

As soon as she said the words I knew who she meant. There was no doubt at all in my mind. I was duly led across to confront the girl I'd now admired from a distance for many weeks.

'Hi, I'm Claudia,' she said.

It was an exotic name, fitting of her exotic appearance.

'I'm Simon,' I replied.

Once we started talking that was it. We couldn't be separated. We chatted longingly to each other for the rest of the night. Claudia was twenty-seven years old. She was studying to be an occupational therapist. She wasn't married, but she was in a similar position to me. She was trapped in an unhappy relationship she wanted to leave. We seemed to have so much in common. When we said our long goodbyes at the end of the night, I had an overwhelming feeling it wasn't the last I'd be seeing of her. I knew I'd see her again very soon. When I drove down to see Roxanne and Grace the next day I mentioned nothing of this liaison of course. I didn't mention I'd met someone I felt very drawn to and wanted to see more of. I kept it all to myself. I pretended all was all right. This carried on for weeks, all the way up to Christmas.

PART THREE – CLAUDIA

Chapter Seventeen

I somehow maintained the pretence of being the dutiful husband and father. Every weekend I still drove down to see my wife, who was drifting inexorably away from me, and the daughter I loved. But increasingly my heart was elsewhere. I was confused. I didn't know what I wanted. Sometimes when I took my wife and daughter out for the afternoon we still seemed like a family. Things were almost normal and as they should be. Roxanne was always dressed up when I came to collect them. She was still attractive. I was still attracted to her, but I was falling in love with someone else. I was falling in love with Claudia. I couldn't help myself. I couldn't make it stop. I seemed hopelessly set on a new course, for better or worse and whether it was right or wrong. It seemed too late to turn back. I was getting in too deep. I didn't even feel that bad about it. Roxanne no longer wore her wedding ring. She'd shown contempt for our marriage. She no longer shared the same bed, or even the same house, with me. She only saw me when it suited her. When I drove down to see her and Grace she still didn't invite me to stay the night. Once I'd taken them out and dropped them back she had no further use for me, and I was sent home, alone. It would have been too much to bear, except my thoughts were now preoccupied with Claudia.

Christmas drew ever nearer. The Friday before, as soon as I finished work, I went out with Paul and Sandy and the rest of the gang, as I almost always did every weekend now. Claudia and her friends were there too of course. As soon as Claudia and I started chatting we closed everything but each other out of our minds. We could have been alone in the room. We became almost oblivious to anything else. We were barely mindful of the loud music and other people there. We only had eyes for each other, although I was vaguely aware as I chatted to Claudia that Paul was getting friendly with Claudia's friend, Sam. Cally, Mattie, Sandy and Cliff meanwhile all went off to dance. Steve went off to get drunk, or drunker, by himself. I think they'd grown bored of us. Claudia and I were so engrossed in each other we barely spoke to anyone else. When we chatted like this we were a bit anti-social in truth. We couldn't help it. We both had other partners. Time alone together was rare and precious. We had to make the most of it.

'What's your most hated food?' I asked Claudia.

It was a random question, but I was still intrigued to hear the answer.

'Butter,' she replied. 'I can't stand it; awful, slippery, slimy, yellow stuff.'

'Me too. That's how I feel. I can't stand it either,' I said, surprised we'd both hate the same thing.

Our faces lit up and we beamed at each other.

'What's your second most hated food?' I continued.

'Celery,' Claudia said. 'I loathe it. I can taste the tiniest amount in anything. It's evil; the food of the devil!'

'That's amazing. I can't believe it. I hate celery too,' I said.

I couldn't believe it either. I wasn't joking. I wasn't making it up just to agree with her. What a strange coincidence, I reflected. What were the chances of that? I wondered to myself. Both our two most hated foods were butter and celery. Furthermore, we agreed our third most hated food was gravy. It was clearly a sign, I decided. This was it. We were obviously meant to be together. It was an odd thing to reach some kind of decision on, but if I'd ever been wavering on where my loyalties truly lay it swayed me all the same. I started to believe it was more than mere coincidence that we hated exactly the same food items. Most people loved butter, celery and gravy after all. I didn't, and it seemed Claudia didn't either. Maybe Claudia was the one I'd been looking for all my life. I was now thirty-six years old. Perhaps belatedly I'd finally found my ideal partner. We'd been looking for each other.

At the end of the evening I offered to walk Claudia home. She was hesitant at first. Her friends had gone. She was worried about being spotted alone with me. I persuaded her it would be all right. Slightly reluctantly she agreed. It was cold outside. It was the middle of winter. We walked closely together. It wasn't far to where she lived. Perhaps to spend a little more time alone together we slipped down a dark alleyway near her house. No one was about. We were truly alone. She was so close to me I could feel her cold breath on my face. I put my arm on her shoulder and pulled her closer. She was wearing a thin, leather jacket. I kissed her on the lips. Our tongues touched. We could no longer hold back and we embraced much more passionately. I felt no sense of guilt. It felt amazing. I hadn't realised quite how much I'd been longing for this moment, until it finally happened. After a while Claudia suddenly pulled away. She looked shy and embarrassed.

'I can't,' she said. 'I feel bad. I have a boyfriend.'

'I have a wife,' I said simply. 'We're both as bad as each other.'

With that we carried on kissing, thrusting our tongues deep into the other's mouth, gripping each other tight, pulling the other as close as we possibly could. Except we weren't as bad as each other. I was worse than Claudia. I had a wife and a daughter. At that moment I thought little of them. I thought only of Claudia. Furthermore, I realised I simply had to have her. Whatever the consequences, whatever the costs, from then on I was determined we would be together. When I finally let Claudia go we swapped email addresses and telephone numbers. Claudia was going back to her family for Christmas in a day or two, and much as I tried to persuade her to come out the next night it was clear I wouldn't see her again until she was back after the festive break.

We agreed to keep in touch. It would be hard not seeing her after what had happened. I'd have to spend Christmas with Roxanne and Grace and say nothing of the fact I'd kissed another woman. I'd also have to keep it to myself that in the new year I planned to start a new life with Claudia. Of course it wasn't all my fault. It was true I'd now met someone else, but in truth Roxanne had already left me and our marriage many months before. She'd taken off her wedding ring. She no longer behaved like a wife in any shape or form. She'd gone on unexplained holidays without me. She'd entertained other men to meals in our home. She'd chatted online to them. She hadn't slept with me in longer than I dared remember. Whilst part of me felt bad for what I was doing I didn't feel I could really be blamed. It was now a year since Roxanne had suffered her breakdown. I'd given her that long to get back on track and to sort her head out. It hadn't happened. That year had gone. There had been little or no improvement. She was as far away from me as ever, and now I'd grown equally distant from her too.

Bizarrely, in a bid to maintain some small sense of normality for Grace's sake, Roxanne and Grace were spending Christmas with me at my parents' house. I had seen it as the very last chance to salvage our marriage. I supposed it was still that, but after what had passed between Claudia and me it was probably just too late to be saved, however Christmas went and whether it was good or bad. It was actually OK, but I couldn't wait for it to pass to see Claudia again. Right through Christmas that was the main thing on my mind, not seeing Grace enjoy her fourth Christmas, although obviously that was important to me too. Superficially at least Roxanne and I actually got on in a polite, civil manner, but there was no real reconnecting or coming back together. It was hard when I'd kissed someone else. It was pretty much impossible in fact. With Christmas over Roxanne and Grace returned to her parents. I rang Claudia at almost the first opportunity I had. I told her I'd missed her. I asked when she'd be coming back. I couldn't wait to see her, I said. She was more reticent than I was. She reminded me she still had a boyfriend. Even so we agreed to meet up as soon as we possibly could.

Between Christmas and New Year I took Claudia out in the car. She was very paranoid about being spotted or seen. I was less concerned. For some reason I was no longer that bothered. Perhaps it would have been a relief to be caught and found out, and have had to admit the truth. Aware of Claudia's concerns, by a strange twist of fate we ended up driving the narrow country lanes near where Roxanne and I had got married some four or five years before. So much had happened since. I could hardly believe it myself. I could hardly believe where we were now. I couldn't have imagined it, out with another woman and on the brink of separation. Yet here we were. That was the reality that now consumed my life.

Claudia and I stopped at a quiet, village pub, where no one was likely to know us. We held hands as we ate. We kissed. We were happy just to be together. Neither of us wanted to drive back. I took the longest detour I possibly could, but eventually I returned her to her road, eager to see her again as soon as we could arrange it. We agreed to go out on New Year's Eve together. By happy chance Claudia's boyfriend was away then, and Roxanne had made no arrangement to see me. It was too good an opportunity to miss. We agreed to meet and get ready at Paul's flat. By another coincidence Paul and Claudia's friend Sam had now got together too. It seemed we'd be two new couples going out to welcome in the New Year not just one. The new year would be 2002 and so much had changed, just about irreversibly.

On New Year's Eve 2001 I finished work early. There were no late film screenings that night. The cinema shut in time to allow staff to join in the evening's celebrations and festivities, and to go out and enjoy themselves in whatever manner they wished to do so. I'd planned for the occasion and taken some suitable clothes with me to work to change into. I wanted to look my best for Claudia. It was still very much early days in our blossoming relationship. I didn't want to mess things up, before they'd had a proper chanced to develop. I certainly didn't want to look a state or dress in a way that might cause her embarrassment, still in my work clothes for instance. I wanted to retain her interest and hopefully see it develop further. I was anxious it didn't begin to wane before we'd even properly got together. Hopefully that wasn't going to happen. From what had happened so far there was every sign and indication we were besotted with each other, and we were heading for a long and meaningful liaison.

We met at Paul's flat, the same flat that Paul and I sometimes jammed music together. When I arrived Claudia and Sam were already there. They were sharing some wine and Claudia was rolling a spliff. I hadn't really smoked weed since my student days. I'd momentarily forgotten that Claudia and Sam were a little younger than Paul and me, and as students still themselves, even mature ones, were still into such things. Paul had been a big pothead in his younger days, and it wasn't long before Paul and I were rolling back the years and joining in with the spliff smoking. I also opened a bottle of lager, to put myself further in the mood for the evening that lay ahead. After a couple more drinks we headed into town. We stopped briefly at a bar en route to the club we always went to. Some of our friends were already there, including Sandy who was already slightly drunk and strutting his stuff on the dancefloor.

The evening went well. I spent most of it with Claudia. There was a happy mood in the air, as if my problems of the previous year had suddenly lifted. As the clock struck midnight and the New Year was welcomed in we said goodbye to 2001 for the last time. I was glad to see the back of it. It hadn't been the best or happiest year for me by any means. I sensed my life truly was about to change. I believed I was about to move on to better things and better times. I knew that whatever happened, now that I'd met Claudia they wouldn't be the same as they had been before. They couldn't be. They couldn't go on as they had done. It wasn't possible. It was in all probability the end of my marriage to Roxanne. At that moment, as I held Claudia in my arms, that was the only and inevitable outcome of matters as they were unfolding and I was unconcerned. Events, many of which I hadn't asked for or chosen, had brought me to this situation and to this moment in time. Now I embraced it. I was happy that finally it was happening.

As fate would have it, just as Claudia and I were getting to know each other, as soon as New Year was over and out the way, she had to go away. She was being sent on a college work placement to a medical institution near Brighton, where she could get some hands-on experience of the job she would hopefully be doing in time.

Unfortunately for me the placement would last the whole of the spring term. Furthermore, Brighton was nowhere near where we lived. Neither was it a particularly convenient place to travel to. Yet, we were stuck with it and would have to make the best of it until we could get together again in the spring. Despite the fact that Claudia still had a boyfriend and was actually staying with friends of her boyfriend whilst she was away, and I still had a wife, through emails, texts and telephone calls we kept in touch as closely as we could. Although it wasn't always easy, and sometimes it was very hard to talk freely, we rang each other every night.

I missed Claudia terribly. I longed to be with her. I knew I simply had to have her. The fact she was away only made my heart grow fonder. It was a situation I knew I had to resolve. I'd become no closer again to Roxanne. We'd drifted as far away as ever. I barely saw her. I barely saw Grace. I lived in the house we'd bought for our family to all intents and purposes by myself. God knows what the neighbours made of it. I'm sure they were intrigued. They knew better though than to ask. My face probably betrayed the fact I had no wish to be interrogated on the matter. I maintained my solitary life. I came and went as I always had done, but now alone. I knew I needed to clear up my position with Roxanne. I also knew I needed Claudia to leave her boyfriend. She also knew that she needed to do so, but she was hesitant. They had a flat together. They had many mutual friends. It wouldn't be easy for either of us. But one way or other our various domestic circumstances did need sorting, or we couldn't be together.

In the end I decided I'd be the one to grab the bull by the horns. I felt Roxanne was continuing to make a mockery of our marriage and our family. She'd make promises to bring Grace up to see me, only to let me down at the last. She'd ask me to come down to see them, only to change her mind at the final moment. She was far more interested in her college and online friends than having anything to do with me. Not seeing my daughter, my only child, was devastating. Of course I was now making a mockery of our marriage too by seeing Claudia. It couldn't go on. Something had to be done. After another weekend of being let down I decided to ring Roxanne.

'We need to talk,' I said in a serious and solemn voice.

'I know,' Roxanne replied.

'I've hung on for a year, but things haven't got any better,' I told her. 'I think we need to separate. I'm sorry that it's come to this, but I don't see we have any other choice. I just no longer feel we have a future together.'

I didn't mention Claudia. There didn't seem any point. Even without her on the scene things hadn't been right between me and Roxanne for a very long time. We were simply formalizing and finalising something we'd both known in our hearts for many months. Our marriage was over. Roxanne didn't protest or disagree. It was probably a relief to her too. She hadn't been happy. Indeed she'd been very unhappy. She was now free to pursue whichever of her college or online friends she wanted to. And I was free to pursue Claudia.

Prompted by my actions Claudia ended her relationship with her boyfriend too. As with Roxanne and myself things hadn't been right for a long time. He was sad, but he took the news calmly. It wasn't as if he hadn't seen it coming. They'd grown ever more distant over an extended period, just as Roxanne and I had done. Such relationships can't be maintained forever. In the end something had to give, and give it did. They agreed to stay friends. He maintained a quiet dignity on the matter. He refused to attribute blame. It was one of those things. They had grown apart. And then I had come along. It had been the straw that broke the camel's back. As with Roxanne and myself it had been a long time in the making. If everything is right in a relationship these things don't happen.

I didn't want to start a new liaison on the back of someone else's unhappiness, but occasionally it couldn't be helped. I had no wish to be the villain of the peace, to be the bad guy in all of this, but it was unavoidable if we wanted to be together. Claudia's ex had his suspicions that there was someone else involved, but had been too much of a gentleman to ask. I think he preferred to believe they'd simply drifted apart. It was better for all of us he thought that. Claudia and I meanwhile agreed to keep a low profile, until such a time when it seemed appropriate to announce ourselves as a couple. In the meantime we were still desperate to see each other. We'd been apart too long. Unknown to anyone else we agreed to meet up one weekend on neutral territory, where we'd know no one and no one would know us. I booked us into a picturesque hotel in Bournemouth, which was roughly halfway between where I lived and where Claudia was staying. I planned to drive there, and Claudia was getting the train. We kept our plans to ourselves. We didn't tell anyone else what we were doing. It would be our secret.

When I arrived at the hotel a little ahead of Claudia to check in I could scarcely believe it. It looked like a Tudor mansion. It was secluded, enchanting and beautiful, far better than I'd anticipated. It wasn't even particularly expensive, perhaps because we were staying out of season. I couldn't have expected such a perfect setting for our romantic tryst, but I was delighted by the totally random choice I'd made. I'd just been looking for anywhere to stay. By chance I'd stumbled on a real gem. When Claudia arrived she was as blown away as I was. Things only got better when we were shown to our room. With its Tudor four-poster bed it looked like a honeymoon suite.

'Is this for us?' I barely dared to ask.

'Yes, does it suit?' the hotel staff member enquired.

'It suits very well,' I replied.

We couldn't wait to be alone. We had a lot of catching up to do. I'd brought wine and nibbles with me to enhance our stay. I wanted Claudia to be as happy and comfortable as possible. As it was we spent most of the weekend in our room, kissing and cuddling and getting to know each other better. We hardly went out at all, even though I didn't know Bournemouth all that well. I should have done, as my sister had once had a teaching job there, but I'd never properly visited at the time. Now I had the chance to look around I had better things to do. It was a lovely room to spend time in. It couldn't have been nicer.

We ventured out only twice during the whole weekend. On the first night I persuaded Claudia we should at least get something to eat. We had a meal in a curry house just down the road from where we were staying. As soon as we'd finished eating it was back to our room. On the Saturday afternoon we had a little browse around the shopping centre. It was pleasant, but once we'd looked at a few shops and picked up some more provisions we headed back to our hotel. Besides, I'd come to see Claudia not Bournemouth. And she'd come to see me. We could have been anywhere. Just being together was all mattered. The only disadvantage about dating a student was that I had to pay for everything. But I was unconcerned. I wasn't in a well-paid job myself, but I was better off than Claudia. I was happy to treat her in any way I could.

When the weekend was over and it was time for us to part it was hard. We'd grown closer and more fond of each other, but it would be some weeks before I could see her again. I begged her to do something similar in the meantime, before she finished her placement. She refused to commit. We had to be patient, she said. We'd be together soon enough. It wasn't soon enough for me. I was finding it hard to play it as cool as she was. I wanted to be with her each and every day. I wanted to be with her all the time. I didn't know how I'd get through the next few weeks without her.

Chapter Eighteen

Of course Roxanne got wind I was seeing someone. I don't know how. I hadn't said anything. I'd done my best to keep it very quiet. Even so she still found out. Perhaps one of her former work colleagues had spotted us. Perhaps one of our mutual friends had heard and said something. Either way, once Roxanne found out there was someone else involved, she went into overdrive. She'd been happy to separate, whilst she thought she could snap her fingers and have me back at any point she wanted. Now she realised she couldn't things were very different. I was no longer her pathetic plaything. I was moving on. Roxanne was distinctly unhappy about this. She quickly turned all our former friends against me; all the couples we used to hang out with. None of them would talk to me anymore. Roxanne played the abandoned wife and daughter card well. She was happy to be the victim now, who'd been cruelly dumped and cast aside for a younger woman. She didn't tell anyone she'd initiated the split, taking off her wedding ring and effectively leaving our marriage nearly a year earlier. I didn't put people right on the matter. I maintained my quiet dignity and said nothing. If they wanted to think I was the callous ex-husband, who'd brutally left his wife, let them believe it, I decided. I just had nothing more to do with our former friends. I let Roxanne have them all. Little did they know I'd done everything humanly possible to save our marriage. My efforts had just been insufficient. I'd loved Roxanne. She'd just fallen out of love with me. She just wasn't ready to see me with someone else. But sadly I was.

Roxanne insisted we put the house on the market immediately. I felt powerless to argue. Within days it had been valued and was up for sale, although it hurt me to see it. It seemed strange passing the *For Sale* sign on my way to and from work every day. It seemed no time since we'd bought the house and had been moving in. Perhaps Roxanne's mother had cursed it after all. It certainly hadn't brought us the happiness we'd hoped for. It wasn't long before we had a buyer and I had to start making plans to move out myself. Every weekend when I was at work Roxanne came up to clear her possessions from the house. She threw out dozens of our joint belongings and many of Grace's toys. I could always tell when she'd been. There would be piles of black bin bags outside, waiting to be picked up by the bin men. I knew inside would be many items I wanted to keep, but I didn't have the heart to go through them. If Roxanne wanted to throw out our old life en masse, let her do it, I thought.

I was interested to know how she was managing to move so much stuff. By chance I learned from Grace on a weekend that I had her she was being helped by a man with a van. Apparently the man was called Roy. I was intrigued. I made it my business to learn more. It turned out Roy was someone Roxanne had met online, but happened to live locally near Roxanne's parents. They were now meeting up regularly and were becoming almost inseparable. It didn't take too much to figure this Roy was more than just a friend and helper, although Roxanne was quick repeatedly to deny there was anything between them. Despite her assurances I simply didn't believe her.

Roxanne didn't waste any time. It wasn't long before I was served with divorce papers. I wasn't too happy that I was being named as the guilty adulterer and Roxanne the injured party. She was also getting custody of Grace. I could have fought for custody myself, but with my working hours it just wasn't practical. I could also have disputed the details of the divorce papers, particularly as I'd now learnt of Roxanne's plans to move her and Grace in with what she described in the legal documents as *her friend* Roy and his children. But I couldn't be bothered to dispute anything. I simply signed the papers, to have done with it and get it over with as quickly as possible.

The papers also covered my rights of access and the maintenance I had to pay. At least I had the right to have Grace every other weekend, when I wasn't working. That was something. I also signed the papers to sell the house. Things had moved very quickly. I now just had to wait for Claudia to come back from her work placement. As soon as she did everything I'd put myself through would prove worthwhile. I could also look forward to being a relatively wealthy man by my modest standards by the time she came back. Even during the short time we'd had it the house had gone up considerably in value. I was due to make quite a handsome profit from the sale, even after Roxanne had claimed her half of it. Of course that wasn't why I was getting divorced. It just made the sad situation we'd arrived at in our marriage slightly more bearable.

With the house sale complete, I started looking for new accommodation for myself and my belongings, of which there were many. I was quite lucky that somewhere suitable for my needs came up almost immediately. Although it was more than I could really afford, with the cash windfall from the house I could manage to pay the extra for the foreseeable time to come. The new flat had a large front room, where I could potentially entertain, a big enough bedroom for Grace to stay over, and a light and roomy kitchen, which also doubled up as a breakfast and dining room. For what I was paying there was a lot of space to accommodate all the many and varied possessions I'd built up over thirty odd years. The only downsides were that it wasn't very well heated and I had to share a bathroom with the tenant above. But I could live with that, as in other ways it suited me pretty well indeed. I picked up the keys immediately and made arrangements to move everything I could as quickly as possible. It was hard saying goodbye to the house we'd bought, the scene of all our broken dreams, but it had to be done. Both Roxanne and I were moving on with our lives.

Whilst Paul and Sam were able to publicly and openly flaunt their newfound love it was the opposite for Claudia and me. We had to continue to do our best to keep it quiet and under the radar. When I went out every Friday and Saturday night I couldn't help but feel a little twinge of jealousy to see my friend Paul so happy. Of course I was also pleased for him, but I realised that because of the manner in which Claudia and I had got together it could never be the same for us. We'd have to continue to keep a low profile for the time being. We wouldn't be free to enjoy the honeymoon period that other new lovers did. We'd have to keep our love as quiet and secret as we could.

Even so it appeared Claudia's former boyfriend had also now learned about my existence. Perhaps our phone calls had been overheard. Perhaps we'd been spotted talking intimately once too often. Whatever the reason he now knew who I was, and I knew who he was. He was called Mike. Like me he was a fellow Arsenal football fan. In different circumstances we could have been friends. In fact we had some mutual friends already it seemed. But these weren't the circumstances in which we could possibly be friends. Newly single he was now starting to go out again. It wasn't long before our paths crossed. Clearly I'd been pointed out to him. On several evenings when Claudia was still away there were some awkward stand-offs between his friends and mine. It was obvious to me he was being encouraged by his mates to do some physical damage to me. He was a big guy, as I was myself, but he was more muscular and I had no wish whatsoever to tussle with him, if it could possibly be avoided. On several occasions I feared the simmering tension might boil over into blows. Fortunately it didn't, but I understood that for the time being going out would never be quite the same again, and wouldn't be an option for Claudia and me whilst Mike was still on the scene.

After what seemed like an eternity of waiting, and a ton of long-distance phone calls, texts and emails, Claudia eventually finished her placement and came home. My first hint that our relationship might not be quite as simple as I hoped came on the very first day she arrived back. I'd arranged to cook lunch for her in my new flat. I'd been out in the morning and bought a plentiful supply of food and wine. I planned to present her with a starter, main course and dessert, washed down with as much alcohol as she could drink. My new kitchen was more conducive to the enjoyment of cooking, and I was looking forward to making a meal for Claudia on her return. I had most of the food preparation done and had started the cooking, when I texted her to check what time she was coming over. She was having trouble with her hair and was in a mood, she replied. I had hoped she was as desperate to see me as I was her. Apparently not, she was more concerned with her hair and that it wouldn't sit right. When she failed to arrive at the agreed time I decided to ring her. She was still more concerned about her hair than the meal I'd cooked that was about to be spoilt.

'I don't care about your hair,' I said. 'Hair doesn't matter. I just want to see you.'

'It does matter,' Claudia replied. 'It looks awful. I can't go out like this,' she continued.

'But I've gone to a lot of effort to cook for you, and the food is ready,' I said. 'We haven't seen each other for weeks. I've been looking forward to this more than you can imagine. I've been counting the days off. They couldn't pass quickly enough for me.'

Claudia simply let out an irritable grunt. What had happened to the lovely, sweet girl I'd been entranced by on so many evenings in our local nightclub? What had happened to the darling companion I'd taken to Bournemouth? Clearly Claudia was rather more complicated than I realised. To my cost I was soon to discover with every day that passed she was very much more difficult than I could ever have imagined. But I didn't care then. It was early days. I was totally besotted and totally in love. I just wanted to see her. I just wanted her to come over. I just hadn't anticipated this peculiar complication. I could scarcely believe what I was hearing. She was all for cancelling altogether, simply because her hair wouldn't sit exactly as she wanted.

After a huge amount of cajoling and persuasion, that it would be a pity to waste the food I'd prepared, Claudia was eventually persuaded to come over several hours later. She only lived down the road, but it was late afternoon before she finally turned up. I gave her a huge welcoming hug and kiss. I didn't feel it was entirely reciprocated. She sat and ate her food in rather moody silence. Still I was thrilled simply to have her there. I hadn't seen her since Bournemouth. My face was beaming with pleasure, just for her finally to be with me. I fired all kinds of eager questions at her, anxious to find out how she'd been and what she'd been doing, but to my disappointment all I got was rather short, monotone replies.

'Do you like the new flat?' I asked, changing the subject.

'It's all right,' she answered rather gloomily and unenthusiastically.

'I like it a lot,' I said. 'I think it will be perfect for me.'

'It's a bit cold,' Claudia said, letting out a fake shudder, as if it was freezing, when in fact the kitchen was illuminated by bright, balmy sunshine and warmed by the heat of the oven.

'I got the cheque from the house this week,' I continued. 'I'll be a rich man, at least for a few months.'

'All right for some,' Claudia retorted. 'I'm as poor as a church mouse,'

I decided to ply her with more drink to try and improve her mood. Slowly she cheered up, but it was hard work. I started to wonder quite what I'd got hold of and what I'd let myself in for. Even so I was still pleased to see her and persuaded her to stay the night with me. Claudia's moodiness also extended to the bedroom. I soon found out she was a bad combination of being both demanding in bed, yet awkward and unrelaxed at the same time. It put me on edge and ill at ease when we were making love. On the one hand she expected to be generously pleasured. On the other hand she had all kinds of hang-ups about how and where she was touched. I found it hard to get it right with her, and pretty soon started to feel more than a little inadequate in that department. Sex was meant to be fun, a pleasure, but with Claudia I found that it was an ordeal to be endured rather than enjoyed. Often I just wanted to get it over and done with, rather than it bringing any real pleasure and enjoyment. It was totally stressing me out and putting me off. I confessed to both Paul and Sandy that I found sex with her difficult and it wasn't the natural, easy experience I'd anticipated and hoped for. Maybe we just weren't right for each other, I wondered.

If that wasn't enough, when the sex was over she had all kinds of peculiar bedtime rituals before she could sleep. She was paranoid about staying awake, and if she couldn't nod off to sleep quickly it was an excuse for another terrible and terrifying mood. I came quickly to dread bedtimes with her. I daren't make the slightest noise or movement, lest it disturb her. As a result it often caused me to lie wide awake far longer than I needed, just to try and ensure that Claudia had slept. If she hadn't I knew that in the morning she would be like a bear with a sore head. She'd be in a frightful temper and there would be absolutely no speaking to her until the afternoon.

Our relationship was further complicated by the fact that I continued to get long, depressed phone calls from Roxanne at all hours of the day and night. She was Grace's mother. I felt I had to answer them. Despite the fact she'd finally admitted this Roy was more than just a friend, she was still clearly far from happy. A lot of the time she felt suicidal, she said. I didn't know what to say. I reminded her she had much to live for – a new home, a new man, money from the house, a new job to look forward to when her course ended. But it wasn't easy hearing her so down and lonely. I felt sorry for her, but she'd pushed us down the route towards divorce. She'd no longer wanted to be together. She'd pushed me into the arms of Claudia.

On weekends I had Grace, Claudia often chose to go away to see old university friends. She had frequent reunions with them, often with her ex-boyfriend Mike in attendance. For the sake of their friends and friendship they remained on polite and superficially good terms. Mike had allowed Claudia to stay on in their old flat until the end of her course, for that year at least. I even stayed there myself with her some nights after we'd been out, as it was nearer to town. It was an odd situation all round. It was strange for me, that Claudia and Mike still saw so much of each other in a social environment. Her weekends with him were invariably drug fuelled, as they enhanced them with late-night cocaine and ecstasy binges, something as a young father I wasn't tremendously comfortable with. That said, under Claudia's bad influence, most nights I too now accompanied my regular bottle of wine with an increasing number of spliffs.

Even so, as with most things, the early days with Claudia were the best. Thanks to the money I'd received from the house I was able to cut back my hours at work a little. And because of the problems going out where we lived I regularly took Claudia away for weekends, paying for guest houses in Bristol, Bath, Glastonbury, Wells, Padstow, Boscastle and Newquay, among other West Country destinations. For the time being I could afford it, so why not make the most of the opportunities to escape? I thought. They might not come again. Those times were the nicest, when life was like one long holiday. Claudia was tall, slender and striking. Despite her moods I was delighted to have landed her. I was like the cat that had got the cream. I also cared about Grace of course, but hardly cared about anything else in my life. That was it. I had Claudia. That was all I needed to be happy. When we were away together I felt like I didn't have a care in the world. After all I'd been through life was to be enjoyed. I wanted to treat Claudia. I wanted to show her my love and appreciation. I paid for everything. She didn't pay for a thing. I was so in love that I didn't even notice at the time.

I was mystified by her moodiness and tendency to sulk over trivia like her hair, but I put up with it. I didn't complain. I wasn't the easiest person in the world to live with myself. I was a mild sufferer of Obsessive-compulsive disorder, and as such was something of a control freak. I liked things as I liked them. I liked everything in its place. It almost physically hurt when things weren't as I wished them to be. But I wasn't a patch on Claudia. She could be extraordinarily difficult. Because of her sleep issues, at weekends she often didn't emerge until late morning or the beginning of the afternoon. Very early on both Grace and I learnt to tiptoe around her, lest we dare wake her from her slumber before she was ready. If we did it was unlikely she'd have a good word to say to anybody that entire day. I quickly learned to fear her moods. She could keep them going longer than any person I'd ever known. If something set her off it was likely the entire weekend would be a write-off.

Despite this moodiness of character we still had some great times in those early days. When we didn't go away for the whole weekend we often enjoyed long day trips out in the car, sometimes travelling great distances to get away from where we lived, leaving the controversy our love affair had seemingly caused far behind. It was now summer. The evenings were long and light. We often enjoyed a drink or a meal in a picturesque town or city far away, before contemplating the drive back. When we eventually returned to my flat we'd sit at the glass table in my newly rented kitchen, sharing a bottle of wine or two, whilst watching the sun go down. On some Sundays when I had Grace, Claudia would

160

join us on a visit to some local, child-friendly destination or attraction. They seemed to get on all right. Claudia wasn't that keen on children, but despite that she was polite and pleasant to Grace. I could tell she was making an effort and trying her best to befriend my young daughter.

As we were still keeping a low profile in terms of going out, sometimes at weekends we invited friends over to the flat. It had a large front room and was ideally suited to the purpose. Paul, Sam, Sandy, Steve, Cliff, Cally, Mattie and the rest would all come over and join us. Our parties soon started to become the stuff of legend. Thanks to the house sale I wasn't short of money at that time. I could afford to be generous. There were always copious supplies of alcohol and food to be enjoyed by our guests. The drink flowed. The pizzas and nibbles never stopped coming. There was plenty of weed to be smoked, for those who wanted it.

On other occasions we organised big communal gatherings of all our friends at the local curry house. We normally ended up booking a table for at least a dozen. Again wine was drunk in industrial amounts. We almost all ended up highly inebriated by the end of the night. At these meals Sandy liked to take centre stage. Giddily drunk he would stand up and serenade fellow diners with a selection of eighties' classics, despite all of us imploring him to shut up. He wouldn't listen. Once in full swing there was no stopping him. But it was harmless fun. Yes, they were good times then. My marriage was almost forgotten. I was dating a younger woman. I felt like I was young again. I only had responsibility for Grace every other weekend. To all intents and purposes I was free to do what I wanted. It must have been harder for Roxanne, but that wasn't my fault. She too had a new house and a new man.

As our summer of love continued Mike announced he was selling his flat and Claudia would have to move out. In fairness to him he'd let her stay on until the end of the summer term, but he couldn't let her stay there forever. It wasn't fair. Besides, he needed the money. He also wanted to move on with his life and put the memories of what had happened behind him. I didn't blame him. I still felt a degree of shame for what I'd done to him. It wasn't like me not to behave like a gentleman. I can only say on this particular occasion I just couldn't help myself. My feelings of desire for Claudia had just been too strong. I would have done almost anything to be with her. I had to have her, whatever the consequences and whoever got in the way. Sadly this time

Mike had got in the way. I didn't know what had come over me. It was as if I'd been possessed and bewitched by longing and desire. All logic on the matter had vanished. It was nothing personal against Mike. I'd just done what I had to do and what was necessary to get Claudia. I was very sorry I'd hurt someone in the process. It wasn't my wish or intention to do so. It was just an unfortunate and difficult situation. I wouldn't have blamed him if he had beaten me up. I would probably have deserved it in truth. Now Claudia had to move out there was the question of where she was going to live. As she'd been contributing towards the mortgage for some years she was getting a small percentage of the flat sale. That at least was good news to her.

'I'll get a flat with Sam,' she announced.

I wasn't quite sure if she was joking or if she was being serious. She spent most nights at my place anyway, so that was the obvious choice. I wondered if she was just testing me, in her usual contrary and contradictory manner.

'Don't be ridiculous. You'll come and live with me of course,' I stated in response.

'I refuse to be a burden on you or anyone,' she said.

'You wouldn't be a burden,' I explained. 'I want you here. I want you to live with me. It will be just perfect,' I said.

'No, it will be better if I get somewhere with Sam,' she insisted.

I wasn't sure if she meant it, or if she was just playing a game. Of course in the end I ended up begging her to move in, probably as she'd planned all along.

'You won't even have to pay any rent at first; only when you can afford it,' I promised.

The prospect of rent-free accommodation seemed to sway her to my way of thinking. Slightly reluctantly, she agreed. I gave her a huge hug and a kiss on the lips.

'I love you,' I said. 'You're amazing.'

'I love you too,' Claudia replied.

I'm not sure if she did and if she truly meant it, but it was still nice to hear. So by the end of the summer Claudia had moved in with me. Our happiness was short lived, however. As soon as she returned to her course for the start of the autumn term it was announced she'd have to go away again. This time she was being sent on a placement to the delights of Swansea Prison. At least it was a city I was familiar with, from my years spent at university in Wales. That in itself was a small blessing.

Chapter Nineteen

Having not long got Claudia back I was dreading her having to go away again. After all she'd only just moved in with me. She was still settling in. We were still getting to know each other. It had turned out she wasn't quite the bright, pleasant, easy-going girl I'd imagined her to be. She was indeed bright, but she was also complicated, moody and difficult. At her worst she was the most stubborn, bloody-minded, awkward person I'd ever met in my life. In fact I wasn't quite sure how I'd come to choose her. I'd just been uncontrollably drawn towards her, as if by some mystical power I couldn't resist, deny or argue with. It had seemed beyond my control, and beyond all rationality, logic or reason. I simply had to be with her, whatever the costs, whatever the price involved and the consequences. It had been the final nail in the coffin of my marriage to Roxanne. But that was a price I'd had to pay and been willing to pay. Now I was with Claudia, just as I wanted. And yet almost immediately she was forced to leave me again for most of the autumn academic term. It wasn't a fantastic prospect after all I'd been through to get her, but nothing had been easy for us. We'd both had partners when we'd first met. We'd had to keep our relationship secret. Even when we became an official couple we still had to keep a low profile. This was just yet another obstacle to be overcome.

As it turned out the time Claudia was away again passed quite quickly and was nowhere near as bad as I feared and anticipated. In fact, as Claudia herself observed, they turned out to be some of the best times we'd spent together to date. Claudia came home as often as she could at weekends during her placement, and I took the train up to see her a number of times. Flush with money from the house I could afford to take time off work pretty much whenever I wanted. So whenever Claudia felt she could fit it in I took a few days off to go up and see her. It wasn't like the period she'd been in Brighton, when I'd hardly seen her at all. This time it worked out quite well. It didn't matter that Claudia had to work at the prison during the majority of the daytimes. I was happy to wander round the streets of Swansea, reacquainting myself with the sights and landmarks I'd known as a history undergraduate from the ages of eighteen to twenty-one several decades earlier. I'd enjoyed my days in Swansea, and I was only too happy to go back to see how the city had changed. In some ways it had changed quite a lot. In other ways it had barely changed at all.

I was much taken with the new Dylan Thomas Centre, which was an addition to the city's cultural and artistic heritage since the time I'd been a student there, and a considerable asset in my humble opinion. It had its own café bar, and on a number of occasions I enjoyed lunch in the gently impressive surroundings. More than once Claudia joined me. It was a pleasure to be able to treat her. I was inspired by the words and images of the late, great Welsh poet that were on display. It encouraged me to pick up a pocket notebook and start jotting down some new poems myself. The nearby marina was also much improved and visually far more welcoming than when I'd lived in Swansea. It had once been a scene of post-industrial dereliction. Now it had been redeveloped and could have been a harbour in a glamorous Mediterranean resort. It wouldn't have seemed out of place.

The city's museum also lay in the Maritime Quarter, and I was happy quietly to idle away some time there, recalling exhibits I'd known as a student. Even better was the refurbished industrial museum, now known as The National Waterfront Museum, also on the marina, which I was happy to go back to time and again. With numerous displays and artefacts on the industrial past of Wales it was a joy to visit. I also took the opportunity to revisit The Glynn Vivian Art Gallery and the famous Brangwyn Hall. I looked round the shops of The Quadrant Shopping Centre and stalls of the legendary Swansea Indoor Market, known for its Welsh food produce, including cockles, laverbread and Welsh cakes. When I'd lived in Swansea it had always had more than its fair share of rain. By contrast on the occasions I visited in the autumn of 2002 the weather was largely fine.

I took the opportunity to walk down Oystermouth Road, with its views of Swansea Bay, to the main university campus. There were many more cafés and bars on site than there had been in my day. I was happy to sit in more than one, taking in the scenery and recalling my time as an undergraduate. Of course it brought back many memories. I remembered the faces of friends not seen since. I wondered how they were and what they were doing now. I reflected on my own life, both its successes and failures. Some things had worked out as I wanted them. Some hadn't. I hadn't done all I wanted, hoped for and expected. I hadn't become the great writer I imagined I would be. There was still time, I told myself, though it was slowly slipping away.

I took a bus down to The Mumbles and enjoyed a few beers in some of the pubs Dylan Thomas had frequented as a young man. His photographs adorned the walls, as did some of his poems. I'd drunk in many of these pubs as a student. They hadn't changed much. Their significance had meant less to me then. It had been lost. Now as an adult, and as a minor published poet myself, they held more importance to me. I hoped they would be allowed to remain as they were, basic, rustic and unaltered, a small part of the Welsh literary and drinking heritage. It would be a shame to see them turned into modern theme bars. That would be a tragedy, I thought, though at the same time it seemed inevitable with ever-changing tastes and social habits.

It was nice to get away. It was nice to have a little time by myself. I was able to make sense of some of the events of the last year. I was able to come to terms with them. I was able to understand and digest them a little more. I was no longer married. I was no longer a homeowner. Grace no longer lived with me. I now had a new girlfriend, and a largely new circle of friends. The friends I'd had when I was with Roxanne had in the main vanished from my life. They'd stuck with Roxanne. They'd deserted me en masse. It didn't matter. It wasn't important. I had new people to hang out with, like work colleagues Paul and Sandy, both of whom I'd grown very fond of.

The time away was actually good for me and Claudia. In the evenings I took her out for dinner in the city's restaurants, or we enjoyed wine and food in the room where she was staying. It worked wonders for our sex life too. For the first time I felt able to relax when I was making love to her, and it felt much better for both of us. Of course it wasn't all perfect. Several times she came home and for some reason or other was in a terrible mood. If she arrived in a bad mood from being overtired and travelling after a hard week, in all likelihood she would stay in the same foul temper the whole weekend. More than once this happened. Several times I booked a romantic meal out for us on the Saturday night, only to have to cancel at the last moment, because her hair wouldn't sit as she wanted, or she had a cold sore or some other minor ailment. It was very frustrating, but I learnt to live with it. When times were good they were very good, and during her months in Swansea there were many more good times than bad ones.

When her placement finally finished and she was back for good, I looked through all the poems I'd written during my various stays in Swansea, as well as the poems I'd scribbled down during the months of my dying relationship with Roxanne and our eventual splitting up. There were more than enough to form a new collection, even though I now considered myself more of a novelist than a poet. I got in touch with the publishers at *Poetry Now*, who'd been supportive of my work in the past. They were more than happy to help me put another collection out. It was entitled *Miscellaneous Thoughts*. It was part of their *Slim Volumes* series, and in many ways it was my first properly bound, full collection of poems in book form. Most of my previous efforts had been small pamphlets. After twenty odd years of writing it was nice finally to have a proper book of poetry out. It wasn't quite Dylan Thomas, but it wasn't bad and I was quite proud of it.

During the daytimes when Claudia was at college and before I had to go to work myself I continued typing my latest novel, *Daydreamers*. It was progressing at a fair pace. I was enjoying the escape of writing it. It took me to another place, one which in my mind was almost as real as the actual world I lived in. To me at times the two seemed to merge and I could barely tell them apart. It was one of the joys of writing. It allowed me to create parallel universes in my head, with characters and events that to me seemed as genuine as those that really existed and occurred in real life. I was completely lost and absorbed in the project. It wasn't long before it was finished. As always I had high hopes for it and sent it off to prospective publishers and agents with a high degree of expectation. One or two showed a little interest, but again it came to nothing. As with previous ventures it wasn't long before I got over my sense of disappointment and dejection and was starting something new.

I decided to write a novel set against the background of the first gigs I'd attended as a teenager. I'd been a middle-class punk rocker at the time, into the bands that were popular then like *The Clash*, *The Stranglers* and *Siouxsie and The Banshees*. As soon as I'd turned sixteen, together with a childhood friend we'd gone to as many gigs as we could. Attending many of them also was a girl I'd had a huge, schoolboy crush on. Dressed in black leather, to me she was a vision of pure loveliness. Of course in reality I never got to date her. I knew her well enough to talk to, but no more. In my novel, which I titled *Young Punks*, I imagined what might have happened if I had got together with her. My novel allowed me to live out my teenage fantasy. In my story I got the girl that I had no chance of getting in actuality. Pretty soon I was absorbed in the writing of this latest novel. I loved working on it, metaphorically putting pen to paper as often as time allowed, and very soon a number of chapters were complete.

In fact I did have a girl, just not the one in my novel. It was no longer Roxanne either. It was Claudia, someone altogether more complex and difficult. Though I had by now become accustomed to some of her peculiarities and learnt to live with them and cope with them as best I could. It was still a learning process. Claudia was one of the most paranoid people I'd ever met. She imagined the entire world was staring at her, talking about her behind her back and commenting on her appearance. Naturally they weren't. They had no interest in her at all, but she wouldn't be convinced. She was certain fate and the world in general had it in for her. She was jealous of anyone and everyone who appeared to have anything better, even though for the most past this perceived better luck and good fortune others had was entirely without foundation and a complete figment of her imagination. Often those she resented were nowhere near as well off as she was herself. I found it strange. Her distorted perception was odd, but nothing could persuade her otherwise. In her head she was the ugliest and unluckiest girl on the planet. It couldn't have been further from the truth. Nothing I said could reassure her. She lived with this false view of what she looked like and how she was perceived.

Her paranoia extended to almost all avenues of life. If we went out for a meal and ordered the exact same dishes, when they came out she'd be convinced I'd been given a bigger portion than she had. An angry scowl would start to spread across her face, and then quickly turn to raging fury. She'd complain bitterly that I'd been given more chips and would start counting them. She'd comment I had a larger slice or even a bigger plate. What's more the waiter or waitress had deliberately given her less. She'd be certain of it. I'd have to offer to swap. I'd let her have my plate. I didn't care. I'd do whatever it took to keep her in a good mood. I feared her temper and her moods. I couldn't bear it when she sulked. The sulks would last for hours, sometimes even days. But for all that I loved her totally and completely. I remained besotted, for all her faults and awkwardness. I have no idea why. A spell had been cast on me.

In the summer of 2003 Claudia finished her degree. She got a first. I wasn't surprised. At least I was right about something, that she was bright. She was difficult. She was hard work, but she was intelligent. She deserved her first-class degree. She'd worked hard for it, and she'd got the reward. She did better than all her friends, who mainly got 2:1s and 2:2s. It would put Claudia in an advantageous position to get a decent job, and she started applying for suitable positions straight away. It wasn't long before she secured interviews for a number of possible jobs. She prepared carefully for each of them, and got offered one almost immediately, which she was happy to accept.

The job was located at a hospital about ten miles from where we lived. The money was very good. Claudia talked about getting the bus there in the morning, but like the fool I was I wouldn't hear of it. Despite the fact that I worked evenings, when Claudia took up her new post I got up early every day and drove the ten miles there to drop her, before driving the ten miles back to get ready for my own work. Of course Claudia didn't appreciate it. She didn't thank me. She just took it for granted. She never contributed towards the cost of the petrol either. I always paid for it, despite the fact Claudia was now earning much more than I was. She rarely showed any appreciation for anything anyone did for her. She probably saw the kindness as a form of weakness and stupidity that she was happy to take advantage of. She did at least start to contribute towards the cost of our rent now she was working, though I continued to pay the lion's share.

It was peculiar. As soon as she began her new job, Claudia was earning twice as much as I was but still looked to me to pay for our days out and weekends away whenever we had them. If we had Grace with us of course I had to pay for her too. I was getting through a small fortune, keeping Claudia in the lifestyle she had grown accustomed to. Every night we drank wine and smoked weed, all of which I paid for. Claudia was very happy to share these pleasures, but never once paid for them. She never even offered to contribute. She simply took it for granted that I would provide. I was living way beyond the modest income I earned from the cinema. I was having to dip into the money I'd got from the sale of the house more and more. It had been a fair sum. Slowly but surely it was shrinking, as I paid out for pretty much everything Claudia and I did together.

Meanwhile, unknown to me, she was saving hand over fist. As I splashed out she diligently saved, it turned out for a house she would eventually buy without me. But for now we were living in relative domestic bliss. Or I convinced myself we were. We couldn't have cats or dogs where we rented, so as a compromise we got ourselves a pair of house rabbits. They contributed to the sense of being settled and being in a lasting relationship. Now Claudia had finished her course and had a job I raised the question of marriage. I was keen to commit further,

169

but Claudia wasn't. She wouldn't hear of it. She knocked me back. I was disappointed. She had no interest in it.

'I don't want to get married, and I don't want kids,' she said.

I was quietly devastated. I'd taken it for granted we'd get married one day, and indeed that I'd get the chance to expand my family. I loved children. I wanted more. I wanted to add to the one wonderful daughter I had in Grace. I started to wonder if it would be with Claudia. I retained hope. I was convinced she'd change her mind. I believed once her university friends started getting married and having families of their own, as I knew some were now considering, Claudia would reconsider. She'd become fearful of getting left behind and would become desperate to get married and have children herself. I kept asking her. The answer didn't alter. It was always the same. I eventually realised Claudia was simply too selfish, too self-absorbed and too narcissistic to ever get married, let alone to have children. But still I persisted.

She wasn't willing to get married to me or start a family, but she was willing to let me teach her to learn to drive. So for the ensuing weeks and months I gave up my time and my car, including paying for the increased insurance, and devoted hours to teaching her. She was a good learner, and eventually when it came to take her test passed first time. She bought herself a small car. At least I didn't pay for that, and I didn't have to drive her to work every morning anymore. But I was slow to see I was being used. I existed mainly for Claudia's benefit. But I was to blind and too lovestruck to realise it.

Chapter Twenty

Looking back I find it hard now to recall the years I spent with Claudia and my relationship with her. It's all become a blur. Maybe it was the wine we drank, or the weed we smoked. There were times when we hosted parties and consumed so much we simply fell asleep and woke up to find everyone gone. Whatever the explanation large chunks are now forgotten and I've erased them from my memory. For a long time I wanted to forget. I wanted to blot them out of my mind altogether. I couldn't bear to think about them. I couldn't bear to think about her. What I do recall is largely through a series of weddings and weekends, some I attended, some I didn't.

The early ones were largely good. As time passed they became less successful and increasingly a source of argument, bitterness and recrimination between us. At some point during the early years of our relationship we attended a wedding in Birmingham. At the time it was another welcome opportunity to get away and stay at another hotel together. It went pretty well. Few of Claudia's other friends were attending. It was generally much better when they didn't, and we were able to spend some quality time alone. Claudia got extremely drunk, so much so by the end of the evening she was struggling to stay on her feet. She fell over repeatedly as she tried to dance and I had to help her back up. By at least she was having fun. We both were. It was a pleasant occasion, and apart from a sore head in the morning little lasting damage was done.

It was surprising how often we had reason to go away at weekends. Every few months something else came up. We were invited to a wedding in Kent. A girl called Emma, who'd been on Claudia's course, was getting married to a guy called Nick. They were a nice couple. They lived locally but were getting married on the other side of the country, where Emma had originally been brought up. It was a long trek for us. As Claudia had only just passed her test I was doing most of the driving there and back. I was also paying for the petrol. Emma and Nick were getting married in a local church. The reception was being held in the vast garden and grounds that adjoined Emma's parents' country house, and in which lavish marquees had been erected. The venue was perfect for an outside wedding. Unfortunately despite being high summer they were unlucky with the weather. It rained all day. They didn't take it to heart and made the best of it. Everyone did. Some brides would have been devastated. Emma wasn't like that. She took it in her stride. They still enjoyed their wedding day. To them it was just perfect.

In my experience a wet wedding day can in fact bring good luck and normally leads to a lasting marriage. As far as I know it did in this case and the couple are still together. Wonderful weather on a wedding day conversely doesn't always lead to a lasting marriage in my observation. I had beautiful weather for my first wedding, but that didn't last. Enough said perhaps? I realise my assertion isn't exactly scientifically proved or backed up by empirical evidence. My comments are merely based on personal experience. A few more test cases would be needed, but it's amazing how often it's worked out like that with weddings I've attended.

Despite the weather this one was another success. Claudia and I had a nice time together. Sam also attended, but without Paul. Their relationship had become strained. They had been very close, spending all their time together, but it seemed to have hit the rocks of late. Sam appeared keener to get serious than Paul was. He seemed to have commitment issues, as many of my friends did, like Sandy, Steve and Cliff. I feared Sam and Paul might split up. I wondered what impact that might have on my relationship with Claudia if they did. Sam had become moody and distant, as if she resented the fact Claudia and I were still close, or as if it was somehow my fault she was experiencing problems in her relationship. Paul was a good friend, but very much his own man. Nothing I said was likely to influence him.

The weather the day after the wedding was much better, and they were able to take advantage of the marquees, lighting and garden features that had been carefully erected to host a lavish barbecue. It was a fitting end to a nice weekend. Afterwards Claudia and I began the long journey back. It took about six hours of solid driving to reach home. When we got back to the flat I opened a bottle of wine and Claudia rolled a spliff. It was time to relax, unwind and perhaps celebrate. Claudia had managed to stay in a good mood the entire weekend. That was a rarity in itself and worthy of some form of celebration.

Other weekends weren't as good. Often Claudia went off to Bristol or London to meet up with her various former university friends without me. Despite the fact Claudia now had a new partner and was part of an established couple who lived together, Claudia's ex-boyfriend, Mike, often still went too. It was a rather odd situation for me to find myself in and one I wasn't entirely happy about or comfortable with. Yet I felt powerless to object. Partly consumed by guilt Claudia was determined to remain on good terms with Mike and not cut him out of these events. His presence also meant it was very difficult for me to attend. Instead I stayed at home and looked after Grace, taking her to children's adventure centres, play farms and petting zoos. Claudia meanwhile enjoyed a somewhat different weekend of heavy drinking and hard drugs. When she got back she always delighted in giving me the details, even though she knew how much it annoyed me.

'We were taking MDMA in the club and then snorting lines of coke afterwards until 6am in the morning,' Claudia would proudly announce.

'Why do you tell me this stuff?' I'd ask, wondering why she didn't pick up on the fact it made me irritated and pissed off. 'I really don't want to hear it.'

'We had a great time. I can't wait to go again,' she'd continue, with an underlying implication that the times she had with me weren't as great and were boring in comparison.

'Well I was asleep then, and my daughter was asleep too,' I'd respond, not wanting to hear any more.

These kind of conversations highlighted the fact there was a significant age difference between us and a clear difference in the relative levels of responsibility we each had. I had the responsibilities of a father to a young daughter. Claudia had none of that. She could go off any weekend she wanted and get wasted if the desire so took her. I came to dread her weekends away. They became the source of growing tensions and resentments between us. I imagined her up to all kinds of things. I wished she'd never told me what she did on them. It was best I had no idea, but still she insisted on telling me. Her friends sounded like a bunch of middle-class arseholes, who thought they were being clever taking drugs. They should have known better by now. They were too old for it, but they hadn't grown up yet. I didn't mind a bit of weed, but they could keep the rest of it. They could flush their ecstasy and coke and anything else down the toilet as far as I was concerned. I preferred to spend quality time with my daughter.

Meanwhile Paul and Sam did split up. It had been on the cards for a while, and it finally happened. Sam was devastated. She often came round to our flat afterwards and had tea with us, so she wasn't lonely, but did little more than sulk. Of course it made things awkward when we went out, as I was still friends with Paul. It made things even more awkward when before long Paul started seeing someone else. We tried to keep it quiet and a secret from Sam, but it was inevitable she would find out and eventually she did. She became even more resentful then. It meant there were events we couldn't invite them both too. For a while Sam seemed to hold out a hope they might get back together. It soon became clear it wasn't going to happen. Paul was getting serious with his new girlfriend, Anna. Sam had had enough. She got another job and moved away. This wasn't good news for me. It just meant another person for Claudia to visit at weekends without me.

On one rare occasion I was actually allowed to join Claudia on a weekend in London. I'd started to complain that I was never invited and was always the one to miss out. After all Claudia was always invited to anything I did with my friends. Indeed, she'd started to take over some of the friendships and now texted and rang many of my friends more than I did. She insisted on having the numbers of everyone I knew. Of course she didn't reciprocate. I didn't have the numbers of any of her friends. She guarded that information jealously. Indeed she was obsessed with developing friendships whenever and wherever she could, and at any opportunity that arose. Friends meant far more to her than either family or partners. I wondered if it stemmed from some trauma in her childhood. Perhaps she hadn't been popular as a child. Perhaps she didn't have any friends then. In my observation she clung to friends in grim desperation, like a drowning person clings to a piece of floating debris. I didn't have many friends when I was at school, but I didn't care. It meant nothing to me. During her teenage years Claudia had been packed off to boarding school by parents only too happy to offload her. That was probably the reason she had an almost unnatural dependency and reliance on having friends around her at all times, and had to cultivate new ones whenever the chance presented itself.

I was only allowed to go to London as Mike couldn't go. It was the one and only time I did. I didn't really want to go that much in truth, but I was fed up with never being included and had grown somewhat resentful of that fact. I was included this once. That was enough. For a start it meant a long drive to London. Worse still it meant driving in central London itself, something I had no experience of and was entirely ill-prepared for. Even so one way or another we made it to Claudia's friend's flat where we were staying.

On the first night we went to a rather dull bar in the West End, where we were joined by all of Claudia's other former flatmates from her university years and their partners. There Claudia did something she was prone to do from time to time, which really annoyed and frustrated me. She started talking to a complete stranger. Rather than return to me and her friends after an appropriate period had passed, as most people would, she continued to talk to this younger man for most of the evening. I grew ever more bored, lonely and fed up. I started to sulk, and as the minutes passed and turned into hours my mood darkened. It was as if Claudia had completely forgotten I was with her. She'd become oblivious to my existence. I sat and fumed in silence, not talking to anyone. One of the other boyfriends offered to buy me a short to cheer me up. I wasn't interested. I was quietly livid. I was in such at mood by then I knew I'd find it hard to snap out of it. Even in the taxi back at the end of the night Claudia and I barely spoke.

She'd pulled the same stunt on me several times back at home. Because of the circumstances in which we'd met it was hard for us to get quality time out together. We were always afraid Mike or his friends might show up. Even when we did occasionally get time in a club alone Claudia was prone to spoil it. She would see some guy she was mildly acquainted with or half knew by sight or had met once before and would go off and chat to them. But she wouldn't just say hello or chat to them for five minutes or quarter of an hour and then come back. That would be it for the rest of the evening. I'd see it happening. I'd see it unfolding before my eyes and my heart would sink. Wild horses couldn't drag her away from her conversation. God knows what rubbish she found to talk about. God knows how she kept it going. Maybe it was just some perverse way she had of annoying and upsetting me. It certainly worked. I would silently seethe with rage. When it was eventually time to leave, the evening ruined, we'd walk back not talking to each other.

It wasn't a good start to the weekend. It didn't get a lot better. None of her friends could get up in the morning. I was so bored I took myself off shopping both days. I thought I might as well get to see a bit of London as we were there. Come the afternoons they didn't want to do much more, but laze around chatting. They were happy to smoke the weed I'd bought and brought with me though, whilst not providing any themselves. In the evening we just went out for a meal and to a couple of local pubs. I was only too happy to get the weekend over with. I didn't know then I wouldn't be going again, but if I had known I probably wouldn't have been too bothered. It wasn't my kind of thing.

Little did I know that my one visit to London came at a price. I was expected to reciprocate. A month or two later I had all Claudia's friends and their partners crashing in sleeping bags in our large front room, where our house rabbits also lived. Claudia didn't cook for them or entertain or buy the wine they drank. I had to do all that. I provided and cooked the food. I arranged and paid for the takeaways they ate. I was the lavish host. I gave Claudia's friends the biggest portions. I thought she'd want me to do that. Of course I was wrong. She had such a tantrum over receiving a smaller portion on one occasion that I had to cook a second meal just for her. Of course she didn't thank me. Neither did she thank me for looking after her friends, even after she'd had to go to work and left me with them on the last day. She just expected it. She just took it for granted. For my part I couldn't wait for them to go.

Meanwhile the wedding invitations continued to come thick and fast. More and more of Claudia's old university friends were getting married. Only Claudia steadfastly refused to follow suit. Whenever I mentioned it I got a flat and determined no. I was beginning to despair that she'd ever change her mind, as I'd hoped she would. Indeed it became increasingly obvious she never would do. It wasn't on her agenda. She had no interest in marriage or children. She never would have. I was just wasting my time and my money on her. I was deluded to think otherwise. The more I poured into the relationship, the less I got back and the worse she treated me. I did everything I could to make her life comfortable. I was rewarded with coldness bordering on contempt.

We were soon invited to another wedding in the Home Counties. I don't recall the exact destination, but it was somewhere on the Eastern side of London near the border of Kent and Essex. Again it involved a long drive for us. This time Claudia shared a bit of the driving. Former University friend Caroline was getting married to a posh bloke, who had the appearance of a portly and well-off London stockbroker or similar. Almost everyone there appeared to be ex public school and of rich and well-bred stock, middle class bordering on upper class, except me of course. I was a middle-class Socialist from a state-run comprehensive school. No expense had been spared on the wedding. The wine flowed in abundance. I availed myself of rather too much of it, glass after glass, and peaked too soon. I even fell off my chair at one point during the speeches. When we got back to the hotel where we were all staying I just wanted to go to bed. Claudia and her friends of course wanted to party through the night. I let them get on with it.

Sometime in the middle of the night I woke with a start. I looked at my watch. It was nearly 5am. I realised Claudia still hadn't come back. I felt a little sick, confused and worried. I had no idea where she was. I went to look for her. I knocked on the door where a number of the other girls were staying. They didn't answer for a long time. I knocked again and kept knocking. I was getting more concerned. Eventually someone stirred.

'Do you know where Claudia is?' I shouted through the keyhole. 'She hasn't come back yet.'

'She isn't with us. She left ages ago,' someone replied.

'Do you know where she went?' I asked. 'She hasn't been back to our room.'

'No idea sorry. Now we need to get some sleep,' the voice continued rather grumpily.

'Are you sure she didn't say anything about where she was going?' I pressed.

'Maybe she went to the shop. There's a 24-hour garage opposite,' I heard someone suggest.

'OK, thanks,' I replied.

I wasn't really dressed for it, but I went to the garage. Of course she wasn't there. I was suddenly even more worried. Her friends had gone to bed, but Claudia hadn't. It was nearly morning. Where on earth could she have gone? I went back to our room to see if she had turned up there. She hadn't. I splashed some water on my face to wake up fully and put on some proper clothes. I went in search for her again. Eventually some time between 6am and 7am I found Claudia sitting on a grass verge outside the hotel with one of the other boyfriends from the wedding. I could tell she'd been crying. Furthermore my intuition told me she'd been talking about me, or more accurately complaining about me I suspected. It was a very odd scene and an odd situation. The other man jumped up. I could tell he was about to protest his innocence and that nothing untoward had happened.

'I don't want to hear it,' I muttered angrily.

I then turned to Claudia.

'Let's just get to bed,' I said to her and started to trudge back.

Reluctantly she followed me back to our room. On the long drive back afterwards I had to stop the car several times to allow Claudia to be sick. In many ways the wedding was the beginning of the end of our relationship. I became increasingly aware that Claudia was slagging me off behind me back, both to her friends and to her parents, who lived near Leeds and we occasionally went to stay with. She was turning them all against me. She was making me out to be the villain of the peace. If only they knew what she was really like behind closed doors. If only they had the slightest inclination how difficult she was and what I had to put up with. She complained I was controlling and wouldn't let her do anything. It was ironic. She was the most controlling person I'd ever met. She controlled and manipulated every situation through her moods.

What was true and what I was increasingly coming to realise was we simply weren't suited to each other. I started to think I'd have been better off staying with Roxanne and making a go of my marriage. I started to think I'd made a massive mistake, one I was beginning to regret. My money was running out, and Claudia was slipping away with it. Meanwhile Roxanne's relationship with Roy had also disintegrated. She and Grace were back living at home with her parents, but Roxanne had already met someone else. She was seeing a fireman called Chris, but even that seemed to be on and off. It seemed that neither one of us could forge a relationship that lasted. Despite everything I still loved Claudia, but now it seemed more an act of desperation. I was clinging on, unable to let go. I'd poured so much effort and affection into our relationship. It was hard to admit it wasn't working. I couldn't admit to myself I was failing again. Although I noticed when I told Claudia I loved her now she rarely or never said it back. She clearly didn't love me anymore.

Another wedding followed, this time in Cambridge. I was anxious for there to be no repeat of what had happened at Caroline's wedding. I didn't want to wake up in the middle of the night with Claudia missing again, wondering what had happened to her. I didn't want to have to go looking for her once more. I could tell her friends were unimpressed that I'd looked for her the last time in the way I had. One even said as much. They left me in no doubt that I was now on some kind of probation with them, guilty until or unless I proved otherwise. They were much less friendly towards me now. They behaved in a more cool and distant way, barely speaking in my direction. I was getting the cold shoulder from all of them.

I could tell Claudia had been poisoning them against me. God knows what she found to tell them. Heaven knew what she'd been saying. I'd been nothing but a loving and dutiful boyfriend. Apparently that wasn't enough. Not that I was bothered what they thought. It just turned me against them in equal measure. At the wedding I barely spoke to them. At the end I whisked Claudia off in a taxi back to our hotel. She was drunk already. She didn't need to stay up the entire night, taking drugs and drinking more. I didn't give her so-called friends a chance to tempt her. When the wedding was over we left immediately. Frankly it was a relief just to get her back to our room without the same shit happening, and without having to stay up half the night. We were drunk enough. We didn't need to spoil it.

One more weekend followed. We went to stay with some of Claudia's friends in Bristol. One had a new boyfriend she wanted everyone to meet. I cut a solitary and lonely figure. I was present, but there was a growing distance between myself and the rest of them. I'd started to resent Claudia's friends. She'd poisoned their minds against me, with her litany of unjustified complaints made when I wasn't there. I was certain they were all telling her it was time she left me. I was holding her back. I was stopping her doing what she wanted. She played her part of the abused, controlled victim well. They had no idea about the truth of our relationship and what she was really like. They had no idea the hoops I jumped through for her and the eggshells both Grace and I trod on around her. They'd never know.

I'd financed Claudia through the end of her degree and whilst starting a new job. I'd let her stay in my flat free of rent. I'd lavished her with gifts. I'd paid for our food, our wine, our day trips and weekends away. I hadn't complained about her continued relationship with her ex-boyfriend and their many weekends together without me. I'd tolerated her drug taking. I'd taught her to drive. I'd helped her find a car. I'd offered to marry her and have a family with her. I even found myself agreeing to move into a new flat, even though I didn't want to. I was happy where we were. But none of it was enough. Nothing ever was.

One more wedding came up. This time it was in Switzerland. A girl Claudia had got to know in her gap year was getting married there. It was a girl I'd met at the wedding in Birmingham, when things had been altogether better between us. She was a nice girl, but there was no way I was going to Switzerland for her wedding. I couldn't afford it for a start. I couldn't get the time off work. And it included a weekend I had Grace anyway.

'I can't go by myself,' Claudia shouted aggressively.

'Of course you can,' I replied. 'You're always complaining I don't let you do stuff. Now here's your chance. Go and enjoy yourself.'

Maybe Claudia wasn't quite as keen and ready to do things without me as she claimed. She was furious. I barely noticed. I'd been drinking wine and smoking a little pot. I went to the kitchen to refill my glass. When I opened the door and went back into our front room, I was dimly aware of Claudia's glass whistling through the air in my direction. It was coming straight towards me and it caught me just above the eye. The glass shattered in an instant, breaking into dozens of glittering, glistening shards and sharp, angular pieces, which crashed onto the floor beneath me. I couldn't believe it. She'd finally gone mad. She'd actually thrown a glass at my head. It was hard to comprehend. A trickle of warm blood ran down the side of my face. I ignored it and sat back down to continue drinking my wine. I knew then at that moment our relationship was as good as over.

To take my minds off things I feverishly continued to write as much and as often as I could, particularly in the mornings when Claudia had gone to work and I had the place to myself. I finished my latest novel *Young Punks*, and whilst I started editing it I immediately began work on a new book. It was a nostalgic, mainly autobiographical reflection on my childhood entitled *Growing Up in the Seventies*. With things rapidly unravelling with Claudia I wrote it as a means of escapism. It got me thinking about happier times when I was young. I also took the time finally to compile an anthology of all the best short stories I'd written and been stockpiling for the last few years in one collection. I called it *The Word*. With the help of the fiction department of *Forward Press*, who produced the *Poetry Now* series I regularly appeared in, I managed to publish a limited edition of the collection in bound book form.

I also pressed on with the poetry writing in a near frenzy of literary activity, which continued throughout 2004. I'd had a few poems published in a poetry magazine called *Rubies in the Darkness*. The magazine also published small pamphlets and collections through their inhouse imprint *Feather Books*. I got in touch and managed to arrange publication of a new short collection titled *An Essentially English Voice*. It was my usual wistful and melancholic musings on love, life, regret and disappointment. A number of the poems were no doubt inspired by Claudia. They explored my continued failure to achieve a lasting relationship. It was an ongoing theme. I didn't seem to have trouble meeting women. I moved in with them, and for a while it usually worked, just as it had worked with Roxanne initially, and Judy at first before that. I just wasn't very good at making things last, it seemed. Now things were falling apart with Claudia too.

Even so a few weeks later, and despite the fact I didn't want to leave where we were living, on Claudia's insistence we moved into a new flat. The people who lived both above and below us where we'd been were probably delighted to see us go. They'd no doubt grown sick of hearing our unruly social gatherings, fights and arguments. Those above and below us in the new place, where we again had the middle flat, wouldn't be so lucky. I wasn't quite sure why we were doing it. We clearly weren't getting on. I was happy where I was. The new place was smaller and more expensive. As I was letting Claudia go to the wedding in Switzerland without me, so if I'd had any sense I should have let her move to the new flat without me. I didn't. Out of some false sense of loyalty I went with her. It was another mistake. I was learning Claudia wasn't just psychologically abusive she was physically abusive too. She would only get worse.

Chapter Twenty-One

By the beginning of 2005, just three years after we'd first officially got together, Claudia and I found ourselves living in a new flat, but our new surroundings didn't bring a change in fortune. Our relationship had deteriorated badly during that time. Things weren't the same between us and as they had been when we'd first met. We no longer even had the escape of hosting lavish, drunken parties, as we'd had before. Our very first party, a housewarming one, prompted complaints to the landlord from our neighbours above about the rowdy behaviour. We couldn't have any more. In our new home we had to live in near total quiet. I found it highly restrictive and I never felt comfortable or relaxed there. I regretted moving almost immediately. I'd been happy where we were. Our new flat might have looked a little tidier and smarter, but looks could be deceptive. I couldn't even strum my acoustic guitar or play a CD in the daytime without our neighbours complaining. They were totally unreasonable. They expected us to live as if we were on some kind of communal retreat and had taken a vow of silence. I couldn't live like that. The floors and walls were clearly paper thin. Even whispered voices travelled and could be heard. They could hear us. We could hear them. It didn't suit me at all. I wasn't sure Claudia could live like that for long either. But as moving had been her idea, for a while at least she put on a brave face about the problems it had inadvertently created. She falsely maintained the pretence that all was well.

She'd also cultivated a new friend and was feeling rather pleased with herself. Several years earlier, before he'd met Sam or his latest girlfriend, Anna, Paul had briefly dated a young German au pair called Cynthia. As usual it hadn't been long before he'd moved on to another female companion, as soon as boredom had started to set in, and before the relationship with Cynthia had a chance to go anywhere. I liked Paul. He was mild-mannered, good-natured, gentlemanly and charming. If he had one fault it was his reluctance to commit to a single woman long term. Ever since I'd known him he'd had a habit of moving from one female to the next at almost indecent speed, always oblivious to the destruction he left in his wake at each failed relationship. He was the ultimate serial monogamist. He was never alone long. With his charm someone new always quickly entered his life. Sam had been very hurt when he'd left her somewhat abruptly and with little warning. Cynthia had taken it a little better, when earlier the same had happened to her, but I still felt bad for her. As a result ever after I'd continued to go out of my way still to involve her in our social activities. It was a kindness on my part I was to come to regret.

Cynthia started to come round to our flat for tea. Claudia and I would take turns cooking for her. Cynthia started to come round a little too often for my liking, but Claudia seemed to be in her element. She loved it. Pretty soon Cynthia started accompanying us on our trips to the cinema. As a manager there I was entitled to free tickets, popcorn and drinks. Cynthia began to share these privileges. She expected them, as far as I could tell. She thought they were hers by right. I noted there was no question of her going if she ever had to pay for her own ticket and drink. She only liked a free trip. She started to join us all the time. I wouldn't have minded if she occasionally offered to buy me a drink when we were out in return, to say thank you. She never did. Neither did she ever reciprocate by offering to cook for us. As far as I could see it was a totally one-way street, an arrangement to favour her only. Some weeks she was round at our flat having tea with us as many as two or three times, just like Sam had done before. I wouldn't have minded so much, except Claudia wouldn't allow my friends, Paul or Sandy, to come over at all. It hardly seemed fair. I was beginning to grow resentful. I felt I was being taken for a ride. My good nature was being taken advantage of. I stopped thinking of Cynthia by name. I started to think of her as just *The German*, or as things deteriorated more simply as *The Germ*.

Things took a further turn for the worse when Claudia stopped coming out on Saturday daytimes altogether. For some years we had enjoyed regular day trips in the car, sometimes just the two of us, sometimes with Grace as well. Suddenly these stopped. Claudia announced in future she'd be meeting Cynthia for coffee in town on Saturdays. I was hardly pleased. I was furious in fact. Our Saturdays had been the main quality time we'd had together. Now that was being taken by someone else. But it appeared that was how things were going to be, and I was stuck with it. Partly out of a sense of bloody-mindedness I carried on going out on Saturdays anyway, one weekend by myself, one weekend with Grace too. I started to invite Sandy along. He was now single again. He'd left his partner Joan in search of new and greener pastures. They hadn't materialised. He realised too late he'd made a terrible mistake, but there was no going back. The damage had been done and he had to make the best of it until he found someone new himself. It would take a while. Until that time he regularly started tagging along with us. I found I had much in common with him. We grew close. We engaged in long, thoughtful conversation. We were sometimes mistaken for a gay couple. We even jokingly called ourselves *The Odd Couple*, after the Jack Lemmon/Walter Matthau film. The description seemed to fit. We felt as if we were exactly that. Though I'm not sure which of us was which of the two late, great actors.

As no doubt Claudia was complaining about me to Cynthia, I started to tell Sandy some of the horror stories of Claudia's antics and behaviour behind closed doors. I told him her about her forty-eight-hour tantrums, her sulks and moods, some of which even extended to seventy-two hours or longer. I told him about her peculiar bedtime rituals and performances. I explained she was no better in the morning. Often she complained she felt too sick to speak when she woke, as we were forced to tiptoe around her. Of course there was nothing wrong with her. I told him about the incident when she'd thrown a glass at my head. I said about the drug-fuelled weekends with her ex-boyfriend, and her habit of spending entire evenings talking to other men, when she'd gone out with me.

I explained I found sex with her an ordeal not a pleasure. I said it was impossible to relax with her. Her demands put me on edge. I almost preferred to avoid sex altogether. I complained that she continued to expect me to pay for everything we did, despite the fact that she now earned double what I did. I complained she would fly into a rage if she thought my identical meal was marginally bigger than hers. I explained she'd refuse to go out if her hair wouldn't sit as she wanted. She'd force us to cancel meals and other events. I'd lavished her with gifts and love. I never got any love back. I felt I received little more than contempt. She refused marriage. She refused to have kids, though she was willing to share the same roof. She expected me to buy the wine we drank nightly and the weed we smoked. She never paid for it once. Overall I didn't paint a picture of domestic bliss. I said she was the most difficult person I'd ever met. Sandy was surprised. Outside Claudia tried to portray herself in a very different light, as sweetness personified. The truth was very different, I explained.

Pretty soon Sandy found out for himself what she was really like. At the time, when I had breaks from the cinema, I was continuing to take regular film extra work. I enjoyed doing it. It was a bit of extra cash, and naively I even thought it might be a way into working in the film industry. Sometimes I took Paul along with me for the day. We didn't get our big break, but we did have a lot of fun on the various film sets and locations where the filming took place. In one film I found myself playing a German businessman, for which I needed a cream suit. I didn't have one, but Sandy did. I'd warned him never to ring late, in case he disturbed Claudia's sleep. But anxious to make arrangements to get me the suit he forgot and rang late one night, waking Claudia up. She'd already gone through her bedtime ritual and had started to fall asleep. Sandy woke her up. She went absolutely ballistic. She went berserk. He was still on the phone and could hear her yelling *I'll kill them both!*

'I better go,' I said. 'Speak soon, I hope.'

Claudia took off her mask and pulled out her ear plugs. She marched to the kitchen and I saw her picking up knives, pots and pans. After what had happened with the wine glass I was genuinely scared. I wondered what she had in mind. I ran to the toilet and locked myself in. She started banging on the door with her pots and pans, trying to break it down. I half expected a blade to come splintering through the wood. I stood back and hoped the lock would hold. She carried on banging. I was certain our neighbours would complain about the fearful din she was making. After a while she stopped.

'I'm going to get something heavier,' I heard her mutter.

She came back and continued banging, trying to force her way in. The door held firm.

'How dare you disturb my sleep,' she shouted. 'I'll kill you, and I'll kill your stupid friend.'

She carried on banging for a while longer, until she eventually gave up. I remained scared to come out. I realised I'd become truly fearful of her. She was wild, irrational and unpredictable. I suspected she was unhinged, borderline insane, or at least on the spectrum. I cowered in the toilet for at least an hour, until I was certain she'd gone back to bed and was asleep. I slept on the couch that night. I was scared to go near her. Sandy too kept his distance from her in future. I think he was worried she night actually carry out her threat to kill him.

Whilst I continued to live with a mad woman I got a phone call from Roxanne that made my heart sink. She was pregnant. It was typical, I thought. Roxanne hadn't wanted another child with me. Claudia certainly didn't want one. Now Roxanne was having one. I felt quite jealous. It should have been mine, I thought. The sad thing was she didn't even know the father that well. It was someone she hadn't long met and wasn't sure if she wanted to be with him or not. Of course I said all the right things like congratulations, but I was dying inside. Roxanne even started to make hurried plans to move herself and Grace in with the new boyfriend, whose name was Luke. They even started preparing and decorating a children's bedroom for Grace and the new arrival to share. She'd never move in. She'd never live there. Perhaps sensibly Roxanne changed her mind at the last moment. She didn't love Luke. She split up with him during the pregnancy and would have the baby alone.

Claudia and I continued to soldier on, but things weren't the same. Most of her old university friends were married now. Some like Roxanne were even pregnant. Claudia showed no inclination to do the same. I realised I was wasting my time with her. We'd never get married. We'd never have a family. We'd never settle down properly. Furthermore, I'd wasted almost all my money from the sale of the house I'd shared with Roxanne on her. It was almost gone, and I had nothing to show for it, except a broken heart. I'd done everything I could to make Claudia happy. I'd showered her with love and affection in the hope I might get a small amount of love back. I never did. I'd come to realise it was a lost cause. Nothing good or positive would ever come of it.

Suffering from mild Obsessive-compulsive disorder as I did I noticed small changes. I noticed when things had been moved. I was aware when they weren't the same. I registered when something went missing, or when it wasn't in its usual place. I noted when habits had been altered or broken. Over a number of nights, when I came home from work I realised that Claudia had changed her routine. Normally she came in and cooked. The usual signs she'd been in the kitchen were absent. There were other small indications that she wasn't spending the time in our flat she usually did. I didn't say anything, but I started to get suspicious. I knew for reasons unknown she'd been somewhere else. Then by chance, as I walked to work one day, I happened to run into Nick, whose wedding to Emma we'd attended. Emma had been on Claudia's course.

'Sorry to hear Claudia didn't get that job in Bristol she went for,' he said.

I didn't allow my face to betray the fact I knew nothing about it.

186

'I'm sure there will be others,' I said. 'Did she tell you she was applying?'

'She just mentioned to Emma that she'd been staying late at work to write her application, and going to the library to do extra research for the interview. Pity though. With her first I'm surprised there was a better candidate,' he remarked.

'Yes indeed,' I said. 'Just one of those things I guess. Anyway I'd better be of to work. Nice to see you again.'

At least I now knew the truth. She'd applied for a job in Bristol behind my back. She'd written and submitted the application without saying a word. She'd prepared for the interview and maintained her silence. Presumably she'd even taken a day off work and travelled to Bristol by herself and still never mentioned it. She just hadn't got the job. Doubtless if she had she'd been planning to move there without me. I felt quite hurt. I felt betrayed, almost as if I'd discovered an affair. It was the same sense of betrayal. She'd been sneaking around behind my back, making plans that I wasn't part of. It was all the proof I needed that she was indeed planning to leave. For all her faults, her moods, her eccentricities and peculiarities, I did in fact still love her. But it was pointless, I realised. There could be no future with her. She didn't want marriage and she didn't want a family. On top of that I had now discovered she couldn't be trusted. She was deceitful. She was secretive and conniving.

I went for a long walk by myself down the country lanes and paths where my parents lived, to clear my head and think things through. Despite the fact I loved her I started to make plans to leave Claudia. For me this was the final straw. I needed to get her out of my life. She was a toxic and cancerous presence that I knew I had to get rid of. I started to think of my life without her. I started to imagine something beyond our existing negative and unhealthy relationship. I knew she was planning to leave me. I knew both her friends and her family were encouraging her to do so. I decided to hasten those plans. Yet I wanted Claudia to be the bad guy. I'd play the victim. I'd play my part well. I'd milk it for all it was worth. I'd make things terribly difficult for Claudia to leave. It wouldn't be easy. I'd pay her back for some of the suffering and unhappiness she'd caused me. I'd make it hard for her to go. I would make her suffer just as she'd made me suffer. She'd be the guilty party in the eyes of all our friends she was so anxious to impress and keep on the right side of. Yet at the same time unknown to her I was now planning to leave too. I'd had enough. I realised I simply had nothing left to give, and what I had given was completely meaningless. It meant nothing to Claudia at all. I'd come to appreciate that. I would never be the person she wanted. And she could never be the person I needed.

'When were you going to tell me?' I asked, confronting her with all I had discovered.

'What does it matter? I didn't get the job anyway,' she replied, avoiding directly answering the question.

'Were you planning to move without me?' I continued.

'I hadn't thought.' Claudia said. 'I was going to think about that if I got the job.'

It didn't really matter what she replied, the trust had gone. It had been irrevocably broken. Over the summer of 2005 the arguments got worse. I spent less and less time with Claudia. I spent more and more time taking Sandy out instead. We generally didn't share the same bed anymore. Claudia slept in our double one. I slept in the small single bed we kept for Grace on the weekends she visited. The last social event I recall us attending as a couple was a birthday meal for Paul's friend, Steve. It was actually quite a nice occasion. When we got back to the flat Claudia and I had sex. It was the last time we did. By the time the next birthday meal came round in just a couple of months we'd split up. As the arguments worsened both of us had had enough. We'd reached the end of our tethers. There was nothing more to be done. Our relationship couldn't be saved. We'd arrived at the end of the line. After a particularly vicious argument Claudia announced that one more row and she was leaving me. For some reason on this occasion we both knew she meant it.

Living with someone as difficult as Claudia I knew very well another argument couldn't be put off for long. I could have tried to tread on eggshells and tiptoe round her a little longer, but I couldn't be bothered. I'd become a little fatalistic about our relationship by that time. I saw no point in delaying the inevitable. I thought we might just as well get on with it and move on to the next chapter and start living the rest of our lives. As it happened it was Cynthia's birthday next. I'd come to loathe *The Germ*. Her interfering and meddling had done nothing but further harm to our already fragile relationship. She'd been happy to stick the knife in, whilst still expecting free food and cinema tickets from me. It was now my opportunity to get my own back. I decided that

Cynthia's birthday, when we were due to go out for another communal meal with our friends, was the time to provoke the final argument with Claudia. I knew Claudia was looking forward to the meal. I decided she wouldn't get to go to the ball after all. I can't remember what started the argument, but once it got started there was no stopping it. It quickly gained momentum and got out of control.

'That's it. That's the end of our relationship,' Claudia announced. 'We've officially split up.'

'Thanks for that,' I said. 'After all I've done for you, and after all I've spent on you. You're the most selfish and ungrateful person I've ever met in my life.'

It was the middle of the day, but to stoke the fire I cracked open a bottle of red wine and started drinking heavily from it. I also rolled and lit a giant spliff.

'Give me some,' Claudia insisted.

'Get your own,' I told her. 'You said it. We're not together anymore. I'm sick of sharing my stuff with you. You've never paid for a damn thing since I've known you. This time I'm keeping it all to myself.'

'You bastard. I hate you,' she said.

'Not as much as I hate you,' I said.

'I'm going to kill you. I'm going to get a knife and stab you in the heart,' Claudia promised.

'Go ahead,' I said. 'I really don't care. You've already ruined my life anyway. I've given you everything. I've asked you to marry me. I've asked you to have a family. All I've had in return is coldness, moodiness, sulking and loathing. Do what you want. You've broken my heart anyway.'

So it went on through the day. I continued to drink and smoke. We both shed our share of tears. But there was no going back. I just sat on the floor, getting off my head.

'We can still go to the party,' Claudia suggested at about six o'clock.

'What, go and pretend everything is all right?' I laughed. 'I'm sick of doing that.'

'Why not? It is Cynthia's birthday,' Claudia said.

'Don't be ridiculous,' I replied. 'Of course we're not going. What's more you can ring *The Germ* and tell her why we're not going.'

Claudia dutifully rang. The meal went ahead, but I heard afterwards there was an odd atmosphere. There was bound to be. All our friends now knew Claudia had dumped me. Our splitting up was effectively the end of the group. We never socialised as a unit all together again. It was over in more ways than one. I retained the friendships of Paul, Sandy, Steve and Cliff. Cynthia and the rest went with Claudia. Afterwards I never again had anything to do with any of them. That was it. They'd chosen, just as the friends I'd shared with Roxanne had chosen. They'd shown where their allegiances lay. They'd gone with Claudia. They could have her. Their friendship with me was at an end. At least I now knew who my real friends were. As they attended Cynthia's party without us I continued to drink. I polished off two bottles of strong red wine and countless joints. Claudia was convinced I was going to be sick. I wasn't. Instead I took myself off to bed, to forget all about it.

An odd period followed. Claudia and I continued to live together but were no longer a couple. I left her in no doubt that I was the injured party, and my life had been ruined by what she was doing and what she'd done. I never for a moment let her forget how much she'd hurt me and how much she was killing me by her actions. I'd left my wife and daughter for her after all. Even so a strange truce of sorts developed, as both of us started the search to find new accommodation. These things couldn't be done at the drop of the hat. They took time. We also had to give notice where we were living. In the meantime each had to tolerate the other for the time being. Odder still there were even rare moments between us when we were nice to each other. More than once we ended up on the couch, arm in arm, cuddling like we had done when we first met. These moments were almost surreal.

'Sometimes I don't know why I'm doing what I'm doing,' Claudia said.

'I don't know either,' I replied.

'When I look at you I don't understand why I'm leaving. It makes no sense and seems like a mistake perhaps,' she continued.

'Then don't, if you feel like that,' I said,

'But it's too late. It's too late for us,' she pleaded, looking sadly up into my eyes. 'Things have just gone too far to get back on track.'

For once she was almost being sweet. But she was right. It was too late for us. And I knew why she was leaving. Her friends and parents had told her to. But apart from that we just weren't suited. We wanted totally different things. We could have no future together. We were splitting up and it was the right thing to do. Like many couples before us we had tried but failed. We had reluctantly come to the inevitable but correct decision to part. We each had to let the other free, to live a life they were more suited to. The truce and sense of near tenderness between us didn't last. It abruptly ended when I started seeing someone else. Peace had been short lived. All-out war was suddenly declared.

Chapter Twenty-Two

I met Victoria one Friday night when I was out with Paul, Sandy, Cliff and Steve. We were at our usual club. Claudia had gone somewhere else with Cynthia and some of my other former friends. We'd quickly come to realise we could no longer socialise in the same places. Neither of us was mature enough to handle the fallout. There was bound to be disagreement, resentment and argument. Although we still lived together under the same roof it was best we kept our social lives completely separate. It meant we could never go out as a big group again. Half of my friends had remained loyal to me. The other half had gone with Claudia. They could keep her as far as I was concerned. Their disloyalty meant they were as good as dead to me. I knew Cynthia in particular was someone I would no longer even be able to speak to with any degree of civility or politeness. My only course of action was to blank her completely. Ensuring we didn't meet or cross paths with this antitheses group was difficult. It meant that going out once more became something of a minefield. Splitting up with Roxanne some years earlier had destroyed some of my long-standing friendships. Now splitting up with Claudia was destroying more.

I met Victoria just as she was leaving. It was unfortunate but couldn't be helped. I thought I recognised her. She looked vaguely familiar. Our eyes met. She thought the same. She thought she recognised me. She actually looked like a girl who used to hang out with a female friend of many years earlier, I realised, but that wasn't it. It was something else. I knew her from somewhere, but I couldn't quite place where. She was blonde, curvy and pretty. I'd have put her in her mid to late thirties, a little younger than me. We got talking, but just as her friends were beckoning her to the door. It was a pity. I hadn't seen anyone at the club all evening even slightly to interest me. Now that I had she was leaving.

'Can't you stay a little longer?' I pleaded.

'I'm sorry. I'd like to, but I really can't tonight. We're all sharing a taxi back,' Victoria explained.

'Fair enough, but nice to have met you,' I said.

'Tell me your phone number. I'll remember it,' Victoria promised.

'I'll give it you by all means, but you'll never remember it,' I said.

'I will. You see,' Victoria assured me.

I gave her my number. She repeated it. She then gave me a quick kiss, before running after her friends. She'd seemed really nice. She was certainly very attractive. I only wish I'd bumped into her a little earlier in the evening. I never expected to hear from her again though. I was certain she'd have forgotten my number, just as I'd have done after a few drinks if I'd tried to remember hers. I just hoped I might see her another week in the same place, hopefully before too long and too much time had passed. In fact I needn't have worried. As these thoughts were running through my mind Victoria texted me from the taxi just a few minutes after leaving. *See, I told you I'd remember*, the text stated simply. It was signed with a kiss. I texted her back, saying it was nice to have met her and saying I was sorry we hadn't met earlier. She agreed, saying it was nice to have met me too.

I felt a little odd about asking her out. Having only just split up with Claudia it didn't feel quite right and I wasn't quite sure I was ready. Another side of me told me it was too good an opportunity to pass up. It was also a chance to get back at Claudia for the pain she'd caused me over a prolonged period, and to show her I was ready and able to move on. I could have a life without her. I quickly weighed the arguments up in my head, before texting Victoria back. I asked if she wanted to meet up and I suggested a time and a place. She wasted no time replying, agreeing to my suggestion. I texted saying I'd see her then.

As I walked home I was struck by a new dilemma. Should I tell Claudia, or should I not? My first thought was to keep it to myself. I then thought perhaps honesty was best, as she might find out anyway. I was also slightly intrigued by how she'd react. At this point she held all the aces in our relationship. She'd split up with me. No doubt she thought she could have me back at the drop of a hat anytime she wanted, just by clicking her fingers. It wasn't quite like that anymore. I was genuinely moving on and not just pretending to. Part of me wanted Claudia to suffer a little of what I had suffered; to experience a little of the torment she'd put me through. Part of me also realised her spell had now been truly broken. Despite all her faults, her weirdness and her difficult nature, I had genuinely loved her when we'd been together. Heavens knows I'd loved her through all of it, though it was hard latterly to understand why. I'd started to realise that my love for her was misplaced and ultimately pointless. She could never provide the things I wanted, like more children and marriage, and I couldn't provide her with the things she wanted. I still loved her in some ways, but I knew we could have no future together. We simply weren't compatible.

Now our relationship had finally ended, I was almost surprised by the sudden and dramatic extent to which I was waking from what felt like a bad dream. Once her spell had been broken it was utterly broken. My love was diminishing by the minute. I began to see her more than ever as she really was – a selfish, self-obsessed, unpleasant, narcissistic individual, who only really cared about herself, but who was desperate for the approval of others, notably peers and friends, at whatever cost to her most personal and intimate relationships. To Claudia friends mattered much more than family, partners and lovers and always would. She had a distorted view of the world, which revolved round herself and her needs and no one else's. It wouldn't change. She had a sharp mind, but she wasn't all that pleasant underneath. She wasn't a very nice person in truth. For most of the time we'd been together she'd treated me pretty contemptibly. I'd showered her with love and affection, gifts and generosity. I'd got nothing in return. I doubted she'd ever loved me in all honesty. Most of the time she'd just been using me for what she could get out of our relationship. That swayed my thinking. I would tell her about my date. She'd broken my heart. I'd give her a little of that hurt back. Predictably when I told her she was shocked at first. Then she went mad.

'A date? What do you mean a date?' she asked.

'I met someone. That's all. It's nothing serious, only casual. We're just going out for a drink. I just thought it best to tell you. I'm just trying to be honest,' I explained.

'When did this happen?' Claudia continued.

'Last week,' I answered.

'When are you seeing her?' Claudia pressed.

'On Wednesday,' I replied.

'What's her name?'

'Does it matter?'

'Yes.'

'Victoria.'

'Did you know her before?'

'No.'

Claudia then stopped her interrogation, to think and consider for a moment. I could see the implications of what I'd said begin to churn around in her head. She was slowly digesting them. I wondered what

194

her response would be. She was starting to scare me. Her face started to twist into a violent rage.

'To think I've been living in this house under the same roof as you, and you were starting to see another woman…' she began.

Claudia didn't even finish her sentence. She got up and ran towards the kitchen. I saw her pick up a huge, gleaming carving knife in her hand. I knew for a fact it had a very sharp blade. It had the potential to slice right through me in an instant. I was frightened. I thought this time she might actually try to kill me. I didn't doubt she had potential to do so. She'd always been borderline psychotic. She gripped the knife tightly and started to run back in my direction. I didn't wait around to ask questions or reason with her. I didn't have any shoes on, but that was the least of my concerns. I ran barefoot straight out of the front door, down the single flight of stairs and out into the road. I didn't stop there. I ran round the corner and hid there, trying to listen out to hear if Claudia was following. I think she followed for a bit, then gave up and went back inside. She probably felt conspicuous holding a long knife. I thought about phoning the police. In the end I rang my mum and asked her to come and pick me up. I explained I didn't feel safe at the flat anymore. I stayed at my parents' house for the next couple of days, whilst Claudia calmed down. When I did eventually feel confident enough to sneak back in Claudia didn't say a word. She just got on with whatever she was doing. But she had truly terrified me this time. I had no idea where her madness would stop. I knew it wouldn't end soon.

I was very nervous when I went on my date with Victoria. I'd been with Claudia for four years, when I hadn't so much as looked at another woman. Now I was meeting one. I suspected that she sensed that I was nervous. I felt it only fair to explain my rather odd situation, that I had recently split up with a girlfriend, but we were still living together whilst we served out the notice on our flat and both looked for new places to live. Victoria took it all in. The date went reasonably well. We even kissed at the end of it and agreed to meet again.

Our second date was a daytime one, when we met in town for a coffee, a cake and a chat. Again it was fine. We seemed to get on and find things to talk about. It certainly wasn't awkward or uncomfortable for either of us. Victoria was an attractive woman. I was happy in her company. Yet I didn't hear from her for a while after that, or I'd hear from her and we'd arrange something only for her to cancel on me at the last moment. It started to get a little frustrating, but at least it had broken the ice for me. It had got me back into the dating game, even if it had been a little too soon for me to be fully over Claudia just yet.

I remained in touch with Victoria and we stayed friends. She later told me she'd liked me, but had been worried by my situation with Claudia. I said I fully understood. It was indeed complicated, I agreed. For my part I liked Victoria, found her engaging and pleasing to the eye, but doubted long term that I was likely to be the man for her. I was an overgrown indie kid after all, with lots of hang-ups, phobias and insecurities. I wasn't one for all women. I wasn't everyone's cup of tea by any means. I knew deep down I probably wasn't Victoria's. It was just as well it didn't go anywhere. But it wasn't long before I was out again, this time on a Saturday night with Steve, looking for someone else to fill the void that Claudia had left in my life.

The night was drawing to a close. We'd done the rounds of pubs we liked and had ended up in a live music venue, that later in the evening doubled up as an indie dance club after the live music had finished. It was only a little, basement place, but it was cheap and cheerful and normally rammed on a Saturday night. As Steve and I sat down supping our pints, Steve also rolling cigarettes, I noticed a girl I knew. She was a regular at the cinema, and had hung around the local indie clubs at the height of Britpop a decade or so earlier with her sister. They were both small, slim, dark and attractive. I'd had a slight crush on the pair of them, but neither had a particularly good reputation with men. They'd both dated friends of mine at various points in the past, and it had never worked out terribly well. The younger sister was now living away. It just left the elder sister, Julie, living locally. By chance she happened to be out on this particular night and was sitting with friends very close to where Steve and I were sitting. I was vaguely aware Sandy also had a crush on Julie and had kissed her just a week or two earlier. But they weren't actually dating, and in truth Sandy had a crush on just about every woman he met, and pretty much every woman we mutually knew. If I'd ruled out talking to every woman he liked and made a half claim on there literally wouldn't have been any women left, at least not where we lived.

Anyway I was just drunk enough to think this Julie was fair game, at least to talk to. She wasn't entirely my type in truth. She was a bit loud and bit too much of a ladette for me, too keen on lager and football for a girl. I suspected she was also a bit loose with her virtue, but she was attractive, had a nice smile and I did quite fancy her. There was no harm just talking to her, I thought. I wasn't planning anything more. Just saying hello didn't mean I had to get with her. When I went over her face immediately lit up. She beamed at me with a mixture of instant recognition and genuine pleasure. Her warmth and enthusiasm were quite infectious. She seemed delighted that I was there.

'Come and sit down. Pull up a chair. Bring your friend over too,' she announced, insisting that Steve also join us.

We did what we were told and duly sat down. Julie was very talkative and sociable. She chatted at length on all kinds of things and quickly put me at my ease. There were no awkward gaps in the conversation whatsoever. Maybe after the sulky moodiness of Claudia this was perhaps what I needed, I thought to myself. Perhaps I'd benefit from someone loud, gregarious and energetic to coax me out of myself and back to form? My relationship with Claudia had caused me to lose confidence. It had been stifling and claustrophobic. I'd never been able to relax with her. Julie was a different sort of person altogether. In superficial terms she was vocal, opinionated and boisterous, when I tended to go for quieter, more demure, gentile women. But she was bright and she was fun, and we were definitely getting along. It was refreshing and I found myself grinning in her company. She seemed like the kind of girl who could show me a good time, bring me out of my shell and start getting me enjoying life again. At the end of the evening we kissed and exchanged phone numbers.

I didn't waste too much time waiting to text her. I texted Julie the next day. I suggested meeting midweek. I offered to take her for a curry and to a pub I was keen to try out that neither of us had been to before. She didn't take long to text back. She quickly agreed. I had another date. When I told Claudia she pretty much stopped speaking to me altogether. Yes, in one way I was punishing Claudia, not just for ending our relationship, but for being a total pain to live with for the last four years. In another way I just wanted to get on with my life. I wanted to cleanse all feelings and memories concerning Claudia. As I say I'd woken up from the spell that had been cast on me. I now saw her as she truly was, and I didn't like what I saw very much. She was spending her nights hanging out with Cynthia and other of my former friends, slating my behaviour. What did they expect? She'd finished with me. I had every right to start dating other people. It wasn't my fault we were both still stuck living under the same roof. I didn't like it any more that she did.

Claudia's birthday came and I had to sit and watch her get ready to meet Cynthia and the other friends who'd deserted me. I didn't find such moments easy. By this time we'd both found new places in which to live, and could move as soon as our notice expired and we got keys to our new homes. Neither of us had done particularly well. Claudia had a room in a shared house, with a couple into rave music and ecstasy. That part would suit her at least, I thought with a touch of irony. Her druggy weekends had always been a source of friction between us. For my part I was planning to rent a tiny, ground floor bedsit in an old, Victorian, terraced house. It was at least conveniently situated near the city centre shops, but it was a far cry from the space I'd enjoyed in the flat I'd had when I first met Claudia. I was definitely going down in the world. I'd sunk a long way since being the young, aspiring homeowner I'd been with Roxanne.

As Christmas 2005 approached the last couple of weeks I spent in the flat with Claudia became beyond awkward. We both tried to avoid the other as much as possible. Claudia had taken our small, spare, folding bed, that Grace had used when she stayed, and put it in the front room. She was sleeping there. She let me have our big, double bed, mainly as she suspected that I was enjoying carnal pleasures with Julie on the weekends that she went to stay with Sam. Claudia had bizarrely even taken to examining the sheets on her return, searching for proof and semen stains. Whilst I had let Julie stay there several times whilst Claudia was away, our relationship hadn't become sexual yet. Julie was keen, but I just wasn't ready for a physical relationship. I had more respect for Claudia than she realised, though after the way she'd treated me I wasn't bothered if she thought we were at it like rabbits. Julie had probably never had a man refuse her before. She probably wondered what was wrong. I'd already had to ask Sandy if he minded if I dated her. Luckily he wasn't too put out. I still wasn't ready to rush into anything too serious. It suited me to keep everything more at the level of friendship for the time being.

As I prepared to move into my poky, new bedsit, Julie and I grew closer. We now spent most nights together. I often stayed with her in her flat, which coincidentally was very near to where Roxanne and I had owned our house together. Life was strange, I often reflected. I'd fallen in love several times. I'd been married. I'd got divorced. Then I'd got with another woman I'd seen around and been drawn to like a moth to a flame. It hadn't worked out. Now I was dating someone I'd known

198

by sight and to say hello to for many years, but had never imagined I'd end up with.

I see Julie now as a bit like Pluto. She was an important part of my life, but I can't quite give her planetary status. Despite a promising start, we didn't date long enough for me to devote a section of this book to her. It could have been different. As I got to know her I thought it would work out differently to how I imagined it would at first. When we met I thought of her mainly as a friend; someone to hang out with and enjoy a good time with. As I got to know her better I started to think we might in fact forge a more lasting relationship. In the end it turned out to be not quite either. It had potential though, and despite my first impressions I grew increasingly to like her and to enjoy and rely on her company more than I'd anticipated. Initially she'd been the keener one, anxious to move the relationship on to a more serious footing. As time went on I started seeing things more as she did. It was a relief when I could finally move out of the flat with Claudia and turn my back on that chapter of my life for good.

We both finally moved out over Christmas, almost exactly four years to the day since we'd first started dating. In the end I actually moved out a few days before Claudia. I'd even had the embarrassment of being there when her new flatmates had arrived to pick up some of her stuff. Someone else had also come round with a van to buy some storage units she wasn't taking. Each time I sat there in meek silence playing the docile idiot that had been dumped. When it actually came to say goodbye I put my arms round Claudia and gave her a gentle hug.

'Good luck,' I said, trying to turn back the clock to recreate the affection we'd once shared.

'Do we have to do this?' she said, shying away from any emotional scene that might take place.

'Apparently not,' I replied rather brusquely, releasing my grip on her.

So she was still a heartless bitch after all. I had genuinely loved her. It was a pity to see it end like this, but it couldn't be helped. It was inevitable. As I was going she stopped to speak one more time.

'I'd like to stay friends,' she said.

'Maybe,' I replied, although I didn't really see how we could.

In fact, after we were both settled in our new places I did see Claudia once or twice. I met her once at the cinema and I also invited her over to see my new place.

'I see you've landed on your feet,' she said.

199

She hadn't changed. The place was an absolute dump. Only Claudia could be jealous of it. The last time I met her she invited me over to her place. It wasn't that much better than mine in truth, but I said she'd done well for herself.

'I've been up all night, taking drugs with my flatmates,' she announced, rather pleased with herself.

I imagined she was saying it to taunt me. I didn't make any comment, but I decided there and then not to see her again. I couldn't do the being friends thing. I was better off with Julie, I thought. Even so at the end of the evening I politely said goodbye to Claudia. I knew I was saying a real goodbye this time. The next time I saw her I blanked her. We didn't speak again. I was too bitter at the way she'd treated me. I felt she'd played me like a fool. It wasn't possible for me to be friends with such a person. We became sworn enemies. I grew pretty much to hate her. I just hated Cynthia even more. In future I'd have nothing to do with either of them. It was a new year and I'd begin a new life with Julie. That prospect actually made me feel quite happy.

PART FOUR – HEATHER

Chapter Twenty-Three

By the beginning of 2006 I was seeing Julie most nights when I wasn't working late. Mostly I stayed with her at her place. Occasionally we stayed at mine, as it was nearer to town. Though much less often, as Julie found it small and damp, and she wasn't happy with some of the other tenants we had to share a toilet and bathroom with. They were mainly a mix of middle-aged and elderly drunks, it had to be said. But they largely kept themselves to themselves and didn't bother me too much. They drank quietly alone in their rooms most of the day and night. They weren't very sociable or contributing much to society, but they were harmless and not bothering me. But I could see why Julie preferred her place. She had a large kitchen and lounge we could relax in. She had a spacious bathroom. She shared with several other girls, who had proper jobs and were pleasant, polite and easy to get on with. I never felt awkward or out of place there.

Indeed 2006 was a very good year. It started well and only got better. It turned out to be one of the best years I'd had in a long time. I could perhaps only compare it to the time when Roxanne and I had got married and Grace had been born. True I was now living in a squalid, old, Victorian house, but my life was finally moving on. Yes 2006 was a good year for me. Away from her evil clutches I finally managed to forget all about Claudia. I consigned her to the darkest depths of my memory and shut her out forever. I dismissed her like a bad dream. In fact I found it much easier than I imagined it would be. I had genuinely been in love with her. I'd truly wanted to marry her. Yet I'd left all my love with her on the doorstep where I'd last seen her. My love had gone for good. It was totally broken and could never be recovered. I found it hard even to think about the time I'd been with her. I preferred to blot it all out. I wished instead I'd spent those wasted years just devoting myself to Grace, or had made more of a go of my marriage to Roxanne even. It was too late now. I'd done what I'd done. I couldn't turn back the clock. I couldn't change anything. Claudia had cast her spell on me. I'd found it impossible to resist. It had turned me into a fool. It had made me do things I now regretted. It had brought me to the meagre room and humble surroundings I now lived in. At least I had Julie. That was something. It was actually quite a lot. And as I say for the first time in several years I felt content and at ease.

With Claudia now safely out the way Julie and I could at last start to develop a physical relationship. It had been difficult and awkward with Claudia. I'd never felt comfortable sleeping with her. I'd been put off at the start of our time together, and despite the best efforts of both of us it had never been quite right. I was worried it would be the same with Julie. I needn't have been concerned. When we first slept together we were instantly far more compatible. The sex was good, much better than it had been with Claudia. It felt natural and unforced. It actually reawakened my interest in sex. I'd started to avoid it with Claudia. Now it was fun again. It gave me renewed confidence in the bedroom department. I'd started to think with Claudia I just wasn't very good at it. Now I actually wanted to have sex again. Julie and I had waited, mainly because I hadn't been ready, but it had been worth the wait. It was nice sleeping with her.

It was a cold winter. On some nights we went to see films where I worked. On other nights we went to pubs or clubs or met up with friends. Julie was a friendly and sociable person. I was being introduced to a whole new group of people. There were so many it was almost hard to keep track of them. Thanks to Julie my social circle was rapidly increasing. On other nights we just stayed in and ordered takeaways or watched DVDs. Sometimes we lay in her bed, me drinking wine, Julie smoking cigarettes. I took the occasional puff, but now I was free of Claudia I'd ditched my weed habit. I'd turned my back on it for good.

At weekends Julie liked to go to the pub to meet friends. Sometimes they had lunch. Sometimes they watched football and just got drunk. I generally met her later in the day, if I wasn't working. I preferred to get out in the fresh air than head straight to the pub at midday. I offered to take Julie for walks or drives out in the car, as I had Roxanne and Claudia. It was much too cold for that, she said. She would perhaps come out in the summer when it was warmer. I wasn't deterred. Instead when I wasn't at work I took Sandy out. Grace joined us on the weekends I had her. She was now nearly eight years old and rapidly growing up, almost too quickly for her father, who was now forty.

Sandy still hadn't found a new girlfriend and was very much regretting his decision to leave his ex, Joan. He'd believed the grass would be greener single and on his own. Of course it wasn't. It hadn't worked out like that at all. Although he went out drinking all the time he hadn't met anyone and was lonely and a bit down. I still felt a bit guilty about dating Julie, one of the many women he'd also been vaguely

204

after. To make up for it I spent a lot of time helping him compose texts to the various myriad of other ladies he was potentially interested in. Occasionally he even got a date out of it, but sadly it never seemed to go out any further than that.

Sandy liked to sing. I told him I played the guitar. To cheer him up I started going round to his flat from time to time and playing the guitar for him. We started playing cover versions of rock, punk and indie classics, but quickly moved on to some songs I'd written and ones I'd done with Paul from work. Before long Sandy and I were writing and performing our own compositions. Sandy had the infectious enthusiasm of a child. Pretty soon he was talking about forming a band and doing some live gigs. He was full of unbridled passion and excitement for the project. There was simply no stopping him. It had started as just a bit of fun. Now he was making all kinds of plans for indie rock stardom. Sandy had helped me through some difficult times with Claudia. He'd been a shoulder to cry on and someone to vent my emotion and anger with. Now I was helping Sandy back with music.

Meanwhile Julie and I were growing closer. I'd been reluctant to commit at first, for fear of getting my fingers burned. She didn't have the best reputation with men. She had a history of dating one after another. I didn't want to be just another one of her conquests. So I held back committing too much. Even so I'd grown more fond of her and felt we were a proper couple now. On Valentine's Day we exchanged cards, as lovers do. She wrote that she hoped it would be the first of many happy Valentine's Days together. It was a sweet thought. It struck a chord in me. I took her out for a meal after. I gazed at her over our food and over the table. She had sparkling eyes and had nicely defined features. She was pretty. She wore elegant clothes. She was intelligent. She was confident. She liked good conversation. She was never short of something to say. And despite the fact that she wasn't really like any of my previous girlfriends, maybe that was a good thing. She was fun to be with. I was enjoying myself and I was happier with her than I expected. By the time we wandered slowly back to her flat we'd both had quite a lot to drink.

'Love you,' she said slightly dreamily.

She then looked a little aghast at what had slipped out.

'Is that too soon?' she asked.

'Not too soon,' I assured her. 'Love you too,' I repeated.

It was true I was falling for her, but I was aware I was still always holding something back. Maybe it was too soon after Claudia, that I could never fully commit. Maybe I was too aware of the failed relationships in Julie's closet. I don't quite know what it was. Given time I might have fully committed, but as time passed I noticed small changes in her. For the first few months she'd been total sweetness and light. She'd been the perfect partner and the perfect companion. She'd done everything right, to get me where she wanted me. Once she'd done that she stopped making such an effort. Her real character started to come out more. She could be tired, moody, angry or simply sad. Sometimes I'd go round and she'd just want to go to bed early. Other times she'd be moaning about work or something a friend had done. She could get quite annoyed and aggressive about little things, trivia in fact. She'd blow them up into something significant, and in turn blow up about them. At first I dismissed it as perhaps the time of the month or just having an off day, but the moodiness became more common. Things were still largely fun, but there were occasions when I was round at her flat relaxing and drinking wine that I suspected she would have preferred I wasn't there at all. A few times when I thought we were meeting she announced she was just having a night in.

One such occasion was a Friday night when I'd arranged to go round after work. She'd texted to say she wasn't feeling great and it was best we leave it until the next day. I was a bit disappointed, as I'd been looking forward to seeing her, but said she was better resting if she wasn't well. I texted a few of the usual suspects to see if anyone else was about, but unusually no one had plans to go out that night. Even so, as it was on my route home, I decided to stop off for a quick pint at our usual indie club anyway. When I got there I didn't see too many familiar faces. I did see one, a very old friend called Dan I'd known from the local pub circuit for over twenty years, so I went over and started to chat to him. The club was quite busy. We couldn't get a seat, so just hovered on a step on the edge of the dance area. Two younger girls then came over to chat to Dan. They evidently knew him. One was dark, the other was blonde. They were both pretty in their own but quite different ways. After a bit I joined in the conversation. The blonde was more obviously striking, but I was quite taken by her dark-haired companion. She had the kind of cute, innocent, fresh good looks that some indie girls have. She looked sweet, friendly and appealing all in one, though she was smoking a cigarette, so she wasn't entirely sweet I realised. It was at times like these I almost regretted not being single.

'I'm Heather,' she said.

'I'm Simon. Nice to meet you,' I replied.

'I think I've seen you before,' she continued.

'Probably. I work at the arthouse cinema,' I explained.

'Maybe, or perhaps I've seen you here,' she said.

'It's likely. I come here a lot,' I said.

'I do too. I'm surprised we haven't met before,' Heather said.

'You probably wouldn't have noticed me. I'm a bit older than you,' I said. 'Too old still to be coming here in truth.'

'How old are you, if it's not a rude question?' Heather asked.

'I could just lie, or shall I tell you the truth? Which would you prefer? No, it's not a rude question. I'm forty,' I said truthfully.

'That's OK. It's not that old,' Heather replied.

'How old are you then?' I asked in return.

'Twenty-five,' Heather said.

She was fifteen years younger than I was, quite an age gap. I was about ten years older than Julie.

'You should also know I have an eight-year-old daughter,' I said, although I didn't know why I had to tell her that.

I still hadn't introduced Julie to Grace. I didn't want to rush things. It had seemed too soon. Now I was telling someone I'd only just met about my daughter.

'Anyway, it's nice to meet you now,' I said. 'Although I'm not stopping long. I just finished work and was only having a quick drink on my way home.'

'Well, I hope we meet again soon,' Heather said.

As I left the club and headed home I also hoped I would meet Heather again soon. It was an odd feeling to have, as in general I was happy with Julie. But meeting Heather had sparked something inside of me that I didn't quite know what to make of. Needless to say when I saw Julie the next day I said nothing of meeting Heather to her. It was hardly appropriate to, and I simply carried on seeing Julie just as I had before. But it had been a night to remember and one that I wasn't about to forget. Secretly I rather hoped that Heather and I would cross paths again and sooner rather than later. Though if and when we did meet again I wasn't quite sure what I'd do about it, particularly if I was out with Julie. It was a rather odd and unusual position to find myself in.

In the circumstances I tried not to think about my chance meeting with Heather too much. A couple of weeks passed and I didn't see her again, though I hadn't forgotten her or put her out of my mind altogether. In the meantime things continued more or less as they had done with Julie. She still seemed quite into me, at least on the surface. Outwardly she remained pretty keen, or appeared to be. Mostly we got on very well and had nice times together, whether we stayed in, went out as a couple, or met up with friends. Her periods of relative moodiness, when she wasn't much fun to be around, did become more common though. I decided to confront her about them, just in case there was something wrong.

'Have I been a moody cow?' she asked in such a way as to suggest she was half offering an apology.

'A bit,' I replied. 'I just wondered what was up.'

'I'm all right. Just a bit exhausted with work,' she explained.

'Fair enough. Just checking that everything was OK with us?' I said.

'It's fine,' she said, reassuring me.

A few weeks later Julie announced she was going away for a weekend, to see a band at the National Exhibition Centre in Birmingham. It was one of those big, American touring acts like Billy Joel or Bruce Springsteen, that I had no interest in seeing. I told her I was fine about her going, but had no wish to join her. I had Grace anyway. She said she was going with a friend, who was driving her. It turned out it was a male friend called Miles and they were staying in a hotel together. Still I trusted her. As I say she gave every impression of being very keen on me. I'd met the guy once or twice. He seemed pleasant enough, and I didn't really perceive him as a threat. He had a bit of a beer paunch and whilst not ugly certainly wasn't a handsome man either. I understood he'd lost his wife and had been left to bring up their only child by himself. It was a genuinely sad story. If Julie did have any interest in him I imagined it to be more out of sympathy. But I wasn't concerned. She seemed happy with me. I saw no reason to object to her going with this male friend, Miles. Later I realised I'd been a bit of a mug.

My first clue that all wasn't quite as it seemed was when Miles pulled up outside in his flash sports car to collect her. It was a modern, expensive model and the roof was down. Julie seemed only too delighted to jump in with him, throwing her luggage into the back in a carefree manner, like they were setting out on holiday together. She gave me a cheery wave, as they sped off. The wind was blowing through her hair, and a huge smile of pleasure spread across her glowing face, as they disappeared into the distance. They looked quite the young couple on a romantic getaway. They could have been heading off on honeymoon. She looked gleeful. He looked anything but a man mourning his wife. Even then my suspicions weren't aroused. They should have been.

I have no idea what happened that weekend and whether Julie was unfaithful or not, but whatever did happen when Julie returned she was never quite the same. She was less friendly and more distant, though nothing was ever said. Even so things changed between us. About the same time I decided to move out of the bedsit I was renting and find somewhere else to live. Even I had become fed up with it. A couple of the drunks who lived in the other rooms were regularly getting so drunk that they were weeing all over the toilet and bathroom. It was pretty disgusting. I wasn't prepared to tolerate it. I even told the landlord, who was a nice man, the reason I was going. He understood. It had happened before, he said.

It was then things started to get pretty weird between Julie and me. Mainly out of politeness, as I was looking for a new place, I asked Julie if she wanted to look for a new place together. I really wasn't bothered about living with her. Whilst she was fun to have around a lot of the time I knew she could be moody and confrontational on occasion. I was by no means desperate to live with her, and was far from totally set on the idea myself after my experiences with Claudia. Even so I thought I should at least sound her out, rather than just go ahead and get a place by myself without so much as asking her opinion. She was silent at first when I mentioned it. Then she was non-committal.

'Maybe it's a bit soon to move in together,' she said at last.

'That's fine,' I replied. 'I just thought I should ask.'

It really was fine. I was perfectly happy living on my own. I was in no rush to cohabit with a girlfriend again. Things got odder when I got a text from Julie that clearly wasn't meant for me. *Oh my God, Simon wants to live with me. How shall I put him off?* it read, before being finished with a kiss. I actually received it when I was at work. It gave me quite a jolt. For a moment I felt a little sick. Was it intended for Miles? Had it been intended for her sister? It certainly hadn't been meant for me. I texted Julie back saying I'd received the text by mistake and asked if she could perhaps explain its meaning. She didn't reply for ages. I was certain her error had sent her into a big fluster at being caught out and she was probably firing off other texts in panic. Eventually I got a text offering some feeble excuse and trying to laugh it off as a misunderstanding. I didn't believe her this time. I was certain something fishy was going on.

Her mood and offhandedness didn't improve. My birthday was coming up. We were going out for a curry with friends. I felt certain her humour would improve then and that she would be back to her old self. I was wrong. Even when we went back to her flat after the meal we didn't sleep together as I was expecting. She remained quite aloof and distant. I was growing tired of it. We'd only been together six months. It was far too soon to be going through all the crap that I'd been through with Claudia again. Frankly I had no intention of doing so. I decided to bring things to a head. Something was going on behind my back that she wasn't saying, whether it was seeing another man or whether she'd just had second thoughts about our relationship. Whatever it was I was determined to get to the bottom of it. After the failure of my birthday weekend I sent her a short and sharp text demanding she explain herself. I didn't get a reply straight away. When I eventually did she said we should meet for a drink one night later that week after I finished work. I agreed.

Arsenal were playing Barcelona in the Champions' League Final that week, so for the next day or two I put Julie out of my mind. I went to see the game in the local pub with Sandy. I was gutted Arsenal lost, their ten men losing to two late goals after Arsenal had led for much of the match. When I met Julie, who happened to be a Tottenham fan (we didn't discuss football much together), she was wearing a Barcelona scarf. It immediately put my back up. I couldn't be bothered to comment, but I wondered why she was wearing that shit. At least Arsenal had pipped Spurs for the final Champions League slot that season, after the Tottenham players had suffered a bout of unexplained food poisoning. Julie had been gutted. I of course had been quietly delighted. We got drinks and then sat down. Julie had a serious manner about her. She was almost staring ahead, unwilling to look me directly in the eye.

'I've been giving it a lot of thought all week,' she began. 'I haven't been able to sleep. I've wrestled with myself. I've weighed it up. I've shed tears about it, but I've decided we should finish. It's over between us. I really think it's for the best,' she announced.

'OK,' I said.

'Is that it? But don't you want to discuss it?' she asked, a little disconcerted.

She obviously wanted some kind of scene or drama that I wasn't prepared to give her. Perhaps she thought I was going to beg her to reconsider. I had no intention of doing so. Sure I liked her, but I'd never been that convinced by her. Her recent behaviour had just made me think I'd simply been right about her all along. She was no good and not to be trusted.

'What's to discuss? You said it's over,' I pointed out.

'I thought you'd want to talk it through though,' she said.

'Not really. You've made your decision. There's nothing to talk about. I'm actually quite annoyed you've dragged me to this pub just to tell me this. I could have been doing something else tonight,' I said.

It was true. I could have gone to see a film. It was the last night, the last showing. I knew I'd missed it now.

'But I thought I should tell you in person,' Julie said.

'Fine. You've told me. Now I'm going,' I said.

I didn't even finish my drink. I just got up and left my drink and left Julie sitting where she was in the pub on her own. As I walked towards the door I turned round to face her one last time.

'And take that stupid scarf off,' I said. 'It really doesn't suit you.'

So that was the end of that. I was back on my own once more. I was proved right about one thing, however. Within a week or two I saw Julie and Miles out together. It wasn't long before I heard they were an official item. I actually wasn't too bothered about being single again. I'd never been entirely convinced Julie was *Miss Right* anyway. I'd had my doubts about her all along. I'd never introduced her to Grace for a start. If I'd been really sure of her I would have encouraged her to meet my daughter. But I wasn't sure and I hadn't arranged for them to meet. That spoke volumes in itself. When all was said and done I wasn't in fact too disheartened by losing Julie. I'd rather enjoyed 2006 so far. I'd just continue enjoying it, but without her. I did rather hope I might bump into Heather again. That would certainly make things very much better, as far as I was concerned. In the event I'd have to wait just a bit longer for that to happen. But it did happen in time, and like all good things it was worth waiting for.

Chapter Twenty-Four

After what had happened with Julie I planned to hit the town hard that weekend. I felt disgruntled and rather fed up with women in general. But I was happy to console myself in alcohol and revelry. I'd drink, dance and have a good time. During my entire adult life I hadn't been single all that much. I'd generally jumped from one relationship to another, just as my work colleague and friend Paul had a habit of doing. Now I was on my own this time I'd enjoy it for a bit, I decided. I'd started to think relationships were overrated. I'd been very close to Roxanne. I'd married her. It hadn't worked out. I'd started dating Claudia. That hadn't worked either. Now Julie had disappointed me, having begun the relationship seemingly with great keenness and enthusiasm. For once I wasn't accountable to anybody. I could stay out late if I wanted. I could get as drunk as I liked. I could go anywhere I wished and talk to anyone I liked the look of. If one of those people happened to be Heather so much the better.

As it happened I didn't run into Heather. For some reason I found myself out in my usual club on my own that Friday night. As so often I went there as soon as I finished work. I sat in the downstairs bar, nursing my pint, contemplating whether I could be bothered to go upstairs to the proper dancefloor. Paul, Sandy, Steve and Cliff must have been otherwise engaged. If they weren't I'd surely have been with some combination of them. I wasn't on this occasion, but I wasn't too concerned. I was certain some familiar faces would come along before too long. They always did. It was unlikely this particular night would be any different. I went to the club so often over such a long period of time there were always some people there I knew. I was sitting alone, actually quite happy. I wasn't even thinking too much of Julie. Knowing that she'd probably been seeing Miles behind my back I was quite glad to be shot of her in truth. I was a little sad about it of course, but it was better to be single than with a partner who was cheating. I was just getting lost in my own thoughts, when a pretty, young blonde came and sat at my table.

'Mind if I join you?' she said.

'Go ahead,' I replied.

I guessed she was in her early twenties. I was a bit surprised she'd want to chat to a man in his early forties, nearly twenty years older, but who was I to argue or complain? I was on my own and I had no one else to talk to.

'I was dancing upstairs and I got a bit bored,' she explained. 'I thought I'd come downstairs for a change of scenery.'

'Why not? Sounds sensible,' I said. 'Would you like me to get you a drink? I was just about to get one for myself,' I added.

'Yes please. Can I have a vodka and coke,' she said.

'Whatever you like,' I replied.

I got her a drink and sat down beside her. We started chatting. She said her name was Natalie and she was a nurse. She'd just got off a long shift. She took a cigarette out of a packet and lit it. She had a long gulp of her drink. I quickly surmised she liked to work hard and play hard too. She clearly liked her alcohol and tobacco, and it wasn't long before I realised she liked her drugs as well. She said she had a bit of an ecstasy and cocaine habit and had blown a fortune on them. Bit odd for a nurse, who was meant to be safeguarding our health, I thought, but I didn't say anything. There was no doubt she was very attractive. I was just pleased she'd singled me out to talk to.

'Do you want to dance?' she asked after a while.

'I won't dance, but I'm happy to watch you,' I said.

I did indeed watch as Natalie joined a group who were dancing near our table. I noticed she danced in quite a sexually provocative way, sticking her bottom out as she did so. She was getting quite a few looks from the other men around us. I imagined she might go off with one, but it was me she came back to. She threw her arms round my neck and gave me a kiss full on the lips. It was time for another drink, I realised. We had a few more and still Natalie hadn't decided there were any better options in the club than me.

'Apologies for being forward, but do you want to come back with me?' she suddenly blurted out, looking a little embarrassed.

'I'll come back for a drink,' I said. 'But I'm not promising anything else.'

I didn't really do one-night stands. I wasn't about to start, even for someone as attractive as Natalie, but I was happy to go back and share her company. She had a nice flat in the basement of an old Georgian property. It had probably once been the servant's quarters for a wealthy family. Perhaps a nurse's wages weren't so very bad after all, I reflected. It was certainly a lot nicer than where I lived, even though I'd just moved into a new place. My new bedsit was positively humble compared to the spacious surroundings Natalie enjoyed on her own. She poured me a drink and then led me into the bedroom. She invited me to sit down.

'Make yourself at home. I'm just going to change out of my clubbing clothes,' she said.

She changed right in front of me, taking off her top and throwing it down. She made sure I got a very good eyeful of her naked breasts, before putting on another, more comfortable top. It left little to the imagination and little doubt as to what was on offer. Despite the obvious temptation I spent the night with Natalie but didn't make love to her. Having no other commitments and nothing much else to do (I had no Grace that particular weekend) I did end up spending most of Saturday and Sunday hanging out with Natalie. She was very pretty. Indeed she was too much to resist for a whole weekend, and before it was out we did end up having sex. I was really quite smitten, though I had no idea what she saw in me. I ended up taking her out quite a few times over the coming weeks. Then she suddenly stopped texting. I learned later she'd found another man. I did like her, but it was fair enough she'd found someone nearer her own age. They later ended up marrying and having kids together, I heard.

Meanwhile I got asked out by a female customer at the cinema. She'd been in quite a few times over a long period and had always taken the trouble to talk to me. She was skinny, red-haired and pretty. Her name was Louise. I recognised her from the local art college and had always been a little bit attracted to her. She was a bit of a hippy and a bit of a free spirit, in her early thirties at a guess, but I was happy to go out with her. She lived in a caravan on a farm out in the country. A couple of times I drove out to see her. A couple of times she drove into town to see me. She was intelligent, interesting company, though I wondered if she was a little too arty and a little too feminist for me. In one respect she reminded me of Victoria I'd briefly dated before Julie. I'd see Louise and we'd enjoy a nice date together. Then I wouldn't hear from her for a week or more. Added to the fact she lived out of town, after a few dates I decided I was wasting my time with her. We were better off as friends, I thought, and friends we remained.

My social life was expanding all the time. When I wasn't out with Paul, Sandy, Steve or Cliff I was out with some of the younger guys from work. On one occasion I found myself chatting to a colleague I'd never really chatted to or noticed before. She was called Tess. She wasn't conventionally good looking, but she was intelligent, articulate and interesting, and the more I chatted to her the more I realised we had much in common. I started to think she was someone I could perhaps get to know better. She wasn't pretty like Natalie had been, but looks weren't everything and there was something about her knowledge and conversation that was attractive. She also played the guitar, she said. I told her she should come over and jam with Sandy and myself the next time we played. She said she would be happy to do so. As we chatted I found myself warming to her.

'I can never get a date,' she complained at one point.

'I'll take you out on a date,' I said.

I don't know why I said it. It just came out. Maybe I was a bit drunk. It was too late to take it back now. She jumped at it. It had only been said in semi seriousness, but I was committed to it now. I'd have to take her out on a date.

'That would be great,' Tess said, her face positively beaming. 'I haven't been out on a date for nearly seven years.'

'That's a long time,' I agreed.

'Believe me it is,' she said. 'I was a bit messed up in my last relationship, so I've avoided another one since then.'

'Understandable,' I said, though my general habit after a failed relationship was to launch straight into another one. 'I should explain I've only just come out of a relationship myself, so I'm not looking for anything serious,' I added, just so we had things clear and upfront. 'I'm happy to go out on a date, but I'm not ready to commit to anything,' I elaborated.

The truth was I was actually quite enjoying the single life, after so many years in relationships that had turned sour and hadn't worked out. I wasn't desperate to get tied down again any time soon. Just at that moment casual dating seemed more fun. I was quite happy continuing with more of the same for the time being. As it was I went out with Tess a few times. I started to see another side of her. There were a couple of occasions when I introduced her to friends she just cut them dead with some acerbic remark. I was positively shocked and aghast. She could be the life and soul of the party when she wanted to be. Other times she was almost narcoleptic to the point of falling asleep, or simply in a very foul mood and would hardly speak. When she was like that she was rude and aloof to an extreme I'd rarely seen in a person. She had a habit of stalking off without so much as a word. It set the alarm bells ringing straight away. I couldn't have another complicated, difficult

215

girlfriend like Claudia. I'd had four years of that, and it had been too much.

Whilst I continued to hang out with Tess and she continued to jam with Sandy and me (she was now pretty much a fully paid-up member of our embryonic band), I distanced myself from her as a potential partner. She was far from happy about that and indeed gave me hell in work and out of it for that choice for months and years after. I tried to explain we'd only ever enjoyed a fling. We'd never been an item or in a relationship together, I protested. I reminded her that I'd been honest and open from the start, that I wasn't seeking anything serious. It fell on deaf ears. Nothing I said seemed to placate her. I well and truly got my fingers burned this time. Tess reacted as if I'd broken off an engagement to her. From my point of view there was nothing to finish. We'd had a couple of dates, but that was it. I just wanted to keep it plutonic, to be friends and nothing else. It seemed that wasn't and would never be enough for Tess.

'I thought we had real potential,' she said, the tears welling in her eyes.

'We do get on,' I agreed. 'I'm just not ready for another relationship yet.'

In truth she'd scared me off by the way she was round other people. I started to think maybe the casual dating scene wasn't for me after all. Maybe I needed something more settled, just not with Tess. I wanted someone relaxed and easy going, who wasn't hard work. It was a real shame I hadn't run into Heather again by now. I was always in the club where I'd met her. It was amazing that around four months had now passed and we still hadn't bumped into each other again. It was about time that changed. I'd even tried to initiate a meeting, but that had gone wrong. I'd happened to bump into the other girl, the blonde, who was with Heather on the night we'd first met. Her name was Emily. I casually mentioned that Sandy and I would be out the following night, if she wanted to join us. I suggested she invite Heather too. To my surprise Emily did join us. We even had a nice evening, but she didn't bring Heather. She'd only invited her at the last moment, too late for Heather to come. Emily was certainly pretty, but she wasn't the girl for me. Very quickly I picked up the fact that she didn't like kids. It could never work. No Heather was the one I was desperate to meet up with. Very soon I'd get a slice of good fortune and I would meet her again.

It was a Tuesday night. I arrived late at the club. I was joining Paul, Steve and Cliff for a quick drink after finishing work. By the time I got there, around half eleven, they'd already been out some time. I wasn't planning to stay long. I certainly wasn't expecting to meet anyone. As we stood with our drinks on the edge of the dancefloor I started to look around. I suddenly realised with a jolt there was Heather dancing with some other girls. I wondered if she'd even remember me, as much had happened since our last meeting. There were no guarantees. Perhaps I'd made less of an impression on her than she had on me. She was after all fifteen years younger than I was. I didn't rush over straight away. I thought I'd bide my time and wait for her to come across to the bar. She'd surely want another drink at some point. She was wearing a feather boa. She was clearly in party mode. I wondered if it was someone's birthday. I guessed she wasn't working the next day. It was my day off too. Eventually Heather came nearer. It was now my chance.

'Hi,' I said.

'Oh hello,' she replied in a friendly voice, but also sounding a little surprised to see me. 'You'll have to excuse me,' she said. 'I'm a bit drunk. I'm out with my sisters. One of them is back from America, so we're celebrating.'

She was indeed out with two other, slightly older girls. They were both blonde. Heather was dark, but I could see a slight family resemblance between the three of them. Heather completed the introductions. I also introduced them to my friends.

'We've seen you here before,' the middle sister, who was called Vicky, announced loudly. 'I tried to get your attention at the bar once. We thought you might suit a friend of ours, but you ignored us.'

She then laughed. The eldest, who I gathered was called Lisa, joined in the laughter.

'Sorry about that. I wouldn't have ignored you. I just didn't notice,' I apologised, trying to recall the incident.

'I pinched you quite hard, but you never turned round,' Vicky continued.

The mention of a pinch did vaguely ring some bell in my head. I think I'd felt it at the time, but not knowing who or what it was had thought it best to ignore it.

'Don't tell him that. You'll scare him off,' Heather protested.

'Oh he's made of sterner stuff than that,' Vicky said, giving me a friendly slap.

They were all clearly slightly tipsy.

'I can see I have some catching up to do in the drinking department,' I said.

'You can come and join us anyway if you want,' Heather said, beckoning me to a table, where earlier they'd been sitting.

I spent the rest of the evening chatting to Heather and dancing with her. My friends and her sisters were with us all the time, but I only really had eyes for Heather. We were instantly almost inseparable. At the end of the evening I made sure I got her number and walked her and her sisters to a waiting taxi. I was planning to walk back to my new bedsit, which was further away from the city centre than the place I'd recently left, but was still near enough. It was only ten to fifteen minutes away, if I walked briskly. Besides, I liked a little fresh air to clear my head after I'd been drinking. And I had much to reflect on this particular evening.

'There's a gig this Friday night. Some of my friends are playing,' Heather said. 'Would you like to come along?'

'If it's the one I'm thinking of I'm already going,' I said.

When Heather explained where it was it turned out it was the same gig. That was a happy coincidence. I was only invited as some friends of Sandy were also on the bill. I hadn't even been that bothered about it in truth, but it suddenly became an altogether more interesting event if Heather was going too.

'I can meet you there, or we could meet for a drink in the pub first?' Heather suggested.

'That sounds great,' I said. 'I'll text you and we can arrange it.'

It did indeed sound great. Everything was working out at last. Ever since I'd first met Heather I'd hoped to meet her again. Ever since things had started to turn sour with Julie I'd hoped our paths would cross and I'd get an opportunity to get to know Heather better. Now I had that chance. I wasted no time texting her. We exchanged texts the very next day and arranged where to meet on the coming Friday. It was funny. When we arrived at the club together Julie was there. I said a polite hello and no more. I was with Heather. I had no need for Julie now. She was a distant memory. I'd moved on. I bore Julie no malice. I had a feeling she'd actually done me a favour. If I'd stayed with her I wouldn't have been where I was now, with someone who actually suited me much better.

Over the coming days and weeks I started to see Heather most nights. I introduced her to my friends. She introduced me to hers, many of whom were musicians. Suddenly I had a whole new set of younger acquaintances. Sandy was ecstatic. There was talk of us doing gigs with them, although to my mind we were hardly ready. Tess was furious. Why was I willing to date Heather when I hadn't been willing to date her? The simple answer was Heather was a gentle, good-natured girl. Tess had been always on the edge of kicking off. I didn't want the drama. Heather was temperamentally the polar opposite of both Tess and Claudia. It was just what I needed at that moment in my life. Whilst Tess continued to play in our band, as I felt sorry for her and didn't have the heart to fire her, she gave me the cold shoulder at work. It was just something I'd have to put up with until the dust had settled. It wasn't going to change anything though. I had Heather now. There was no going back to Tess, however much she tried to engineer a change of heart on my part. It would never happen, although I continued to feel a little guilty about the situation. It was just unfortunate. I hadn't meant to hurt Tess. I'd just met someone I liked more. Often Heather stayed with me at my flat, though we didn't sleep together immediately.

'I'm not very lucky in love. I want to be sure it's right,' Heather said.

'That's OK. There's no hurry,' I agreed. 'Let's get to know each other first.'

When we did finally sleep together it felt good. It felt lovely in fact. We were very compatible in that department. Things obviously felt right between us and it wasn't long before I introduced Heather to both my parents and Grace. I'd been enjoying the single life. I thought that was what I wanted. I didn't want to commit to anyone for a bit, I'd insisted. Heather had changed all that. Very quickly I was very committed. After just a few weeks dating I invited Heather for a weekend away together. We decided to go somewhere quiet, where we could just relax and chill out. We chose a sleepy little village near Glastonbury, where we stayed in an old coaching house for the weekend. We didn't do very much. We had a few drinks, some nice food, enjoyed each other's company and got to know each other a little better. It was enough to cement our relationship. 2006 had been a good year so far. I had a strong feeling it was going to continue. Despite the age difference I felt Heather and I were going to be together for some time to come.

'I imagined myself with an older man with a young daughter,' she quietly confided in me whilst we were away. 'Now I am.'

'And I'm glad you are,' I said.

She also made another small admission.

'You know the first time we met wasn't actually the first time I'd seen you. Neither was the time my sister pinched you,' she said. 'I saw you out on New Year's Eve. I liked the look of you then, but you were with someone else. I was disappointed when she came over and gave you a kiss. Not her, I thought.'

She meant Julie of course. Her reputation preceded her.

'So meeting me wasn't entirely an accident?' I asked.

'Not exactly,' Heather said. 'I knew Dan, so I asked him who you were and if he'd introduce us.'

'Well I'm glad he did,' I said.

'I'm glad too,' Heather agreed.

'And I'm glad I'm not with Julie anymore,' I said. 'I'm very glad I'm with you instead.'

Chapter Twenty-Five
(An Epilogue)

The summer of 2006 proved to be a memorable and happy one. And not because England brought the World Cup back from Germany as hoped. A very strong team featuring the likes of Beckham, Gerrard, Terry, Lampard and Rooney, the so-called *Golden Generation*, played with a distinct lack of energy and crashed out at the Quarter Final stage on penalties again. I didn't care too much. I had other things on my mind. My life was changing direction. Having spent much of my twenties and thirties on fruitless attempts to get a novel published, racking up one failed venture after another, in my early forties, partly inspired by Heather and partly inspired by Sandy, I returned to my first love, which was music. I decided to have a break from any serious writing and put it on the backburner for a while. Until otherwise inspired for the time being and foreseeable future I'd enjoy making music as my main outside interest.

I'd never completely turned my back on music. For much of the previous decade I'd jammed intermittently with work colleague Paul. Now thanks to Sandy and others I had the opportunity to do it in a more serious way. Sandy was keen to get a live, gigging band up and running. I was quite interested in the possibility of recording. Most of Heather's friends and the new people I was meeting were musicians. It was too much of a coincidence to ignore. They could assist me in bringing my musical ideas to some kind of fruition. After all I'd been writing songs since I was fifteen years old, and to date I'd done precious little with any of them.

As fate would have it another work colleague called Alan was getting interested in the whole recording process. He wasn't really a musician himself, but thanks to the new music recording programmes that could now readily be downloaded on computers he was keen to record others. The new digital recording programmes were far more sophisticated that the old four-track recorders that relied on hissy tapes that Paul and I had been left to experiment with, and that I'd tried to record with in previous musical enterprises. Suddenly with a home computer, a musical interface, a few instruments and bits and bobs, it was relatively easy to make quite sophisticated music. During much of that summer I spent many of my spare afternoons and evenings round at Alan's, recording songs both for a solo album and a band album with Sandy and Tess.

Alan added little bits of keyboard, and also got one or two musician friends to guest on some of the tracks. A few of them sounded terrific, a great improvement on anything I'd achieved in the past.

As I got more engaged in music and it became a more important part of my life I saw an opportunity to get more involved in it at work. The cinema where I worked had a café bar. On my suggestion we started having a weekly live acoustic music event under candlelight. Heather's musician friends provided many of the first acts to play there. Pretty soon more and more acts wanted to play, as it became an established and popular local venue for live music. Social media was just getting going and would soon become an explosion. I found no shortage of acts to book on *Myspace*, and then later *Facebook*. I never seemed to struggle finding someone exciting and new to put on. Many who played were keen to book up again. Heather kindly kept a look out for other indie, folk and Americana singers that might suit the vibe we'd established. She too found plenty.

It quickly became a big social night out for just about everyone I knew. Paul had another new girlfriend, so we didn't see much of him, but almost everyone else I was close to came along. Sandy, Steve and Cliff were there most weeks, as was Heather and hordes of her friends. Her sisters often came too. And of course as time went on I got to know many of the other musicians who played and was soon able to count them as friends. Swayed by Sandy's constant nagging it wasn't long before he and I, backed by Tess, were doing short sets too. We weren't very good at first. I was very nervous and had something close to stage fright. I wondered what the heck I was doing up there, but I stuck at it, we practised regularly, and as a unit slowly improved.

My newfound interest in music brought me into the orbit of another ageing indie kid like myself. His name was Stuart and he'd once been in a moderately successful band who toured with *The Wedding Present* in the early 1990s. Stuart lived in a small village out of town. I booked his band without even hearing them, solely on the basis they were fans of cult indie band *The Television Personalities* and their eccentric singer, Daniel Treacy. It appeared Stuart was also just getting back into music, after taking a decade long break to have a family. He knew the ropes much better than Sandy or I did. He even had a friend who had a recording studio. Stuart was keen on launching a local independent record label, to release some of the music all our various bands were making. Stuart had energy and enthusiasm. He also had an ear for a good tune and an eye for captivating indie artwork.

It wasn't long before all these things were happening, and Sandy and I were just swept along with it. Everything seemed to come together at once. I provided a venue for our acts to play in. Stuart provided a studio we could hire at reduced rates and a little label to promote our music. Very soon Sandy and I found ourselves going along to the studio to put some of our first tracks down. Tess played bass on the first few recordings and then quit. She found it all too much after our fling, and left both the band and the cinema to join another band and start a new life in Bristol. Stuart replaced her. As his mate who ran the studio was a drummer we even had someone to drum for us now and could play gigs in bigger, louder venues.

In time we'd release professionally recorded studio albums, get national reviews and even get played on the radio, none of which I'd ever imagined doing in my wildest dreams. I thought music had passed me by. It seemed it hadn't entirely. I'd also start recording and releasing proper solo albums, playing almost all of the instruments on them. I'd started to learn the bass myself and began to play in other bands, as well as playing guitar for Sandy. It all happened so suddenly and so quickly, partly thanks to Sandy, partly thanks to Heather, partly thanks to Stuart. But we didn't make any money and we didn't become famous. We were a little bit old for that. No one wants pop stars in their late thirties and forties after all. But it was fun whilst it lasted and indeed it lasted for more than the next decade, as our music gradually became more serious. Other acts fell by the wayside, even Stuart's in time. We kept at it and once Stuart stopped we carried on. We'd learnt everything we needed from him to record and release the music ourselves and appear on *Amazon* and *iTunes* and *Spotify* and all the other digital platforms. In a relatively short period of time we achieved far more than I thought was possible, and in many ways more than I ever had with writing.

Even so I didn't turn my back on writing entirely. Perhaps inspired by my love affair with Heather I once more collaborated with Feather Books to produce a small pamphlet of poetry called *At Heart A Romantic*. I was a little bored of poetry as a medium in truth, but from time to time poems just came into my head and I felt obliged to write them down. I still quite enjoyed working on a new collection. It had always provided a welcome break from novel writing. Now it was providing an occasional break from music. This one was no different. It was a pleasure to put it together and see it published.

I also hadn't lost my love for sport. Despite suffering lingering ill health for years since having glandular fever I continued to play tennis and badminton whenever I could. I played my last serious tennis tournament in 2006. I had a match on a Friday night, but I was so keen to get to my date with Heather I found myself barely concentrating on the game. It made me realise it wasn't worth playing any more serious singles matches of that kind. On another occasion I entered a club tournament, but was having such a good time away with Heather in Glastonbury and Wells that I rang my prospective opponent and gave them a bye rather than rush home to play. It made me appreciate where my priorities lay. Surprisingly in my early forties I did find myself playing football again. Alan, who I'd spent time recording with, was very keen and launched a works team. Before long I was leading the team out as Captain, against a host of other local teams, businesses and organisations. It brought back happy memories of playing when I was young, and even in my more advanced years I found it was still fun.

But what made that time really special was my relationship with Heather, which continued to flourish. We saw each other most days, and most nights she stayed with me at my bedsit, whatever we'd been doing beforehand. Most of our leisure time when we weren't working we spent together. She joined me on my trips out with Grace. She came with me when I went round to see my parents. I went with her to her mum's, where in theory she was still living, though in reality she spent far more time at my place than her own. I was happy to have her. Sometimes we went out to the pub or for a meal together. Other times we met friends or went to gigs or went to the cinema. Once in a while as a treat we went away. On other occasions we just stayed in watching films, drinking wine and nibbling snacks. It didn't really matter what we did. We were happy just being together. Tess had now gone. We no longer had to worry about her. Predictably enough she'd been nothing short of horrible to Heather. Heather had just taken it in her stride and never reacted. Now that small blot on our happiness, which had been largely my fault, had disappeared. We were free to enjoy the new life we were making together.

Just then I got some unexpected news at work. I was unexpectedly promoted to the position of General Manager. I'd always been a manager of sorts there, Box Office Manager, Duty Manager, Marketing

Manager etc, but finally I was in overall charge of the cinema. It meant both an increase in status and a big increase in my salary. The previous Manager had left suddenly. I applied for the job. I was interviewed in London, but I never seriously thought that I would get it. I wasn't even the leading candidate. But thanks to some of the innovations I'd introduced at the cinema, including the thriving live music nights, I landed the job.

One of the first consequences of getting the promotion was that I had to go away to Edinburgh for a few days. Despite the long train journey there and back I found it to be a most delightful city, with fabulous museums and galleries. I was impressed with Scotland in general and I loved Edinburgh in particular. The other major consequence of my improved job situation was that Heather and I could plan a real future together. I'd never really earned enough before. Suddenly I did. My income pretty much doubled overnight. So did my responsibilities and workload of course. But at the time that part didn't seem to matter too much. What did matter was that it made a big difference to the kind of life I could potentially enjoy with Heather. That prospect filled me with a mixture of excitement and anticipation. Then early in 2007 Heather made a surprise announcement.

'I think I'm ready to have a baby, she declared.

She slightly took me back, but I was privately delighted by the revelation. I'd wanted a second child with Roxanne, but she'd never wanted one. It had hurt me a little when she'd gone on to have a second child, with someone else after we'd split up. I'd been desperate for a second child, but I'd been stuck with Claudia, who hadn't been in the slightest bit interested. What a waste of time, effort and money that relationship had been! It was now nearly a decade since I'd had Grace. I'd begun to think I'd never be a father again. Now here I was with a young woman, who was telling me in an open and honest way she wanted to start a family with me.

'Are you sure?' I asked Heather. 'I'm ready to try if you are.'

'I'm twenty-seven now. It's as good a time as any,' Heather replied.

She had indeed just turned twenty-seven. She'd been twenty-five when I met her. She was twenty-six when we started dating. We'd now been dating a little over a year. I was now forty-two. We were very happy together. We started trying for a baby straight away. To my surprise and to Heather's surprise she conceived very quickly. Only a month or two passed and she missed her period. We held our collective breaths when she took a pregnancy test. It was positive. I'd been due to play badminton that evening. I never played badminton again. I was already having to devote an increased amount of time to band practices. Now we had a baby on the way too. There was no way I had the time to keep up two racket sports. So having been a badminton player for thirty years or more I stopped on the spot. In future, if and when I had the time, I'd just continue playing tennis.

The pregnancy was soon confirmed by Heather's doctor. We both decided that with Heather pregnant it was time at last to move in together. We got a place just round the corner from where I already lived almost straight away. I warned Heather beforehand that I wasn't the easiest person in the world to live with, but she didn't seem put off or to mind that fact too much. Amazingly I was able to move most of my possessions by foot. We didn't have that much stuff between us, and very quickly we were both settled in our new place. I'd left a lot of my belongings in storage at my parents' house, and most of Heather's things were just clothes, CDs and books, which I brought over from her mum's in my car. I'd got rid of most of my furniture when I'd sold the house I had with Roxanne. We didn't own much else of any size, apart from my double bed, which I simply took apart and moved.

Meanwhile the pregnancy progressed, but it wasn't without its complications. More than once during the early stages Heather suffered severe bleeding and we thought she'd lost the baby. They were stressful days. It was touch and go, but the baby was strong and it clung on to its infant life and continued to grow and develop in Heather's womb as it should do. Heather was told to take things gently and we did everything we could to ensure that she did. Luckily she had a clerical job in an office, so nothing too physical was required. She stopped drinking. She stopped smoking, which on occasion she had done prior to being pregnant. She watched what she ate. She hardly went out. She tried to stay calm and relaxed. As things started to settle she did come out once or twice with me. On one occasion it was to a gig to see old punk band *The Vibrators*, who I'd liked when I was a kid. It wasn't really Heather's kind of thing, but she was happy to come along. The gig wasn't very busy. In fact the venue was two-thirds empty. That actually suited us ideally of course. Heather and I just stood at the back and watched from there. We didn't want to upset the baby. To our surprise an ageing, female punk, who was rather drunk, approached us. She was a bit unsteady on her feet.

'You're pregnant. I can tell,' she announced. 'There will be a few problems, but it will be all right, and you'll have a healthy girl,' she promised.

'I hope you're right,' Heather replied, a little taken aback by the unexpected revelation. 'I've always wanted a baby girl,' she admitted.

I don't know if the woman was a mystic. I don't know if she was some kind of clairvoyant, but her predictions were to prove to be correct. There were further complications when Heather went for her next scans. It seemed our baby was the wrong way round, what medics call a breech birth. The doctors weren't too worried, however. They were still optimistic the baby would turn before Heather's due date. Because of work commitments and the odd hours I worked, I was unable to attend many of Heather's antenatal classes. Her sister Vicky went to most of them with her instead. I tried to recall everything I'd learned when Roxanne had been pregnant some ten years earlier. I did at least remember some of it, which I hoped would prove useful. Heather's nine months of pregnancy was now nearly over. The impending arrival of our new baby drew ever closer. Still the baby hadn't turned.

We went for further meetings with Heather's doctors. They decided in the circumstances the best option was for Heather to have a caesarean section. Heather was booked in for a date at the hospital to have the operation. We had to pack bags for her to have an extended stay there. I of course went with her. We even got as far as changing into our surgical gowns in readiness for the procedure. At the last minute scans revealed the baby had turned. There was no need for a caesarean after all. Heather was a little disappointed at first. She'd gone into hospital expecting to come out with a baby. She'd been sent home with nothing. It was a bit of an anti-climax, after we'd built ourselves up and got prepared, but once we were home we got over it soon enough. A few days later Heather was called back to the hospital and they began the process of inducing her. I spent most of the day with Heather but was sent away at nighttime. I got a phone call first thing in the morning. It was just after seven.

'Come quickly, the baby's on its way,' I was told. 'You better hurry. It won't be long.'

I got to the hospital about fifteen minutes later. Just ten minutes or so after that our baby daughter was born. Heather actually gave birth standing. Once she'd gone into full labour it had been really quick.

Roxanne had taken ages. I couldn't believe this was so fast. I was handed our baby girl as they cleaned Heather up. The baby was quiet and still on my lap, with her big, blue eyes gazing up into mine. She seemed a fit and healthy child.

'I think we'll call her Rose,' Heather announced.

Who was I to argue?

'Rose it is,' I said.

Over the next few days we were showered with visitors, flowers, cards and gifts from an array of family, friends and well-wishers. Heather only spent a couple of nights in the hospital before we took Rose home. It reminded me of when Roxanne and I had first taken Grace home. We lay her down on the floor in the middle of our front room.

'What do we do now?' Heather asked.

We soon learnt. We had to, though Rose was never a good sleeper and spent most nights in with us. We quickly outgrew the flat we were renting, as Rose's toys, cots, prams, buggies and other things soon multiplied beyond expectation. There was also disturbing noise in the night from the tenants above, which was keeping both Heather and Rose awake. It wasn't long before we moved into a proper house on the other side of the city. There Rose had her own room, and we had a separate front room and kitchen, an upstairs as well as a downstairs, no neighbours above us, as well as a small outside patio and garden. Inspired by the arrival of our wonderful new daughter I put together another modest collection of poetry. I did it with *Masque Publishing*, who regularly published my poems in their magazine *Decanto*. I called the collection *Celebrations of Life*. It seemed rather fitting. I never formally proposed to Heather. I never even bought her an engagement ring. But one early evening when we were sitting downstairs together with Rose the thought of marriage popped into my head.

'Maybe we should get married?' I said. 'We've done everything else. We've moved in together. We've had a baby daughter. What else is there left?'

'Why not get married then?' Heather replied.

So as simple as that it was agreed.

We got married in May 2009 in an historic mansion set in the grounds of the city's university. The weather was splendid that day, the warmest it had been all year, just as it had been for my first wedding. Heather looked beautiful, as I knew she would. All our family and friends were there. I was particularly pleased my dad was able to attend. He was in his late seventies and in declining health, but lived long enough to witness both the arrival of Rose and our wedding. Sandy was best man of course. Heather's sisters and Grace were among the bridesmaids. Both the bands I played in performed, as well as Stuart's band and another friend's band we all liked. It was a lovely occasion. It all went perfectly. Afterwards we honeymooned in Cornwall. We even took Grace with us.

That's the end of my story. After twenty years of trying I did finally discover true love. It was just a long and arduous journey through many ups and downs to find it. I hear little of either Judy or Claudia these days, though I don't bear either of them any malice. They went their own ways and presumably have lived their lives since as they wished to. I've remained on good terms with my ex-wife Roxanne. I still see Grace often, though she is now a grown woman. Now as I write I am in my mid-fifties. More than another decade has passed. We haven't had any more children, as I might have hoped, but Heather and I are still together. Rose is growing older. And we're happy.

Printed in Dunstable, United Kingdom

68174293R00131